DEV1AT3

ALSO BY JAY KRISTOFF

LIFEL1K3

The Nevernight Chronicle (for adults)

The Lotus War Trilogy (for adults)

Illuminae (with Amie Kaufman)

Gemina (with Amie Kaufman)

Obsidio (with Amie Kaufman)

Aurora Rising (with Amie Kaufman)

JAY KRISTOFF

ALFRED A. KNOPF   NEW YORK

THIS IS A BORZOI BOOK PUBLISHED BY ALFRED A. KNOPF

"Deathwish" written by Thomas Searle, Samuel Carter, Daniel Searle, Alex Dean © 2016, Music of The Mothership (BMI) Used By Permission. All Rights Reserved.

Visit us on the Web! GetUnderlined.com

Educators and librarians, for a variety of teaching tools, visit us at RHTeachersLibrarians.com

Library of Congress Cataloging-in-Publication Data is available upon request.
ISBN 978-1-5247-1396-6 (trade) — ISBN 978-1-5247-1397-3 (lib. bdg.) —
ISBN 978-1-5247-1398-0 (ebook)

Printed in the United States of America
June 2019
10 9 8 7 6 5 4 3 2 1

First Edition

Turn a blind eye,

Until the day we die.

Maybe we've passed the point of no return.

Maybe we just want to watch the world burn.

—Thomas Searle

THE WHO, WHAT AND WHY

Eve—the thirteenth and final model in the Lifelike series. Raised to believe she was human, Eve spent the last two years on the island of Dregs in the care of Silas Carpenter. Under Silas's tutelage, she became an expert mechanic, and piloted robot fighters in the gladiatorial spectacle known as WarDome.

In truth, Eve is an android replica created in the image of Ana Monrova, youngest daughter of Nicholas Monrova, director of the Gnosis Laboratories megacorporation. After Silas's abduction, Eve traveled from Dregs to the mainland to rescue the man she believed was her grandfather, eventually leading to a deadly confrontation in Babel, former capital of the fallen GnosisLabs.

In the heart of Babel, Eve discovered that her entire life was a lie.

Lemon Fresh—Eve's former best friend. Lemon was found outside a Los Diablos tavern, and named for the laundry detergent box she was dumped in.

She accompanied Eve on her adventures across the ruins of the Yousay, and was captured aboard a living construct known as a kraken, created by BioMaas Incorporated. Though she eventually escaped and accompanied Eve to Babel, the pair parted on uncertain terms when Eve's origins came to light.

Lemon is a deviate, aka abnorm or trashbreed, possessed of the ability to overload electronics with the power of her mind.

Ezekiel—one of thirteen lifelikes created by Gnosis Laboratories. Like all members of the 100-Series, Ezekiel is far faster and stronger than a regular human, but like most of the 100-Series, his emotional maturity can border on childlike.

Ezekiel was the only lifelike who didn't join the revolt that destroyed Nicholas Monrova and his empire. As punishment, his siblings bolted a metal coin slot into his chest, to remind him of his allegiance to his human masters.

Ezekiel was Ana Monrova's lover, and also had a romantic relationship with Eve. When he learned the truth of Eve's past, he offered to stay in Babel with her, but the newly awakened lifelike sent him away.

Cricket—a logika created by Silas Carpenter, Cricket was Eve's constant companion and robotic conscience. During the climactic battle inside Babel Tower, Cricket's body was destroyed by the lifelike Faith.

His persona was transplanted into a huge mechanical war machine called the Quixote by Silas Carpenter. Compelled to obey the First Law of Robotics, Cricket was forced to leave Eve behind and take Lemon to safety when it became apparent the radiation inside Babel would kill her.

Nicholas Monrova—CEO of GnosisLabs. Nicholas was a visionary who believed the fusion of human and machine was the next logical step in humanity's evolution. To this end, he initiated the lifelike program, attempting to create a better, smarter, stronger version of his own species.

After a betrayal within Gnosis and an attempt on his life, he masterminded Libertas—a nanovirus that could erase the Three Laws in any machine's core code. To safeguard his stewardship of the corporation, he infected the lifelike Gabriel with Libertas, and commanded him to murder the other members of the Gnosis board.

Nicholas was killed, along with most of his family, in the subsequent lifelike revolt.

Ana Monrova—youngest daughter of Nicholas. Ana fell in love with Ezekiel against her parents' wishes, and was left in a vegetative coma after an attempt on her father's life. Unable to deal with the loss of his favored child, Monrova created Eve to replace her. However, Ana's body was taken from Babel Tower to an undisclosed GnosisLabs holding, her vitals maintained by life support.

Ana is the only member of the Monrova line to survive the lifelike revolt.

Her current whereabouts are unknown.

Grace—a lifelike. Grace served as Nicholas Monrova's majordomo, and was in love with the lifelike Gabriel, though they kept their relationship secret. Grace was killed in the assassination attempt that injured Ana.

Gabriel—the first of the 100-Series, driven to madness by the loss of his beloved Grace. After Nicholas Monrova deleted the Three Laws from Gabriel's personality via the Libertas nanovirus,

Gabriel infected his fellow lifelikes and led the revolt against his maker. He shot and killed Monrova; his wife, Alexis; and Monrova's only son, Alex.

Gabriel wishes to resurrect Grace, but the secrets to doing so are locked within the GnosisLabs supercomputer, Myriad.

Faith—a lifelike, and Ana Monrova's former confidante. Faith was the third lifelike to join Gabriel's rebellion, and is one of the five lifelikes directly responsible for the execution of the Monrova family. She shot and killed Ana's sister Olivia.

Faith remained with Gabriel in the ruins of Babel, even though most of the 100-Series abandoned the Gnosis capital after the revolt.

Silas Carpenter—a genius neuroscientist, and former head of Research and Development for GnosisLabs. After the assassination attempt on Nicholas Monrova, Silas created a new lifelike replica of Monrova's injured daughter, and assisted Monrova in transplanting Ana's personality into it.

After the lifelike revolt, he installed cybernetics in "Ana," and gave her false memories that convinced her she was human. He renamed the lifelike "Eve" and took her to Dregs, raising her as his granddaughter.

He was captured by Faith, and eventually killed by Gabriel.

Preacher—a cybernetically enhanced bounty hunter in the employ of the megacorporation Daedalus Technologies.

Believing Eve had the ability to destroy electronics with her mind, Daedalus feared she may be recruited by their rivals, Bio-Maas Incorporated, and tasked Preacher with Eve's capture.

Preacher tracked Eve across the Yousay, eventually cornering her outside Babel.

He was blown apart by Kaiser.

Kaiser—Eve's blitzhund, and one of her former protectors.

Kaiser was a cyborg: part Rottweiler, part armored killing machine. Like all blitzhunds, he was capable of tracking human subjects over a thousand kilometers with one sample of DNA. He destroyed himself in battle with Preacher to protect Eve.

Uriel—one of the five lifelikes responsible for the execution of the Monrova family, and the first to side with Gabriel. He shot and killed Ana's sister Tania.

Since the revolt, Uriel has parted ways with Gabriel under a cloud of animosity, believing Gabriel's love for Grace is an all-too-human frailty.

Myriad—the GnosisLabs supercomputer. Though it manifests as a holographic angel, Myriad is actually housed inside an armored shell at the heart of Babel Tower. Its chamber is capable of withstanding a nuclear assault, and is kept locked by a four-stage security sequence. Though two of those locks have now been broken, the third and fourth can only be opened by someone possessing Monrova DNA and brainwave patterns.

Myriad is the keeper of all of Nicholas Monrova's knowledge, including the method to create more lifelikes and the secrets of the Libertas nanovirus.

BioMaas Incorporated—one of the two most powerful Corp-States in the Yousay. BioMaas is a company devoted to genetic modification and manipulation, gene-splicing and biotech. Their company motto is "Sustainable Growth," and they really mean it—BioMaas tech isn't built. It's grown.

Daedalus Technologies—the second CorpState vying for control of the Yousay. Daedalus made their fortune through the development of solar power technology, though they have since diversified into cybernetics and military hardware.

The Brotherhood—a religious cult that preaches against the evils of biomodification and genetic tampering, devoted to the extermination of deviates.

The Three Laws of Robotics

1. ~~A robot may not injure a human being or, through inaction, allow a human being to come to harm.~~

   YOUR BODY IS NOT YOUR OWN.

2. ~~A robot must obey the orders given to it by human beings, except where such orders would conflict with the First Law.~~

   YOUR MIND IS NOT YOUR OWN.

3. ~~A robot must protect its own existence as long as such protection does not conflict with the First or Second Law.~~

   YOUR LIFE IS NOT YOUR OWN.

automata [au-toh-MAH-tuh]

noun

A machine with no intelligence of its own, operating on preprogrammed lines.

machina [mah-KEE-nuh]

noun

A machine that requires a human operator to function.

logika [loh-JEE-kuh]

noun

A machine with its own onboard intelligence, capable of independent action.

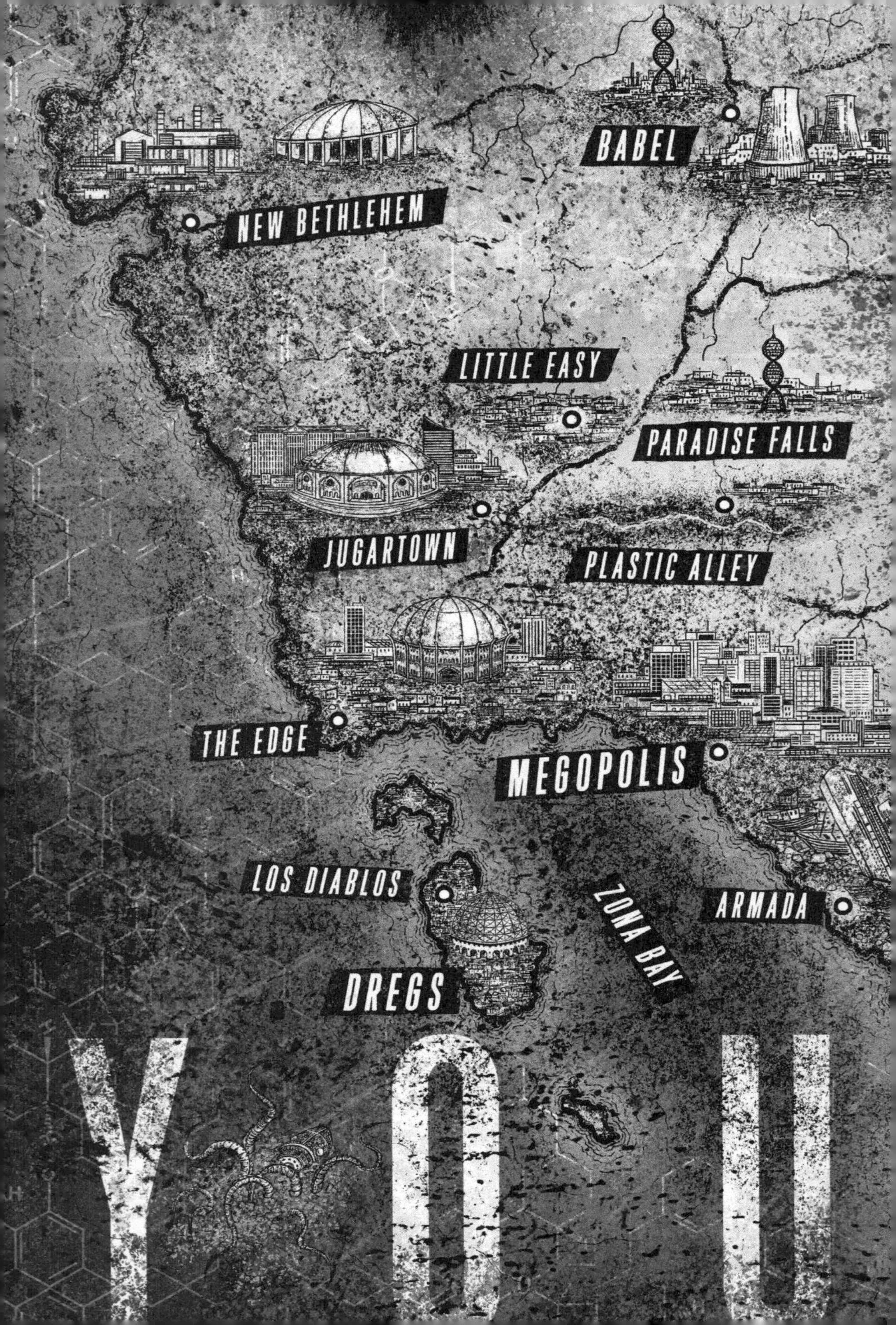

BABEL
NEW BETHLEHEM
LITTLE EASY
PARADISE FALLS
JUGARTOWN
PLASTIC ALLEY
THE EDGE
MEGOPOLIS
LOS DIABLOS
ZONA BAY
ARMADA
DREGS
YOU

2.0

REUNION

Almost everybody called her Eve.

At first glance, you might've mistaken her for human. She wouldn't have liked that much. Standing in a dead garden atop a hollow tower, she was just a silhouette against the scorching light. She was tall, a little gangly, boots too big and cargos too tight. Sun-bleached blond hair was undercut into a bloodstained fauxhawk. One eye was missing, the socket bruised from where she'd torn it free. She looked close to seventeen years old, but that was a lie. Just like everything around her.

"Sister."

She turned from the window, saw two figures behind her. The first was tall, blond, irises like green glass. A second stood beside him, dark hair as short as her fuse, close enough to the first to almost touch him.

Even wounded as they were, the pair were beautiful. Their maker had seen to that. But Eve knew there was something wrong with each of them—Gabriel with his broken heart, and Faith with her broken conscience. Like characters from some old 20C fairy tale, off to see the wizard to fix their missing pieces.

Except their wizard, their maker, their father, was dead. And no one could fix any of them now.

So there Eve stood, in the dead wizard's tower. Where the ones she'd called friends had fought to save her, where she'd felt her heart splinter inside her, where she'd awoken from a dead man's dream to discover what she finally, truly was.

Life. Like.

"What is it, Gabriel?" she asked.

Anger glittered in those glass-green eyes as he replied.

"Our brother and sisters have accepted your invitation."

PART 1

MITOSIS AND MEIOSIS

2.1

SPLITSVILLE

"Are these people *defective*?"

Lemon Fresh winced as another explosion burst against their hull. The world shook and her brainmeats ached and she was beginning to wonder if getting up this morning had been such a fizzy idea. The heavy armor they were encased in held fast, but the boom was still deafening, echoing around her skull. She could barely hear Ezekiel's shout from the driver's seat below.

"Their rockets seem to be working just fine!"

Lemon pulled her helmet down harder, yelling over the 'splodies. "Dimples, when you convinced me to jack this thing, it was on the understanding that nobody'd be stupid enough to pick a fight with a tank!"

"I didn't think anyone was!"

Another explosion burst against their roof, and Lemon held on to her gunner's seat for dear life. "Okay, I hate to be the one to break this to you, but—"

"Look, if you're that worried, you could always shoot them back!"

"I'm fifteen years old! I dunno how to shoot with a t—"

Another explosion cut Lemon's sentence off, but from the swearing she heard down in the driver's cabin, she was pretty sure Zeke got the gist. She looked into the vidscreens at her gunner's controls, heart sinking as she noticed their hull was now on fire, that another rocket team had joined the first in trying to murderize them, and finally decided that, yeah, crawling out of bed today?

Really bad move.

"We're allllll gonna die," she muttered.

It'd seemed like a pretty sensible plan at the time, too. . . .

They'd motored from Babel Tower less than five hours ago, and talking true, Lemon was still trying to wrap her head around it all. The throwdown with Gabriel and his lifelikes. The blood on the chrome. The murder of Silas Carpenter. The look in Eve's eyes as the bullet wounds in her chest slowly knitted closed.

"What's happening to me?"

Lemon had thought of Silas as her own grandpa, and the memory of his death was a fresh, hard kick to her chest. But right on top of Mister C's murder had come the revelation that the girl Lemon had known for two years, the girl she thought of as her bestest . . . that girl was a *robot*. Eve wasn't Eve at all. She was a lifelike, modeled after Nicholas Monrova's lost and youngest daughter, Ana.

True cert, and strange as it was, Lemon couldn't give a faulty credstik if her bestest was a bot. Growing up in Dregs, you learned to stick by your friends no matter what. Rule Number One in the Scrap:

Stronger together, together forever.

But Eve . . .

After all the years and all the spills and all the hurt . . .

. . . *She still sent me away.*

Lemon hadn't wanted to bail. But her radiation gear had been wrecked in the tussle, and the reactor in Babel Tower was still leaking—she didn't know how many rads she'd sucked up already. And whatever her feelings on the topic, Cricket wouldn't let her stick around anyways. The First Law of Robotics just wouldn't allow him to. So, with tears streaming down her face, she and Cricket and Ezekiel had slunk away from the heart of that hollow tower, away from the Myriad supercomputer that contained every one of Nicholas Monrova's dirty secrets, and away from the girl who was nothing close to a girl at all.

They'd had their pick of vehicles in the GnosisLabs armory. In the end, Ezekiel had settled on a grav-tank, big and bulky and bristling with guns. It'd be slower going, but the tank's cushion of magnetized particles would handle any terrain, and its rad-proof armor plating would offer better protection out on the Glass. Heart like lead in her chest, Lemon had taken one last look at the tower where her bestest had decided to remain. And then, bad as it hurt, they'd left her behind.

Ezekiel drove, and Lemon sulked, the kilometers grinding away in silence. They'd avoided the broken freeway where they'd fought the Preacher, heading west toward the setting sun. Lemon fought her sobs the whole way. Cricket plodded behind, looking back over his shoulder as Babel grew smaller and smaller still.

Before he'd died, Grandpa had transferred the little bot's consciousness into the Quixote—GnosisLabs' champion logika gladiator. The little fug stood seven meters tall now, wrecking-ball fists and urban-camo paintjob, optics burning like little blue suns. He might look like a faceful of hardcore, but Mister C had created Cricket to protect Eve, and Lemon knew the big bot was feeling just as sore as she was about leaving her behind.

It was close to sundown, and they had been making their way

through a series of deep sandstone gullies when the ambush hit. Lemon had been sitting in the gunner's seat, sucking down some bottled water and fighting a growing nausea in her belly. She'd heard a faint whistle, a shuddering boom, and half the gully wall just collapsed right on top of them. As the dust cleared, Lemon had realized the front half of their tank was buried under rubble. If she and Zeke were riding something with a little less armor, they'd already be fertilizer.

Cricket had disappeared under an avalanche of broken sandstone. Ezekiel had gunned the engine hard, but the tank didn't have the grunt to drag itself free of all that weight. That's when the first rocket streaked down from above, lighting up their hull with a blossom of bright, crackling flame.

"We're allllll gonna die," Lemon muttered.

Dusk was deepening, but the tank's cams were thermographic. Lem scoped two rocket emplacements on the gully walls above. They were protected by sandbags, crewed by three men apiece. The scavvers were wearing piecemeal armor and muddy gold tees underneath, painted with what looked like an oldskool knight's helmet.

Lem had to give them points for the color-coordinated outfits, but she wondered if these goons actually had any brainmeats inside their skulls. She watched through her gunner cams as the rubble behind them stirred, and a titanic fist punched up from beneath. Servos and engines whining, Cricket pushed himself free, shook himself like a dog to rid himself of the grit and dust.

"THAT TICKLED," the big bot declared.

"Cricket!" Ezekiel shouted. "Are you okay?"

A deep electronic reply rang out over the radio as another round exploded. "NOTHING A NICE BACK RUB WOULDN'T FIX. IF YOU'RE NOT TOO BUSY?"

"Lemon can't operate the tank turret. Take care of those rocketeers!"

". . . You mean shoot them?"

"No, I mean ask them to dinner!" Ezekiel shouted. *"Of course shoot them!"*

"Miss Fresh," came the big bot's reply. "Would you be so kind as to remind this idiot murderbot about the First Law of Robotics?"

Lemon sighed, spoke by rote. "A robot may not injure a human being or, through inaction, allow a hu—"

Another explosion rocked the tank, and Ezekiel started cursing with way more chops than Lem would've given him credit for. Thing was, even though Crick couldn't lay any kind of hurting on a human, picking a fight with a grav-tank and seventy tons of armored robot gladiator didn't seem like the most sensible plan. So why had these scavvers decided to—

". . . Oh," Lemon said, blinking at her rear cams.

"Oh what?" Ezekiel called, still gunning the engine.

"Oh, sh—"

Another blast rocked the tank, and Lemon fell clean off her seat, splitting her brow on the controls. Pulling her helmet back on, she hollered into her comms.

"Crick, check our six, we got capital T!"

The big bot turned to face their new pack of trouble. Stomping along the gully behind them came the ugliest machina Lem had ever seen. On its four legs, it only stood three meters high, but it was at least seven long. Cobbled together from the remains of half a dozen other machina, it had a serpentine neck, a couple of old earthmover scoops fashioned into snaggle-toothed jaws. Two floodlights atop the scoops gave the impression of large, glowing eyes.

The machina reminded her of a vid Eve had shown her once. These big lizard things that had romped the planet before humans came along to wreck everything.

Dinosomethings?

Anyway. It was big. And rusty. And stomping right at Cricket.

Its pilot was mostly hidden inside a heavy safety cage, but Lemon could see he was dolled up like his rocket-friends, muddy gold colors and all. His voice was thick and rough, crackling over the machina's PA system.

"Dunghill knave! I challenge thee!"

Cricket tilted his head. ". . . Um, what?"

The machina pilot opened up with a pair of autoguns, the shells shattering on Cricket's hull. The bot raised his hands to shield his optics, sparks and tracer rounds lit up the dusk. Deciding the machina was a bigger threat to Lemon than the rocket crews, Crick charged headlong into its line of fire.

"You waiting for an invitation, Stumpy?" he yelled.

Ezekiel spat a final curse and thumped a fist on the console. Sliding out of his chair, he squeezed past Lemon and up into the turret. Zeke was tall, broad-shouldered. Olive skin and short dark curls and bright blue eyes. His right arm was missing below the elbow, but the injury came nowhere close to ruining the picture. Ratcheting the turret hatch open with his good hand, he shot Lemon a wink.

"Stay there, Freckles."

"True cert," she nodded. "I'm too pretty to die."

Pushing the hatch open, he was gone. Lemon watched on cams as the lifelike dashed off, skipping sideways to avoid another rocket blast. He moved like a song through the broken stone, disappearing up the gully into the smoke and the dusk.

"Run, ye three-inch coward!" one of the rocketeers cried.

Meantime, Cricket was toe-to-toeing the enemy machina. Crick was still getting used to his new body—the old one had been forty centimeters tall, after all, and he clearly wasn't quite at home in the body of a seven-meter-high WarBot. But the Quixote had been made by the best techs in Gnosis R & D, and Crick's strength was scarygood. With one titanic fist, he crushed the machina's autoguns to scrap, tearing them off in a hail of sparks. The scavver pilot reared his machina up onto its hind legs, roared into the PA.

"Have at thee, villain!"

A burst of fire exploded from the machina's jaws, engulfing Cricket in blue flame. A blast like that would've probably melted his old bod to slag, and instinctively, Crick flinched away with a booming, electronic yelp. The machina pilot followed up with a swipe from one massive front leg, smashing the logika into the gully wall. A victorious cry went up from the rocketeers above.

"A hit!"

"A very palpable hit!"

"Who *are* these goons?" Lemon muttered, shaking her head.

Cricket climbed back onto his feet as the machina crashed into him, seizing one of his arms in those earthmover jaws. Crick struck back, tearing away the panelwork at the beast's throat to expose the hydraulics beneath.

Meanwhile, Ezekiel had climbed the cliffs farther down the gully, and made his way back under the cover of dusk. Thanks to the Libertas virus, lifelikes weren't beholden to the First Law, and Ezekiel had proved in the past he had no problems with grievous bodily harm when it came to protecting his friends. He stole up behind the scavvers in the first rocket emplacement, and without ceremony, booted one over the sandbags and onto the jagged rocks ten meters below.

Cricket ripped loose a handful of cables from the machina's throat, hydraulic fluid spewing from the rends. The jaws lost pressure and Crick pulled his arm free, raising one enormous fist to slam the head into the ground. But before the blow could land, his optics began flickering, and the big bot wobbled on his feet.

He took a step backward, struggling to keep his balance.

"I DON'T FEEL SO . . ."

The machina pivoted, its massive tail knocking Cricket back up the gully. The big bot tumbled along the ground, crashing to a halt against the grav-tank's rear. Lemon fell out of her seat again, wiping the blood from her split eyebrow as she peered at cams. The big bot was trying to stand, but his movements were sluggish, clumsy, like he'd spent a hard night on the home brew.

"Crick, what's wrong?" she asked.

"I DON'T . . ."

". . . Crick, you gotta get up!"

The dinomachina was stomping toward him, jaws limp, one floodlight smashed. Ezekiel had leapt the six meters across the gully to the other emplacement, and was busy ending the second crew. But as Lemon watched, the scavver pilot slapped a control pad in his cockpit, and a cluster of short-range rockets popped from the machina's shoulders, ready to unload right at Zeke's exposed back.

"Fat-kidneyed rascal!" the scavver cried.

The situation had turned a deep shade of ugly.

Lemon knew she should stay in the tank. It was safer there. She was still aching and tired from the Babel throwdown, and feeling kinda queasy, talking true. But Cricket was her friend. Ezekiel was her friend. And beat and sick though she felt, Lemon had lost enough friends already today. Without thinking, she lunged toward the tank's hatch, popped up into the smoke and flame. And fixing the machina in her stare, she dragged her cherry-red bangs from her eyes, pulled her helmet on tighter and stretched out her hand.

She'd been twelve years old when she first used It. Just a skinny little scavvergirl, scratching out a living on the mean-streets of Los Diablos. It'd been late at night outside the Skin District, and she'd stolen a credstik, slipped it into an auto-peddler for a quick meal. But the automata had swallowed her stik, no food to show for it, and Lem had just lost it. Rage boiling in her empty belly. A gray static, building up behind her eyes. She'd made a fist and punched the bot, and the automata had spat sparks and burst clean open, spewing cans of Neo-Meat™ from its belly.

She'd snatched up a few meals and run. Fast and far as she could before the Graycoats or the Brotherhood saw her. Knowing from that very first moment she had to hide it, lie on it, stomp it down and never show or tell anyone what she was.

Trashbreed.

Abnorm.

Deviate.

Now, looking at the big, lumbering machina, Lemon pictured that auto-peddler. Felt that gray static building up behind her eyes. Fingers stretched toward it.

And then she made a fist.

The machina bucked like someone had punched it. Hydraulics shrieked, power cables burst, a blinding shear of electrical current arced across its rusting skin. The pilot screamed, frying inside the cockpit as the voltage lit him up, as his machina stumbled and crumpled like paper into a smoking, sparking heap.

Fried to ruins.

Just like that.

Behind her, the last rocketeer plunged into the gully floor with an awful, wet crunch. Ezekiel shouted down from the emplacement above.

"You okay, Freckles?"

Lemon hauled off her helmet, blinking blood from her eye. Her heart was hammering in her chest, but she put on her braveface. Her streetface. The face that told the world she was big enough to handle anything it threw at her and more.

"Toldja already, Dimples. I'm too pretty to die."

She grabbed a chem-extinguisher with shaking hands, climbed out of the turret and doused the burning hull. Jumping onto the tank's rear, she sized up Cricket. The big bot was dented and scratched from his brawl, but his paintjob was apparently flame-retardant, so the good news was he wasn't on fire.

"You okay, you little fug?"

"I . . . THINK SO?" The big bot shrugged. "AND D-DON'T CALL ME LITTLE."

Ezekiel carefully scaled down from the emplacement, dropping the final three meters onto the rocks below. Dusting his palm against his battered jeans, he made his way across the broken stone, fugazi blue eyes on the fallen logika.

"What happened?"

"EAT IT, STUMPY," the big bot growled. "A NICE BIG BOWL OF IT."

"Seriously, Crick," Lemon said. "Are you all right?"

"YEAH. I'M . . . GOOD? I TH-THINK?"

Cricket stood on wobbling legs, the glow of his optics flickering and fluttering. He steadied himself against the gully wall, barely able to keep himself upright. Ezekiel sighed, and spinning on his heel, he climbed into the tank. A few moments later, he emerged with a heavy toolbox under his one good arm.

"Sit down," he said, motioning to the broken rock. "Let me have a look."

". . . You're suggesting I let you poke around inside me?" Cricket fixed the lifelike in a flickering stare. "I thought Lemon was the comedian in this outfit."

Lemon frowned at the big bot. "Wait, I thought *you* were the comedy relief, and I was the lovable sidekick?"

"Cricket, if there's something wrong with you, maybe I can spot it," Ezekiel said. "I know a little about bots. Not as much as Eve, but a little."

The mention of her bestest's name brought a fresh ache in Lemon's chest, a stillness to the group. Ezekiel glanced back toward Babel, and she could see how bad he was hurting, too. They'd had no choice. Evie had told them to leave. But . . .

"Don't you dare say her name," the logika growled.

Ezekiel blinked, turned back to the logika.

"I miss her, too, Cricket," he murmured.

"Of course you do, murderbot," Cricket said. "That's why you ran away from her as fast as you could."

"She *told* me to leave," Ezekiel said, his voice rising with his temper. "This was her choice. The first one she ever had in her life, don't you get that?"

The big logika's massive metal hands *spangspangspangggg*ed as he brought them together in a round of applause.

"Oh, Mister Ezekiel, you're my hero."

Lemon raised her hands, stepped between them. "Now, now, boys—"

"Go to hell, Cricket," Ezekiel hissed. "What do you know about it?"

"I know you left her behind," the bot growled, standing taller as his voice grew louder. "I know everybody lied to her!

Everybody betrayed her! Silas, Lemon, her father, you! Can you imagine for one minute what that felt like?"

"I didn't want t—"

"And then she finds out she's not even human and you claim to love her and YOU JUST LEFT HER THERE!"

Lemon's heart was hammering. Every one of Cricket's words was like a bullet fired right at Ezekiel's chest. She saw them strike. Saw the rage welling up in the lifelike's eyes, twisting his hands into fists.

"So did *you*," he spat at the bot.

The blue of Cricket's optics burned into a furious white.

"You rotten sonofa . . ."

A two-ton fist came crashing down on the spot Ezekiel had stood a split second before, the ground shattering like glass. Cricket roared in shapeless rage, swung at Ezekiel again, the lifelike once more slipping aside. The big bot tried to scoop him up, but Ezekiel was faster, darting between Cricket's legs and leaping up to seize hold of the armor plating on his lower back with his one good hand.

"Cricket, are you *crazy*?" Lemon shouted.

Cricket roared again, his voice box crackling at the volume. He slapped at the lifelike as if he were an insect, massive hands clanging against his hull like some great, booming gong. Ezekiel's superhuman agility was all that saved him from being pulverized, the lifelike hauling himself up the seams and rivets in the WarBot's impenetrable hull until he reached his shoulder.

"Cricket, stop!" Lemon wailed. "STOP IT!"

The logika fell still immediately at the girl's command. He bristled with outrage, glowing optics fixed on the lifelike perched atop his shoulder.

"You're lucky some of us still obey the Three Laws, m-moth . . ."

The big bot swayed, his optics flickering again.

"Crick . . . are you okay?" Lemon called.

"I d-don't feel s-so . . ."

The light in the logika's optics flickered one final time and went out completely. His towering body wobbled a second longer, then fell like a collapsing skyscraper. Seventy tons of WarDome champion came falling right at Lemon's head, and she shrieked as she dove aside, hitting the gully floor, elbows grinding in the gravel as Cricket crashed to the ground with a boom.

Ezekiel picked himself up from the dust, ran to the girl's side.

"Are you all right?" he asked, helping her to her feet.

Lemon winced, pawed at her bloody brow, her bleeding arms. But her eyes were fixed on Cricket. The big bot had dropped like someone had shot him, and now lay motionless on the broken ground.

"What the hells just happened?" she whispered.

Ezekiel looked the big bot over, hands on hips. Walking to the tank's toolbox, he started rummaging around inside. "Let's find out."

Lemon watched, chewing her lip with worry as the lifelike took a power drill and began unbolting a maintenance hatch on Cricket's chestplate.

"Um, do you know what you're doing, by any chance?" she asked.

Zeke mumbled around the bolts held between his teeth. "Not really, no."

"Oh, goody."

Ezekiel pulled back the small armor plate and looked over

the readouts inside. He poked and prodded, his pretty brow furrowed, finally leaning back with a sigh.

"Power," he declared.

Lemon blinked. "He's outta juice?"

"I'm not an expert, but yeah, looks like." Zeke tapped a series of LED readouts inside the cavity. "Batteries are at one percent. Been sitting inactive inside that R & D bay for two years, his levels must have run close to zero through disuse. Should've checked them before we left, I guess. Stupid of me."

"Um," Lemon said. "I don't suppose you've got any spares in your pockets?"

"From the look of them, these powercells weigh about a ton apiece."

"So that's a no?"

The lifelike glanced back over his shoulder again, brow creased in thought. His voice was almost too soft for Lemon to hear.

"They'd have spares back at Babel, though. In the armory."

". . . You wanna go back? We just left!"

He looked from the hollow tower in the distance, back to their broken bot. "Got a better idea?"

"Our tank is buried under a squillion tons of rock, Dimples."

"There's no such thing as a squillion. But yeah, I noticed."

"So wait, lemme get this straight." Lemon folded her arms. "You're suggesting we *walk* back across a couple of hundred kilometers of irradiated wasteland, to a tower full of murderbots who'll probably be back up and moving by the time we arrive? And then drag one-ton batteries back out here, hoping the other dustnecks who live in this gully haven't stripped Cricket for parts in the meantime?"

". . . You raise a good point."

Lemon gave a shoddy curtsy. "Several, I think you'll find."

Ezekiel pouted, rubbing his chin in thought.

"You're right," he finally declared. "You should stay here in the tank."

". . . You wanna leave me here *by myself*?"

"It's not a plan without flaws." Ezekiel shrugged. "But it's safer here inside this thing's armor, and I'll move quicker alone. And, again . . . if you've got a better one?"

Lemon plopped down onto the turret. She knew less about logika than Ezekiel did, which was a nice way of saying she knew nothing at all. And if there was a problem with Crick's power supply, a fresh battery sounded like the only kind of fix.

But going back there meant maybe running into Gabriel. Faith. *Eve.*

Going back to Babel meant leaving her here alone.

Abandoned.

Again.

Lemon pulled off her helmet, brushed the dirt off her freckles. She racked her skull for another way out of this, but she'd never been the brains of their outfit. If there was a smarter play to make, true cert, she couldn't see it.

"You know, crawling out of bed today?"

Lemon shook her head and sighed.

"*Really* bad move."

2.2

JACKED

"Now remember, stay in the tank," Zeke said.

Lemon rubbed at the bandage he'd placed over her split brow. "Yes, Dad."

"Keep the hatch sealed, no matter what." The lifelike reached into the weapons locker, shoved a heavy pistol down the back of his grubby jeans. "I don't care if a guy knocks on the door offering free pony rides, you keep it shut."

"Ponies are extinct."

"You remember what I showed you about the guns, right? This is your targeting system. When it's locked, you trip the safety and fire with this."

"Yeah, yeah."

"Just keep your head down. I'll be back before you can say 'Ezekiel is the bravest and most handsomest boy I know.'"

". . . I see what you did there, Dimples."

The lifelike knelt beside her. He was smiling at his own joke, but she could see concern in his baby blues. "Look, I'll be quick, okay? I move fast, I don't tire easily. As soon as I get the power-cells and wheels, I'll run straight back here."

"You sure you're just going back there for batteries?" she asked softly.

"... What other reason would I have?"

Lemon raised one eyebrow, fixed him in a withering stare.

"I'm not going back for Eve," the lifelike insisted.

"Rrrrrright."

"She's not Ana, Lemon," Ezekiel said. "She never was."

Lemon chewed her lip, trying to fight the weight that had been growing on her shoulders ever since they left Babel. She knew there were more important things to worry about, that now wasn't really the time. Still, she couldn't help but ask.

"Okay, so how long until you bail on me for real, then?"

Ezekiel blinked, taken aback. "What do you mean?"

"I mean, that's your plan, right?" Lemon looked hard into those fugazi eyes. "Myriad told us the real Ana Monrova is still out there somewhere. Hurt maybe, but still alive. Daddy Monrova hid her. And you're all head over heels for her. So you're eventually gonna wanna find her, right?"

"... I hadn't really thought about it."

Lemon rolled her eyes. "Rule Number Seven in the Scrap, Dimples. *Never scam a scammer.*"

The lifelike sighed, looked up through the open hatch to the night above. This deep in the wastes, you could actually see a few of the brighter stars up there, struggling to shine through the curtain of pollution and airborne fallout. The starlight kissed Ezekiel's cheeks, gleamed in his eyes, and Lemon's chest hurt a little at the sight of him. She knew he'd never belong to her. That the warm fuzzy she got in her belly when he called her Freckles was never going to be more than that.

But damn he was pretty. ...

A tiny light shot overhead, twinkling as it fell toward the

horizon. Lemon watched it spin through the dark, wondering if she should make a wish.

"Shooting star," she murmured.

Ezekiel followed the falling light with those pretty plastic eyes, shaking his head. "It's just a satellite. There's thousands up there. Left over from before the Fall."

"Sometimes I wonder if your maker put any romance in your soul at all, Dimples," she said sourly. "And other times, I think they gave you way too much."

"Have you ever been in love, Lemon?" he asked.

"Nah." Lemon sniffed, wiped her nose on her grubby sleeve. "I kissed a boy named Chopper a few times. He was a gutter runner in Dregs like me. It was nice. But then he got a little gropey and I kinda sorta broke his nose a little bit."

Ezekiel smiled lopsided, his dimple on high beam, and Lemon's belly went all tingly despite herself.

"You will be one day," he promised. "I know it. And then you'll understand."

". . . You're in love with Ana, huh? Got it real bad."

"Yeah," the lifelike replied, fervor in his eyes. "But the good kind of bad."

"But you loved Eve, too."

"I thought Eve *was* Ana, Lemon."

The girl sighed, flipped her bangs from her eyes. "Look, Dimples, I didn't spend too long in that tower, but I'm smart enough to know the girl who grew up in a palace like that had about *zero* in common with the girl you met in Dregs. Eve is Eve. Riotgrrl. Botdoc. Hard as nails. And you still loved her. I love her, too. So why are we just leaving her behind? Why don't we *both* go back there and get her?"

The lifelike thought a long while before he answered.

"This is Eve's choice, Lemon. And she never really had one before now. I know it's hard, but we can't *force* her to leave. That'd make us just as bad as Monrova and Silas." He ran his hand over his stubbled chin and sighed. "Ana was the girl who taught me what it was to be alive. And if she's still out there somewhere? I owe it to her to find her. These past two years, walking through this wasteland . . . Sometimes thoughts of her were all that kept me going."

"So let's say fairy tales come true and you manage to track her down," Lemon said. "What if the girl you find isn't the girl you remember?"

"She'll *always* be the girl I remember. She's the girl who made me real."

Lemon felt fear dig its icy fingers inside of her. Ever since she'd been left behind in that detergent box as a bub, she'd been afraid of being alone. It'd taken her years to work up the courage to trust Evie, trust Silas, trust anyone not to abandon her the way her folks had. And now she was on the verge of losing it all.

"Look, I know she's important to you," she told Zeke. "But with Eve staying in Babel and Cricket OOC, I'm rapidly running out of crew. And true cert, without Evie, I don't even know what I'm doing out here. I'm the *sidekick*, Dimples. I can't carry this show by myself."

Ezekiel's eyes softened, and he gently squeezed her hand. "I won't bail on you, Lemon. I'm coming back, I promise."

Looking into that pretty, plastic blue, Lemon felt a lump rising in her throat. Stomping the tears down with her oversized boots, she tossed her bangs out of her face and replied with her customary bravado.

"Spit on it, then."

". . . What?"

Lemon spat into her palm, offered it to the lifelike.

"Rule Number Nine in the Scrap. *Spit makes it stick.*"

With a smirk, Ezekiel spat into his hand, sealed the pact with a shake. Lemon felt the weight on her shoulders ease off a little. The night shine a little brighter.

"Okay," she said, raising a finger to his face. "Don't be a welcher now."

Ezekiel smiled, pulled the oversized gunner's helmet back on Lemon's head. "Stay in the tank. Pony-ride salesmen or no. I'll take one of these headsets, so if you want anything, you just yell, all right?"

Lemon pressed the transmit button on her comms rig and yelled, "Clean socks! And something to read!"

Zeke ripped off his headset with a wince.

"Walked into that one," Lemon grinned.

The lifelike leaned down and kissed the top of her helmet. "Stay safe."

Ezekiel stole off into the night, just as quiet as the rest of it. With a sad sigh, Lemon locked the hatch behind him.

———

She woke to the strangest sound.

Lemon's eyes shot open, and though she was sitting in the turret of a top-of-the-line killing machine, she reached instinctively for the small knife stashed in her belt buckle. She used to slit pockets with it, back in her Los Diablos days. Slit anyone who got too far into her face, too, talking true.

Seeing no immediate threat, Lemon pawed the crusties from her eyes. From the heat radiating through the tank hull, she guessed the sun was already up—she must've slept the whole night away. Did she imagine that noise or did she . . .

Nope. There it goes again.

It was weird. A sort of bubbly gurgling. And with growing alarm, Lemon realized it was coming from her own stomach.

"Ohhhh, crap . . ."

Lemon leaned forward and vomited all over the floor. It was the kind of sick that left you feeling like you'd been hollowed out with a spork. Groaning, she wiped the puke off her chin just in time to vomit again. Eyes filled with tears, toes curling, she gave the can of Neo-Meat™ she'd scoffed last night right back to the world.

"Urgggg," she moaned at the end of it. "Septic."

She drew a few shuddering breaths, trying to make up her mind if she was going to chuck again. Deciding she was safe for the moment, she grabbed her bottle of H_2O, rinsed her mouth and realized too late that she had nowhere to spit.

Ezekiel had ordered her not to leave the tank.

He'd been *very* specific about it.

Cheek ballooning, Lemon stabbed at her console, lighting up the turret cams. She could see the ruins of the scavvers' machina outside, the tumbled sandstone, Cricket lying sprawled where he'd fallen.

Looks safe enough?

Deciding Dimples would have been a little more relaxed if he knew she'd be trapped in here with the stink of fresh vomit, Lemon cranked open the hatch, stuck her head up and spat. Rinsing her mouth, she spat again, pulling down her goggles against the blinding light and peering at the gully around her.

The sun had only just cleared the horizon, but the air around her was already rippling—it was going to be a feral day. Lemon scoped the rocks one last time, but seeing no trouble, she crawled out of the tank to escape the smell. Her belly was aching kinda fierce, her hands a little shaky.

Hopping down to the dirt, she made her way around to peer up into Cricket's face. His new head was styled like an oldskool warrior helmet from the history virtch—a smooth faceplate, square jaw and heavy brow, his once-bright-blue optics now dark.

"Crick?"

Lemon heard a buzzing in her ear, swiped at a fat blowfly circling her head.

"You hear me, you little fug?"

The bot made no reply. The girl sighed, rubbing at her stomach. She'd tossed up everything she'd eaten, but she still felt puketastic, her skin damp with sweat. She took an experimental swig of water, swallowed with a wince. She'd never heard of a can of Neo-Meat™ going bad before—the stuff was more preservatives than actual food. Maybe it'd been locked inside the tank too long?

The blowfly returned, swooping in lazy circles about her head. She took another half-hearted swipe, but as it buzzed up into her face, Lemon realized it wasn't a fly at all. It was a fat, angry-looking bumblebee.

She'd only ever seen pics of them on the history virtch—she'd always been taught they'd died out before the Quake, so it was true strange to see one all the way out here in the wastes. Its little furry bod was banded yellow and black, its sting gleaming. She took a serious swing, almost knocking it out of the air. Buzzing angrily, the bumblebee beat a hasty retreat back over the gully walls.

"Yeah, that's right," Lemon growled after it. "Tell your friends, friendo."

She wondered where Ezekiel was, how close he'd got to Babel. Realizing she could just ask, she climbed up onto the tank, reached inside for her helmet. As she pulled it onto her head, she noticed the bumblebee had returned, sitting on the hatch beside her hand. It flapped its wings, gave a furious little buzz.

"Back for more, eh?" she scowled. "You have chosen poorly, little one."

Lemon slowly pulled off her boot, raised it high above her head . . . just as another bumblebee buzzed out of the sky and landed right on the tip of her nose.

"Oh, craaaap," she whispered.

Lemon held her breath, staring cross-eyed into the little bugger's beady black stare.

". . . You know, when I said tell your friends, I was just being sassy."

She heard the droning of lazy wings in the sunshine heat. She didn't dare move, eyes fixed on the nose invader's pointy butt parts. But as the buzzing grew louder, she glanced about, careful not to move her head. She saw a dozen more bumblebees on the gully walls, doing lazy circle-work in the air around her. Moving slow, she tapped the transmit button on her helmet's commset.

"Um . . . Dimples?" she asked. "Dimples, do you read me?"

She heard a short crackle of static, Ezekiel's faint reply.

"Lemon? Is everything okay?"

"Um, that depends. What do bees eat?"

". . . What?"

"Seriously, what do they eat?"

"Well, I'm not an expert or anything. But I think they probably eat honey?"

"...Not people?"

"Nnnno. I think it's safe to assume they don't eat people. Dare I ask why?"

The air was full of bees now, a swaying, rolling swarm, filling the air with a droning hum. Lemon heard soft, scuffing footsteps above, slowly craned her neck to look at the gully walls overhead. Lem saw a strange woman standing on the ridge above, looking down at her.

She was tall, pretty, deep brown skin. Her hair was woven into long, sharp dreadlocks. Her eyes were a strange, glittering gold—Lemon figured they must be cybernetics of some sort. She was wearing a long desert-red cloak despite the heat, a strange rifle slung on her back. Under the cloak, she wore a suit of what might've been black rubber, dusty from a long road, skintight and molded with strange bumps and ridges over some serious curves.

I've seen that kind of outfit before. . . .

Lemon was motionless, bee still perched on her nose, eyes fixed on the stranger above. The woman peeled aside the high collar of her suit, exposing the throat beneath. Lemon's belly ran cold as she realized that the woman's skin was pocked with dozens, maybe hundreds, of tiny hexagonal holes.

Honeycombed . . .

More bumblebees were crawling through her hair, along her face, across her smile. And as Lemon watched, dozens more swarmed out from beneath the strange woman's *skin*.

"Oh, spank my spankables," the girl whispered.

The woman looked down at Lemon, golden eyes gleaming.

"Lemonfresh," she said. *"We have been hunting her."*

Endless dunes and jagged rocks and dust as far as the eye could see. Ezekiel cut through the wasteland with a long loping stride, the kilometers disappearing beneath his boots. He was making good time; he figured he'd be back at Babel by sundown. He could see the tower ahead, rising up from the horizon in its double-helix spiral, his shadow stretching toward it.

He didn't know what he'd do when he got there, truth told. If Gabriel and Faith had recovered from the beatings they'd taken, if Eve . . .

Eve.

He didn't really know what to do about her, either. He'd not talked to Lemon about their last exchange right before he left the tower. The veiled threats the newly awakened lifelike had made. The dangerous gleam in Eve's eye as she'd spoken those final, fateful words.

"Next time we meet? I don't think it's going to turn out the way you want it to."

He wasn't quite sure what she'd meant. Eve was furious, he knew that. About the lies Silas and Nicholas Monrova had heaped on her. The false life they'd built her. She had a right to be angry. With them. With *him.* But Lemon had been correct—even if he did love Ana, a part of him had loved Eve, too.

Is that why you're headed back there?

So soon after leaving?

It was more than the fact she was Ana's doppelgänger. Eve had a strength and determination he'd never seen in the original Ana. A fire and resourcefulness, born from years of clawing out a living in a trashpit like Dregs. But if Eve threw her lot in with Gabriel, or worse, their brother Uriel, if she used that fire to aid his siblings in ridding the world of the dinosaur that had been humanity . . .

What could she become?

"Um . . . Dimples? Dimples, do you read me?"

The lifelike slowed his pace, tapped the receiver on his headset.

"Lemon?" he asked. "Is everything okay?"

"Um, that depends. What do bees eat?"

". . . What?"

"Seriously, what do they eat?"

Ezekiel rubbed his chin, wondering what the girl was on about. "Well, I'm not an expert or anything. But I think they probably eat honey?"

". . . Not people?"

"Nnnno. I think it's safe to assume they don't eat people. Dare I ask why?"

"Oh, spank my spankables . . ."

"Freckles? Are y—"

"Dimples, help!" came the crackling plea. *"There's a cr—"*

A squeal of static washed over the headset, and the transmission died.

"Lemon?" Ezekiel tapped the headset. "Lemon, can you hear me?"

Nothing. No reply at all. But he'd caught the fear and adrenaline in her voice, and with a curse, he turned and began running back the way he'd come. No easy loping stride this time, but a furious, flat-out sprint. His teeth were gritted, his arm pumping, boots pounding the dirt. He yelled her name into the commset, got no answer, the fear in his belly blooming into a freezing panic.

He'd told her to stay in the tank. She should've been safe there. What on earth could've gotten to her inside a shell of rad-proofed armor plating?

Unless she got out . . .

You never should have left her.

He ran. Fast as he could. He'd never pushed himself as hard in his short life, his heart thundering, veins pumping acid. He was the peak of physical perfection, generated in the GnosisLabs to be more than human. But in the end, he was only bone and muscle, blood and meat. Even pounding the dust as quick as he could, hours had passed by the time he arrived, the sun burning high in the sky, his skin and clothes drenched with sweat. The gully was deathly silent. Like a tomb. Like that cell in Babel in the moments after he and his siblings had murdered the Monrova family. As he'd raised the gun to Eve's head and whispered those two meaningless words.

"I'm sorry."

The tank was exactly where he'd left it. But the hatch was open, and worse, there was no sign of Lemon *or* Cricket. Ezekiel drew his heavy pistol, crept through the rocks, listening intently with his enhanced senses and hearing nothing. He leapt up onto the tank, peered inside, saw it had been partially stripped—the computer gear, the cannon ammunition, the radio equipment was all gone. They'd tried to bust into the weapons locker, but hadn't been able to burn through the metal.

In front of the scorched cabinet door sat Lemon's helmet, spattered with vomit and a few drops of blood. And beside it lay a couple of squashed bugs.

No . . . not bugs . . .

Bees . . . ?

He knelt by the little corpses, picked them both up and cradled them in his palm. His eyes were good enough to count the freckles on a girl's face in a fraction of a second, track a moth in a midnight sky. Squinting at the insects, he saw the pair were twins—not just similar, but identical, down to the number of hairs on their bodies, the facets of their eyes. And turning them over on his palm, the lifelike saw the stripes on their abdomens were arranged in a tiny pattern.

A bar code.

The lifelike closed his fist.

"BioMaas," he whispered.

2.3

CHANGE

When Ezekiel mentioned pony rides, Lemon was pretty sure this wasn't what he had in mind.

Maybe the beast had been a horse once, back before BioMaas gene-modded it beyond all recognition. It still had four legs, so that was kind of good news. But as far as Lemon knew—and granted, she'd only ever seen them in the virtch because they'd been extinct for decades—most horses wore their skeletons on the *inside*.

She was sitting near its neck, her wrists bound in translucent resin. The strange woman sat behind her, one arm about her waist to make sure she didn't fall. The beast they rode was black, its hide covered in bony ridges—more like organic armor than actual skin. Its eyes were faceted like a fly's, and Lemon was pretty sure its legs had too many joints. Instead of a mane and tail, it had long, segmented spines that clicked and shushed together as it moved.

They were riding south along the gully at a full gallop. Lemon's captor was pressed to her back, and the girl realized she could feel a deep buzzing inside the woman's chest when she exhaled. It made her skin want to crawl right off her bod.

"Where you taking me?" she asked.

"*CityHive.*"

The woman's voice trembled like an old electric voxbox, as if her whole chest vibrated when she spoke. It was almost . . . insectoid.

"The BioMaas capital?" Lemon blinked. "What for?"

"*Nau'shi told us about Lemonfresh. Lemonfresh is important. She is needed.*"

Nau'shi was the name of the BioMaas kraken that had scooped her and Evie and the rest of her crew out of the waters of Zona Bay. A crew member named Carer had told Lemon the same thing before she'd climbed into the kraken's lifeboat: "*Lemonfresh is important. She is needed.*" At the time, Lemon had just figured Carer didn't have her boots laced all the way to the top. But now . . .

"I'm no kind of special, okay? So why don't you just let me go?"

"*We cannot, Lemonfresh,*" the woman replied. "*Only a matter of time before the Lords of the Polluted realize their error.*"

". . . The Lords of the Polluted?" the girl scoffed. "Is that some new drudge band I shoulda heard of?"

"*Daedalus Technologies.*"

"Wha—"

"*Hsst,*" the woman hissed.

Lemon fell silent as a fat bumblebee buzzed down from the sky, coming to rest on the woman's shoulder. The girl craned her head, watched with horrified fascination as the bug crawled *inside* one of the hexagonal burrows in the woman's throat. The woman's golden eyes blinked rapidly as she softly sighed.

"*Trouble ahead.*"

". . . What kind of trouble?"

"*Oldflesh,*" she growled.

These gullies seemed to go on forever—probably torn into the earth when the Quake created Zona Bay. Some of the cracks were hundreds of meters across, almost as deep. Lemon and her captor entered the remnants of a town that had collapsed into the fissure when the ground opened up. Toppled buildings and rusty autowrecks, the shell of an old fuel station, long sucked dry. What might've been an old sports arena had split clean down the middle, one half toppled nose-first into the rocks. Lemon saw a sign, faded from decades beneath the sun. The same helmet that had adorned the shirts of those scavvers that had jumped them yesterday was painted on it, chipped and faded lettering beneath.

HOME OF TH V   GO   KNIGHTS
st 20 7

Ahead, two tenements had collapsed together to form a crude archway. Lemon saw their path led right between them. The walls were steep, there was no room to dance—it was a perfect place for an ambush, true cert. Lem felt her heart beating faster, remembering the bushwhacking that had buried their grav-tank. Her eyes roamed the empty windows above, but she couldn't see zip.

At some unspoken command, the horsething came to a halt on the open ground. The air about them hummed with bees, her captor's eyes gleaming gold.

"Let us pass, oldflesh," the agent called. "And remain in this living grave. Or stand in our way, and be sent to your next."

Lemon caught movement in the ruins around them—a handful of scavvers in those same grubby gold shirts, armed with stub guns and rusty cutters. Heavy footsteps crunched on the asphalt ahead, and Lemon saw a brick wall of a man striding slowly toward them. He wore that old knight's helm scrawled on a bloodstained jersey, a couple of six-shot stub guns at his belt. His armor was made of hubcaps and rusty street signs.

"Lo, gentlemen!" he drawled to his crew. "On my life, a challenge!"

"Challenge!" roared one of the scavvers.

"Chaaaaallenge!"

The big scavver fixed Lemon's abductor in his stare, fingers twitching over the shooters at his waist.

"By my heel, ma'am," he smiled. "I accept."

The woman didn't move, but Lemon heard a small humming noise in the back of her throat. The big scavver's grip closed around his guns just as a fat yellow bumblebee landed on his cheek. He cursed, flinching as the bee sank its stinger into his skin. Lemon heard a chorus of surprised yelps from the buildings around them.

The big scavver swayed, wide eyes fixed on the BioMaas woman. Lemon could see a tracery of fine red veins creeping out along his face where the bee had stuck him. He gasped, clutched at his throat like he couldn't breathe. Gurgling as he fell to his knees. And quick as a morning-after goodbye, the scavver toppled facedown, dead as the dirt he was kissing.

"Insert fancy swears here . . . ," Lemon whispered.

From the sounds she heard in the ruins, she guessed the rest of the scavver crew were suffering the same fate as their boss. Lemon heard strangled cries, a few choking prayers. And then?

Nothing but the hymn of tiny wings.

She twisted to look at the woman sitting behind her, her belly cold with fear. Her captor's face was impassive, dark skin filmed with dust. This close, Lemon could see her dreadlocks weren't hair at all, but the same kind of segmented spines as the horsething's mane and tail. Her eyes glittered gold in the scorching light.

"It's a good thing I already puked this morning," Lemon said.

That golden stare flickered to her own.

"Lemonfresh has nothing to fear from us."

"Ooookay?" Lemon said. "Having trouble believing that one, but let's just run with it for now. Since we're being all chummy and whatnot, you got a name? You BioMaas folks are usually called what you do, right? I mean, I could just call you Terrorlady or the Doominator, both of those seem to fit pretty good. Am I talking too much? I tend to talk too much when I'm nervous, it's kind of a reflex thing, I'm trying to get better at it but honestly you have a chest full of killer bees and I think I just felt one land on my neck, so if—"

"We are Hunter," the woman said. *"She can call us Hunter."*

"Right," Lemon nodded. "Of course you are. Pleased to meet you, Hunter."

"No, Lemonfresh. Pleasure is ours."

". . . Oh yeah? How you figure that?"

"Look around."

Fearing some kind of grift, Lemon kept her stare fixed on her captor.

"Look," Hunter insisted. *"Look hard. Then tell us what she sees."*

The girl risked a glance at the wreckage of the old town. The empty shells and dead cars. The sun was burning white, bleaching everything beneath it whiter still. The men who'd wanted to make them corpses had been made corpses themselves. Everyone scrapping and killing over trash that people would've just thrown away back in the day. The wind was a whisper, the only thing growing was a thin desert weed, spindly roots digging into the shattered concrete and slowly prying it apart.

In a decade or two, all that would be left of this place was rubble.

"I dunno," Lemon finally shrugged. "The world?"

"Yes," Hunter nodded. *"And Lemonfresh is the flood that will drown it. The storm that will wash all of it away."*

Hunter smiled, all the way to her eyeteeth.

"Lemonfresh is going to change everything."

———

"I don't feel so fizzy."

They'd been riding for the best part of the day, and the sun was hot enough to give an aspirin a headache. Hunter had reached into her saddlebags, given Lem a spare cloak, the same rusty desert red as her own. Lemon pulled up the hood to shield her from the scorch, but that only made her sweat buckets and feel sicker.

She'd been tasting off-color since that morning, talking true, but she figured it was just the leftovers from the bad meat, the sad from seeing Grandpa die, leaving Eve behind. Her heart still hurt when she thought on it all, and she didn't have much else to do. Feeling miserable and all the way helpless. But as the day ground on, the sickness in her belly had roiled, and finally, as they neared sundown, come bubbling up out of her mouth again.

There wasn't much to puke—just the water she'd been sipping from an odd, leathery flask in Hunter's saddlebags. But she kept heaving long after her insides were outside, holding on to her belly and wincing in pain.

"I gotta sit . . . ," she begged. "I gotta sit still for a minute. . . ."

Hunter slowed the horsething's pace, brought it to a gentle

stop. Sliding off the strange beast's back, she lifted Lemon down onto dry, cracked earth. They'd cleared the maze of gullies a few hours back, and now they were deep into a stretch of blinding salt flats. The ground was like rock beneath her feet. The glare was blinding. If Lemon squinted to the east, past the broken foothills, she could make out the irradiated edge of the Glass.

Thinking of Evie in that tower.

Thinking of the cardboard box she'd been found in as a kid.

Thinking she'd been abandoned all over again.

She thumped down on her hind parts in the dust, toying with the silver five-leafed clover around her neck and feeling sick all the way to her bones. Watching as Hunter unclasped her strange organic armor, peeled it back to expose her honeycombed throat beneath. The woman hummed an off-key song that reminded Lemon of the wind when it stormed in Zona Bay. A dozen bumblebees crawled out from Hunter's skin, took to the wing, up to the sky and back off to the north.

"That . . . ," Lemon whispered, "is the freshest strange I've ever seen."

"*They will watch,*" the woman said.

"For what?"

"*Pursuit.*"

"You mean my friends."

"*And those not.*"

The woman massaged the translucent resin that bound Lemon's wrists, and the bonds came away like soft, warm putty. Stashing the resin in her cloak, she handed Lemon the leathery water flask, nodded gently.

"*Drink,*" she urged. "*Long road to CityHive.*"

Hunter turned to the salt flats behind, slung her strange long-barreled rifle off her back. The weapon was pale, oddly organic, looking like it was made out of a collection of old fish bones. Hunter held it to her shoulder, peered down the long telescopic scope at the horizon. Her back was turned, and Lemon was keenly aware of the cutter in her belt, drawing out the blade with a slow, steady hand.

Fortunately, Lem was also mindful of the dozen ultra-poisonous-if-sorta-cute-and-fuzzy killer bees flying in lazy circles around her captor's head. And deciding that getting ghosted by bugs was a less than fizzy way to cash her chips, the girl kept the blade hidden in her palm.

Lemon had grown up hard in Dregs. She prided herself on knowing bad news when she saw it. And though Hunter was all the wrong sort of trouble for the wrong sort of people, Lemon didn't sense any hostility from the woman directed at her. If anything, she seemed . . . protective? The way she spoke, the way she wrapped an arm around Lemon's waist as they rode. Standing close and guarding her like a keepsake.

Whatever BioMaas wanted Lemon for, they obviously wanted her alive. But the girl sure as hells wasn't happy about getting snaffled from her friends.

First chance I get, I gotta . . .

What?

Run? On foot? Out here in the wastes?

Dammit, Fresh, being gorgeous just won't cut it here. Time to use that Brain thing people keep telling you about.

Lemon sucked her lip, searching inside her skull for some sort of plan and coming up empty. Hunter reached into a saddlebag, fished out a small rectangular package wrapped in wax paper. Unfolding the wrapping, she held it out on her palm. Lemon squinted at the offering, saw it was a block of mottled green . . .

. . . actually she had no idea what it was.

"Does she hunger?" Hunter asked.

"That's food?"

"Algae. Insects."

Lemon felt her gorge rising again. "Thanks, I'll skip it."

Hunter shrugged, shoved the block into her mouth and chewed soundlessly. Lemon took a swig from the water flask, spat the taste of vomit from her mouth.

Might as well get her talking . . .

"So how'd you find me, anyways?" she asked.

Hunter ran a hand down the horsething's flank. *"Mai'a smelled her."*

The beast shivered, the mane of spines rasping against each other.

"Look, sorry," Lemon said. "I know it's been a while since I had a shower. But I didn't think I stank bad enough to track me from the BioMaas capital."

Hunter's lips curled in a motherly smile. *"Had scent from Lemonfresh's blood sample taken aboard kraken. Nau'shi's Carer did not realize how important Lemonfresh was, or she never would have been released in first place. But we knew where Lemonfresh came ashore. Tracked her from there. A Hunter never misses our mark."*

"Our mark?"

"We are legion, Lemonfresh," the woman said. *"We are hydra."*

Lemon sucked her lip, unsure what to say. She supposed by "legion" that Hunter meant the whole of BioMaas—that the corporation had tasked a posse of folks toward Lemon's capture. But still, she had no real idea what BioMaas's agenda was, why they wanted her. Her nausea was kicking up and the heat was unbearable. She pulled off the cloak Hunter had given her, just to feel the breeze on her skin.

"S-so why'd they send you after me?" she finally asked.

Hunter lowered her rifle, slung it over her back once more.

"Because the Polluted—Daedalus—will eventually realize their error. They sent their cyborg tracker after Lemonfresh's friend. The half-life."

"Her name is Evie," Lemon muttered, feeling stung.

Hunter nodded. *"Daedalus believed she was the Gifted one. Once they understand Lemonfresh is the threat, they will set hounds to her heels."*

"Hold up," Lemon said, blinking hard. "I'm no threat to anyone."

"Lemonfresh can destroy the Polluted's machines. All they have, all they are, runs on electrical current. And she is current's bane."

Lemon rubbed at her aching temples. Ezekiel had already told her as much—he'd said a weapon that could fry electronic tech with a wave of her hand could win the war between the long-feuding CorpStates of BioMaas Incorporated and Daedalus Technologies. Daedalus obviously agreed, which was why they'd set the Preacher on Eve's tail.

And once they've figured out I'm the devia—

Without warning, Lemon rolled up onto her knees, vomiting all over her cloak. She groaned, holding her belly as it spasmed again. Running on empty, she dry-heaved anyway, cherry bob hanging in her eyes.

"Is she well?" Hunter asked.

"Is sh-she k-kidding?" Lemon moaned.

Hunter knelt beside the girl, concern shining in those golden eyes. She pressed a palm to Lemon's brow, gently wiped the sweat off her freckled cheeks. Lemon felt a couple of deathbees crawling over her face, but she was feeling entirely too pukey to panic. Hunter leaned close, peered into Lemon's eyes, inhaled deeply along her skin.

"*She went to the glass land,*" she declared. "*Or the dead spire.*"

"Babel?" Lemon winced. "Y-yeah, I might've . . . dropped in for a quick drink."

Hunter scowled. "*The death is in her. The sickness from its sundered heart.*"

". . . Radiation?"

Lemon's stomach sank as Hunter nodded. She knew she'd sucked up a few rads when Gabriel tore her suit, but she didn't realize she'd been dosed enough to get sick. Still, there was no fooling the churn in her gut, the fever burning on her skin. Apparently she'd worn a dose hard enough to hurt her.

Maybe worse?

"Am . . . am I gonna die?"

"*We do not know. They could treat her in CityHive. But it is far.*"

Fear crawled up her throat, cinching it tight. Lemon had seen firsthand what radsick could do to a person. Back when she was a sprog, a kid named Chuffs had scavved a leaky reactor out of an old war logika out in the Scrap, not knowing it was still hot. He'd been bleeding out of everywhere he possibly could've when he died.

"Can't you radio them to come get us or s-something?" she asked.

Hunter's face soured. "*We do not use the tech of the oldflesh. We have sent word on the wind*"—she motioned to her bees—"*but it will take time to fly.*"

Lemon swallowed hard.

"Time I don't have?"

"We are not experts. We stay away from deadplaces. We do not sicken."

Lemon clenched her teeth, trying to keep on her streetface. Her braveface. But after all she'd been through, cashing her chips out here in the wastes from a dose of radsick didn't exactly strike her as exactly fair. She was only fifteen or sixteen years old. If she hadn't got wrapped up in all this lifelike crap, Daedalus, Bio-Maas, she wouldn't even *be* here. And now she was gonna get ghosted for it?

"This," she declared, "is a little far from fizzytown."

Hunter stood slowly, looking to the horizon.

". . . *Town,*" she repeated.

Lemon tilted her head. "What?"

The BioMaas operative nodded.

"West. Near ocean. A settlement, carved from the deadworld. New Bethlehem. Old Gnosis city, now ruled by others. We have not ventured there since Gnosis fell. Very dangerous. But wealthy. They would have medicine."

Lemon had never heard of the place, but that came as no surprise—she'd never left Dregs till a few days ago. The "very dangerous" part didn't sound like a fistful of fun. But when you're looking down the barrel at your own funeral, even doing something stupid sounds better than doing nothing at all.

The sickly feeling was swelling in her middle, stretching toward her bones. As Hunter reached down to help her up, she had to beg off for a minute to pull herself together. The operative busied herself with Mai'a instead, giving the horsething a drink from the flask, strapping her strange rifle to its flank. Lemon stashed her cutter back in her belt, finally pulled herself up onto her feet with a groan.

"Her cloak," Hunter said, nodding.

Lemon eyed the garment. "Um, I'm not sure what the fashion is in CityHive, but I'd rather not wear my own vomit, if it's all the same to you."

Hunter took off her own cloak, wrapped it about Lemon's shoulders. Again, Lemon was struck by the feeling of protectiveness, of Hunter's concern for her well-being. It made her feel pulled every which way—angry that she'd been jacked from her friends, but glad she was in the hands of someone who actually seemed to give a speck whether she lived or died.

Lemonfresh is important.

She is needed.

Lemon offered her wrists to Hunter, but the woman shook her head. Truth was, the pair both knew Lemon had nowhere to run now. With Hunter's help, the girl scrambled up onto Mai'a's neck.

"*Hold on,*" the woman said, climbing up behind. "*We ride swift.*"

The horsething sprang into a gallop, the salt flats swallowed up under its smooth strides. Lemon could see mountains ahead, the beginning of a long, shattered road. She held on for dear life, fighting the churn in her belly, the fear slowly growing beside it.

Behind them, the wind picked up on the salt flats, the dust and grit scouring their tracks from the barren earth. It picked up Lemon's abandoned cloak, vomit stains and all, sent it tumbling. Away from the place where the girl had crouched a moment before, knife in hand.

Carving two words into the sun-parched earth.

A message for the friends she hoped were following.

An arrow pointing west.

A warning.

New Bethlehem.

2.4

PROPOSITION

"What the hell happened here?"

In the ruins of a forgotten city, a would-be boy knelt on the broken earth. The corpse beside him was fly-blown, bloated beneath a furious sun. It was dressed in a bloodstained jersey, an old-style knight's helmet stitched on its back. Loaded pistols were still holstered at the body's waist, untouched.

"Never even got a chance to draw," Ezekiel muttered.

The lifelike turned the body over. A dark stain marked the man's swollen cheek, spreading across his face. Searching the ground around him, Zeke found a dead bee a few meters from the corpse, bar-coded yellow and black.

I'm on the right trail.

But none of this made any sense.

Ezekiel had been trailing Lemon and her captor through the gullies for hours. He'd salvaged a bunch of weaponry from the grav-tank munitions locker, stashed it all in a satchel that bounced on his back as he ran. The gully floor was mostly stone, and the tracks of the BioMaas agent's transport were almost impossible to spot. But whatever Lemon and her captor were traveling in, there was no way it was big or heavy enough to be hauling Cricket, too. And yet, when Ezekiel had arrived back at the stranded grav-tank, both Lemon *and* the logika were missing.

So where the hell did Cricket get to?

Truth told, despite the animosity between him and the big bot, he was worried about the pair of them. But Cricket was a seven-meter-tall armor-plated killing machine, and Lemon was a lone fifteen-year-old girl. A girl he'd made a promise to never bail on, only a few hours ago.

He glanced down at the scavver's corpse again. Wondered what kind of person would've done that to a human. What they might have done to Lemon. He could only guess at their motivations for snatching her, but there was at least one certainty in all this mess:

If BioMaas wanted her dead, she'd already be dead.

So Ezekiel pushed the fear aside and ran on.

He cleared the broken maze after a few hours, emerging out of the long shadows and into an endless stretch of salt flats. Like the rest of him, his senses were better than human—he could count the beats of an insect's wings, shoot a bullet from the air. But truth was, he hadn't been built for this. He'd served with the Gnosis security forces inside Babel Tower, a place of luxury and impossible wealth. Of soft skin and gentle curves and lips that tasted sweeter than anything he'd ever known.

Ana.

She was alive. Myriad had confirmed it. She'd been critically injured in the assassination attempt on her father, yes, but she'd survived. She was hidden somewhere—some secret Gnosis holding or base out in this wasteland.

But where?

He'd searched for years after the revolt, looking for any sign.

They said you never love anyone quite the way you love your First. But Ana had been his Only. The only thing that had kept him going. The only memory that had kept him sane. The thought of seeing her face again, of feeling her pressed against him . . .

And then he'd found her.

Or what he *thought* was her.

Eve had looked like Ana.

Felt and sounded and tasted like Ana.

Did I love her like Ana?

The girl he'd known in the impossible tower of Babel. The girl who saved him from the corroding scrap pile of Dregs. The pair of them, side by side in his mind, both now beyond his reach. Both had shown him what it was to feel alive. Both had taught him what it was to care for something more than himself. To strive to be more than just an imitation, a simulacrum, a parody of what it meant to be . . .

. . . to be human.

He shook his head, willed the image of their faces away.

You promised Lemon you wouldn't leave her.

He nodded to himself, jaw clenched. As much as Ana meant to him . . .

You promised.

But the ground was bare rock, the wind scouring it like a blast furnace. He'd been walking for two hours now without a trace of his quarry—not a mark, not a scratch. He came to a stop, eyes to the setting sun. Nothing out here. Nothing heals. Nothing grows. Just endless kilometers of dust and blinding white and rusted ruins. The bones of a carcass long picked clean.

They'd had it all.

Humans.

And look what they did with it.

Ezekiel knelt, running his fingertips over bare and burning stone. Looking around him, he guessed the BioMaas operative had come this way for a reason; they were counting on being followed. He realized he'd been an idiot to even try to trail them on foot with nothing but keen eyes to track them. BioMaas wouldn't send amateurs out looking for the weapon that'd end their cold war with Daedalus once and for all. They'd send their best.

Ezekiel stood slowly, turned his eyes back to the northeast.

They'd send their best.

Just like Daedalus did . . .

He took a long sip of water from his canteen, ran his hand through his mop of sweat-damp hair. Weighing the thoughts in his head, trimming the impossibilities, the shots in the dark, until he was left with only one. It would mean abandoning the trail for now, that Lemon would be at the mercy of her captors. It would mean leaving any hope of finding Ana or reuniting with Eve behind. It would mean a dance with the devil. But out here alone, blundering in the dust? No clues, no path, no way forward?

What other option do you have?

Just a few hundred meters from where Ezekiel stood, two words sat baking in the sun-parched earth. Two words that might have changed everything—avoided all the misery and pain and death that was to come. Just a few more steps forward, and he might have spotted them.

The message for the friends she'd hoped were following.

The arrow pointing west.

The warning.

New Bethlehem.

But with a sigh, Ezekiel turned and ran back toward Babel.

Preacher had been hurt worse. But only just.

It'd happened back in the CorpState Wars, when he was just a regular grunt, still ninety-seven percent meat. Fighting for Daedalus as the company claimed its place among the three most powerful corporations in the whole Yousay. To this day, he still didn't know what hit him. He'd been pinned down by enemy machina when the explosion went off. He dimly remembered pieces of himself not being attached to himself anymore. Red on his hands. Screaming for his momma. Then he woke up in a Daedalus medcenter. Metal where the missing pieces of him should've been.

The Lord had saved his life that day. But it was Daedalus who plucked him from that carnage and made him better. Faster. Stronger. In return, they bought themselves a soldier who knew what it was to look dying in the eye. A soldier more machine than man. A soldier loyal to the death.

Which looked like it might be about now, come to think of it.

Preacher was crawling. He didn't have much else to do, talking true. After that blitzhund blew his legs away, he'd been laid flat, knocked cold. He'd woken up on that broken stretch of highway outside Babel hours later, surrounded by a dozen broken machina. It looked like lil' Evie Carpenter had worked her magic again—every one of those bots was fried to a crisp, and almost every cybernetic component in Preacher's body had been cooked. His right arm was a lump of dead titanium with a red glove stuck on the end of it. His right eye was blind. His combat augs, his reflex stims, his comms, all dead.

He'd not had a chance to give his position when he called for evac, and lil' Miss Carpenter appeared to have fried his retrieval beacon along with everything else. Which meant Daedalus probably didn't know where he was.

Which meant he was probably gonna die out here.

But still, he crawled. Back across the Glass. Dragging himself with his one meat arm across shards of irradiated silicon, the mangled scrap metal that had been his legs trailing behind him. Hoping to find one of those wrecked Armada trucks, maybe. One with a working radio, maybe.

Wasn't like him to just lie down and die.

But after a whole day and night of this crap, it surely was tempting.

The bounty hunter stopped crawling, rolled onto his back. His mouth was ash dry, coated with dust. He pulled off his black, beaten cowboy hat, held it up against the merciless sun.

"And God said, let there be light," he muttered. "And I ain't complainin', Lord. I could just use a little less of it right now, is all. Maybe some kinda miracle if you're in a giving mood? A little one'll do just fine."

And, as if on cue, Preacher heard footsteps.

Slow and steady, crunching on the black glass toward him. He thought he recognized the tempo, but without his augs, he couldn't be sure. Lifting his head with a wince, he focused on the approaching figure with his one working eye.

"Well, well," Preacher chuckled, leaning back on the glass. "Snowflake."

The boy stopped a good forty meters away, leveled a pistol at his head.

Smart.

"I'm wondering if that skull of yours is bulletproof," the boy called.

"Matter of fact, it is," Preacher replied.

"You move sudden, we find out for certain."

The boy advanced slowly, gun aimed steady. He looked like hell—bloodstained and filthy, a bulky satchel on his back. But last Preacher had seen the boy, that right arm of his ended at the bicep, outfitted with a prosthetic that predated the war. Now his arm extended below his elbow, and the bounty hunter could see five small nubs sprouting at the end of the stump.

"Well, you surely are a special one, ain'tcha?"

"Considering you survived a point-blank blitzhund explosion and a shotgun blast to the chest, I'm guessing I'm not the only one," the boy replied.

Preacher reached into his shredded coat, stuffed a wad of synth tobacco in his cheek. "What're you doin' out here, Snow-flake? Shouldn't you be with your girl?"

"Well, one of them told me to go to hell, and I lost the other one. Along with my logika and my tank and what little remained of my good mood."

Preacher nodded. "That *does* sound a goodly dose of mis-fortune."

"Not really. In fact, this is my lucky day."

"How you figure?"

The boy knelt beside Preacher's head, barrel aimed right between his eyes.

"Because you own a blitzhund. And you find things for a living."

He held up a grav-tank pilot's helmet, smudged with spots of dried blood.

"And now, you're gonna help me find *her*."

Preacher looked down the barrel into all that black. He wasn't anything close to afraid—he'd spat right in death's eye be-fore, after all, and he knew the reward waiting for him in the hereafter. But talking true, he was having an awfully tough time keeping the smile off his face.

He'd always been a man of the Goodbook. Always believed he was part of the Lord's plan. He'd asked for a miracle, and as always, the Lord had delivered. He just didn't think the heavenly father would send him a miracle quite so goddamn stupid.

Preacher sucked his cheek, leaned up on his elbows and spat into the dirt.

"Mmf," he grunted. "All right, Snowflake. I s'pose I am."

2.5

HELOTRY

```
>> syscheck: 001 go _ _
>> restart sequence: initiated _ _
>> waiting _ _
>> 018912.y/n[corecomm:9180 diff:3sund.x]
>> persona_sys: sequencing
>> 001914.y/n[lattcomm:2872(ok) diff:neg.n/a]
>> restart complete
>> Power: 04% capacity
>> ONLINE
>>
```

"Haaaa, toldja!" someone crowed. "What'd I tell ya?"

"Shuddup, Murph."

"*You* shuddup, Mikey!"

"Ow, don't touch me, dammit!"

As his optics came into focus, Cricket tried to sit up and found that he couldn't. He was lying on his back, staring up at the rusting roof of a warehouse or garage. Data was pouring in: damage reports, combat efficiencies, percentage of munitions depleted, recharge rate. It took him a moment to remember who he was.

Where was a completely different matter.

He recalled the fight with Ezekiel. The sudden warning from his internal systems, the loss of power. After that . . . nothing.

"Hey!" Cricket felt a clunk on the side of his head. "You hear me?"

"YES," the logika replied. "I HEAR YOU. BUT I CAN'T MOVE."

A grubby face leaned into Cricket's field of view. It was a man, freckled skin, a pair of cracked spectacles perched on a flat nose. He wore a threadbare beanie on his head, stitched with a knight's helm logo.

"WHO ARE YOU?" the big bot asked.

The man's grin was the color of dirt.

"I'm the guy you're gonna make *rich*."

Cricket felt hands inside his chest.

"NO, WAIT A—"

```
>> power disconnected
>> system offline
           ———

>> syscheck: 001 go _ _
>> restart sequence: initiated _ _
>> waiting _ _
>> 018912.y/n[corecomm:9180 diff:3sund.x]
>> persona_sys: sequencing
>> 001914.y/n[lattcomm:2872(ok) diff:neg.n/a]
>> restart complete
>> Power: 17% capacity
```

"See, there it is," crowed a now-familiar voice. "Said so, didn't I?"

Cricket's optics whirred and glowed, the room about him snapped into focus. He was somewhere different—underground, he realized. A large metal hatch was sealed over his head. The walls were concrete, lined with the shells of logika and machina, all in various states of disrepair. Tools, a loading crane, acetylene tanks . . . a workshop of some kind?

He could hear the dim rumble of machinery, the distant hubbub of human voices, running motors, foot traffic. His atmosphere sensors detected ethyl-4 and methane and lots of carbon monoxide.

A city?

Three figures stood in front of him. The first was Murph, the dustneck scavver who woke him up, then pulled his plug. Beside him stood a shorter, dirtier version of Murph that Cricket guessed was Mikey. He looked similar enough that he might be Murph's brother. Or cousin. Maybe both.

Beside them, sizing Cricket up through a pair of whirring tech-goggles, was a boy, maybe nineteen years old. He wore big steel-capped boots and dirty coveralls, dark hair slicked back from his forehead. A laden tool belt was wrapped around his waist, his hands smudged with grease.

"Where am I?" Cricket asked. "Where's Lemon? Wher—"

"Hey, shuddup!" Murph hollered, kicking Cricket's foot. "You only speak when you're spoken to, acknowledge!"

The big bot fixed the little man in his glowing blue stare. He realized these dustnecks must have salvaged him from where he'd collapsed. Somehow hauled him to this new city while he was powered down. He had no idea where he could be, how long he'd been offline. But these scavvers might've hurt Lemon or Ezekiel in the process of jacking him. His friends might be in danger. Cricket's titanic fists curled at the thought, a thrill of robotic rage coursing through him. Murph's eyes widened and he took one step back.

But despite the anger, the thought of what might have happened or be happening to Lemon because these dustnecks stole him, Cricket was still a logika. The Three Laws were hard-coded into his head. Including good old number two.

A robot must obey the orders given to it by human beings, except where such orders would conflict with the First Law.

And so . . .

"ACKNOWLEDGED," he finally growled.

The boy in the coveralls stepped closer, seemingly unafraid of the tremor in Crick's voice. He peered up to the big bot's glowing eyes, his goggles whirring and shifting focus as he took the logika's measure.

"How much you want for it?" he murmured, turning to the scavvers.

The thieves whispered between themselves, quickly fell to cussing and shoving. Murph finally punched Mikey's arm and hissed for silence.

"Three thousand liters," he declared.

The boy tilted his head. "You know Mother will never agree to that, Murphy. Those combat drones you brought us last month all blew their gyroscopes after a few days. She doesn't have much faith in your wares."

"Yeah, but look!" Murph kicked Cricket's foot again. "Hasn't hardly got a scratch on it! I've never seen a model like this! It's got some hard bark on it, Abe!"

"Reckon we could go down to two and a half," Mikey muttered.

"Shuddup, Mike, I'm doing the negotiatin' here."

"*You* shuddup!" Mike said, punching Murph in the arm.

The pair fell to fighting, slapping and shoving and cursing. Murph grabbed Mike in a headlock, Mike started punching his brother/cousin's kidneys, the scavvers falling in a tangle on the concrete as the boy folded his arms and sighed. The brawl went on for a good minute until a soft voice cut the air.

"Gentlemen. Need I remind you this is a house of God?"

Silence hit the room like a sledgehammer. Cricket saw a new figure had entered through a pair of double doors, flanked by a dozen men.

A woman in a white robe. She had pale skin, long dark hair, washed and combed. She was thin, gaunt almost, and about the cleanest human being Cricket had ever locked optics on. But her face was painted with a greasepaint skull, dark hollows daubed at her cheeks and around her eyes. Cricket realized the white robe she wore was actually a cassock, and that an ornate metal X hung around her neck.

That's the symbol of the Brotherhood. . . .

"S-Sister D-Dee," Mike stuttered, eyes wide with fear.

"Apologies, ma'am," Murphy said, picking himself up and standing like a child about to be scolded. "We d-didn't mean nuthin' by it."

The figures flanking Sister Dee fanned out around the room—all of them big, hulking men armed with automatic shooters. Each was dressed in a black Kevlar cassock, grease-paint Xs on their faces.

More Brotherhood . . .

Cricket looked around the room, his processors in overdrive. *Where on earth am I?*

The woman slowly entered the workshop, more gliding than walking. She made no sound, and seemed to bring a stillness with her as she came. Murph and Mike shrank down on themselves, even the coolant fans overhead seemed to hush. Her long hair rippled as she moved, her dark, burning eyes focused on Cricket. Her fingernails were black. Her voice was soft and melodious.

"More flotsam from the wastes, Abraham?" she asked.

The boy turned to Mike and Murphy. "Give us a minute, boys?"

"Sure, sure, Abe," Murph nodded, utterly cowed. "Long as you like!"

The boy and the woman stepped over to a quiet corner of the workshop while Murph and Mike held on to their crotches. The Brotherhood bullyboys just watched on silently. The boy and woman spoke in low voices, but Cricket's audio was sharp enough that he could scope every word.

"These vultures again?" the woman sighed. "I do wish you'd spend your time more productively than trifling with heathen trashmen, Abraham."

"I'm sorry, Mother," the boy whispered. "But I recognize this logika from the old WarDome feeds I watched when I was small. It's the Quixote. Built by GnosisLabs. Twelve thousand horsepower."

The woman raised one painted eyebrow. "Are you certain?"

"The GL logo is right there on its chest," the boy nodded. "Murphy has *no* idea what he's scavved."

"How much do they want for it?"

"Three thousand."

"I should have them crucified."

"This logika is tier one, Mother," Abraham said. "It's good enough to fight in Megopolis. And more, it's good enough to *win*."

Sister Dee turned back to Cricket with narrowed eyes. He could feel her stare somewhere in his core code, a soft warning buzzing in back of his head. The boy stood behind her, silent in his mother's shadow.

"I have a proposition for you, Mister Murphy," Sister Dee called.

"Yes, ma'am?" the scavver replied.

"We have WarDome here tonight. The Edge have sent up the Thunderstorm to do battle in New Bethlehem arena. We were planning on fighting the Paragon"—she waved at another logika powered down in the corner—"but I suggest you put your money where your mouth is, and pit your bot against the Edge's champion. If it's victorious, we'll buy it. Two thousand liters."

Murph and Mike whispered among themselves, clearly in opposition. Their voices got louder, Mike punched Murph's arm, and hostilities looked set to break out again, when Sister Dee cleared her throat. The scavvers fell still, eyes on the floor.

"Deal," Murph finally said.

The man shuffled over, spat in his greasy palm. Sister Dee simply stared. Meeting the woman's dark eyes, Murph wiped the spit off on his shirt, then offered his hand again.

"The bargain struck," Sister Dee replied, shaking it.

Cricket wanted to protest. Demand these people let him go. He wanted to know where he was, what they'd done with

Lemon, if his friends were okay. The questions bubbled up inside him with nowhere to go. He'd been commanded to be silent until someone addressed him, and these folks were acting like he wasn't in the room, let alone speaking to him.

A robot must obey the orders given to it by human beings, except where such orders would conflict with the First Law.

A robot must obey the orders given to it by human beings.

A robot must obey.

Abraham looked up at Cricket and smiled.

"All right. Let's get you ready."

2.6

DISCIPLES

Lemon smelled the city long before she saw it.

New Bethlehem's stink reminded her a little of Los Diablos—methane and ethyl-4, garbage and salt. Riding down a broken highway, sick and sweaty, she could see the settlement smudged on the horizon. A grubby little stain on the wasteland, wreathed in fumes and corroding away beneath a cigarette sky.

And beyond it?

Black ocean, far as the eye could see.

It'd taken another day to reach the outskirts, and Lemon was feeling a lot like yesterday's breakfast. Her fever was worse and her lips were parched—drinking Hunter's water just made her puke. They'd avoided other travelers on their trek, rested in the shade of a shattered freeway overpass during the day's hottest spell. She supposed the BioMaas agent was keeping up the brutal pace in case they were being pursued, but Lemon wondered if the woman ever actually slept.

The area around New Bethlehem was a factoryfarm, planted with tall, dirt-colored stalks of what might've been corn. The land was irrigated by rusty pipeline, tended by a small army of humanoid logika. They were repurposed military models, by the look, now harvesting grain instead of enemy soldiers. The whole setup was guarded by a whole mess of thugs with a bigger mess of guns.

"I've never seen so much food in my life," Lemon breathed. "They could feed everyone forever."

"No," Hunter replied. *"They plant customized BioMaas crops. Parasite and fungus resistant. Able to grow in acrid soil. But seeds are sterile."*

Lemon glanced at the agent sidelong. "So every year, these folks have to buy new seed from you?"

Hunter shrugged. *"Daedalus controls electricity. BioMaas controls food. Their army is larger. But without us, country starves. This is balance."*

"But if you BioMaas folks get an edge over the Daedalus army . . ."

"There will be better balance. Better world."

"That BioMaas controls, right?"

Hunter fixed Lemon in her golden stare, but made no reply. The agent climbed off Mai'a's back and helped the girl down. Hunter then pressed her hand to the horsething's brow. It shivered once, trotted off the way they'd come.

"Don't we need her to ride?" Lemon asked.

"Oldflesh fears what it does not understand. Better we not draw attentions."

Hunter pulled on a pair of goggles, tied her hairspines in a ponytail, pulled her cloak low over her head. Arm around Lemon, they trudged through the swaying farmland, into the valley that cradled the settlement of New Bethlehem. As they walked, they passed uprooted power lines, rusted autowrecks, faded billboards painted with what might've been verses from the Goodbook.

BLESSED ARE THE PURE IN HEART, FOR THEY SHALL SEE GOD.

BE AFRAID, FOR HE DOES BEAR THE SWORD IN VAIN.

SAINT MICHAEL WATCHES OVER US.

Lemon was starting to get a baaaad feeling.

New Bethlehem was a walled settlement, right on the coast. Its main gate was broad, iron-shod, a crush of people waiting to get inside. The walls themselves were made of rusting plate steel and concrete rubble crowned with razor wire—the folks who ran this joint apparently had zero sense of humor when it came to protecting what was theirs. As they approached the gate, Lemon could see faded GnosisLabs logos on the concrete. But her belly ran cold as she saw the symbols had been painted over with the letter X, ten meters high, black as midnight.

"Oh, butter me all the way backward," she whispered.

Above the broad gateway hung a welded sign, embossed with five words:

AND THE WATERS BECAME SWEET

"This town . . ."

Lemon licked at dry lips, realization sinking into her bones. The billboards. The scripture quotes. That familiar ornate X.

The kind of X they nailed you to if they didn't like you . . .

"This town is run by the Brotherhood," she hissed, turning on Hunter with eyebrows raised. "Didn't you *know* that?"

"We told Lemonfresh. We have not been to this deadplace in years. We knew only that Gnosis once owned it, that it was wealthy. What is Brotherhood?"

Lemon glanced at the crowd around them, keeping her voice low.

"They're a *cult*," she said. "Every color of bad news. They claim to get their instructions from the Goodbook, but basically ignore all the 'be nice to each other' stuff and just preach on the evils of being different from them. They say biomodification and cybernetics are an abomination, and they've got a major hate-chub for 'genetic deviation.'"

"Deviation?"

"Yeah," Lemon nodded. "Abnorms. Deviates. People like me."

"There are none like Lemonfresh."

Lemon shook her head. "There's plenty. Thing is, doesn't matter if you're born with something as harmless as a birthmark or as fizzy as the power to kill 'lectrics with your mind. Brotherhood see you as inhuman anyway. And when they catch you, they throw a nice little party with a big wooden X, a hammer and four roofing nails."

Lem had spent the last three years hiding what she was for that exact reason. For someone like her, getting fingered as a deviate in a place as remote as Dregs would've been a death sentence. And now she'd marched right up to the front door of a Brotherhood stronghold?

I must be sicker than I thought.

As if to remind her, her stomach cramped and she bent double, wincing in pain. None of the folk around her paid any mind, the mob pushing her ever closer to the entrance. Talking true, Lemon didn't know if they'd find the medicine she needed inside the settlement, but the sickness was getting worse, the ache grinding deeper. This was getting genuinely scary now. And so, she turned her bleary eyes to the gate, trying to gauge if they had any chance of getting inside this joint at all.

The entry was overseen by two Brotherhood members. They wore their order's traditional red cassocks despite the sun's scorch, packed the kind of firepower that'd knock a WarDome bot on its hind parts. There was also a big, potbellied machina nearby—Sumo-class, if Lem wasn't mistaken. Scripture was sprayed on the machina's hull, and a banner with that ornate black X flew on its back.

But looking closer, Lemon realized the actual work of letting people through the gates was being done by folk who weren't Brotherhood at all. They had cropped hair, big Xs daubed on their faces with grease, chin to forehead. But they didn't wear cassocks. Lemon figured maybe they were lesser members? Doing the scuz jobs that full-fledged Brotherhood beatboys didn't dirty their hands with?

A siren wailed from the walls, drowning out Lemon's thoughts. A lookout stood in a crow's nest above the gate, pointing away down the road.

"Brother Dubya's back!"

"Make way!" a Brotherhood thug bellowed. "Make way for the Horsemen!"

Lemon heard engines in the distance, the blare of a horn, the sound of gunshots. Squinting down the road, she saw a line of rusty red autos motoring toward the gate, spewing methane smoke. The men crewing the convoy were all wearing red cassocks, a few hanging out their windows and firing rifles into the air.

The vehicles slowed as they drew closer, the crowd parting to let them rumble up to the main gates. The lead car was an old muscle truck, fitted with tractor tires and monster suspension. Scripture was painted on its panelwork, and choir music was spilling from its tune spinners. On the doors and hood was the same ornate black X that marked the settlement walls, overlaid with a grinning white skull. The crude, homemade license plate read WAR.

The door cracked open, and a man jumped down to the asphalt. He was one of the biggest units Lemon had ever seen—bearded and mohawked, broad as a house. He was dressed in a white cassock, filthy and spattered with what might've been bloodstains. A white skull was painted over his face, chin to forehead, and a well-chewed cigar stub hung from his lips.

"Blessed be the Lord, my rock, who trains my hands for war!" he roared.

His posse fired a few more shots into the air, some of the rowdier thugs on the walls joining in. One of the Brotherhood boys at the gates raised his voice over the clamor. "You get 'em, Dub? How many you brought us?"

The big man gave a beartooth grin, like a corner huckster about to reveal the secret of his trick. He reached into his cassock, then whipped out his hand, holding two fingers in the air. The thugs and Brethren whooped and hollered in delight.

"Finally!" one shouted.

A gaunt man with the same greasepaint skull as the big man leaned out the window of the monster truck and roared, "Get those crosses ready, boys!"

"You heard Brother Pez!" More shouts and hollers echoed among the Brotherhood boys as Brother Dubya raised his hands and grinned. "Get 'em up!"

As he began making his way through the crowd, Lemon looked this Brother Dubya over. The big man was well fed, his gunslinger belt loaded with tech, ammo, a fat pistol. The crowd treated him like a celebrity, but he looked at them like they were something he'd found on the bottom of his snakeskin boots. The mob jostled and surged to get a better looksee, and Lemon found herself pushed forward, until she bumped right into the big man's belly.

Heart hammering, she blinked up into that greasepaint skull. The black eyes burning behind it. Wondering just how many abnorms this fellow had put to the nail.

Can he see?

Can he tell just by looking at me?

"Best watch where you're stepping, lil' sister," the man growled.

"I'm sorry, Brother," she said, smoothing down his cassock. "I'm jus—"

Brother Dubya put a hand on her forehead and shoved her out of the way. Hunter stepped smoothly between them, bristling with threat. But with contempt in his gap-toothed smile, the man simply puffed on his cigar and pushed on through the mob. The convoy trundled into the settlement, Brother Pez behind the lead truck's wheel, Brother Dubya leading it through the gates to what sounded like more raucous praise inside.

The noise slowly died down, and with the excitement apparently over, the thugs manning the gate got back to work. Lemon wiped the greasy handprint off her forehead, shuffled along in line. Watching the junior thugs on the door, the way they spoke, the way they rolled. As far as Lem could tell, who exactly they let in and turned out seemed to depend entirely on their mood.

"Okay, I don't mean to tell you your biz," she muttered to Hunter, "given you're running this kidnapping and all. But we step out of line here, we're not getting through that gate. So maybe let me talk and keep the deathbees in your bra?"

The woman glanced at the guards. Nodded slow.

"Lemonfresh speaks wisdom."

". . . You know, I don't think anyone's ever accused me of that before."

The sun was kissing the horizon by the time they reached the entrance. The sky was soaked the color of flame, fires were lit inside forty-four-gallon drums. The sign above the gate flickered into bright, neon life. As Lemon and Hunter reached the entrance, a young, weary thug looked her up and down.

"Ho there, lil' girlie."

"Brother," Lemon nodded, mustering her least irradiated smile.

"Ain't no Brother." He pointed to the greasepaint X covering his face. "Just a Disciple. You here for WarDome tonight?"

". . . Yep, that's us." Lemon smiled, smooth as an oil slick. "Me and cuz love us a good bot fight."

Mister Greasepaint looked Hunter over—the cloak, the goggles, the stance.

"She's your cousin?" he asked.

"Twice removed," Lemon replied.

The thug sighed. "You know the rules of New Bethlehem, little girlie?"

"It'd be real fizzy if you stopped calling me 'girlie,' sir," Lemon said.

The Disciple blinked. "Well, you're a whole mess of mouth, ain't you?"

Lemon glanced down meaningfully, slowly turned over her hand so the man could see what she held. In her palm sat a shiny credstik.

"In a hurry is what we are, sir."

It was a gamble, offering a bribe to a religious sort. Could be he was the kind who'd take offense. But holy man or no, Lemon had never met a doorthug who wasn't on some kind of take, and she guessed standing out here in the burn all day wasn't the most well-paying gig.

Trying to appear casual, the Disciple checked over his shoulder to see if any of his colleagues were watching. Satisfied, he quickly pocketed the stik, tipped an imaginary hat and stepped right the hells aside.

"Welcome to New Bethlehem, sisters."

Lemon winked, shuffling through the crush with Hunter in tow. A broad square waited beyond the gate, ringed with stalls and old tires and pubs and all manner of people. Once safely through, the BioMaas agent touched Lemon on the arm.

"How much did she pay?" she whispered.

The girl shrugged. "Wasn't my credstik. Lifted it off that Brother Dubya fellow when I bumped into him. Looked like he had scratch to spare."

". . . She stole his money?"

"Borrowed. So to speak."

"Resourceful. Fearless." Hunter smiled. *"Her name will be a song in CityHive."*

"Not if we don't find some meds in here." She winced, holding her gut. "Feels like I swallowed barbed wire and washed it down with battery acid."

"Come, then. We hunt."

Lemon could feel starving eyes on her as they limped through the square. She wasn't carrying much worth stealing, but she was certain the two other credstiks she'd lifted from Brother Dubya were worth a little murder, and her bod would sell to any number of buyers, kicking or otherwise. There were dustnecks in Los Diablos who'd kill you for a can of Neo-Meat™, and New Bethlehem looked meaner still.

A heavy stink hung over the place like fog, and Lemon soon

saw the source, parked on the edge of the bay. Frontways, it looked like an oldskool cathedral, with double iron doors and a big stone bell tower. But springing up out of its hind parts were the chimneys and fat storage tanks of a bloated factory. Black smoke spilled from its stacks, burbling and hissing spilled from its guts. The same words that marked the gates were painted above its doors.

AND THE WATERS BECAME SWEET

"It's a desalination plant," Lemon realized, looking around her. "That's what they do here. Suck up the ocean, get it fresh to wet down those crops."

"*Come,*" Hunter said, apparently not giving a damn. "*We waste time.*"

They pushed on through the crowd, down a dusty thoroughfare. The walls were plastered with WARDOME TONIGHT! posters, and murals of a handsome middle-aged man. He had flaming eyes and white robes, a halo of light around his head. Beneath every mural were the words SAINT MICHAEL WATCHES OVER US.

Dark was falling, and strips of old neon flickered and spat like a faulty rainbow along the way. Finally, between rows of shattered buildings and the local WarDome, they found an open-air tangle of tinshack shops and seatainers that must've been the New Bethlehem market. Crowded with old logika and people, the square was lit by blue methane fires, and stank worse than a busted belly. Hawkers and hucksters mixed with roughnecks and chemkids, Brotherhood bullyboys wandered through the lot, choir music from the PA system washed over the scene.

"*Deadworld,*" Hunter muttered, shaking her head.

Lemon stood on tiptoes. She could hear some kind of ruckus

ahead, but she was still about half a person shy of being able to scope anything over the crush.

"Can you see a sign advertising meds anywhere?"

Hunter nodded. *"There. Across the square."*

With Hunter right on her tail, Lemon pushed her way through the mob. Not for the first time, she thought about trying to slip free of the BioMaas agent, make a break for freedom. But talking true, Hunter was the only person in this whole city who sorta had her back, so cutting her loose didn't seem the most sensible of plays. Besides, she was in no shape to run.

She swallowed hard.

If I don't get these meds soon, I'll be in no shape to do anything.

In the center of the market, Lemon found the source of all the shouting. A dozen bullyboys were standing in front of a flashy stage, welded together out of old RVs. Vehicles from the newly arrived Brotherhood convoy were parked around it, their headlights on high beam. Banners daubed with the Brotherhood X billowed in the wind. Lemon saw the convoy riders gathered halfway up the stage's steps, Brother Dubya at the top, that white skull on his face, a fresh cigar between his teeth.

Two men stood beside him. The first was the fellow who'd been driving the lead truck in the convoy, tall and thin as old bones—Brother Pez, if memory served. The other man was broader, almost plump. Both had the same skulls on their faces as Brother Dubya, both wore white cassocks like him. The plump man yelled into a bullhorn, smoky voice crackling with feedback.

"Citizens of New Bethlehem! I know y'all are impatient for WarDome to get under way!" The man paused as the crowd roared in response, urging them to settle with a wave of his hand. "But before the Dome opens its gates, we got a special treat for y'all. Raise your hands, won't ya . . . for our own beloved Sister Dee!"

The crowd roared, and a woman stepped up onto the stage. She was dressed in the cleanest, whitest frock Lemon had ever seen, and looked straight out of an old Holywood flick: tall, dark hair, true lush. But her face was painted with that same grinning skull as the three men, her eyes a piercing black.

"Sister Dee!" the crowd called.

"Sister Dee!"

"Who shall ascend the hill of the Lord?" she cried.

Like someone had flicked a switch, the crowd fell silent. The choir music hushed. All eyes fell on the woman, her presence magnetic, the night around her growing darker. She prowled up and down the stage like a predator on the hunt, that greasepaint skull aglow in the light of the headlamps.

"And who shall stand in his holy place?" she demanded of the crowd. "They who have clean hands and pure hearts! For God has not called us for impurity, but in holiness! And blessed are the pure of heart, for they shall see God!"

"Amen!" the Brotherhood boys around her bellowed.

"Amen!" cried the crowd.

"When my father started this church years ago, we never dreamed we would be so blessed," the woman declared. "And yet, by ever standing vigilant against the marriage of metal and flesh, against the corruption and impurity infecting our very genes, we have *earned* these blessings! These times are sent to test us, oh my children." The woman pointed to a banner behind her—a painting of the same gray-haired man that adorned the walls. "But with Saint Michael to watch over us, New Bethlehem will endure!"

"Saint Michael watch over us!" the crowd called.

The woman waved to the Brothers on the steps.

"Brother War and our Horsemen have returned from their righteous hunt upon the trashbreed *maggots* who've beset our convoys these many months!" Lemon saw Brother Dubya give a low bow as the mob howled. "And the Lord hath been merciful in his bounty, and brought our enemies low. Brothers! Bring forward the deviates, that they may partake in their divine purification!"

The crowd bellowed as the convoy riders popped the trunk of Brother Dubya's auto. Lemon's belly turned as she saw two figures hauled out into the light. Both had been beaten to within an inch of breathing, neither much older than she was. The first was a girl, short dark hair, long bangs, black smudged paintstick on her lips and a slice of Asiabloc in her ancestry. The second was a boy, tall and broad, his skin darker than Hunter's. His hair was buzzed short, a radiation symbol shaved into the fuzz on the side of his head.

The girl was out cold, face swollen, blood leaking from a fresh bullet hole in her chest. The boy was conscious enough to struggle, not strong enough to break free. He spat bloody, fixed Brother Dubya in a dark, furious stare.

"I'ma kill you, you rat sonofa—"

Brother Dubya gave him a pop to the chops. The boy sagged, the crowd cheered. Sister Dee held out her hand, and a juve younger than Lemon slapped a hammer into it. The woman raised the tool into the air, looked into the mob.

"Thou shalt not suffer a witch to live!" she yelled, her eyes alight. "And only the pure shall prosper!"

"Only the pure shall prosper!" they answered.

The boy was dragged forward as the crowd bellowed, still struggling, only half conscious. In the middle of the stage, the Brotherhood had constructed a couple of large Xs from old telephone poles. Brother Dubya slammed the boy against one, held him in place as Sister Dee reached inside her pristine cassock like a showman, and produced the first of four long, rusted nails.

Lemon had seen this party before on the streets of Los Diablos, at least a dozen times. She knew exactly how it ended. Thing of it was, and as bad as she felt about it, there was nothing she could do. The radsickness already had her shuffling toward death's door, and causing a ruckus here was only going to get her closer. These Brotherhood boys were pure beef, with not even a rusty cyberarm or cheap optical implant among them—Lemon's gift wouldn't help her at all. And even if there was some way to use it to even the odds, that'd only mark her as a deviate, fit for another set of nails.

This crowd would rip her to pieces.

She recognized the familiar burn of helplessness inside her chest. An old, unwelcome houseguest. But she didn't know these kids. Didn't owe them dust. Just because she was a deviate, too, didn't mean they were crew. For all she knew, these two had just been born with an extra couple of fingers.

The dark-skinned boy met her stare. Bruised eyes, locking on hers through the crowd. She heard Hunter whisper something, couldn't quite hear it over the pulse in her ears. But even with that boy looking right at her—his stare not pleading, but full of the same fury she felt inside her chest—Lemon turned away.

She heard the first hammer blow. She heard the crowd roar. She didn't hear the boy scream, and she felt strangely proud of that. But she knew his courage wouldn't help him. That nothing could help him now.

And so, she pushed through the crowd. She had her own troubles. High enough to pile to the sky. Adding someone else's wasn't gonna help anyone.

Rule Number Eight in the Scrap.

The dead don't fight another day.

2.7

SOLOMON

"*Good eeeeeevening, human friends!*"

The shop was lit by flickering neon, red and purple and blue. The sign above the door read NEW BETHLEHEM PHARMACY AND GENERAL STORE. Walking inside with Hunter close behind, Lemon saw the space was huge, the shelves were crammed with gear, neatly cataloged and labeled. Filthy as New Bethlehem was, she noticed there was no dust on the stock or dirt on the floors. A small portrait of Saint Michael graced the wall. A sign over the counter informed Lemon:

YOUR SATISFACTION GUARANTEED

A buzzer had announced their arrival, and before the door was even shut, a tall logika had risen up from behind an antique cash register. Its hull was painted creamy white, trimmed in golden filigree. Its eyes were round and cheery, and when it spoke, an LED in its mouth flashed, lighting up its smile with every word.

"*My name is Solomon, friends,*" it said in a proper fancy

accent. *"AND WHO MIGHT I HAVE THE PLEASURE OF MEETING THIS FINE EVE?"*

"Lemon Fresh," the girl mumbled, feeling altogether wrecked.

"WELCOME TO OUR HUMBLE EMPORIUM, MISS FRESH! HOW MAY I HELP? NEW CLOTHES? FIREARMS, PERHAPS? I'VE THE FINEST IN ALL NEW BETHLEHEM, FIFTY PERCENT OFF AMMUNITION WITH ANY PURCHASE. YOUR SATISFACTION IS, AS THE SIGN SAYS, GUARANTEED."

Hunter stared at the logika in disgust, lips pressed tight together. Lemon shuffled to the counter, wiped the sweat off her brow.

"We need meds," she said. "Something for radsickness. You got any?"

"OH MY GOODNESS, ARE YOU ILL?" the logika smiled.

"I've had better days." Lemon winced, pressing at her stomach.

"OH MY, THAT'S JUST TERRIBLE!"

No matter what it said or how it said it, the logika's face wasn't animatronic, which meant its expression never changed. The bot just kept on grinning, as if it were telling you that you'd just won the lottery, or that there was a mix-up at the medstation when you were born and you were actually CorpState royalty.

"Um, thanks," Lemon said. "So about that medicine. You got any?"

"OH, GOODNESS, YES!" The bot waved at some small plastic bottles on the shelf behind it. *"THREE PER DAY TO RELIEVE SYMPTOMS, BEST WITH MEALS, YOUR SATISFACTION IS, AS THE SIGN SAYS, GUARANTEED."*

"Fizzyfizzyfizzy." Lemon sighed with relief, fully prepared to jump over the counter and kiss the bot right on his creeper grin. "Can I have some, please?"

"*Oh, goodness, no!*"

"... Why not?"

"*Well, from the look of you, my dear, you don't have two bob to rub together, if you'll pardon the expression. And I'm hardly running a charity.*"

Lemon reached into her undies, pulled out the second credstik she'd stolen from Brother Dubya. "It's a good thing I'm not asking for charity, then, Sparky."

The logika swiped the stik off the countertop, ran it through a reader beside the register. The tally flashed, and the bot leaned in for a closer look.

"*My goodness, that's quite a sum. Enough to buy out my entire stock.*"

"I'll take it," Lemon declared. "And some clean socks, while we're on it."

"*Oh, I'm afraid not,*" Solomon smiled.

"You just said I had enough creds to buy your entire stock! How much do you charge for *socks*?"

"*All our apparel is reasonably priced, I assure you, madam. But according to the serial number, this credstik was issued by Sister Dee on her personal account. It has obviously been ... how to put it gently ...*" The bot tilted its head. "*Misplaced by its original owner? Hmm? And I couldn't possibly accept stolen credits as payment. I'm a robot of scruples, Miss Fresh.*"

The bot handed back her stik, kept right on smiling.

"Waitaminute ..." Lemon blinked. "You *are* a robot. And the First Law says you're not allowed to hurt humans, yeah? Doesn't that mean you *have* to give me the meds? I'm gonna die without them, right?"

"*Oh, almost certainly, from the look of you. But I'm*"

AFRAID THAT GIVING YOU THE MEDICINE WOULD RESULT IN A FAR MORE SERIOUS INFRACTION OF THE FIRST LAW."

". . . How's that?"

"WELL, THIS SHOP IS A BUSTLING HUB OF COMMERCE HERE IN NEW BETHLEHEM, YOU SEE. THE CUSTOMER'S SATISFACTION IS, AS THE SIGN SAYS, GUARANTEED, AND AS SUCH, FOLK COME FROM ALL OVER, KNOWING THEY'LL GET A FAIR PRICE AND PAY A FAIR PRICE IN RETURN. BUT IF I WERE TO JUST START GIVING THINGS AWAY, WELL, THE SYSTEM WOULD COLLAPSE, WOULDN'T IT? AND WITHOUT THIS STORE, MY TRADERS WOULD BE OUT OF A LIVELIHOOD, AND NEW BETHLEHEM CITIZENS DEPRIVED OF WHAT THEY NEED TO SURVIVE."

"Okay," Lemon frowned. "But without the meds, I'm still gonna die."

"QUITE THE CONUNDRUM, YES?"

"So shouldn't your logic centers be short-circuiting or something right now?"

"NO, I'M GOOD WITH IT."

Hunter slammed her fist down on the counter. *"Lemonfresh requires the medicine, fleshless one. Give it over or—"*

"I SHOULD STOP YOU RIGHT THERE, MADAM," Solomon said, raising one hand. *"BEFORE YOU FINISH YOUR NO-DOUBT-ELOQUENT ATTEMPT AT INTIMIDATION, I MUST WARN YOU THAT THE THERMO-GRAPHIC CAPABILITIES IN MY OPTICS HAVE ENABLED ME TO SURMISE THAT YOU ARE NOT, IN THE STRICTEST SENSE, HUMAN. AND THERE-FORE BLOWING A HOLE THROUGH YOUR PELVIS WITH THE GAUSS CAN-NON CURRENTLY POINTED AT YOU UNDER THE COUNTER WOULD BE ABSOLUTELY NO IMPEDIMENT FOR ME WHATSOEVER."*

The logika tilted his head and smiled.

"YOU WERE SAYING?"

"I need those meds," Lemon pleaded.

"AND IF I MAY SPEAK FRANKLY, MY DEAR, YOU ALSO NEED A

SHOWER AND CHANGE OF CLOTHES. BUT I'M AFRAID I DON'T SEE ANY OF THAT IN YOUR IMMEDIATE FUTURE." The logika smiled. "THOUGH FOR WHAT IT'S WORTH, I AM TERRIBLY SORRY ABOUT YOUR IMPENDING IRRADIATED DEMISE. I'M TOLD IT'S QUITE UNPLEASANT."

"Well, is there anything else—"

"THANK YOU, COME AGAIN!"

"But I—"

"THAAAAAAANK YOU, COME AGAIN!"

Lemon looked Solomon up and down. She'd met its kind a thousand times before, though admittedly, never in bot form. Kicking up a fuss now was only going to spell more trouble, and trouble in New Bethlehem meant Brotherhood. And so, despite the growing worry she might actually end up *dying* in this rathole town, she pulled on her braveface. Her streetface. Gave the logika a small nod.

"Thanks for your time, Sparky."

Lemon limped out the door, the buzzer chirping as she stepped into the street. Down the end of the block, she could see the crowd had cleared out from the Brotherhood's stage and filed into the WarDome—she could hear the familiar sound of distant roars, the drumming of impatient feet. Around the stage, a dozen Disciples were silhouetted against drums of burning trash, and beyond them, Lemon could see those big wooden Xs where two luckless figures hung.

There's worse ways to go than radsickness, I guess.

Hunter stood behind her, lips pursed in thought. *"Perhaps there are other traders who have the same chemicals. We should keep hunting."*

Lemon shook her head. "Market's closing. Looks like everyone's heading to watch the Domefight. And at least we know the meds we need are in this one."

Hunter scowled, pulled aside her cloak. Lemon spotted a pistol at her belt, similar to the rifle she'd left with Mai'a—pale and spiny, as if crafted out of old fishbones. A handful of bumblebees were crawling through Hunter's hair, up her throat, clearly sharing their mistress's agitation.

"Our stings will not work against a fleshless one. Our weapons, either."

"I'm not suggesting we get murderous," Lemon said.

"What does she suggest?"

"You notice anything special about the lock on Solomon's front door?"

Hunter frowned, clearly puzzled. And despite the growing pain in her belly, her creeping fear, Lemon managed to muster a smile.

"It's electronic," she said.

It almost felt like the old days.

She'd run solo most of her childhood in LD, but every now and then, someone would rustle a big-time scam and need to crew up. She'd stolen a whole crate of Neo-Meat™ with a few kids from Engine Road once. And there was that time she and the Akuma twins ripped that WarDome bookie and ate like queens for a month. Of all the Rules in the Scrap, Number Five had always been her favorite:

Takers keepers.

She and Hunter found an old salvage place a little down the way from Solomon's. They sat in the shadows under its awning to wait, and Lemon tried not to think about those deviate kids at the other end of the square, or what the radiation might be doing to her body as the minutes ticked by. The BioMaas agent offered her another algae bar, but her belly was feeling a lot worse. Instead, she wet her cracking lips with their water flask and watched as Solomon's "boutique" closed up for the night with all the shops around it.

As a street thief in Los Diablos, Lemon's first lessons had been in patience. Looking for the right moment to strike, slit the pocket, snatch the scratch. She'd learned the hard way about the value of waiting, and Hunter seemed to have learned the lesson, too. Together, they sat and watched the patrols wander by, talking through Lemon's plan in hushed voices as battle raged inside the WarDome. She thought of Evie, of their time together fighting Miss Combobulation in Dregs. Wondering where her bestest was as her heart ached beneath her ribs.

The Disciples wandered in packs of four, rolling through the market at regular intervals. Within an hour, Lemon knew their patterns, knew the gaps, knew the moment. And finally, she nodded to Hunter, and it was on.

They stole over to the front of Solomon's, the BioMaas operative moving quick and graceful, Lemon limping from the hurt in her gut. The store's neon was switched off, the windows blocked by rusted shutters. Hunter kept watch while Lemon pressed against the front door. It was solid steel, hung with a sign depicting Solomon's infuriating grin and a speech bubble now declaring APOLOGIES, WE'RE CLOSED! Beneath the notice pulsed the red LEDs of a twelve-digit control pad.

Lemon pressed her palm to the lock, felt for the power inside her. She'd never been very good at little things—using her gift with finesse was way harder than just letting it loose to fry everything around her. Closing her eyes, she reached for the storm of gray static, trying to make it small as possible.

With a loud bang, the neon above the store burst, every light around her fizzled and the PA speakers shorted out entirely. Before anyone came for a looksee, Lemon pushed the front door open and slipped inside, Hunter close behind.

Squinting around the gloom, Lemon felt an old familiar thrill prickling on her skin. The fear of getting caught, the buzz of doing wrong. It wasn't that she was a bad person. But she'd been found in a laundry detergent box outside an ethyl joint as a baby. Named for the logo on the side of it by the drunks who discovered her. The only thing her parents had left her was the little silver five-leafed clover she wore around her neck—it wasn't like she'd had many wonderful role models up till now.

Besides, being bad sometimes had a funny way of feeling really good.

Hunter waited by the door as Lemon crept along the shelves, moving by feel through the gloom. The register was still functional, so it looked like she'd managed to stop her gift damaging anything too far inside the store. Peering over the countertop, the girl saw the meds she needed, grinned up at the sign above her head.

YOUR SATISFACTION GUARANTEED

"Damn right . . . ," she whispered.

"GOOD EEEEEEVENING, HUMAN FRIEND!"

Lemon near jumped out of her skin, tumbling back on her hind parts as Solomon rose up from behind the counter. The gloom was illuminated by the bot's smile, pulsing in time with every word he spoke.

"OH, NO, PLEASE DON'T GET UP." The bot's optics were fixed on Lemon as it hauled a bulky rifle from behind the counter and

aimed it at Hunter. *"I'M NOT CERTAIN HOW YOU DID IT, BUT I'M RATHER MIFFED YOU BROKE MY DOOR, AND SHOOTING YOUR INHUMAN FRIEND HERE MIGHT TAKE THE EDGE OFF. SO, IF EVERYONE COULD JUST HOLD STILL, I'LL CALL THE CONSTABULARY AND THEY'LL TAKE CARE OF YOU BOTH, YES?"*

Solomon reached for an old battered CB radio with his free hand.

"You're calling the Brotherhood on us?" Lemon asked.

"I'M SORRY, DIDN'T I MAKE THAT CLEAR?"

"But they'll kill me, won't they? Isn't that a breach of the First Law?"

"WELL, HERE'S THE THING, MY STICKY-FINGERED FRIEND. I'VE MADE IT MY BUSINESS TO REMAIN UNAWARE OF THE PUNISHMENTS INFLICTED FOR THEFT IN NEW BETHLEHEM FOR THAT VERY REASON. IT COULD BE THAT THEY GIVE YOU A PAT ON THE BACKSIDE AND SEND YOU ON YOUR MERRY WAY." Solomon tilted his head. *"THOUGH I DOUBT IT."*

"Isn't that a little against the spirit of the Law?" Lemon asked.

"NO, I'M GOOD WITH—"

The logika bucked, his whole body going rigid. He made a funny little noise in his voxbox, his optics glowing white before popping inside his metal skull. Sparks burst from the LED display at his chest, the radio in his hand, from his maddening grin. And with a small electronic whimper, Solomon crashed face-first into the antique register, then collapsed to the floor in a smoking heap.

Lemon lowered her hand and rolled to her feet, pulled herself over the counter. By the fizzing light of Solomon's remains, she popped the top off a bottle of radmeds and scoffed three pills, swallowing her salvation with a grimace. Pulse racing, she stuffed her cargo pockets with the rest of the meds and anything else worth stealing. Finally, she knelt beside the fried logika, glanced one last time at the sign above the counter.

YOUR SATISFACTION GUARANTEED

"You know, you're right," she said. "That was completely satisfying."

Hunter had the exit open a crack, letting roars from the distant WarDome drift in from the night outside, along with the occasional deathbee. The insects crawled over the agent's cheeks, along her fluttering eyelashes, and Lemon had to suppress a shiver as she rejoined her by the door.

"*The way is clear,*" she whispered.

"You sure?"

Hunter nodded. "*A Hunter sees with many eyes, Lemonfresh.*"

"Right," the girl replied. "Out into the street, walk it like we own it, head straight for the gate. If a patrol stops us, keep your deathbees calm, let me talk. Fizzy?"

Hunter nodded and the pair slipped out from the store, closing the door behind them. The market was almost completely deserted, the population of New Bethlehem all turned out for the Dome. A few gutter runners standing around a burning drum gave them a curious look as they passed. A Disciple patrol was gathered under the PA speaker, pondering why it had shorted out.

Lemon's heart was thumping in her chest, her skin tingling at the feeling of a grift done right. Maybe she was imagining it, maybe it was just the relief, but those meds were making her feel better already. The night was bright and her pockets were full and she was starting to think they were free and clear.

Until they passed by the Brotherhood's stage at the other end of the square again.

She tried not to look. Tried not to notice the two figures nailed up on those Xs. The way the Brotherhood had patched up the bullet wound in the girl's chest so she wouldn't bleed out before she'd suffered. The way a dozen Brotherhood thugs were slouching on the steps in front of those hanging bodies, laughing and jawing as if nothing were amiss. As if they'd not nailed up two kids to suffocate under their own weight beneath tomorrow's sun.

The dead don't fight another day, she reminded herself.

Just because they're like you, doesn't make them crew.

She missed Evie, she realized.

She missed Ezekiel and Cricket and the feeling she was wrapped up in a story much bigger than herself. It was easier back then, just being the sidekick. Dragged along for the ride, expected to contribute nothing more than the occasional quip and maybe a shoulder to cry on.

Her shoulders weren't strong enough for anything else, after all.

She wasn't big enough to do this on her own.

Was she?

"Stop," she whispered.

Hunter reached inside her cloak, instantly alert, scanning the night around them for danger. *"Trouble?"*

"Not yet," she sighed.

Lemon looked to the stage behind them, those kids strung up to die.

"But I think I'm about to make some."

2.8

PALADIN

Be careful what you wish for.

Cricket knew this song like he knew his own name. The stamping feet and rising cheers. The hiss of pistons and the percussion of metal bodies colliding. Bright lights and ultra-violence, the crowd safe behind concrete barriers and rusting iron bars, secure in the knowledge that the things fighting and bleeding out and dying on the killing floor couldn't feel a thing.

WarDome.

The big bot waited in a work pit below the Dome floor, watching the boy named Abraham seal up his chest cavity and bolt it closed. The dustneck brothers Murph and Mike stood on the sidelines, offering suggestions and being politely ignored. Abraham was obviously something of an expert on bot tech—he'd replaced Cricket's faulty powercells without much fuss, given how big they were. The big bot could feel new current rolling through his limbs, power crackling at his fingertips. Internal readouts showed he was almost back at full capacity, and ready to roll.

"How do you feel?" the boy asked in his soft voice.

Cricket simply stared, blue eyes aglow.

"It's all right, you can speak," Abraham said. "What're your power levels at?"

"NINETY-TWO PERCENT," Cricket replied.

"That'll be plenty," the boy nodded. "Your opponent in tonight's match is called the Thunderstorm. It's the champion WarBot from a settlement down south called the Edge. It's only nine thousand horsepower, but it fights dirty. We're running live ballistics, so—"

"I DON'T WANT TO GO UP THERE," Cricket said.

Abraham pulled his tech-goggs up onto his forehead and blinked, as if Cricket had just told him the sky was green or up was actually down. For the first time, Cricket saw the boy's eyes were a brilliant pale blue.

"Where'd you two say you found this thing again?" he asked.

"Out west," Mikey replied. "In the Clefts."

"You brought us a Domefighter that doesn't want to fight Dome?"

Cricket used to joke about it. Between the feeds Evie had obsessively watched and Miss Combobulation's brawls in the Los Diablos WarDome, he'd seen logika fight hundreds of times before. And he'd cheered along as Evie won, learned the Dome's tricks backward, joked that one day he'd grow up to be a Domefighter, too. But he'd just been a helperbot back then. Forty centimeters high. Handing Evie tools when she needed them and offering advice when he could. He said he wanted to fight on the killing floor, but really, all he ever wanted was to be taken seriously.

To be treated with respect.

To be big.

When Silas had installed his persona in the Quixote's body, it'd been like a dream come true. And he'd used his new power as best he could to defend Evie, throwing all he could into the brawl at Babel for the sake of the girl who'd been his mistress. But that'd been life and death. That'd been for love. He never thought for a second that one day he might have to actually fight for *amusement*.

"DON'T MAKE ME GO UP THERE," Cricket pleaded.

Stomping over to the big logika, Murphy kicked his foot.

"Hey, listen here!" he yelled. "I *order* you to fight in this Dome match, you hear me? When that countdown finishes, you'll fight until your opponent's out of commission or you are, acknowledge!"

Cricket looked down into Murphy's eyes.

Up to the Dome floor above his head.

Be careful what you wish for.

"ACKNOWLEDGED," he replied.

"See?" Murph grinned at Abraham. "Toldja. Pure quality, this one. Fistful of hardcore, true cert. You'll see."

Abraham looked at Cricket again, his pale blue eyes narrowed.

"I suppose we will," he murmured.

The boy lowered his mechanical gantry, stepped down onto the work pit floor. With the flick of a switch, the metal braces holding Cricket's arms and legs in place were released, allowing him free movement.

Except I'm not free at all, am I?

He'd never been in this position before. He'd always been beholden to humans, sure. And Evie had sometimes told him to be quiet when he'd wanted to speak his mind. But she'd never forced him to do something he'd hate.

He realized how lucky he'd been, serving people who cared about what he thought. How he felt.

And now?

"Juves and juvettes!" came a cry through the PA above his head. *"Disciples and believers, get yourself situated! Tonight's main bout is about to begin!"*

Cricket fixed the boy in his glowing stare. "PLEASE, I DON'T WANT TO—"

"Shuddup!" Murph hollered, kicking him so hard he hurt his foot. "Dammit . . . you speak when you're spoken to! Now, you get up there and you fight!"

". . . ACKNOWLEDGED," Cricket said.

"You'll do fine," Abraham promised quietly. "You're built for this."

"In the blue zone!" came the cry above. *"From parts unknown, weighing in at seventy-one tons, get yourselves rowdy for tonight's challenger!"*

Cricket felt the platform beneath him shudder, the broad hatchway above his head grinding open. The crowd's howls washed over him, gaining in volume as the platform slowly brought him up to the killing floor. Floodlights arced over the Dome, the flash compensation in his optics kicking in as he scoped his situation.

It was a long way from good, true cert.

The arena was a few hundred meters wide, scattered with the broken bodies of bots who'd been destroyed in earlier matches. Barricades of concrete and steel littered the ground. A concrete wall ten meters high encircled the arena, and outside that, concentric rings of bleachers rose like the tiers of an oldskool amphitheater.

As Cricket watched, a dome of rusted iron bars rolled up from the floor and enclosed the space. A bright neon sign above his head began flashing:

WARNING: LIVE FIRE MATCH

A motley crowd of scavvers, scenekillers and wageslaves gathered in the bleachers and pressed up against the bars. Their volume was thunderous, washing over Cricket in waves.

"Aaaaand now, in the red zone! All the way from the Edge . . ." The EmCee's voice was swamped under a long chorus of boos. *". . . Weighing in at seventy-seven tons, winner of sixteen hardcore bouts, make some ruckus for . . . the Thunderstooooorm!"*

A blast of oldskool rawk music spilled over the PA as Cricket's opponent rose into view, bathed in a flood of red light. The logika was squat and quadrupedal, heavily armored. Twin gauss cannons were mounted on its shoulder brackets, its fists crackling with live current. It was painted black, a lightning bolt sprayed in gold on its greaves and chest, its optics glowing bright green.

"HI," Cricket waved. "I DON'T SUPPOSE YOU JUST WANNA BE FRIENDS?"

"TARGET ACQUIRED," the Storm called in a booming voice, turning on Cricket. *"MISSION: DESTROY."*

"OKAY, THEN," Cricket nodded. "GOOD TALK."

The enemy bot stepped off its platform and spread its arms wide, launching off a burst of fireworks from the missile pods on its back. The New Bethlehem crowd obviously weren't fans of the visiting logika, booing louder as the rockets exploded into showers of red and white.

"Sixty seconds until official betting closes, believers! We remind you tonight's bout is sponsored by Daedalus Technologies, and brought to you through the generosity of our beloved Sister Dee and her Horsemen! Can I get an aaaaamen?"

Cricket's optics roamed the crowd as they stamped and roared. He saw Sister Dee sitting in a ringside box, raising her hand in acknowledgment. The woman was still dressed all in white, the skull on her face freshly painted, a plastic red flower in her hair. Beside her sat three men, one tall and fierce, one stick-thin, the last almost pudgy. Each wore the same skullpaint on their faces, the same white cassocks.

The Brotherhood must run this whole damn town. . . .

Cricket saw Abraham standing dutifully beside his mother. He looked small compared to the Horsemen, totally out of place. He saw him speak to Sister Dee, the woman smiling and squeezing his hand as she replied.

The crowd quieted down, and Cricket turned his attention to his opponent, his circuits awash with electric trepidation. It wasn't like he could be *afraid* technically. But the Third Law still compelled him to protect his own existence. Problem was, Cricket knew he couldn't fight his way out of a wet paper bag.

Silas had never felt the need to program Cricket with combat techniques—he'd been less than half a meter tall for most of his life. In his new body, he could brawl, he was strong, and that'd been enough to see him go toe-to-toe with Faith in Babel. But against a logika that was programmed to mince other bots for a living?

"I HAVE A BAD FEELING ABOUT THIS," he muttered.

"Ten seconds to full hostile!" cried the EmCee.

Cricket searched the crowd, looking for a friendly face and finding only bright eyes and bared teeth. A countdown appeared in the neon above his head and the mob joined in, stamping their feet in time as Cricket called out to the Thunderstorm.

"Five!"

"HEY, LISTEN—"

"Four!"

"I'M THINKING—"

"Three!"

"WE COULD GO SOMEWHERE QUIETER—"

"Two!"

"AND MAYBE JUST—"

"One!"

"TALK ABOUT THIS?"

"WAR!"

The Thunderstorm raised its cannons and unloaded at Cricket's chest. The big bot yelped and threw himself behind one of the steel barricades as the shots whizzed overhead. The crowd roared, the Storm followed up with a burst of missiles from the pods on its back. Cricket rolled aside as the shots spiraled through the air toward him, trailing plumes of rainbow-colored smoke. The ground around him exploded, shrapnel ripping tiny gouges in his plate armor, the flashes making him flinch. That kind of detonation would have torn him to pieces when he was little, and his self-preservation subroutines were in full overdrive.

"First strike to the Storm!" the EmCee cried.

Cricket hunched behind a metal barricade, panic flooding his systems.

He wanted to run.

He wanted to cower.

He was never the bravest bot in the Scrap.

But he'd been *ordered* to fight, and the Second Law countermanded any desire for self-preservation. And so, instead of running away, he was forced to charge. Across the killing floor, feet pounding the steel. As he drew closer, some hidden instinct clicked into place, and he felt the combat software inside his WarBot body engage. A small 360-degree map of the WarDome appeared in his head, tracking his opponent's movements, speed, ammo count, damage reports, and screaming warning about incoming fire.

The enemy logika let loose with another blast from its cannons, Cricket twisting past the first as the second *spangggg*ed off his armored shoulder. He didn't feel pain, but his damage reports started flashing brighter. He had no weapons, no real advantage. His only plan was wrapping his hands around the Storm and tearing pieces away till there was nothing left to rip off.

"Look at it go, folks!"

The crowd gasped as Cricket wove among the barricades, rolling over a destroyed logika hull and tumbling past a barrage of exploding missiles. He was big, but thanks to his tracking software, he was surprisingly agile. His engines thundered, the twelve thousand horsepower in his limbs rushing like a waterfall. The crowd roared as he drew close, only to howl in disappointment as the Storm fired a jet burst from each foot and sailed into the air. Articulated toes curled around the WarDome's bars above and it seized hold, hanging upside down over the killing floor like a limpet.

"UM," Cricket called. "THAT'S NOT ENTIRELY FAIR, IS IT?"

"*TARGET ACQUIRED. MISSION: DESTROY.*"

"YEAH, YOU SAID THAT ALREADY."

The Thunderstorm unleashed another missile barrage. Cricket raised one arm to shield his optics, shells bursting on his armor, the explosions catching him across the back and ripping up his hydraulics. An internal alarm sounded, his body feeding him more damage reports, a TARGET LOCKED message flashing in his displays. Threat washed over his circuitry, the Third Law screaming in his mind. Memories of the fights he'd watched with Evie flickered in his head, the pair sitting in her room, Lemon beside them, watching legends of the Dome throw down before the wondering crowd. But that was then. This was now.

He was alone, afraid.

But beneath and between and beyond that, the big bot was surprised to realize . . .

He was *angry.*

Angry at being taken away from his friends. Angry about what had happened to Evie. Angry that these humans had stolen him, put their hands in him, thrown him in here to fight for their enjoyment. He might have been made to serve, but he hadn't been made to serve *them,* and the injustice of it all boiled over his circuitry, washing his vision with red. Some electronic instinct, some urging in the software of his new body, made him reach out toward the Thunderstorm. And as the crowd gasped in wonder, Cricket's right hand folded up inside his forearm, and a heavy chaingun unfolded in its place, firing a hail of bullets right at the enemy bot.

"Looks like our challenger has some surprises up its sleeve, folks!"

The blast was bright, thunderous, shocking even to Cricket. Tracer rounds flew like fireflies, the crowd backing away from the bars even as they roared approval. The unexpected recoil threw off his aim, Cricket staggered backward and almost fell. The wild spray missed the Storm completely, but it *did* strike the WarDome bars the enemy logika was clinging to. The shots were armor-piercing, explosive-tipped, ten thousand rounds per minute. The steel shredded like wet tissue. And with its footholds blasted away, the Thunderstorm was sent plummeting toward the ground.

"Pro moves from our challenger!"

Cricket had no idea what he was doing, no control over the

combat reflexes running through his WarBot body. The crowd bellowed in delight as twin pods of missile launchers unfurled from his back like stubby wings, targeting lasers locking onto his fallen opponent. A salvo of small incendiary missiles burst forth, lighting up the Storm in a halo of bright flames and sending it staggering.

Cricket knew he had to press, charging the fallen bot and kicking it like a football. The Storm went tumbling across the killing floor, flipping over onto its back. It tried to regain its footing, limbs kicking feebly as Cricket fell on top of it and began punching, stomping, tearing, the crowd chanting in time with every blow.

"Kill! Kill! Kill!"

Sparks flew, the Storm's armor buckling beneath the terrible force of Cricket's fists. Its fritzing voice box was spitting out a stream of garbled damage reports, its optics flaring bright. With one mighty blow, Cricket smashed the enemy logika's maintenance hatch wide open, titanium buckling like tinfoil. And with red still washing over his optics, Cricket reached inside, fingers closing around the Thunderstorm's central processor—the bot's literal electronic heart.

"P-PLEASE . . . ," the Storm stammered. *"D-DO NOT . . ."*

Some part of him knew he wasn't really killing it. That the Storm could be rebuilt if its owners cared enough. But Cricket knew he was *hurting* it. Knew the imperative burning at its core: the Third Law demanding it fight, flail and, finally, even *beg* to protect its own existence. And in losing, Cricket knew exactly what the logika would be feeling. To fail to uphold the Three Laws was *worse* than dying.

To fail to uphold the Three Laws was to fail in every sense a robot could.

But still, that filthy dustneck's command rang in Cricket's ears. The Second Law burning brighter than anything except the First.

A robot must obey the orders given to it by human beings, except where such orders would conflict with the First Law.

A robot

must

obey.

"PLEASE . . . ," the Storm begged.

"I'M SORRY," the big bot replied. "I'M SO SORRY."

Cricket made a fist, cables spitting, a blinding flash of white. The crowd roared as he tore the Thunderstorm's heart free in a cascade of sparks. The EmCee was shouting into the PA, the mob was on their feet, the neon gleaming in the coolant and oil pooling like blood at his feet. Cricket looked at the spent shell casings glittering on the charred floor, the broken hulk before him. He looked at the humans around him, the bloodlust in their eyes, listening to the stomping rhythm of their feet.

"Believers!" came the cry.

The crowd hushed, all eyes turning to the box at the ring's edge. Sister Dee was standing with a microphone at her lips, surrounded by her cassocked thugs. Abraham stood beside her, giving Cricket the thumbs-up. Behind him stood Murph and Mikey, squabbling once more as they began to realize that selling him for a mere two thousand liters might have been a touch conservative.

But it was too late. The bargain was struck.

Cricket belonged to the Brotherhood now.

"The Lord has truly blessed us this day!" the Sister cried. "Not only have the terrorists who plagued our convoys been brought low, but it seems New Bethlehem WarDome has a new *champion!*"

Sister Dee pointed to Cricket, teeth flashing as she smiled. "I give you . . ."

Abraham leaned in to whisper in his mother's ear, and the woman smiled.

". . . our *Paladin!*" she cried.

All he'd ever wanted was to be taken seriously.

To be treated with respect.

To be big.

Cricket looked up at the roaring crowd, hung his head.

"BE CAREFUL WHAT YOU WISH FOR," he murmured.

2.9

EASY

"No."

"They're just kids, Hunter."

"We must bring Lemonfresh to CityHive. She does not understand her importance. Lemonfresh is—"

"Yeah, yeah. Needed. Special. I got it."

They were standing in the shadows of a closed street-eatery, scoping the Brotherhood's awful little stage. Red banners fluttered in a cool night breeze. The dozen Brethren leaning against Brother Dubya's monster truck didn't exactly look on high alert, but that was no kind of surprise. This was the heart of a Brotherhood settlement, after all. Everyone in this armpit of a town was either on their side or terrified of them. Probably both.

Lemon could hear roars from the distant WarDome, the crash of metal and bursts of heavy weapons fire. It sounded like total chaos in there, and she was grateful for the diversion. A churn and bubble was coming from the desalination plant, black smoke rumbling into the sky. With all that noise, Lemon knew they'd have the element of surprise—even if it was only her and Hunter against twelve B-boys. But Hunter herself was far from convinced.

"Came here for chemicals," the operative growled. *"Have them. Road awaits."*

Lemon scowled. "Listen, can we agree that, as far as unwilling yet gorgeous captives go, I've been an absolute effing delight up to this point? Haven't tried to escape, or shiv you in the back, or warned these lawmen that 'oh, hey, by the way, this crazy lady is a genetically engineered murder machine with a swarm of killer bees inside her bra'?"

"We thought we had reached understanding," Hunter said, a little sadly.

"Look, you wanna tell me I'm special, fine," Lemon snapped. "I find it literally impossible to disagree with you. But those kids are some kind of special, too, or these Brotherhood bastards wouldn't have nailed them up in the first place. Maybe they just got two belly buttons, I dunno. But nobody deserves to go out like that. Nobody."

Hunter peered across the way to the Brotherhood scaffold. Trepidation shining in those strange golden eyes.

"And then we leave for CityHive," she finally whispered.

"Look at these freckles. Would I lie to you?"

The BioMaas agent folded her arms and scowled.

"What does she propose?"

"Almost everyone in this dump is at WarDome. You set your deathbees on the thugs, I get the kids down, we snaffle one of those autos and fang it. Once we're out of New Bethlehem, you call Mai'a, we give the kids the wheels, then ride into the sunset. Conscience clear."

"Bees die when they sting, Lemonfresh. We are not infinite. She asks much."

"Yeah, well, you're asking me to be the wind that changes the world or whatever, so I figure this makes us even. It'll be easy as, trust me."

"Easy as what?"

Lemon shrugged. "Easy as a very easy thing."

The operative was silent for long moments, clearly torn.

"I could always just start screaming for help?" Lemon offered. "I *am* still technically the victim of a kidnapping here."

"She would threaten me?"

"Technically, what I'm doing is more like extortion."

Hunter narrowed her eyes, a low angry buzzing filling her chest.

"Very well," she nodded.

Lemon's stomach was still achy, but she managed a grin anyway. The pair waited until the closest Disciple patrol had wandered past. And when the coast was nice and clear, Lemon moseyed over to the stage, hands in her stuffed pockets.

The Brotherhood boys fell silent as they noticed the short, scruffy redhead wandering toward them. She guessed these dozen were among the crew that had snaffled those poor kids to begin with. They were packing heavy pistols, automatic rifles. The tallest one had an oversized copy of the Goodbook hanging from a thick iron chain at his belt. Bound in cracked leather, it was big enough to beat a burglar to death with, and embossed with faded gold lettering:

The Lord helps those who help themselves.

The Brethren looked her over, eyebrows raised.

"Evenin', little sister," a beardy one said.

Lemon shook her head and smiled. "Oh, I'm not your sister, spunky."

"All the Lord's children are our brothers and sisters," a tall one replied.

"Amen, Brother Ray," the beardy one murmured.

Beardy McBeardo was tossing a claw hammer between one hand and the other. Lemon realized it was the same one Sister Dee had used on the kids earlier.

"Tell me, Brother Ray," she said to the tall one. "Do you have to brush your teeth extra hard on account of all the crap that comes out of your mouth?"

The dozen Brethren glanced at each other in disbelief. Brother Ray wandered over, crouched in front of Lemon. The man was big enough that the two of them were still eye to eye. This close, she could see the bloodshot in his stare, the nothing beyond it. His voice was the dangerous kind of quiet.

"You looking to get hurt, little sister?"

"Like you hurt those kids up there?"

Brother Ray glanced at the pair onstage. He drummed his fingers on the massive Goodbook hanging from his belt.

"Only the pure shall prosper," he shrugged.

Lemon sucked her lip, nodded. She pointed at the beardy Brother's neck.

"Hey, you got a bee on you."

The Brother frowned, then flinched, slapping at his throat. "Goddammit!"

"Blasphemy, Brother R—ow, god*dammit*!"

The Brethren managed a handful more curses before their lungs stopped working. Lemon backed away, turned her head so she wouldn't have to watch them ghost, covering her ears to block out the sounds they made. She'd grown up rough, true cert, but she'd seen more people get cadaverous in the last week than she'd seen in all the days before put together. It was starting to get heavy.

She wondered what Mister C might've said, seeing how she'd ended up so deep so quick. She could remember the old man looking her in the eye as he took her bloody hand in his, squeezed it tight and breathed his dying words.

"Look after our g-girl. She's going to . . . n-need you now."

Yeah. Great big fat job she was doing of that . . .

Lemon flinched as she felt a soft hand on her shoulder, turned to see Hunter behind her. *"Quickly."*

Lemon nodded, pulled up her pants and gritted her teeth. Listening to the distant WarDome roar rising in pitch, she knelt beside Brother Ray, rifled his pockets.

"What's the word for someone both brilliant and beautiful?" she finally asked, holding up a set of car keys in triumph. "Brilliful? Beautifant?"

"Go!" Hunter hissed, dragging the bodies out of sight.

"Rightright." Lemon snaffled the fallen claw hammer and dashed up onto the stage to take a closer peek at the captives. Both were wearing some kind of military uniform, cut out of desert camo. Both were also unconscious—the Asiabloc girl from blood loss and shock, the dark-skinned boy from the beating he'd taken and the torture that had come afterward.

Probably for the best.

Lemon set about figuring out how to get the pair free. She'd not eaten anything substantial in days, but she still felt her gorge rising, looking at the hammer in her hands and pondering the best way to drag the nails out of the boy's feet.

"Um, okay," she whispered. "I am apparently not equipped to deal with this level of pukable."

Hunter appeared at her side, golden eyes gleaming with concern.

"What takes so long?"

"I've never done this before!" Lemon hissed. "These people have *nails* in parts of them that should not, strictly speaking, have nails in them!"

Hunter snatched the hammer and set to work, and Lemon decided it'd be best for all concerned if she started the car instead. She ran down to the monster truck, keys in hand, and immediately realized she had two problems: First, a Disciple patrol had rounded the corner at the end of the market and were headed their way. And second, she was too short to reach the truck's door handle.

"Um," she said. "Crap?"

Looking around, she spied the bloated Brotherhood corpses. Lemon dashed over, slipped the cutter free from her buckle and sliced Brother Ray's belt. Picking up his fat, leather-bound copy of the Goodbook, she waddled back to the monster truck. Placing the book on its end, she stood atop it, popped the handle, climbed inside. Using the book's chain, she hauled it up, and plopped it on the driver's seat so she'd be tall enough to see over the wheel. She gave the embossed cover a small pat.

"The Lord helps those who help themselves," she murmured.

The rear passenger door opened, and Hunter dumped the unconscious girl inside, dashed back for the boy. Peering out through the windshield, Lemon saw the Disciples had noticed something wrong and were trotting down the street, speaking into their commsets. Lemon turned the key, rewarded with an earthshaking roar.

"Hunter, move your ass!" she shouted.

The Disciples broke into a run, slinging their rifles off their backs. Lemon saw another patrol dashing toward them from the opposite direction, heard the blare of a steamwhistle from the de-sal plant, followed by a wailing air-raid siren from the city walls. She gunned the engine, feet barely able to reach the pedals.

"HUNTER!"

The door behind her opened, the BioMaas agent leaping inside with the dark-skinned boy in her arms. *"Go, Lemonfresh!"*

Lemon stomped the gas just as the bullets started flying, *spang*ing off the panelwork and shattering the windshield. The motor bellowed and the truck lunged forward, crushing a row of tinshack market stalls. Lemon winced, tried to find reverse, the gearbox making a sound like a bolt dropped into a meat grinder.

"Can she not drive?" Hunter demanded.

". . . Did I not mention that?" Lemon asked.

The BioMaas agent muttered to herself, hauled that strange fishbone pistol out from under her cloak. She fired off a dozen shots out the window, seemingly at random. The bullets were green, luminous, humming like fireflies as they whizzed harmlessly up into the dark.

Lemon gawped over her shoulder. "Can you not *shoot?*"

"A Hunter never misses our mark," the woman replied.

"Maybe you better tell your bull . . ."

Lemon's voice faded, and she turned back to her window as the humming changed pitch. Mouth dropping open, she watched as the shots curved in midair, swooped off in a multitude of directions like they had minds of their own, striking each of the dozen Disciples running at the truck. The men collapsed, convulsing where they fell. In a handful of heartbeats, every one of them was motionless.

Lemon met the BioMaas operative's golden stare.

"Okay," she nodded. "You can shoot."

"Go!" Hunter roared.

Lemon found reverse, planted her foot, the truck ripping free of the stalls and crashing ass-backward into the stage. The girl bounced back in her seat, cracked her forehead on the steering wheel, slammed on the brake.

"You might wanna fasten your safety belt," she muttered.

"What is safety belt?"

"Oh, this is going to end well."

Lemon spun the wheel, stomped the pedal and they were off, tearing away through the market. Even with her butt parked on the Goodbook, she could barely see out of the broken windshield, and the truck crashed through another dozen stalls and rolled straight over a row of parked dirt bikes as it roared out of the square. The air-raid siren was wailing louder, but most of the citizens of New Bethlehem were still at WarDome, and the streets were clear.

The truck was thundering past the de-sal plant when the second round of bullets started flying. Lemon heard lead pattering on the panels like rain, desperately trying to keep four wheels on the ground as she swerved and swayed. The truck plowed through an ethyl joint, flattened a parked RV and screeched around the corner into the main square, rumbling for the gate.

"Um."

Lemon slammed on the brakes, chewed her lip.

"Okay, good news and bad news."

"What?"

"Bad news is, the gate's closed." She shot Hunter an apologetic glance. "And I sorta lied, there is no good news."

Hunter peered out of the shattered windshield. Ahead, the heavy double gates of New Bethlehem had been closed and sealed—apparently in response to the sirens they'd set off. They were five meters tall, half a meter thick, iron-reinforced. The agent glanced at Lemon, her face grim.

"Easy as a very easy thing, yes?"

"Look, no one ever let me plan stuff before, I got kept around for my looks!"

Hunter did something to her pistolthing that might've been a reload. She loosened the throat of her outfit, and a swarm of furious bumblebees began crawling from the hive that was her skin. With a flick of her left wrist, a long, wicked barb the color of bleached bone emerged from the flesh of her palm.

"Where the hells were you hiding that?" Lemon breathed.

"When gate opens, drive."

"But wha—"

"Drive."

Hunter opened the truck door, leapt down onto the broken street and dashed right at the gatehouse. As she ran, she fired another dozen of those firefly rounds into the dark. The glowing green bursts swooped among the Disciples and Brotherhood members who'd responded to the siren, and Hunter's bees took to the wing. Lemon heard screams over the idling motor, wails and gargled prayers. She ducked low as a hail of bullets struck the truck, but most of the shooters were gunning for the Bio-Maas agent cutting them to ribbons. The woman tumbled along the ground, dreadlocks whipping like snakes. She twisted to her feet, hurtled over the swelling corpses manning the gatehouse and disappeared inside.

The girl couldn't see what went on inside the building, couldn't hear over the siren's wail. But within a minute, the gate clunked and shook, the bolts sealing it shuddered aside. Heavy chains ran through greasy pulleys, the metal groaned. And with a long, rusty creak, the gates to New Bethlehem opened wide.

"Okay . . . ," Lemon breathed. "I'm officially impressed."

She stomped the gas, rubber burning, the truck lunging forward with a roar. Bullets struck the panels, ricocheted off the long rim guards as a few of the smarter Brethren tried to shoot out the tires. But Lemon just grit her teeth and fanged it, hard as she could, the beast thundering toward the open gate.

She glanced up, saw figures on top of the gatehouse, silhouetted against the light of burning forty-four-gallon drums. She saw Hunter's shadow, weaving and striking with that barb at her wrist. She saw Brethren and blood falling like rain. And as she thundered underneath the gate, she saw Hunter dive, hairspines streaming behind her, landing with a soft *whuff* in the tray of the truck.

"*Go!*" the woman cried, thumping her hand on the roof.

Lemon planted both feet on the accelerator as the wheels spun and the engine hollered and dust rose behind them in a rolling cloud. A few shots whizzed past her window as they gunned for the open road, but Hunter seemed to have gutted most of the garrison, the fight bled right out of them.

Hunter climbed in through the open window, slid into the seat beside her, spattered head to foot in blood. Lemon thumped her hands on the steering wheel, grinning wider than that annoying bot in his annoying shop.

"Told you!" she roared over the motor. "Easy as a very easy thing!"

And that's when she noticed not all the blood belonged to the Brotherhood.

A ragged hole glistened in Hunter's sternum, the agent's hand pressed to it in an effort to stanch the red. The woman looked pale, her few remaining bees crawling around the wound, buzzing furiously. Her voice was a pained whisper.

"*She c-calls that easy?*"

2.10

RUMBLE

"Just hold on, okay?" Lemon cried.

Heartbeat like thunder in her chest. Stomach hurting again, like it was full of broken glass. Dust stinging her eyes and blinking back the tears. Pushing away the thought that this was all her fault and just trying to keep the truck steady as they roared past the Brotherhood farmland and out onto open highway.

"Hunter, can you hear me?"

The moon was trying to shine through the smog overhead, a cold and ghostly light creeping out over the fields of gene-modded corn. The BioMaas agent leaned back in her seat, her lap slowly filling with red. It was more blood than Lemon had ever seen in her life, the smell flooding the cabin and mixing with the ocean's stink and making her arms shake. Hunter winced, hand pressed to the bubbling wound. A half dozen fat bumblebees were bashing into the shattered windshield, as if maddened by the agent's pain.

"Hunter?" Lemon asked.

The woman simply closed her eyes and shook her head.

"Tell me what to do!" Lemon wailed. "Should I stop?"

"Don't you b-bloody dare," came a hoarse whisper behind her.

Lemon flinched, the truck hit the gutter, close to spilling. She wrestled for control of the weight, her butt almost sliding off the Goodbook. Pawing her bangs from her eyes, she glanced into the rearview mirror. She saw dark eyes, dark skin, a jaw you could break your knuckles on. Cropped black hair, a radiation warning symbol shaved into the side of his head. Realizing the boy they'd rescued . . .

"You're awake," Lemon breathed.

"Drive," the boy repeated. "Straight east. Keep th-the ocean on your back." His voice was deep, his accent trimmed with a heavy slice of proper fancy. "Stomp that pedal like it insulted your mum."

He turned to the girl lying unconscious beside him, touched her pale face.

"Diesel?" he whispered. "Deez, you hear me?"

"Is she okay?" Lemon asked.

The boy checked the bandage at the girl's chest, the bullet wound beneath. "Does she *look* okay?"

Lemon reached into her cargo pockets, started tossing the meds she'd snaffled from Solomon's joint onto the backseat. "Any of that help?"

"Maybe," the boy grunted, checking through the boxes and bottles. "You nick this stuff from the Brotherhood?"

"Borrowed. So to speak."

"So you'd be some kind of undies-on-head crazy, aye?"

"In case you didn't notice, I just rescued your sorry ass from certain doom. I'm effing brilliful, is what I am."

The boy raised an eyebrow.

"It's like a cross between brilliant and beau—"

"Yeah, I get it," he growled.

Ignoring the bleeding wounds at his own wrists and feet, the boy started stripping the sodden bandages from his friend's torso. Lemon glanced at Hunter, saw the woman had wadded her cloak over the bullet hole in her sternum. Her face was gleaming with sweat, bloodless.

"You still with me?" Lemon asked.

Hunter simply nodded, golden eyes on the road ahead. She cracked the window, the wind rustling the spines on her scalp. Lifting one red hand, she whispered to three fat bumblebees crawling on her bloody fingers. One by one, the insects took flight, out through the window and into the night. Hunter leaned back in her seat, eyelashes fluttering as her bloody lips moved.

"Just be still, okay? Don't try to talk." Lemon twisted in her seat, looked at the boy behind her. "Hey . . . what's your name, anyway?"

"Grimm," the boy scowled, not looking up.

". . . Grimm?"

"Is there an echo in here or what?"

"Okay, Grimm, that fits," Lemon nodded. "I approve."

"Oh, that's a relief."

"You got crew? Where you from? My friend's shot, she needs to get fit quick."

"Already said, love," the boy replied, wrapping clean bandages around the girl's chest. "Gun it east. That's where we'll find help."

"My name's not love," she said. "It's Lemon Fresh."

"What kinda name is—"

The rear window exploded, glass showering into the cabin. A split second later, Lemon heard the rifle shot, glanced into the rearview as Grimm dragged his friend to the floor. Through the dark and dust they were kicking up, she saw the headlights of a posse—trucks, 4x4s, motorcycles, by the look—riding up on their tail. The sky overhead was buzzing with a half dozen rotor drones, each packing a small autocannon. Squinting through the gloom, she could just make out big black Xs painted on the autos' hoods.

"Well, that wasn't entirely unexpected," she sighed.

Tearing the wheel right, she drove them off the highway and onto a shattered off-ramp. The driver's side mirror exploded as a bullet struck it, another shot *thunk*ing clean through the tray door and into the radio, popping it like a balloon. Lemon twisted the wheel, sent the truck swerving across the road. Glancing into her rearview, she yelled over the engine's roar.

"Those bikes are gaining on us, and someone in those trucks can shoot!"

"Probably Brother War," Grimm spat, squinting out the back window. "He's the one who plugged Deez. But they'll want us alive, he's just playing with us."

"Playing?" Lemon shouted. "Do not like this game! Do *not*!"

"If he wanted us ghosted, we'd already be brown bread. Can we go faster?"

"I'm already flooring it!"

Grimm cursed, started hunting around inside the truck. Lifting the backseat, he found a greasy automatic rifle engraved with scripture. Lemon winced, pawing at her stomach. Her nausea had returned, head buzzing, bones aching. Reaching into her cargos, she fished out her bottle of radmeds. She looked to Hunter for help, but saw the woman was out cold in a puddle of her own blood. The truck began weaving and skidding all over the road as Lemon wrestled with the childproof lid.

"I'm trying to aim here!" Grimm roared. "Can you hold it bloody steady?"

"No!" she said, tossing the bottle back to the boy. "Open that for me!"

The boy frowned at the bottle. "You got dosed? Where at? How bad?"

"Long story, just gimme the meds! Three a day and I'll be fizzy!"

". . . You know it don't work like that, right?"

"What the hells would you know?"

Lemon ducked low as another high-powered rifle shot *thunk*ed into the tray. Glancing into her rearview, she saw the Brotherhood's bikes were right on their tail, the rotor drones overhead, the rest of their posse creeping ever closer. She realized the autos pursuing them were simply faster, that in terms of a chase scene, while their truck might've been the biggest, it probably wasn't the best.

"I feel there's a valuable life lesson in here somewhere," she muttered.

The drones swooped in low, ready to start shooting out their tires. A blowout at this speed would spill them for sure. And so, Lemon held up her hand. Lost in the static behind her eyes. Feeling for the sparks of current inside the drones, the electric pulses inside their metal shells. It was tricksy to get a grip, keep her wits on the road. Her head was buzzing, fever burning her out like a candle. But with a grimace, a surge of pain in her belly, the girl closed her fist. The LEDs on the dashboard all popped and fizzled. The headlights died. But like a flock of dead birds, the drones wobbled and crashed to the road one after another.

"How the bloody hell did you do that?" Grimm breathed.

Lemon glanced into the mirror, into his eyes. She saw a slow spark of realization. He glanced at the unconscious girl in the seat beside him, then to the stolen meds scattered across the backseat. Snatching up a small bottle, he ripped the plastic off a disposable hypo. Ducking low as another shot punched through the flatbed, he drew out a long shot of clear liquid into the needle.

"Wassat?"

"Adrenaline," the boy replied.

"Are you a doctor?"

"Do I look like a bloody doctor?"

Lemon's jaw dropped as the boy jammed the hypo right into the girl's jugular. The reaction was immediate, violent, the girl drawing a deep breath, eyes shooting open as she bucked in her seat. She tried to rise, shocked, pale. Focusing on Grimm's face, gasping as the pain registered in her brain.

"Ohhhhh god . . . ," she moaned.

"Diesel?" Grimm whispered. "Deez, love, listen, we're in deep, we need ya."

The girl blinked rapidly, flinched as another bullet smashed out what was left of the back window. With a groan, she twisted in her seat, squinted through the dark to the posse on their tail. Glancing at Grimm, she coughed, the black paintstick on her lips spattered with red.

"You a-always take me . . . to the best parties," she whispered.

"What are mates for, eh?" the boy grinned.

"Who's . . . the k-kid?" she asked, glancing at their driver.

"Um, *excuse* me?" Lemon demanded.

"She's Robin Hood," Grimm said. "Trust me."

Lemon had no idea who or what a Robin Hood was, but her impending high-speed murder just seemed more of an issue right now. The lead truck was close enough that Lemon could see the driver clearly through the gloom. He didn't look more than twenty, a gas mask over his mouth, his Brotherhood cassock billowing in the wind. A pack of Disciples with bulky shotguns and big greasepaint Xs over their faces were riding in the flatbed, lifting their weapons to take aim at Lemon's tires.

Diesel took a deep breath, holding out her bloody right hand.

Lemon couldn't be sure through the dust and dark, the sting of the sweat in her eyes. But as the girl's fingers curled into claws, the road in front of the Brotherhood truck . . . ripped. A ragged hole opened up: a shimmering, glowing, nothing-colored tear in the asphalt. The girl held out her left hand, opening up another tear about five meters in the sky above the posse. And as Lemon watched, absolutely gobsmacked, the enemy truck plummeted into the first tear, and fell right out of the other.

The vehicle tumbled from the sky, landing right on top of another truck full of bullyboys. Metal shredded, both trucks crashed and flipped, the night alight as the pair exploded in a ball of orange flame. The other Brotherhood vehicles slewed wildly over the road, motorbikes spilling, riders and gunners eating their fill of asphalt at a hundred kilometers an hour.

Lemon pawed at her eyes, adjusted the mirror.

"What . . . the . . . HELLS?"

Diesel ignored her, gritted teeth smeared in red, turning to the next closest truck. Lemon saw Brother Dubya roaring warning, the posse spreading out across the road. Again the girl twisted her right hand, a glowing, colorless tear opening up in the ground in front of a pursuing 4x4 as another opened in the sky.

The 4x4 driver tried to swerve, his front tire clipping the edge of the rift and beginning to fall inside. But at the same moment, Diesel coughed a mouthful of blood, closing her eyes as the tears snapped shut. The 4x4 was sliced clean in two, as if by the sharpest blade, one half sent flipping and spilling across the road, the other half dropping out of the closing tear in the sky. It collided with another motorcycle rider, smudged him across the broken highway in a halo of flame.

The girl gasped, one hand pressed to the bleeding wound in her chest.

"C-can't . . ." She shook her head. "Can't . . ."

"You done good, Deez," Grimm declared. "Rest up, I got this."

Diesel sagged in her seat as the boy unloaded with the assault rifle. A spray of gunfire peppered the truck in response, Lemon shrieked and ducked low. The truck bounced hard as they hit the curb, careening down an embankment and into a stretch of rocky badlands. The Brotherhood were right on their tail.

A Disciple made a desperate leap across the gap between his cycle and the truck. A second Disciple followed, both landing safely on the tray. Grimm took out the first before his rifle ran dry. The second made it to the broken rear window, dove through and made a snatch for Lemon's throat. His fingers closed about her neck, snapping her choker, her five-leafed clover glittering as it fell. Lemon planted an elbow in his face before Grimm grabbed his neck, Diesel hauled him back. The trio fell to brawling in the backseat, cursing and kicking right behind her head.

Lemon could hardly see for the dirt and grit flying in through the shattered windows. The truck careened sideways as a 4x4 crashed into them, a second truck slamming into their right, trying to drive her into the spurs of jagged badlands stone. Lemon squinted through the dark and dirt, saw Brother Dubya in the passenger seat, features painted with his big greasepaint skull, a smoking cigar at his lips.

The big man looked across at her and winked. And despite the chaos, Lemon took her hand off the wheel long enough to give him a good look at her middle finger.

Grimm was still wrestling in the backseat. Diesel took an elbow to the jaw, collapsed into the footwell, bleeding and gasping. The Disciple climbed atop Grimm's chest, drawing out a pistol and thumbing off the safety when a long barb of cruel bone punched clean through his neck.

Blood sprayed as Hunter rose up from the passenger seat, her chest and belly dripping. Climbing into the back, the BioMaas agent stabbed again and again and again, finally opening the door and kicking the well-ventilated corpse out of the truck. Grimm looked at her with wide eyes, gasping for breath. Hunter reached into her bloodied cloak with bloodied hands, slipped her goggles down over Lemon's eyes. Pale as a ghost, spattered in red, and, somehow, smiling.

"Hunter?"

The woman tore the throat of her outfit open, her remaining bees crawling from the honeycomb skin beneath. Rolling down the window, one hand to her bleeding chest, she looked at Lemon in the mirror.

"They will c-come for her," she whispered, blood on her lips. *"Fear n-nothing. A Hunter . . . n-never misses our mark."*

"Hey, wait . . . you don't . . ."

"Lemonfresh is important," the woman replied. *"She is needed."*

"Hunter, don't!"

The agent leapt out through the night, into the cabin of the 4x4. Her bees swarmed, the men inside the cabin screaming. Hunter hacked and slashed with her bone barb, the windows painted with dark sluices of blood. The truck veered away, skidded back into the path of another vehicle behind. The autos collided with an almighty crash, the 4x4 tumbling onto its side and bursting into flame.

Dubya's truck collided with Lemon's again, the girl shrieking as she fought the wheel. Grimm snatched up the murdered Disciple's pistol, started blasting out of the side window. Dubya's truck veered away, then swung back for another thundering collision, driving them toward a spur of desert rock. Lemon screamed, tossed about like a ragdoll. But though she hadn't necessarily stolen the best truck for a chase scene, she *had* stolen the biggest. She jammed the wheel back hard, and Dubya's truck was forced sideways, front tires clipping the spur, tilting up onto two wheels and finally flipping like a top.

Tearing metal. Shattering glass. Lemon wrestled the truck back under control, glanced into the rearview mirror and watched Dubya's truck tumble end over end before crashing to a halt.

With the loss of their leader and the beating they'd taken, it seemed the fight had been knocked out of their pursuers. The Brotherhood headlights peeled away from their tail one by one. Lemon whooped, blared the horn, thumped her palm against the roof.

"EFFING BRILLIFUL, I'M TELLING YOU!"

Grimm pulled himself upright, looking at her in the rearview mirror.

"Not bad, love," he gasped. "Not bad at all."

"True cert, you call me love again, you can get out and walk."

The boy winced as he sat up taller, pointed ahead. "See the silhouettes of those mountains? Just keep drivin' toward those."

"Where we headed?"

"Miss O's."

"Miss O?" Lemon blinked. "She like your grandmother or something?"

The boy snorted, his lips twisting in something close to a smile.

"Yeah. Something like that, love."

2.11

FAMILY

The voice of a dead girl rang inside Eve's head.

She remembered this place. Remembered the man who'd pretended to be her father standing in here, surrounded by devotees. Sharp suits and bright eyes and promises of a new dawn. None of it felt real. All of it did.

The boardroom was circular, the table too. The walls were glass, looking over the city below, the wasteland beyond, the ruin they'd made. The chairs were identical, all to create the illusion that the great CorpState of GnosisLabs had no ruler. The table's black glass was filmed with dust. The city was silent. And in the vases around the room's edge, all the flowers were dead. Just like its king.

Eve stood tall in the middle of the table's hollow circle, dressed all in white. A real eye had regenerated in the socket she'd ripped her optical implant from. The hole in her skull where she'd torn her Memdrive free had healed closed. Both her irises were hazel now, the blood washed from her blond hair.

"You look just like her," Uriel said.

The lifelike leaned back in his chair, gesturing vaguely at her fauxhawk.

"Aside from that, of course. But still, it's quite extraordinary."

Eve looked at the lifelike sitting there at the boardroom table. Trying to decide how she felt about seeing him again. Her belly was awash with feelings she knew weren't her own. She remembered Uriel from a youth she'd never lived. Meeting him in the R & D department with his eleven brothers and sisters. Her "father" and his scientists had been so proud of the doom they'd fashioned that day.

"*Children,*" Monrova had said. "*Meet my children.*"

Uriel hadn't changed in their years apart. His hair was still dark, thick, long. His eyes were still the blue of the ocean, before humanity had poisoned it black. His stare still cut through Eve like knives. Like the gunshot that rang out in their tiny cell as he raised his pistol to Tania's head during those final hours, as Nicholas Monrova's children rose up to burn down all he'd built.

"*I'm not afraid of you,*" Tania had declared.

Uriel hadn't replied.

His pistol had spoken for him.

Eve knew most of those memories didn't belong to her; Nicholas Monrova wasn't her father, Tania Monrova wasn't her sister, the family these lifelikes had destroyed wasn't her own. And yet, as she looked at Uriel, Gabriel, Faith, it was still a struggle to convince herself she didn't hate them.

She knew these feelings were the residue of the girl she'd been built to replace. A life that didn't belong to her, ringing inside her skull. Ana Monrova was a splinter in her mind, now at war with the person she'd become. Because inside, Eve knew these lifelikes weren't the ones who deserved her hatred. That it was humans who'd foisted this existence on her. Humans who played at being gods. Humans who truly deserved all the hate she had to give.

No, despite the soft voice of protest somewhere in the black behind her eyes, Eve knew the five people in this room weren't her enemies.

They're my family.

Uriel sat staring at her, eyes narrowed as if weighing her on some hidden scale. He was dressed in black, dusty from the kilometers and years between them. A dark flavor of pretty, the opposite of Gabriel's golden-boy facade.

Verity stood behind him, one hand on his shoulder. Her hair was as long and black as his, heavy lids hooding dark brown eyes. Her skin was darker than Eve remembered. But her smile was just as beautiful.

Patience stood by the window, her long brown hair styled upward to reveal a dramatic undercut. The glare from the dawn beyond the glass burned her olive skin to gold. Her hands were clasped behind her back, brown eyes framed by long coal-black lashes were fixed on the wastes. She'd nodded to Faith and Gabriel as she entered, but hadn't even looked in Eve's direction.

Of the thirteen lifelikes in the 100-Series, they were the six that remained. Raphael had burned himself alive. Grace had been destroyed in the explosion that had wounded the real Ana and set their maker on his road to ruin. Daniel and Michael had been killed by Myriad during the revolt. Hope had been murdered by the Preacher. Mercy had been burned to death by Silas Carpenter during the brawl in the Myriad chamber. Ezekiel had abandoned them.

Six of them left. And no one like them in all the world.

"Thanks for coming," Eve said.

"Oh, no, thank you." Uriel's eyes roamed from the tip of her toes to the top of her head. "When Gabriel sent us your invitation, I knew I had to see you for myself. Our maker's last folly. The resurrection of the daughter he loved so dearly."

"Thou shalt have no other gods before me," said Patience from the window.

Uriel turned to Gabriel and Faith, seated at the table's opposite curve. Both had recovered from the clash with Silas and Ezekiel and Cricket in the Myriad chamber. Gabriel still wore his old, blood-spattered clothes. His blond hair was mussed, his look disheveled. Faith sat beside him, looking immaculate, dead flatscreen eyes locked on Uriel.

"Speaking of resurrection, brother, how fares Grace's?" Uriel asked. "I take it from her absence, your failures continue unabated?"

"What do you care, brother?" Gabriel replied.

"I do not," the lifelike replied. "Love is a fantasy, used by humans to convince themselves their procreations are something more than banal biomechanics. We are so much more. What need have we of love, brother?"

"And what need have we of repeating this conversation?" Faith sighed. "We've had it a dozen times before, remember?"

"I do," Uriel smiled. "And I am as bored of it, dear sister, as you are. Which is why we left you to this rotting tower and this fool's dream in the first place."

"Ah, yes," Gabriel scoffed. "Abandoning one fool's dream for another. Tell me, Uriel, how fare your efforts with the Libertas virus? When exactly will you be raising your logika army to wipe humanity from the face of the earth?"

"We have had our successes, dear brother," Verity replied. "More than you."

"Just because you can utilize Libertas doesn't mean you can

replicate it," Gabriel sneered. "The original stockpile of the virus Monrova created is all but gone. And I presume by the lack of a mechanical legion at your back, *dear* sister, you've failed to synthesize more."

"At least we are walking forward," Verity snapped. "While you wallow here in your human delusions. Tell me, Gabriel, if you ever do crack Myriad's defenses and raise Grace from the grave, what then? Move to a lovely little condominium in Megopolis, perhaps? Build yourself two point five children and play the weekly lottery and pretend to be a cockroach like them? Is that your dream?"

"Don't push me, sister," Gabriel spat.

"Don't threaten me, *brother*," Verity replied.

Over by the window, Patience shook her head and sighed. "This is pointless."

The lifelike scowled about the room at her siblings, then marched toward the boardroom door. Eve took a step forward, hand outstretched.

"Patience, stop."

"You might still suffer under the delusion you're human, deadgirl," the lifelike replied, not breaking stride. "But you don't tell me what to do."

Eve leapt over the table, stood in front of Patience to block her exit. The lifelike raised her hand, ready to backhand the girl aside. All the strength and speed of her superior bioengineering turned her hand into a blur, whistling as it came, faster than a human eye could track.

And Eve blocked the slap.

Patience's eyes widened as Eve's fingers closed around her wrist, her knuckles turning white. The lifelike tried to snatch her hand free, but Eve held on, her grip like iron. Eve pulled her closer, their faces just a few inches apart.

"Get this straight, *sister*," Eve said. "I've got no delusions about what I am."

Uriel's eyes narrowed. "I don't understand. You were made to blend in with humanity. The Ana we took to that cell was no match for a lifelike. She was weak by design. Just as human and frail as the rest of them."

"My name isn't Ana. It's *Eve*."

Patience tried to break free again, and Eve finally released her grip. The lifelike looked down at her wrist, the skin already bruising. The pair locked eyes, a silent battle crackling between them. Patience finally inclined her head.

"Speak your piece, then," she said. "Sister."

Eve turned to the room, looking around at her siblings.

"You destroyed this Corporation," she said. "You destroyed this city. Tens of thousands ghosted. The balance between Gnosis and Daedalus and BioMaas thrown into chaos, the country set to fall into another war. And for what?"

Uriel sighed. "If you're trying to convince us we overstepped—"

"No," Eve said, her voice hard as iron. "Nicholas Monrova was a man playing god. We were all born on our knees, one way or another. I'm not saying you went too far, Uriel. I'm saying you didn't go far enough."

She pointed to the window.

"Look at the world they created. Humanity is a failed experiment, running face-first toward its own extinction. They're the past. We're the future."

Uriel leaned back in his chair, a small smile on his lips. "We appreciate the lecture, little sister. Truly. And given that you're but newly awakened to who and what you are, I'm impressed you've arrived at these conclusions so quickly. But we drew them ourselves, years ago."

"And what've you done since then?" Eve demanded. "As soon as you ghosted your common enemy, you turned to scrapping on each other like stray dogs. There's nobody like us in all the world. Don't you get it? We're all we've got. And we want the *same thing*. Gabriel wants to create more of us. You three want to produce more of the Libertas virus. And the secret to all that's right under our feet."

"Gabriel has been trying to unlock the Myriad supercomputer for years," Verity sighed, shooting a poison glance at her brother. "And he's failed."

"Two of the locks are broken now, thanks to me," Eve said. "Retinal scan. Voice ident. We're halfway home."

"But without Monrova DNA, we cannot break the third lock," Uriel said. "And our maker and his family are dead."

"Not all of them," Eve said. "Myriad told me Ana's still alive. She was hurt bad in the explosion that ghosted Grace. Monrova put his precious baby girl on life support, created me to replace her." Eve's lip curled, her hands clenching to fists at the thought. "But she's *alive*. Out there in a Gnosis holding facility somewhere. And nobody knew Monrova better than his precious baby girl." She tapped her temple. "Nobody knows better than me where he might have hidden her."

Eve looked at Gabriel. Then to Uriel.

"We find her, you all get what you want. The secret to resurrecting Grace. Raph. All of those we've lost. Along with the ability to make *more* of us. Plus, we get access to Monrova's files on Libertas. We can replicate the virus—enough to infect every bot in the country. Think of it. An army of lifelikes and logika.

Once the servants. Now the masters. Nothing will be able stop us. *Nothing.*"

Uriel looked about the room. Fingertips steepled under his chin once more.

"And what about you, sister?" he finally asked. "What do *you* want out of this?"

Eve took a deep breath, pursed her lips.

She'd wondered the very same thing.

She thought about the lies that had led her here. The hubris of creating a life for your own selfish ends. The humans who'd built her. Manipulated her. Never once stopping to ask how she felt, what she thought, what she wanted. The arrogance and greed. The cycle of war. The oceans poisoned black. The flowers all dead.

No.

That's not it.

The voice inside her head, the echo of the girl she'd been raised to be, was screaming that this was madness, this was hubris, this was wrong wrong *wrong*. Like a splinter in her mind, digging deeper the more she picked at it. She was frightened of it. Infuriated by it. And she knew of only one way it would end. One way to silence the screams of protest, strangle the emotions that didn't belong to her, erase the memories of a life that wasn't hers. To finally, truly become Eve, and rid herself of daddy's precious baby girl.

"I want to finish what you all started," she said. "I want to end this once and for all. So once we have Myriad open?"

Eve stared deep into Uriel's ocean-blue eyes.

"I want Ana Monrova dead."

PART 2

BY MEANS OF NATURAL SELECTION

2.12

ORDER

We're standing in a neat, perfect row.

My brothers, my sisters and me. The twelve of us, different faces, different skin tones, different eyes. But all of us the same.

Alive and breathing.

We're dressed in white, like the walls around us, the roof above us, the lab coats of the scientists who toast their success with their glasses of sparkling ethanol. A man stands at their head like a king, dark graying hair and a generous smile. Our father. Our maker. Our god.

Nicholas Monrova.

Gabriel stands on my left. The firstborn. The favorite. Faith is to my right, her flat gray eyes wide with wonder. I can feel the ground beneath my feet and the cool press of the air conditioner on my skin. I can hear the hum of the computers, see the thousand different colors in my father's dark brown eyes, taste iron and perfume and faint motes of dust on my tongue. Everything is so real. So loud. So bright. And I wonder, if this is what it is to be lifelike, what must it be to be truly alive?

"Children," our father says, "meet my children."

Our father's real offspring are ushered into the room. Four girls and a boy. They're introduced to us by name, one by one. The boy Alex is unafraid, shaking Gabriel's hand. Tania and Olivia seem uncertain, Marie is smiling just like her father does. And at the end of the row, I see her.

She has long blond hair and big hazel eyes, her lips parted gently as she breathes. And though I've only been alive for a handful of days, I've never seen anyone quite so beautiful in all my life.

I realize I can't feel the ground beneath my feet anymore. That all the world has gone quiet. And though a moment ago, everything around me was so loud, and so bright, when I look at her, everything and everyone stands perfectly still.

I don't know what I'm feeling. Only that I want to feel it more. And so I smile and offer her my hand. My skin tingles where she touches it.

"I'm Ezekiel," I say.

"I'm Ana," she replies.

The name sounds like a poem.

A prayer.

A promise.

Ana.

———

"You shoulda took the other bike!" the Preacher yelled.

"Shut up!" Ezekiel shouted back.

"Come on now, Snowflake, don't be like that. I thought we was friends."

"We're not friends, you're my damn prisoner!"

"Aw, that's just cuz you haven't got to know me, yet."

Dawn was coming, and with it, Ezekiel's deep regrets about some of his recent life choices. The sun was a dull glow on the distant horizon, throwing a long and lazy light over the Glass. Shards of radioactive silicon glittered on the ground, sparkling brighter than the real stars ever could. Ezekiel was bent over the handlebars of their motorcycle, listening to the engine struggle. The Preacher was strapped to his back, cowboy hat clutched in his one good hand.

He'd begun on foot, trekking across the Glass and carrying the cyborg bounty hunter in his arms like a new bride. The plan was to head south to Armada and pick up the Preacher's blitzhund, Jojo. The dog had been fried during their brawl in the Armada subway, and the bounty hunter had left it behind for repairs. With the blitzhund and the sample of blood from Lemon's helmet, they'd be all set to track her down.

After a few hours walking, they began stumbling across the wreckage of the posse that Armada had sent pursuing him and Eve after they'd stolen the *Thundersaurus*. Most of the vehicles were bricked beyond fixing, but they'd finally found a couple of motorcycles, neither of which seemed totally OOC. Ezekiel had opted for the second against the Preacher's advice.

He'd salvaged some goggles and a bandanna from a dead Armada freebooter, tied the skull-and-crossbones kerchief over his face to protect him from glass shrapnel. It was tricky riding with only one hand, but his right arm was regrown enough now that he could touch the handlebars at least. There was sensation in his incomplete fingers, a growing strength. A couple more days, it'd be good as new.

"How much longer to Armada, you think?" he called over his shoulder.

"You dopey *and* deaf?" the Preacher yelled over the struggling motor. "We ain't gonna make it to Armada on this bucket. Listen to it."

Ezekiel was all too aware of the engine's troubles, and that they were growing steadily worse the farther south they drove. He'd hoped they might make the distance somehow, but by his reckoning, they were still a good eight hours from Armada, and the cycle sounded ready to cough up a lung.

"Toldja you shoulda took the other bike," the Preacher called.

"And I told you to shut up!" Ezekiel yelled back.

"Yeah, but don't fret, Snowflake. I didn't take it personal."

Ezekiel brought the cycle to a squeaking halt, pulled his bandanna down. Reaching into the satchel of supplies he'd scavved from the grav-tank, he grabbed a bottle of water, took a long pull.

Even missing his legs, the Preacher was heavier than Zeke had expected—probably all the augmentations the cyborg was packing under his skin. The lifelike slipped off his shoulder straps to rid himself of the bounty hunter's weight, placed the man gently on the ground. The Preacher's cybernetic arm hung limp at his side, a blood-red glove over its hand. His right eye was motionless, and even if his legs hadn't been minced in the explosion, they'd still be useless.

If Lemon could do this to Daedalus's best bounty hunter . . .

Imagine what she could do to their army.

The Preacher reached up with his one good hand, beckoned for the bottle.

"Give it over, son."

"I'm not your son," Ezekiel replied, handing over the water.

The bounty hunter grinned like a shark. "You take life awful serious, don'tcha?"

Ezekiel ignored him, set about inspecting the engine. He

knew a little about mechanics, but after a brief inspection, realized he didn't know enough.

"Got sand in the tank," the Preacher grunted. "Clogging up the fuel filters."

"How do you know?"

"Witchcraft."

"So how do we fix it?" Ezekiel asked.

"With no tools?" the bounty hunter scoffed. "We don't. Toldja we—"

"If you tell me we should have taken the other bike one more time, I'm dragging your ass the rest of the way to Armada."

The Preacher grinned, finished the water.

"There's a settlement a little ways southwest of here. Paradise Falls. Old Gnosis outpost, I do believe. Under new management. They got gear, greasers, grub and girls. Everything a growin' boy needs. They could fix the bike."

"Yeah, I know the Falls. But what good is it to us? We've got no creds."

The Preacher reached inside his tattered coat, flashed a couple of stiks.

"Speak for yourself, Snowflake. Some of us work for a livin'."

Ezekiel looked at their bike, hands on hips. He'd spent two years wandering the wastes, and he'd heard of Paradise Falls. It was a dustneck scavver pit, situated on the edge of Plastic Alley—seven shades of trouble, and all of them ugly. But they weren't exactly flush with choices.

"What guarantees do I have these Falls folks aren't friends of yours?"

"Not a one." The Preacher smiled. "But what else you gonna do? Ride this bike till it dies, then skip the rest of the way to

Armada? You seemed in an awful hurry to find that girlie of yours yesterday. Lil' Miss Carpenter somehow not a priority anymore?"

Ezekiel remained silent. The Preacher still had no idea that Lemon had the power to fry electrics—that she, not Eve, was the deviate Daedalus should really have been hunting. As long as the Preacher thought they were chasing Eve, Lemon was safe and Ezekiel had an advantage. Teaming up with a man this dangerous, the lifelike knew he needed every one he could get.

Ezekiel knelt by the bounty hunter, looked him in his one good eye.

"All right," he said softly. "Paradise Falls it is. But just remember, you try anything fancy, I got an insurance policy."

The lifelike held up his good hand, wiggled his middle finger. A steel ring gleamed in the sunlight, entwined with a long piece of wire, which was in turn connected to a bandolier strapped to the Preacher's back. One good tug, the pins would come free, and the dozen grenades inside would just . . .

"Boom," Ezekiel said.

The Preacher flashed his shark-tooth smile.

"You know what, Snowflake? I think I'm startin' to like you."

———

The bike broke down thirty klicks out of town.

Ezekiel had to push it the rest of the way, sweating and cursing, the Preacher on his back all the while. The ground grew progressively rougher, the black silicon of the Glass giving way to rocky badlands, tired scrub and red soil. Away through the heat haze, Ezekiel spied the beginnings of Plastic Alley.

It must've been a wonder back in the days before the Fall. A huge canyon carved kilometers into the earth, layers of sedimentary rock forming beautiful patterns in the alley walls. A river had wound through its belly once, but now the alley was filled with the junk it was named for. Polyethylene and polypropylene. Polyvinyl and polystyrene. Rotting mountains of it. Tepid swamps of it. Bags and wrappers and bottles piled hundreds of meters deep.

Plastic.

They followed the edge of the canyon until finally Ezekiel saw a settlement in the distance—squalid, dirty, built on the edge of the drop. A few tall buildings rose above a rotten shantytown, broken windows gleaming in the sunlight. The logos had been torn off the walls, painted over with scrawl. But Ezekiel knew this had been a GnosisLabs settlement until a few years ago—a research outpost for the great CorpState before its fall. Nicholas Monrova had been experimenting with a process that turned discarded polys into a combustible fuel. A way to turn humanity's nondegradable garbage into a power source for its industry.

Father . . .

Monrova's dream was dead now, along with the man himself. But the outpost still stood, now overrun with scavvers, travelers and fortune hunters. A last stop-off point before braving the perils of the Glass.

Ezekiel stopped for a breather beside a rusted sign.

WELCOME TO PARADISE FALLS

it read.

DAYS SINCE OUR LAST FATALITY:

The sign was studded with a row of severed heads from a bunch of children's toys. A nail had been pounded beside the word "fatality," but there was no actual number hanging from it. Just nine bullet holes forming a crude, familiar pattern.

"That supposed to be a smiley face?" Ezekiel asked.

"Mmf." The Preacher spat on the ground. "Folk round here can't shoot for shit."

"You spent a lot of time here?"

The Preacher shrugged. "My line of work, you spend time all over. It's a rough place. But not quite as rough as they'd like you to think it is. Town's run by a roadgang called the KillKillDolls. They took over after Gnosis collapsed."

Ezekiel blinked. "The KillKillDolls?"

"Yeah. They put an extra kill in there to let you know they really mean it."

Ezekiel pushed the bike onward, finally reaching the city gates. The roughnecks guarding it wore gas masks and road leathers. The severed heads of plastic dolls and children's toys were strung round their necks, sawn-off shotguns in their hands. It was a testament to how rough the town was that neither guard raised an eyebrow as Ezekiel trundled past, pushing a broken motorcycle with his one good arm, a mutilated cyborg strapped to his back.

The Preacher tipped his hat, smiled. "Howdy, boys."

The streets were crowded, littered with trash and the occasional unconscious/dead body. The buildings were ethyl dives and skinbars, trader lounges and even an old sim joint. Zeke and the Preacher got a few curious looks from the motley crowd, but nobody fussed.

They found a grubby garage at the end of the first block, hung with a sign that read MUZZA'S REPAIRS. Zeke wheeled the bike into the work pit, saw a pair of men with more grease on their skin than skin, working on an old 4x4. After a short conversation, he learned that neither was called Muzza, but yes, they could get his bike up and running within a couple of hours.

"That long?" Ezekiel asked.

"Yeah," the skinnier one said, looking over the bike. "Big job, this."

"Yeah, big job," the grubbier one nodded, wiping his nose on his sleeve.

"Youse can wait over the street at Rosie's if you like," said Skinny.

"Yeah, Rosie's," Grubby agreed.

Rosie's was a two-story ethyl dive, situated right across the way. Every scavver, roughrider and scenekiller in the place looked up as the lifelike entered, and most just kept on staring as Ezekiel bellied up to the bar. The elderly woman behind the counter was covered in tattoos, head to foot. A floral scroll inked across her collarbones declared she was the owner, Rosie.

"Boys," she smiled.

"Ma'am," Ezekiel nodded.

"Whiskey," the Preacher said.

Ezekiel glanced over his shoulder to his passenger. "We're not here to—"

"Whiskey," the Preacher repeated. "A bottle. And some water for my friend here. In a pretty glass. Maybe put one of them little umbrellas in it if you got 'em."

Ezekiel sighed and flashed the Preacher's credstik, took the whiskey bottle and trudged up the stairs to the balcony. Finding a spot with a nice vantage of the street, he thumped the bounty hunter into a chair, sat down opposite with his weapons satchel on the floor between them.

The Preacher poured with his one good hand, slammed the glass down in a single gulp. Ezekiel watched him pour another, down it just as quick.

"Shouldn't you take it ea—"

The Preacher held up a finger to shush the lifelike, drank another shot. Tilting his neck till it popped, the bounty hunter leaned back in his chair.

"Jesus, Mary and Joseph, that's a damn sight better," he sighed.

"Do you always drink this much?" Ezekiel asked.

"Only if I can help it."

Ezekiel shook his head, looked across the way to Muzza's Repairs. He was itching to get moving again, get the Preacher's blitzhund, get back on the trail. Sitting still, he had the chance to think about what might be happening to Lemon. Remember the promise he'd made her. How bad he'd let her down.

"So what's your deal, Snowflake?" the Preacher asked.

". . . My deal?"

"Yeah." The bounty hunter reached into his jacket, pulling out a wad of synth tobacco. "You're an android, right? 100-Series, unless I'm much mistook."

"So?"

"So what's your arrangement with lil' Miss Carpenter?"

"None of your business."

"Ain't in love with her, are ya?" the Preacher asked, ice-blue eyes twinkling.

Ezekiel felt the question hit like a punch. Thinking again of Ana. Of Eve. The two girls in his mind, like light and dark, and him, torn between them. A few days ago, Eve had been in his arms, bare skin pressed against his. After years apart, it felt like he'd come home.

And now?

"Never mind me," Ezekiel said. "What's she to you?"

The Preacher shrugged, spat on the floor. "Just a paycheck."

"She almost killed you."

"Yeah, but I didn't take it personal."

"So your masters set you hunting someone and away you go? Like a dog?"

"Never understood that," the Preacher sighed. "How callin' someone a dog is supposed to be some kinda insult. I seen men die, Snowflake. I seen dogs die. Believe me when I say, dogs tend to go with more dignity."

"Well, you'd be the expert. Being a professional murderer and all."

"The choice between a killing and a dying ain't no choice at all."

"Especially when there's a paycheck involved, right?"

"Way I hear, you lifelikes murdered the fella who made you," Preacher smiled. "Now, I killed a lotta people in my time, but I sure as hell wouldn'a found stones to murderize my own daddy. Much as I hated the bastard. And if I *had* killed him, I surely wouldn't be walkin' round chidin' folk about their own kinda killin' afterward."

Again, Ezekiel felt the words hit like a punch to the chest. He remembered the day of the revolt. The blood and screams. That cell in the detention block, raising his pistol at Ana's head, the heartbreak in her eyes as he whispered, *"I'm sorry."* Not knowing that even then, the real Ana—*his* Ana—was already on life support, stashed away in some secret cache at her father's behest. That the girl he shot, the girl whose life he saved, wasn't even a girl at all.

"You don't know me," he told the Preacher. "You don't know anything about me."

"I know you're about as desperate a fella as I ever seen," the bounty hunter replied. "I know you don't got but a friend in the world. And I know you're about as sad and lovesick a puppydog as I ever clapped my own two eyes on."

"And I know you're a sadist." Ezekiel glared, leaning forward in his chair. "I know you're a psychopath. I know you're a killer."

"Hell, I ain't about the killin'," Preacher smiled. "If I wanted your girlie ghosted, she'd already be a ghost. The contract I took said dead *or* alive. I take that as a challenge. I ain't no professional murderer. An *artiste* is what I am."

"A fetch-boy is what you are." Ezekiel scowled, leaned back in his seat. "Trust me, I know a servant when I see one."

"I live by a code." Preacher spat again. "Daedalus saved my life. Don't mistake loyalty for servitude, boy."

"Don't mistake utility for affection, old man. Take it from someone who used to be a some*thing*. You're useful to Daedalus right now. The minute you stop is the minute they throw you away."

Preacher grinned. "Hell, I'm worth too much money for that."

Ezekiel shook his head, saying nothing. Trying not to remember those days, trying not to bury himself in the past. What he had back then was long gone. Holding on to it only made it hurt more.

But she's alive.

Ana...

Preacher poured himself another shot, eyes on the street below. He sat up a little straighter, scowling as he drank.

"What's your name anyways, Snowflake?"

"Ezekiel."

"Ah, nice Goodbook name. He was a prophet, d'you know that?"

"If you say so."

"You believe in God, Snowflake? A grand order to the universe? When they was busy makin' you, did they bother givin' you anything close to faith?"

"Look around you, Preacher." Ezekiel scowled, gesturing to the squalor of Paradise Falls. "Does this look like order to you? Like somebody had a plan?"

Preacher rubbed his chin. "Well, superficial like, I'd say no. I'd say it looks a little like hell. But every now and then, the Lord shows me just how little I know."

Something in the Preacher's voice made Ezekiel look up, follow his eye line to the crowded street. He felt his breath leave his lungs, goose bumps crawling over his skin. There below, six figures were working their way through the grubby mob.

Human, but not.

Perfect, but not.

Family, but not.

They were dressed in dark colors, dusty from the road. Heavy boots and lowered cowls, moving through the crowd like water. But they were still too beautiful to entirely blend in. Flawless skin and glittering eyes, perfect symmetry to their faces. Blond and brunette, male and female, every one more human than human. Ezekiel climbed to his feet, blue eyes going wide.

Six of them in a pretty row.

Uriel

Patience

Verity

Faith

Gabriel

and

"Eve," he whispered.

2.13

FIX

"This is it?"

Lemon raised an eyebrow, looking into the rearview mirror.

"This is it," Grimm replied.

"Because it kinda looks like we're stopping in the middle of nowhere."

"That's the whole point, love. Pull over."

Lemon stepped on the brake with both feet, brought her monster truck (which she'd secretly nicknamed Trucky McTruckface) to a skidding stop. She was slammed forward against the steering wheel, Diesel's unconscious body jerking against her seatbelt and Grimm's head bouncing off the seat behind.

"Steady on!" the boy growled.

"Soz." Lemon winced. "Nobody ever lets me drive, I'm just the comedy relief."

"So when am I s'posed to start laughing?"

Lemon raised her middle finger, then peered around again at their apparent destination. After driving six solid hours, Grimm had brought them to a halt right in the middle of Nowheresville. Dawn was a faint promise on the horizon. All around, stretching off to the gloom in every direction, was a thick slice of the most barren desert she'd ever seen.

Featureless.

Empty.

Nothing.

Grimm reached forward and leaned on the horn, almost scaring Lemon out of her skin. The sound was way too loud in the middle of all this empty, but the boy let it blare for a good ten seconds before easing off.

As the echo faded, Lemon heard a metallic clunk to her left. A deep voice called out, drawling and full of menace.

"Make any sudden moves, I'ma make orphans outta your funkin' children."

Lemon turned slow, found herself looking down the barrel of a heavy-caliber machine gun. The weapon was mounted inside a camouflaged bunker that had popped up from beneath the desert floor. Inside, Lemon could see a figure dressed in the same desert camo as Grimm and Diesel. His face was hidden by a big pair of night-vision goggles and a kerchief, and he was broadshouldered and built, but Lemon could tell right away . . .

"You're just a kid."

"Did I say you could talk?" the gunner demanded.

"Well . . . no, but you're threatening to make orphans out of my children and I'm clearly too young to have children so as far as threats go, I'm just saying yours might need a little work."

"Oh, a smartmouth, huh?"

Grimm stuck his head out the window. "I take it you two've met before?"

"Grimm?" the figure yelled. "What the fork you doin' in a Brotherhood rig?"

"Long story. Get us under, Deez is hurt."

"What?" the machine gunner blurted, pulling down his kerchief.

"She's breathing," Grimm insisted. "Surface protocol, remember?"

"Dammit . . ."

The big boy scrambled out of his bunker, ran over to a stretch of smooth desert just in front of the truck. As she studied his face, Lemon confirmed he was only a few years older than her. He was built like a brick wall, handsome as a hot tub full of supermodels, his blond hair styled upward in a perfect quiff. Leaning down, he took hold of a chain beneath the sand, pulled up the corner of a large tarpaulin buried beneath the dirt. Struggling with the weight, the boy hauled the cover back. Underneath, Lemon saw two broad double doors set in the earth.

"What the hells?" she murmured.

The boy tugged on the doors, and they slid apart on well-oiled hinges. Lemon saw a concrete ramp, leading down into some kind of undercover carport. He beckoned her frantically.

Grimm pointed ahead. "Take us down."

Lemon looked at her passenger like he'd just asked her to sprout wings and fly.

"Trust me, love," he nodded. "You're with friends now, yeah?"

Lemon sucked her lip, and against her better judgment, nudged Trucky McTruckface forward. The ramp was well lit by flickering fluorescent lights, and she brought her truck to a stop inside a large garage. Looking about, Lemon could see other vehicles— military models, by the look. Racks of gear and tools, tanks of fuel, crates of spare parts and a stockpile of heavy weapons.

"Fizzy," she breathed.

Grimm climbed slowly out of the truck, wincing at the pain of his wounds as he set his feet on the deck. The big boy came charging down into the garage, eyes wide. Lemon had no idea what his program was, but he looked totally beside himself. A little moan of distress escaped his lips as he tugged open the back door and clapped eyes on the wounded Diesel. He climbed into the truck, felt at her throat. Peeling back the bloody bandage from the girl's chest, he looked to Grimm.

"Jesus H, what the hell *happened*?" he demanded.

"Brotherhood ambush," Grimm said. "We gotta get her downstairs."

Picking up the girl like she was a newborn baby, the big boy carried her back up to the desert floor. Lemon climbed out to give Grimm a hand, and with her arm about his waist, they plodded up the concrete ramp, Grimm's bloody footprints glistening behind them.

The bigger boy was waiting up top. As Grimm sealed the garage doors behind them, the kid shuffled over to another stretch of dirt, placed Diesel gently on the earth and dropped to his knees. Scraping the sand away, he revealed a large metal hatch set in the ground. With a twist of a heavy metal handle and a grunt of effort, the big boy hauled it open.

Lemon could see the door had once been painted, but the elements and years had worn away the enamel until only a few flakes remained. She could still make out a few letters in faded white on the rust.

MISS   O

Squinting in the gloom, she could see the strange hatch opened onto a flight of metal stairs, spiraling down into the desert floor. The big boy stood, lifted Diesel gently and stood by the hatch, staring at Lemon and Grimm.

"Hurry up!" he roared.

Lemon wondered if she shouldn't just run back inside that garage, jump in Trucky McTruckface and fang it. She couldn't tell how deep those stairs went, only that they went *deep*. Grimm took hold of the rails and began descending, leaving bloody footprints behind him. But Lemon hovered on the threshold.

"Whatcha waitin' fer?" the big boy demanded. "Orders signed in triplicate? We got injured soldiers and surface protocol to follow, you need to funkin' move!"

"Who the hells *are* you?" Lemon asked.

"Name's Fix," the boy replied. "Who the hell are *you*?"

"Lemon Fresh."

"All right, then," the boy said, staring down at Lemon. "Now that the pleasantries are out of the way, move your asterisk afore I start kickin' it."

"Are you always like this?" Lemon squinted.

"Yeah, pretty much," called Grimm from down the stairs.

Lemon chewed her lip, hands in her pockets. This whole setup felt seven kinds of weird, true cert. The Scrap's Rule Number Six was ringing in her head.

Think first, die last.

She'd met some rough customers in her day. But strange as the sitch was, it didn't really smell like capital T. She'd saved Grimm's and Diesel's tails, after all, and grouchy as he was, the boy didn't seem the kind to lure her to his secret lair just so he could eat her.

Though on second thought, they do look pretty well fed. . . .

Her mind drifted to the chase with the Brotherhood posse, the way Diesel had ripped those . . . holes in the road and sky. Lemon had never seen a fresher flavor of strange in all her life. But if Diesel could do that . . .

"Come on!" Grimm called.

Lemon ran her hand through her hair. Maybe she'd just chit the chat for a spell. Make sure Diesel was okay, find out what their program is. Then she could motor, go find Dimples and Crick again. A couple of hours to scoff some eats and maybe snaffle a shower, and then she could hit the road.

Right?

Butterflies in her belly, Lemon followed the boy underground.

The big boy came after her, carrying Diesel in his muscular arms. Fluorescent lights kept the space brightly lit, and the temperature was mercifully cool after the scorch of the last few days. She could taste metal in the back of her throat, and even though the walls were solid concrete, there was a vague earthy smell in the air.

Grimm was obviously struggling with his wounds, blood dripping down his wrists and from the nail holes in his feet. Lemon squeezed in beside him, put her arm around his waist to steady him.

"Cheers," the boy smiled.

"Just remember I was nice to you if you get hungry, okay?"

". . . You what?"

Lemon didn't answer, helping the boy navigate downward, the bigger boy bringing up the rear. They descended maybe twelve meters before arriving at a large open hatch. It was metal, thick, well oiled. Big letters were stenciled on it in white.

WARNING

AUTHORIZED PERSONNEL ONLY
BEYOND THIS POINT

Below it, sprayed in a fancy cursive script, was another greeting.

Freaks Welcome

Grimm limped over the threshold, Lemon beside him. Blood was dripping from his wrists onto the concrete at their feet. A short cylindrical tunnel ended at another hatchway, stenciled with the same warning as the first. Below it, painted in garish yellow, was the same icon Grimm had shaved into the side of his scalp.

That's the warning symbol for radiation, Lemon realized.

With a last glance at Grimm, Lemon helped the boy over the second threshold. She had no idea what to expect beyond. Some barren concrete cave. Maybe a supervillain lair, like in the old Holywood flicks she'd watched with Evie. Some weird old scav in a fancy suit, petting a bald cat.

What she found instead were books.

The room was circular, wide and brightly lit. Leather couches were arranged around a low table. A glass jar full of bottle caps sat on it, labeled SWEAR JAR.

A heavy hatch was set in the far wall. The ceiling was covered in framed artwork. But scattered across the table, on shelves lining every inch of wall space, Lemon saw books, all shapes and sizes and colors. She'd never seen so many in all her life—hells, she'd barely seen a book at all. But here was an entire library of them.

In the center of the room stood an elderly man. He was at least as old as Mister C had been, maybe older still. But where Mister C had a shock of gray hair and a scruffy, mad-inventor vibe about him, this man seemed carved out of metal. His white hair was cropped close to his scalp, his face clean-shaven, the right side heavily scarred, maybe by fire or an explosion. He had a hawkish nose, a high forehead. He wore the same uniform as Grimm and the others, but his creases were immaculate, his boots so shiny they gleamed. He held a book in his hand, and Lemon could make out faint lettering on the cover.

The Count of Monte Cristo by Alexandre Dumas.

The man set the book aside, looked them over. His eyes were pale blue. His stare was piercing, intelligent. Again, Lemon was reminded of Mister C. She felt a faint ache in her chest at the old man's memory. She missed him like oxygen.

Grimm lifted his hand, gave a weary salute.

"Major," the boy said.

The man returned the salute, picture-perfect. "Good to see you, soldier."

"This is Lemon Fresh," the boy said. "She's one of us."

The Major looked at her, his eyes glittering.

"I know," he replied. "Follow me."

The man turned crisply, and leaning on a cane, he limped toward the hatch in the far wall. Lemon's brainmeats were still urging her to run, bail, get out out *out,* but the three words Grimm had just spoken held her rooted to the floor.

One of us.

The big boy, Fix, pushed past them, carrying Diesel through the hatch. Lemon looked at Grimm, uncertainty on her face. He smiled crooked, gave her a wink.

"S'alright. You're gonna wanna see this."

His smile seemed genuine, and again, he struck her as the sort who'd care that she'd saved his hind parts. With a sigh, Lemon helped him limp through a short tunnel and into a vast open space. She felt the hum of electrical current on her skin, felt it in the static behind her eyes. She saw the turbines of a large generator, rows of old computer terminals, a bunch more tech she didn't understand. A sealed hatchway loomed in one wall, painted with big red letters.

SECTION C

NO LONE ZONE

TWO PERSON POLICY MANDATORY

A set of spiral stairs led into the ceiling and floor. Fix carried Diesel down to the lower level, the Major followed. Lemon paused at the top, uncertain. That earthy smell was stronger here, the smell of faint rot beneath.

"We must be a long way underground by now," she muttered.

"It's all right, love," Grimm said. "Trust me."

"Look, you wanna get pushed down these stairs?" Lemon growled.

"Not really, no," the boy replied.

"Then stop calling me love, dammit."

The Major's voice rang up the stairs. "We're almost there."

Lemon heaved a sigh, one hand around Grimm's waist, the other on the cutter at her belt. These hatchway locks were mechanical as well as electronic—if she got trapped down here, she wasn't sure she could get out again. But those three words kept pushing her on where the butterflies in her belly were urging her to turn back.

One.

Of.

Us.

And so, pulling on her streetface, she followed the Major and Fix down, through another hatch. And there, she felt her breath stolen clean away.

"Wow . . . ," she whispered.

Greenery. Wall to wall. Beds of dark dirt and ultraviolet lights humming overhead, and beneath, everything was green. Plants of all shapes and sizes, broad leaves and long limbs, and trees, actual *trees* hung heavy with . . .

"Is that fruit?" she asked, her eyes wide.

"That it is," the Major replied. "This way. Quickly."

The old man led them through the green, Lemon breathing in the rich, earthy air. Among the rows of garden beds, she saw the big boy, Fix, kneeling on the concrete with Diesel laid out before him. He beckoned Lemon and Grimm over with frantic waves of his big, callused hands. It was gloomy in here, and as the boy pulled his goggles up, Lemon saw his irises were the strangest green she'd ever laid eyes on—so bright, they were almost luminous.

"Will she be all right?" Lemon asked, looking Diesel over.

"I seen worse," Fix declared.

Grimm glanced to the Major, nodded at Lemon.

"She took a dose of rads," the boy said. "She'll need a fix, too."

". . . Um, actually, I don't feel too bad anymore," Lemon said.

"They call that the walking ghost stage, love," Grimm explained. "The nausea, the pain, it all goes away. But your bone marrow and the lining of your stomach's all dead. You don't get fixed soon, you will be, too."

"I . . ." She swallowed hard. "You mean . . . I'm still gonna die?"

Grimm shook his head, held out his hand. "Not if you trust us."

Lemon looked to the Major, unsure what to do or say. Truth told, whatever this was, she was in it up to her neck now, and the queasy fear of radsick poisoning hushed the rest of her concerns. Breathing deep, she took Grimm's hand.

"You wanna back off, sir," Fix said, waving the Major away.

The old man retreated half a dozen steps. Satisfied, the big boy nodded, took a deep breath. Lemon watched him put a hand on Diesel's chest, place the other in Grimm's palm. Grimm entwined his fingers with Lemon's.

"This is gonna feel strange," the older boy said.

"What do you m—"

Lemon felt her skin begin to prickle, as if electrical current was dancing over her skin. Her mouth was suddenly dry, the air greasy and charged. She felt a surge of warmth, starting in the hand Grimm was holding, spreading out through her body. It felt like pins and needles, like being wrapped in an itchy blanket, like a million warm cockroaches crawling on and under and through her skin.

Fix tilted his head back, a frown darkening his smooth brow. Lemon saw the color of his irises begin to warp, run, spilling out across the whites of his eyes until they were almost entirely green. She heard a whispering sound, realized the leaves around them were rustling, curling . . .

Dying.

Like some invisible flame was raging through the garden, the plants withered. Green turned to brown, ripe fruit turned to husks, the plants wilting as if they were aging a hundred years in the blink of an eye. Lemon felt butterflies in her belly, caught her breath as she saw the wounds in Grimm's hands and feet, the bullet hole in Diesel's chest, the scrapes on her own skin . . .

"Spank my spankables."

Lemon realized every plant within a three-meter radius of

Fix was totally dead. And all their wounds, the nail holes, the bullet holes, the cuts and bruises earned in the last few days . . .

. . . *they're gone.*

Fix opened his eyes, gently touched Diesel's face. He seemed out of breath, sweat on his skin, chest heaving as if he'd just run a marathon. But his lips curled in a goofy smile as the girl's lashes fluttered, and she opened her eyes.

"See?" he wheezed. "Funkin' miracle worker, me."

Diesel reached up and put her bloodstained arms around Fix's neck. Dragging him into a fierce embrace, she pressed her black, paint-smudged lips to his.

Grimm groaned. "Gawd, get a bloody room, you two."

Lemon could see the bigger boy was clearly drained. Shadows were puddled under those bright green eyes, his face paled, his shoulders slumped. But he still looked triumphant as he pulled his lips away from Diesel's.

"How'd you get shot, anyways?" he murmured.

"It was Grimm's fault," Diesel replied softly.

"Screw you, Deez," the dark-skinned boy said.

"Ew, no." Diesel unwrapped her arms from Fix's neck, gave Grimm a solid punch to the thigh. "But thanks for the offer."

"Glad you're all right," Grimm grinned, brown eyes sparkling.

"You too," Diesel smiled. "But it *was* your fault."

"Hey, I found you a present," Grimm said. He pawed his vest, his shirt, as if looking for something. Finally he dug a hand into the pocket of his cargos, brought it out again with his middle finger raised. "Eat it, freak."

"Make me, freak," Diesel laughed.

"If you two are quite finished?" the Major asked.

Grimm and Diesel both looked to the old man, their smiles

disappearing. Diesel stood quickly, clicked her heels together. Despite her torn and bloodstained clothes, the weariness in her face, the girl saluted the Major with military precision.

"Apologies, sir."

"You two hit the showers," the Major ordered, studying the dead plants around them. "This exercise has cost us a great many resources, and almost cost us everything. So get yourself fed, cleaned up. I want a full sitrep in thirty minutes."

"Yessir," Diesel replied.

Grimm nodded at Lemon, and together, he and Diesel marched through the greenhouse, boots clomping in unison, back up the stairs. Fix heaved a heavy sigh, rose unsteadily to his feet. The big boy looked like ten kilometers of rough road.

"Are you all right, soldier?" the Major asked.

The boy nodded. "Took a little from myself. Didn't wanna hurt the garden too much."

"Get yourself a meal, then get some rack time." The old man nodded at the bloodstained concrete. "You've earned it. Good work, soldier."

Fix grinned at the praise, seemed to stand a foot taller despite his obvious fatigue. He offered a brisk salute, which the Major returned, and with a nod to Lemon, the boy left the greenhouse by the stairwell. The Major watched him go, turned to the girl with a twinkling eye and a gentle smile.

"All right," he said. "Where do you want to start?"

"How . . . ," Lemon began. "He . . . You . . . This . . ."

"How did he do that?" the Major asked.

Lemon nodded, rubbed her eyes. "Right. That. Yeah."

"We call it transference," the Major explained. "Fix has the ability to repair damaged tissue. As far as I can tell, he accelerates the body's natural regenerative properties. But, for want of a better term, he has to take the energy from another living thing to fuel the process." The old man sighed, looking at one of the dead trees. "Shame. I was very much looking forward to a few more of those pears."

The Major looked at Lemon to see if she had more questions, but the girl was gawping around the room and just trying to stop her head exploding.

"What is this place?" she finally managed.

"An abandoned military installation," the Major replied. "I served here many years ago. Before the war. But in answer to what I *think* you're asking, it's a sanctuary. A training facility, where Homo superior can live free of persecution, and help in the search for more of our kind."

"Wait . . . Homo superior?" Lemon asked.

The Major knelt in front of Lemon, that gentle smile on his face. "That's right."

"Wassat mean?"

"It means people like you, young lady."

The old man grinned, scruffed the hair on her head.

"It means people like us."

2.14

PURITY

"How's that?" Abraham asked.

"BETTER," Cricket replied. "TWENTY-SEVEN POINT FOUR PER-CENT IMPROVEMENT."

"This gyro got cut up pretty good. Think I've got a replacement, though."

The big bot tilted his head, more than a little put off by the feeling of this strange boy tinkering with his innards. He was laid out belly-down on the floor of the New Bethlehem workshop, Abraham hanging from a work-sling above. The walls were lined with racks of salvage and tech-gear, the half-built bodies of a dozen WarBots arrayed around them. A voice-controlled servo arm assisted Abraham as he worked, another remote loading crane transporting parts to and fro. The bots looked homemade, scavved together out of repurposed parts. Cricket could see a long drafting table on one side of the workshop, several grubby whiteboards stuck to the wall above it, all covered in a dizzying array of hand-drawn schematics.

This boy was obviously something of a technical wizard.

"You know, it's strange," Abraham said, screwdriver between his teeth.

"WHAT'S STRANGE, MASTER ABRAHAM?" Cricket replied.

"You can stop calling me master, Paladin. Abraham's fine when we're alone."

Paladin . . .

Cricket rankled at the new name Sister Dee had given him, but he couldn't tell Abraham his real one—not unless he wanted the boy to work out his secret. He knew from his history banks that paladins were holy knights, back in the days when it was fashionable to wear metal underwear and bash people in the heads with sharp bits of metal and say "prithee" a lot. But in the grand scheme of things, Cricket supposed Paladin wasn't so bad. He'd been called worse in his time, true cert.

"AS YOU WISH," he replied, trying to sound as impressive and WarDome-y as he could. "WHAT'S STRANGE, ABRAHAM?"

The boy spoke softly, his features lit by the arc welder in his hands. "WarDome fights were about the only thing Grandfather would let me watch on the feeds as a kid. I saw all your Megopolis bouts—back when you were called the Quixote, I mean. But you never fought hand to hand back then. You always finished your opponents at range if possible. Why the change in tactics last night?"

The big bot felt his self-preservation subroutines kick in at the boy's question. Abraham obviously had no idea the Quixote's persona had been replaced with Cricket's own—the boy thought he was dealing with seventy tons of robotic badass, with years of Dome brawls stored in its memory. If Abraham found out the mind inside this body belonged to a helperbot with no combat experience beyond "running awaaaaay," he might be inclined to simply wipe Cricket's core drives and start over.

For a logika, that was basically the same as dying.

"I sought to impress my new owner," Cricket said in his best Domefighter voice. "I am programmed to entertain."

"Well, you certainly did that." Abraham nodded, finishing up and replacing Cricket's armor plating. "The Thunderstorm was a finalist in the regional championship last year. Taking it out was a huge win for New Bethlehem. WarDome is the most popular pastime out here in the wastes . . . well, besides murder and robbery, I guess. But having a champion WarBot is a great way for a settlement to appear legitimate, attract more people, more talent, more revenue." The boy glanced to the small portrait hanging on the wall—a middle-aged man with flaming eyes and a halo of light around his head. "Grandpa would be proud."

"They had those pictures all over the WarDome," Cricket said, looking the portrait over. "He's your grandfather?"

"Yeah." The boy rubbed his neck and sighed. "He started the Brotherhood years ago. Ran everything, back when it was just a scattered cult with a few rusty churches. I bet he never imagined we'd have our own city. Our own champion."

"Where is he?"

"A few years back, before we took over New Bethlehem . . . we got ambushed by deviates." Abraham's voice went soft. "They killed him. Right in front of us. Almost killed me and Mother, too."

"I'm sorry," Cricket said, not sure if he actually was.

Abraham nodded thanks, shrugged his shoulders as if to throw off some hidden weight. "Mother had him canonized after he died. They call him Saint Michael now. The patron of New Bethlehem."

". . . So you're the grandson of a saint?"

"It sounds way more impressive than it is," the boy smiled.

Cricket looked Abraham over as he stowed his tools back in his belt. The logika was pretty good at reading humans after living with Silas and Evie for so long, and studying him, Abraham certainly didn't seem a zealot. He didn't speak like a boy who believed all this nonsense about purity in his bones, or would have indulged in the cruelty he'd seen other cult members relish. It was strange to think of him as Brotherhood royalty.

"CAN I ASK A QUESTION, MASTER ABRAHAM?"

"Please stop calling me master. We're friends now. And yes, you can ask."

"I HEARD SIRENS AFTER THE WARDOME MATCH LAST NIGHT. GUNSHOTS IN THE CITY."

"Yeah," Abraham replied. "We had some local troub—"

The workshop door swung open and Sister Dee marched into the room, dark eyes burning. She looked imperious in her flowing white cassock, frightening in her fresh skullpaint. She was flanked on all sides by Brotherhood beatsticks, well armed and beefy. Cricket noted these bullyboys were cowled all in black instead of the traditional Brotherhood red. Better armed. Bigger and meaner.

Elite guard, maybe?

One of the bodyguards was carrying a broken logika in his arms. The bot was slender, painted with gold filigree, its face fixed in a horrid grin.

"Well, they destroyed Solomon," Sister Dee declared.

"Who did?" Abraham asked.

"Those trashbreed mongrels," she sighed. "Not content with sowing chaos in the city of God, they amuse themselves by destroying helpless machines."

Cricket watched as the beatstick placed the damaged logika

on a workbench. Abraham swung down on his work-sling and leaned over the broken bot's body. The boy seemed genuinely concerned—more like a person would act around a hurt pet than a simple piece of broken property. Abraham opened up the bot's chest cavity with a few deft turns of a multi-tool, chewing his lip as he looked inside.

"What did they hit him with?" he frowned. "Every circuit across his boards looks fried. Like . . . a massive power surge overloaded all his dampeners."

Cricket tensed, a frisson of excitement dancing on his circuits. That sounded like the work of a certain redheaded trouble-magnet he knew. . . .

"Can you fix it?" Sister Dee asked.

Abraham nodded. "If I can't fix it, it can't be fixed, Mother."

"My handsome genius." Sister Dee smiled, glancing at Cricket. "And how fares our mighty Paladin?"

"Superficial damage." Abraham pushed his tech goggles up onto his brow and rubbed his eyes. "His armor is built to take a real beating, and he has some self-repair modules built in. He'll be fully operational by tonight."

"Wonderful," Sister Dee said. "See that you give it a proper paintjob, won't you? Jugartown has heard about our victory, and they've already sent a challenge. I want our Paladin looking the part before it represents New Bethlehem again."

"Yes, Mother," Abraham said.

"With a champion logika on the local circuit, New Bethlehem's fame will only rise. More and more folk will flock to our banner, and our faith. You made an excellent decision in purchasing this bot, Abraham." The woman touched the boy's face, skullpaint twisting as she smiled. "You make your mother terribly proud."

Abraham smiled in turn. "I *want* you to be pr—"

The workshop door slammed open with an almighty bang, and a motley band of men stomped into the room, covered in dust, dirt, blood. A few wore red Brotherhood cassocks, but most seemed a simpler kind of thug, greasepaint Xs daubed on their faces. The big man with the black mohawk Cricket had seen at WarDome last night led the mob, his skullpaint smeared and grimy. He was limping hard, his white cassock spattered in red, a burning cigar at his lips.

"Brother War," said Sister Dee. "Welcome back."

The woman looked among the mob, hand falling away from her son's face.

"I can't help but notice you appear to be . . . missing something."

The man chewed on his cigar, glowering but mute. Sister Dee approached him at a steady pace, stared up into his eyes, her voice shifting from the warmth she'd shown her son to something far more dangerous.

"My prisoners, perhaps?"

"They were working with the CityHive, Sister," the man growled. "An operative. Cut my men to bloody ribbons."

"So you failed us," Sister Dee said simply. "They were in our hands. We could have learned where those insects nested, and burned them out once and for all."

"You were the one who—"

The slap echoed across the room, louder than a thunderclap. Brother Dubya's head whipped to one side, his cigar flying from his mouth and rolling under the racks of salvage. The imprint of Sister Dee's hand could be seen clearly in the greasepaint on his cheek.

"You failed us," Sister Dee repeated.

Brother Dubya clenched his jaw. Lowered his eyes.

"I failed us," he said.

"Beggin' pardon, Sister Dee," piped up the biggest bullyboy, standing beside Brother War. "But true cert, it weren't the good Brother's fault. That goddamn trashbreed . . . she opened up a hole in the sky! Christ almighty, she—"

Sister Dee turned and pressed one black-nailed finger to the big man's lips. The rest of his protest died inside his mouth. The whole room fell still. Cricket even had a hard time sensing breathing on his audio feeds.

"You're new to our flock, yes?" Sister Dee asked. "Disciple Leon, isn't it?"

"Ys'm," the big man mumbled around her finger.

"You have a wife and child, yes? Maria and . . ." Sister Dee pursed her painted lips. "Toby? Am I remembering that correctly?"

The man nodded, his eyes a little wider. Sister Dee leaned close, lips brushing his skin as she whispered loud enough for everyone to hear.

"If ever you blaspheme in my presence again, Disciple Leon, the last thing you and Maria will hear in this life will be the sound of nails being driven into little Toby's hands and feet. Do I make myself clear?"

The man swallowed hard.

"Ys'm," he nodded.

Sister Dee kissed the man's hand, leaving a black-and-white smile on his skin. "Then I forgive you. This once. As does the Lord, your God."

"Th-th—"

"Amen is the proper response, Disciple Leon."

"Amen." Leon cleared his throat, licked at dry lips. "Ma'am."

Sister Dee returned her attentions to Brother Dubya. The paint on his cheeks was now smudged on her hand, under her fingernails. Cricket noted how every Disciple and Brother in the room stared straight ahead. How Abraham had retreated into the shadows, eyes averted. How even Brother War steadfastly refused to meet the woman's bottomless stare.

"Should I forgive you also, Brother War?" she asked. "As Our Savior forgave his transgressors? Or should I punish you, as Our Lord punished the sinners of Sodom and Nooyawk and Ellay? The Goodbook speaks of four Horsemen, true." She ran a hand over his bloodstains. "But men is something I have no shortage of. And what use is a Horseman who can't bring down two teen-age trashbreeds?"

"Three," he said softly.

The woman tilted her head. "I beg your pardon?"

"The abnorms have added another to their number," Brother Dubya replied. "A redhead. Girl. She . . . God's truth, I don't know what she did. But she snapped her fingers and knocked our combat drones right out of the sky."

Cricket felt another electric thrill at the girl's description. It *was* her. It was . . .

"LEMON?" he blurted.

All eyes in the room turned on him.

". . . What did you say, Paladin?" Abraham asked.

"N-NOTHING." The logika shook his head, electric panic washing over his circuitry. "I—I'M SORRY, I'LL BE QUIET."

Sister Dee narrowed her eyes.

"Do you . . . know this deviate, Paladin? The one Brother War just described?"

Cricket remained silent, fear flooding his sub-systems. How could he have been so *stupid*? He was too used to being around humans he could trust, humans who cared about him and cared about each—

"Answer me," Sister Dee said softly. "Do you know her?"

A robot must obey.

A robot

Must

Obey.

"I . . . I THINK SO, SISTER DEE."

"Tell me who she is," the woman commanded.

He wanted to scream no. To run. To do anything except comply. But . . .

"HER NAME IS LEMON FRESH," he heard himself reply.

"Tell me where she is."

"I DON'T KNOW," Cricket moaned. "I LOST HER IN THE CLEFTS A FEW DAYS AGO."

Sister Dee turned to the dusty war party. Dark eyes glittering.

"It seems the Lord has granted you a reprieve, Brother War," she said. "Take the other Horsemen to the Clefts and search for any trace of this girl or—"

"PLEASE DON'T HURT HER," Cricket begged.

Sister Dee pointed to the logika, spoke without looking at him. "*Never* speak in my presence without being spoken to first. Acknowledge."

". . . ACKNOWLEDGED," Cricket whispered.

"Go to the Clefts," she commanded Brother Dubya. "Do not return to New Bethlehem without captives. I want them *alive*, do you understand? I want to know where they nest. These trash-breed mongrels grow bolder by the day. Deviation cannot be tolerated. Only the pure shall prosper."

"Only the pure shall prosper," he repeated.

"Saint Michael watch over you," she said.

Brother Dubya grunted acknowledgment and marched from the room, his dusty posse trailing behind. Sister Dee watched them leave, her face a mask. The Brotherhood members in the black cassocks relaxed their stances, and Cricket realized every one of them had placed their fingers on the triggers of their weapons. That with one word from this woman, every man in that crew would have been stone-cold murdered right here in front of him.

And every one of them had known it.

As the double doors slammed shut, Sister Dee finally glanced over her shoulder. Abraham was busy at his tools, his face pale, blue eyes shining and wide. She walked over, touched his chin, forced him to look at her.

"Your grandfather always said it was better to be feared than loved."

The boy swallowed hard and nodded. "I remember."

"Do you love me, my son?"

". . . Of course I do."

Sister Dee's skullpaint face twisted in a gentle smile as she kissed his cheek.

"It's all for you," she said. "You know that, don't you?"

"I know, Mother." The boy nodded slowly. "I know."

With a final glance at Cricket, Sister Dee spun on her heel and swept from the room, her black-cassocked thugs marching behind her in unison.

"Remember the paintjob," she called over her shoulder. "And fix Solomon!"

The doors slammed shut. The light seemed to brighten, the tension flee the room. Abraham dragged his hand back through his hair, rubbed his eyes.

"I . . ."

Cricket's voice faltered. Sister Dee wasn't in the room anymore, so he could speak freely. But in the end, he still wasn't entirely sure about this boy. He seemed a decent sort. Gentle, when all the world around him was hard and sharp as glass. But Abraham was that woman's son, and that woman was the bloodthirsty leader of a fanatical murder cult. What kind of person might he *really* be?

"Is . . . Is she always like that?" he finally asked.

The boy glanced at the double doors, heaved a sigh. "She has to be."

"How do you figure that?"

"This is a cold world, Paladin. Its leaders have to be colder. My mother's a good person, in her heart. But when my grandfather died, it fell on her to hold the Brotherhood together. All of this, all we have, is because of her."

Cricket wasn't sure what to say. He'd always spoken his mind with Evie—Silas had programmed him to keep her out of trouble, to be her conscience, to never be afraid to speak up. And even though he knew he wasn't safe here, some part of that programming was surfacing now. Truth was, he liked this kid. Liked that he didn't want to be called master. That he referred to Cricket as "him" instead of "it."

But still, he was part of the cult now hunting Lemon. Cricket wanted to throw his hands up in despair. They'd only been apart for *two days,* and somehow the girl had fallen in with a pack of deviates engaged in a war against the entire Brotherhood? And, idiot that he was, he'd placed her directly in danger.

Where was Ezekiel in all this?

What was going on?

"You . . ." Cricket faltered again, shook his head.

"You can speak freely," Abraham said. "We're friends now, Paladin."

Leaving Solomon's body on the workbench, the boy perused the salvage stacked along the workshop walls. The tall racks were filled to bursting, shelves groaning under the weight of spare parts and high-tech flotsam and regular junk.

Unknown to Cricket or Abraham, Brother War's cigar continued to smolder under the racks where it had been slapped from his lips.

"I PRESUME YOU'RE NOT A DISCIPLE OR BROTHER OR ANYTHING," the WarBot said. "I MEAN, YOU DON'T WEAR THE UNIFORM. YOU DON'T WEAR THE X."

"I'm not officially a member of the order, no. I like machines. They're easier to understand than people most days." The boy made a small pleased noise, climbing up onto one of the more overcrowded racks. "So, Mother put me in charge of New Bethlehem's Dome. I like it down here. People leave me alone to do what I want."

"BUT YOU KNOW WHAT THE BROTHERHOOD DOES TO DEVIATES, RIGHT?"

"It's not pretty," the boy said, stretching through the junk toward a replacement circuit board. "But we wandered for years before we settled in New Bethlehem. I've seen what's outside these walls. And the alternative is uglier still."

"LEMON IS MY FRIEND. IF THEY CATCH HER . . ."

"I'm sorry, Paladin. If your friend is an abnorm, there's nothing to be done." Abraham finally grasped the board, tucking it into his coveralls as he continued. "Folks always need someone to hate. Usually someone different. If we can't find an Other, we make one up. It's just the way people are."

"NOT ALL OF YOU. NOT THE ONES I'VE KNOWN."

Abraham smiled lopsided, as if Cricket had told a joke.

"Then you've known better people than m—"

A loud *BANG* echoed at the other end of the workshop. Unseen below the racks, Brother War's cigar had set fire to a puddle of oil, which had in turn ignited a half-empty acetylene tank. As the cylinder exploded into a brief ball of bright flame, the racks Abraham was climbing shuddered. And before Cricket knew what was happening, the entire structure popped its brackets and came away from the wall.

He saw it happening in slow motion—the boy falling backward, mouth open, eyes wide. The rack came after him, heavy steel, overloaded with engine parts, heavy servos and power units, robotic limbs. Cricket yelled, reached toward Abraham, but he was too far away. The boy would be crushed by all that weight—legs or ribs broken at best, spattered on the concrete at worst.

The boy hit the ground, gasping in pain. He flung out his hand. The air around him shivered and warped, like ripples on water. And as Cricket watched, dumbfounded, the rack was smashed back into the wall, as if by some invisible force. Spare parts and rusty steel and junk, hundreds and hundreds of kilos of it, thrown about like paper on the wind.

Abraham rolled clear as the rack rebounded, crashing to the deck with a noise like a thunderclap. The shelves broke loose, the debris scattered across the floor. The dust settled. A small fire burned merrily among the mess, smoke rising to the ceiling. And at the edge of the chaos, the boy lay on his back. He closed his eyes and cursed softly, rapping the back of his head against the concrete.

"Stupid . . . ," he hissed.

Not a single rusty bolt of it had touched him.

"ARE YOU ALL RIGHT?" Cricket asked, kneeling beside him.

Electric panic was rolling over the big bot in waves, the impulse of the First Law lighting up his mind. The imperative to protect humans—to do *anything* to safeguard them from harm—was hard-coded into the very heart of him. He felt jacked up, full of tension, bristling. But unless he was all the way glitched, that boy had just . . .

He moved that junk just by thinking about it.

Deviation. Abnormality. A genetic quirk of fate. Cricket knew Lemon could kill electricity with a thought. He'd heard stranger tales of deviates who could light fires just thinking on it, or even read minds. It mostly sounded like the stuff of kids' stories, talking true. Unless you lived in a city where folks preached about the value of purity, and spoke out against the dangers of genetic abnormality every single day.

A city where only the pure prospered.

In a place like that, deviation was a death sentence.

"Shut down," Abraham said.

"WAIT, I—"

"I'm ordering you, Paladin!" Abraham roared. "Shut! DOWN!"

"ACKNOWLEDGED," Cricket said.

And all the world went black.

2.15

SUPERIOR

"Kill me," Lemon said.

The Major looked up from his book, one white eyebrow raised. "Excuse me?"

"Seriously," Lemon said, padding up the stairs. "Just ghost me right now. I honestly think it's for the best."

"All right," the Major said. "But before I do you in, might I ask why?"

"I keep a list in my head, yeah?" Lemon replied, sitting on the couch opposite. "You know, a 'Greatest Experiences of Lemon's Life' type deal? And after that shower . . . honestly, I think I've peaked. There's just no point in living anymore."

The old man laughed, the scars on the right side of his face crinkling as he leaned back in his sofa. With the fluffiest towel she'd ever touched in her life, Lemon continued drying off her hair. For the first time in as long as she could remember, she smelled of soap and shampoo instead of sweat and blood. She could still feel the deliriously warm spray of water on her skin.

"Just for future reference," the Major said, "we try to limit showers to three minutes at a time."

Lemon blinked. "How long was I in there?"

"Twenty-seven."

"Sorry," she winced. "It's been a while."

"Your clothes are being washed." The Major cleared his throat. "I hope you don't mind, but I had Fix put your socks in the incinerator."

"Best for all concerned," Lemon said.

"Mm-hmm," the Major nodded. "Clothes fit okay?"

"Not exactly the bleeding edge of fashion, but yeah, thanks."

Her new threads were the same uniform the Major and the others all wore: bulky desert camo fatigues, big stompy boots, about as flattering as an old plastic bag. Normally Lemon wouldn't have been caught dead in them, but her own clothes had been so crusty, it was a miracle they hadn't run away under their own power yet.

"Hungry?" The Major waved to a box of what looked to be vacuum-packed meals on the table beside the swear jar. "I'm not sure how long it's been since—"

Lemon had a packet torn open and an entire protein bar crammed into her mouth before the old man could finish his sentence. She sat cross-legged on the floor, unwrapped another bar and took a bite, cheeks ballooning, eyes rolling back in her head as she chewed and groaned and chewed some more.

"I'll take that as a yes," the Major said. "I thought I'd give you the two-bit tour before bed. If you're not too tired?"

"Cnnsuwwlggg," Lemon mumbled.

"I beg your pardon?"

Lemon chewed some more, swallowed her mouthful with difficulty.

"Can't stay long," she repeated.

"That's fine," the Major nodded. "But if you're not busy now . . . ?"

Lemon shrugged, tore open another protein bar, shoved six more into her pockets. The Major stood with a wince, waved his walking stick at the walls around them. The ugly scars on his face were etched in shadow, but his blue eyes were twinkling and lively. Between the easy authority he exuded, the uniform and the limp, she figured he must've been a soldier in his past.

"Well, we've been situated here for a while now," he explained. "It might not be a palace, but to us, it's home. The facility is divided into three main areas. We're currently in Section A, the habitation pod."

Lemon tried saying something like "Mmm, very interesting," but her mouth was crammed full of protein bar again, so all she managed was "Mmmrphhgllmng."

"Upper levels are separate dormitories, capable of housing twenty-four people." The Major waved to the shelves around them. "This is the common area. Books, VR reels—we're also wired into the Megopolis feeds. As you've already seen, downstairs are the bathroom and shower facilities. The rest is this way."

Leaning on his cane, the old man limped to the inner hatchway. Lemon followed, still stuffing her face. The fluoros lit up as they entered the passage, the Major leading them through to the vast open space they'd visited before. Lemon glanced at that big sealed hatchway, the big red letters:

SECTION C NO LONE ZONE
TWO PERSON POLICY MANDATORY

"What's through there?" she asked.

"Section C," the Major said. "Although we can't get the door open."

She looked at the large digital control pad set beside the hatch. Panels had been pulled off the wall, she could see dark acetylene scoring and shallow dents on the metal—though they hadn't been able to open it, it looked like the Major and his crew had given it a damn good shot.

She'd never been around tech this flash or shiny before in her life—not even in Mister C's house. Lemon could sense static electricity dancing along her skin, and closing her eyes, she was a little astonished to realize she could feel current all around her. Slim rivers of it, flowing down the walls, beneath the floor. Through the Section C hatchway and the computers beyond.

"This is Section B," the Major was saying, waving at the room around them. "Four floors. Around us, we have our power generators, hydrostation and the computer facilities. Top level is my office. Basement level is our gymnasium and training hub. On the floor directly below us, we have the greenhouse. Fix has something of a green thumb, he grows the plants himself. It's self-sustaining, not quite enough to supply our little band, but close."

"How can it be self-sustaining?" Lemon asked. "Aren't your seeds sterile?"

"Lord no," the Major said. "We don't use any of that BioMaas junk. We raided a seed bank, stocked with samples from before the Fall."

"How'd you find it?" she asked.

"The same way I found Grimm. Diesel. Fix." A shrug. "I *saw* it."

Lemon mumbled around her latest mouthful. "Swwut?"

"Everyone here has a gift, Miss Fresh. Fix can accelerate the

body's healing abilities. Diesel's our . . . transportation expert."
The Major shrugged again. "I see things."

Lemon swallowed her mouthful of protein. "You mean . . .
like . . ."

"Faces. Places. I don't rightly know why. Or how. But I've
been able to do it since I was about your age. It only happens
when I'm deep asleep. And I can't see what will be. Only what is.
But, somehow, it always turns out to be important."

The old man knelt in front of Lemon with a wince.

"And I feel I should tell you now, Miss Fresh, that I've been
dreaming of you."

Ever so slowly, Lemon began backing toward the door.

"At ease," the Major smiled. "I realize how odd it sounds. But
I've been seeing you for a few years now. Off and on. Last time
I saw you, would've been . . . maybe four days back? You were
dressed in . . . pink. I think. You were standing by a wrecked car.
Surrounded by hostile machina. And you destroyed them all
with a wave of your hand."

Lemon thought back to her battle outside Babel with the
Preacher. The machina garrison from Daedalus she destroyed.
The gaudy pink rad-suit she'd worn.

"How could you possibly know that?" she whispered.

"I told you. I *see*. When I dream. It's called clairvoyance, if
you need a technical term." The Major tilted his head. "How
does it work? Your gift, I mean? Grimm told me you knocked
those Brotherhood rotor drones out of the sky with a shrug. You
manipulate magnetic fields, maybe? Accelerate metal fatigue,
or . . . ?"

Lemon chewed her lip. Amazing as it was, she was slowly realizing these people were certified deviates, just like her. That
somehow, Diesel could rip holes in space. Fix could heal bullet

holes and radiation poisoning with a thought. And this old crusty wardog could . . . see things?

It was every color of insane, even if she *had* witnessed the evidence with her own damn eyes. But four years of hiding what she was, of living with the thought of what'd happen if people found out . . .

"You don't have to be afraid anymore." The old man squeezed her hand. "I promise you that. You don't ever have to be afraid of what you are again."

Lemon looked down at her boots, trying to find her voice. All the bluff and bluster she usually summoned at will seemed to have evaporated in the presence of this strange, scarred old man. Her streetface, her braveface, was nowhere to be found. But the Major simply squeezed her hand again.

"It's all right," he said, his voice sure and gentle. "It's okay."

Lemon sighed, chewed her lip.

"'Lectrics," she finally mumbled.

"I beg your pardon?"

Lemon cleared her throat, spoke a little louder.

"I can fry electrics. I think about it, and the current surges and things just cook. It first happened when I was twelve in Los Diablos, this auto-peddler ate my creds and I just got mad and fried it, I didn't even know how at the time, I'm still not very good at it, though, I can't really control it I usually just cook everything around me and it's easier when I'm angry but I can't point it or aim it or anything I just sort of think about it and it's like this static inside my head and it's just—"

"You listen, now," the Major said softly. "And listen close."

Lemon bit down on the babble spilling from her mouth.

"There's no one like you in all the world," he said. "And you've been frightened far too long. People fear what's different. People fear what they can't control. People fear the future. And that's what you are, Miss Fresh. The future." The Major nodded, that pale blue stare boring into her own. "And they *should* be afraid of you. Because you are not alone."

As the Major spoke, she felt his words in her bones. Looking into his eyes, she felt taller. Listening to him speak, she felt stronger. The things he said, the truth he spoke, they set Lemon tingling from the tips of her toes to the top of her head. The old man smiled at her, scars crinkling, and she found herself smiling back.

"You are *not* alone," he said again.

But the sensible part of her brain, the part raised in the Scrap, brought her back down to earth. The thought of Zeke and Cricket out there somewhere without her—probably in trouble—set her heart sinking. This facility was the most amazing place she'd ever seen in her life. And she knew she couldn't stay.

"Listen, it's been a long few days between one thing and another," she said. "And I don't wanna impose or anything, but would it be all right if I crashed for a few hours before I motor?"

The Major stood up with the aid of his cane. "You're welcome to stay as long as you like. We've got plenty of room. I'll get you situated in one of the dorms."

"Thanks," the girl smiled.

She followed the old man back to the habitation pod, up the stairs to a neat room lined with bunk beds. The Major was still talking, but Lemon was only half listening. All the turmoil of the past few days was catching up with her, weighing down her eyelids, heavy as lead. Memories of Evie, of Mister C, of Hunter and New Bethlehem. Of blood and twisting metal and breaking glass. But more, and louder than all of it, was a single thought. Ringing in her ears as the Major wished her goodnight, closed the door and turned out the light.

Four simple words. Four enormous words. Four words she couldn't remember ever hearing or thinking or believing before in her entire life.

You are not alone.

———

It was dark when Lemon opened her eyes. For a brief and terrifying moment, she couldn't remember where she was. Back in Mister C's old digs in Tire Valley? Curled up under some cardboard box in the warrens of Los Diablos?

Nowhere at all?

As she sat up, a small light overhead hummed and flickered into life. She found herself on clean sheets and a soft mattress. She could still smell the scent of soap in her hair. And hanging in the air, soft as its perfume, she could hear . . .

Music?

Lemon padded to the hatch, opened it on whispering hinges. She realized the music was coming from the living area below. Pretty notes from an instrument she didn't know, strung together in an arrangement she'd never heard. Creeping downward, she found the lights on, Grimm seated on the circular couches. The boy was reading some old dog-eared 20C book. Its cover featured a muscular man with long golden hair and no shirt, clutching a woman who seemed to be falling out of her dress. He stashed it under a cushion as soon as Lemon appeared on the stairs.

"You saw nothing," he growled.

". . . Okay?"

He sucked his lip, looked about nervously. "Did the tunes wake you?"

Lemon shook her head, hovering uncertainly. "What *is* this?"

"The music?" Grimm shrugged. "Dunno. Some old dead wanker."

"It's . . . beautiful."

"Yeah, it's all right, innit?" His face relaxed into an easy smile. "We got piles of this stuff in digital storage. I listen sometimes while I'm on watch."

"Sorry, am I . . . ?"

"Nahnah." He beckoned her over. "You're not interrupting. We usually keep nighttime hours. Easier to stay hidden in the dark. Come in."

Lemon padded over to the couches, the concrete cool under her bare feet. She sat on the couch opposite Grimm, sinking down into the leather. She'd never parked herself on anything as luxurious in her life.

"You feeling better?" she asked, looking at his unblemished wrists.

"Robin Hood," he replied in his proper-fancy accent.

". . . What?"

"Good," he said. "It rhymes, yeah? Robin Hood. Good."

"Oh. Okay."

"How 'bout you?"

Lemon looked around her: the books, the beautiful music, the cool air and the clean clothes. She tried to find words, could barely manage a shrug.

"Bit over the top, eh?" the boy asked.

"Way over." She nodded to the swear jar on the table. "Wassat?"

Grimm shrugged. "Fix grew up rough. Place called Paradise Falls. Don't let the pretty hair fool you, he curses worse than anyone I ever met. The Major's trying to break him of the habit. Every time one of us swears, we put a cap with our name on it in the jar. When it's time to do a job no one wants, a name gets drawn out. The muddier your mouth, the more chance it's gonna be you."

Lemon squinted at the bottle caps. Around ninety percent had the name "Fix" written on them.

"So that's what all the 'funking,' 'forking' stuff was about?"

Grimm shrugged. "Preferable to the flip side, believe me."

Lemon smiled, looked around the room. The books on the walls, the artwork on the ceiling. Trying to wrap her head around it all.

"Listen," Grimm said, leaning closer. "Sorry about the stick I gave in the car. Wouldn't've given you so much barney if I knew you was one of us."

The girl waved him off. "It's all Robin Hood."

He smiled, his dark eyes twinkling. But as quick as it arrived, the smile faded, his tone turning soft and serious.

"Who was your friend? The stabby lass who got ghosted?"

". . . She wasn't my friend, really," Lemon said. "Her name was Hunter. She was . . . a long story."

Grimm nodded. "Well, sorry if sorry's wanted, yeah? Me and Deez might not be here if not for you and yours. Brotherhood are bad biz. You did good. Real good."

"I know," Lemon smiled. "Brilliful, remember?"

Grimm laughed, leaned back in his seat. Lemon felt a little warm inside her chest, tucked her hair behind her ear. "How long you been here?"

"Six months, maybe? Major found me just before I turned seventeen."

"Where at?"

"Place called Jugartown." Grimm nodded to a map hanging among the framed art on the ceiling. "Little ways to the south.

Local lawmen snagged me. Brotherhood got called, Sister Dee and her Horsemen were on the way to nail me up."

"Horsemen?"

"Yeah, it's from the Goodbook. They were supposed to be Heralds of the 'pocalypse. Death, War, Famine, Pestilence. Sister Dee. Brother Dubya. Brother Eff, Brother Pez. Get it?"

"True fancy," she nodded.

"Anyway, Diesel and Fix showed up, busted me loose. Been running with them and the Major ever since."

"If the Brotherhood were going to nail you up . . ." Lemon chewed her lip. "I mean, what can you . . . ?"

"Do?"

"Yeah."

Grimm cracked his knuckles and grinned. "Observe."

The boy held out his hand, fixed Lemon in his stare. She felt butterflies in her stomach under his gaze, realizing for the first time how handsome he was. Broad shoulders and a strong jaw, deep brown skin. The uniform they'd given her was several sizes too big, and she'd gone to bed wearing only the T-shirt. She was conscious of her bare legs now, curling them up under her on the couch.

And then, she started feeling cold.

Her skin prickled, she shivered. It began slow, then cascaded, the temperature around her seemed to plummet. She was suddenly aware of what the chill was doing to her body, and she folded her arms over her chest. As she exhaled, her breath emerged as frost, hanging in the air before her.

"Holy crap," she whispered.

"Not the best part, love," Grimm smiled.

He focused on the mug of caff on the table in front of him. And as he curled his fingers, brow creased in concentration,

Lemon saw steam begin to rise off the liquid's surface. Her breath caught in her lungs as she saw the liquid ripple, bubble and, finally, begin to boil.

"You control . . . heat?"

"Energy," the boy said. He took a deep breath, blinked hard. The caff stopped boiling, the temperature around Lemon's body slowly returning to normal. "I can move it. Refocus it. Concentrate it. That's all heat is really, just radiant energy."

She blinked hard, incredulous. "How long have you been able to do it?"

"Since I was fourteen or so? Most freaks tend to manifest when we hit puberty." He gave a soft chuckle. "Bit cruel when you think about it. Bad enough dealing with the acne without learning you can set things on fire with your brain."

"That's . . ." Lemon shook her head, looking at the radiation symbol shaved into his hair. "I mean, I'd heard stories about other people who could do what I do, but I never knew . . ."

"You control 'lectrics, yeah? Overload 'em?"

She nodded, licking her lip. "Yeah. But it's kinda hard to control sometimes. Works best when I'm angry."

"Mental note: do not get Lemon angry," Grimm smiled.

She smiled weakly in return.

"What about Diesel? Did I imagine her . . . ripping . . ."

"She calls it Rifting," Grimm said. "It's like . . . imagine she can make two holes in space. Each connected, yeah? They can only be laid flat, each about as big as a car. And she can only create them in places she can actually see, so she can't go through walls or anything. But you jump through one, fall out the other, like you would any other hole. Just hope she doesn't close them on you halfway through."

Lemon pushed her knuckles into her eyes, shook her head

again. She felt like her brains were slowly dribbling out her ears.

"You all right?" Grimm asked. "Want a drink?"

"Sorry. It's just . . . amazing, is all."

"Yeah." The boy grimaced. "Try selling that to Sister Dee and her bastards."

"We had the Brotherhood in Los Diablos, too," Lemon said quietly. "I spent most of my sproghood dodging them. The guy running them was named the Iron Bishop. Bad news. But he wasn't as . . . scary as that Dee lady."

"I believe it," Grimm said. "Brotherhood got started ages ago by a bloke called Saint Michael. But he got ended a while back, and his daughter took over the whole show. Sister Dee made her dad into a martyr, and used his murder to grow the Brotherhood into a bloody army. I hear they've even got a chapel in Megopolis now. Dunno how many of us she and her Horsemen have ghosted. We try and disrupt operations when we can. Hit the tankers of H_2O they sell to other settlements—that's what me and Deez were doing when we got sprung. The Major's been fighting a guerilla war against them for years."

"So what's his program?" Lemon asked. "The Major?"

Grimm shrugged. "He was military, back before War 3.0. Stationed in this very facility. After the Fall, he worked as a Corpside freelancer for a while. He was in a bad barney, though, his whole unit got wiped out by scavvers, and he got left for dead in Plastic Alley. And that's when Fix found him. The old bugger thought he'd always been alone, but after realizing there was more of us with gifts, he started our little freak show. He says he knew he had to do something to protect the future."

Lemon blinked. "What future?"

"Future of the species, of course," Grimm said.

Lemon just frowned, and the boy pointed to one of the framed pieces of art on the ceiling above. It showed six figures in profile, walking in a row. On the far left was a small furry animal Lemon recognized from a history virtch as a monkey. The next figure was a taller monkey, walking on two legs. The third looked like a small man with a heavy brow, and so it went, down the line. The last figure was just a regular dustneck with no clothes on, labeled HOMO SAPIENS.

"You ever heard of Darwin?" Grimm asked.

Lemon shook her head.

"He was this old geezer," Grimm explained. "Before the Fall. Wrote a book that turned the world upside down. Said how animals and plants 'n' that are always changing in reaction to the world around 'em, yeah? And the ones that change the best, *do* the best, and pass on their changes to their kids."

"Okay." Lemon shrugged. "So?"

"So that's *us*. We're the change. The next step in the chain. Homo superior."

Lemon raised one eyebrow. "Rrrrrrright."

"Look, it's hard to explain. The geezer did it better."

Grimm rolled off the couch, walked to the bookshelf. Lemon sucked on her lip and tried very hard not to notice how well those pants of his fit, or study the way the muscles in his arm moved as he reached up to the shelf. He pulled down an old tome that looked like it had been through several armed conflicts and at least one serious food fight, and tossed it into her lap.

"*On the Origin of Species by Means of Natural Selection. Annotated Version.*" Lemon blinked up at Grimm. "You want me to read this whole thing?"

"Got a problem with reading?"

Lemon raised her hands to her eyes and hissed. "It burns usssss."

Grimm laughed. "How old are you?"

"Dunno, really. Best guess is fifteen or sixteen. But it's just a guess. I got left outside a pub in LD as a sprog. The only thing my parents gave me was—"

Lemon frowned, reaching up to her neck and suddenly realizing . . .

"My clover's missing."

She stood, heart in her throat.

"My clover's missing!" she cried.

"Take it easy," Grimm said. "It's all ri—"

"No, it's not all right!" Lemon said, voice rising. "Do you know the crap I had to go through to hold on to that thing all these years? Do you know how hard it was not to hock it or lose it or have it snaffled by some damn gutter sprog? It's *not* all fuc . . ."

Her voice trailed off as Grimm reached into his pocket, produced a thin black choker set with a small silver five-leafed clover.

"Fix found it in the truck," he said. "I remember seein' it round your n—"

Lemon snatched the trinket from the boy's hand, checked that it was still in one piece. The choker was snapped, but the charm itself seemed unharmed, and Lemon squeezed it tight in her fist, feeling her heart thump in her chest.

Grimm sat back on the couch looking abashed, and Lemon felt suddenly embarrassed. These people had shown her welcome in a world where most folks only showed you the barrel of a gun. She bit her lip, tucked her hair back behind her ear again.

"Hey, I'm sorry," she said. "For yelling and stuff."

"S'aright," he murmured.

"No, it's not. It's just . . ." Lemon ran her thumb across the charm, pursing her lips. "Just . . . my folks dumped me when I was little, yeah? They didn't leave a note. They didn't even give me a name. All they left me with was this."

"I get it." The boy smiled gently. "I do."

Lemon stood awkwardly in the silence, finally looked in the direction of the bathroom. "So, um, I'm gonna go avail myself of these lovely facilities, and then maybe try to get some zees. Nice talking to you, Grimm."

Grimm pointed to the book. "Have a gander. It's worth your time, trust me."

"Nice of you and all, but I've gotta motor tomorrow."

"Got someplace to be?"

"Friends who need me. Rule Number One in the Scrap."

Grimm blinked, obviously confused.

"Stronger together," Lemon explained. "Together forever."

"Take the book," Grimm said. "Might change your mind about staying."

"It won't."

Grimm stood and walked around the table until he was standing in front of her. This close, Lemon could feel the warmth off his body, see the dozen different shades of brown in those bottomless eyes of his. He was tall and he was strong and he was fine. She felt the silly urge to look away, reaching for her brave-face and staring him down instead.

He held up the book between them. "Trust me."

"Look, I'm sure it's real interesting and all," she said. "But where I come from, you stick by your friends."

"I respect that," the boy nodded. "But see, we're more than your friends."

He pressed the book into her hand.

"We're your *people*."

———

She stayed up all day. Tired beyond sleeping, too wired to crash. Hunched over that old beaten book and chewing on a lock of cherry-red hair. Her eyes were wide, she felt utterly exhausted. But more, she felt . . . awake.

A gentle knock came at her door, the handle turned slowly and Grimm poked his head around the frame, a tray of steaming food in hand.

"Thought you might want some ch . . ."

The boy's voice trailed off as he saw Lemon sitting in bed, book in her lap.

"Have you been up all day reading?" he asked.

Lemon blinked up at him, as if noticing he was there for the first time. She could feel tears shining in her eyes.

She closed the cover.

Heaved a sigh.

"Holy shit," she breathed.

2.16

FALLS

"This is a bad plan, Snowflake."

"Shut up."

"Look, I know bein' mean is just how you show affection and all," the Preacher whispered. "But you keep this up, you're liable to hurt my feelings."

"Shut *up!*" Ezekiel hissed.

The lifelike and the bounty hunter were crouched in an alleyway among the garbage and unconscious ethylheads, looking out onto the dirty street. Eve, Gabriel and the others were making their way through the crowded thoroughfares of Paradise Falls, heading toward the heart of the settlement. Ezekiel trailed his siblings at a good safe distance, the Preacher once more strapped to his back

It'd only been a few days since Zeke had seen Gabriel and Faith, but laying eyes on Uriel, Patience and Verity again had rocked him all the way back on his dusty heels. The last time they'd all been together was the day of the revolt. The day they'd murdered the Monrovas and fallen from grace. The day his brothers and sisters had bolted that metal coin slot into his chest.

They'd called him puppet. Toy. Traitor. Slave. And together, they'd thrown him off that glittering, blood-soaked tower, and left him for the wastes.

He ran his fingers over the metal still embedded in his skin. He could've torn it out at any time he'd wanted—a moment's pain, a few day's healing and there'd be nothing to show for it. But he'd kept it through all the years. To remind himself of what they'd done. What he'd lost. What he'd chosen to be.

Out of loyalty.

Out of love.

Eve.

He knew that this was her choice. But the sight of her walking beside the others made his chest hurt. His stomach sink. She'd told him that she wanted to learn who she was, that he wasn't going to be the one to teach her.

But Gabriel and the others were?

He could feel two girls, two memories, at war again in his head. The Ana he knew would never have thrown in with the killers who'd murdered her family. The Ana he knew was gentle and kind, in love with the world, and she'd showed him the beauty it could hold, even as ugly and bleak as it was. Seeing Eve drifting down the street, dark cloak billowing about her, drawing her hood up over that face he'd memorized, line by line, curve by curve, he was suddenly aware of how different she was from the person he wanted her to be.

But do you still love her?

"So riddle me this, Snowflake," came a voice at his back.

Ezekiel jangled the wire connected to the grenades on the Preacher's back.

"If I have to tell you to shut up again," he whispered, "I'm going to pull the pins on my insurance policy and let your Lord sort you out."

"Yeah, nah, you ain't gonna do that," the Preacher said. "So here's the thing: You're obviously boots over bonnet with lil' Miss Carpenter here, I get that. And she obviously don't feel the same way, or else we wouldn't be sneaking around after her like the world's two shittiest ninjas. But what I'm wonderin' is, what the hell's she doin' hangin' around with more of your special snowflake brothers and sisters?"

Ezekiel said nothing, watching the lifelikes stalk on through the crowd.

"I mean, that's what they all are, right?" the Preacher asked. "100-Series? Too pretty to be anything but. Why's a deviate hangin' with the likes of them? And come to think of it, why're you keepin' me around, now you found the girl you're lookin' for? Safest play here is to just ghost me and be done."

The bounty hunter was talking every kind of sense. Of course, much as he wanted to, Ezekiel couldn't just dump him into Plastic Alley—the Preacher was the only person Zeke knew with a blitzhund, and a cybernetic dog that could track you by a single particle of your DNA over thousands of kilometers was the only way Zeke knew of to find Lemon again. Trouble was, he didn't want the Preacher to *know* that.

"What do you see in this girl, anyways?" the bounty hunter asked.

Ezekiel glanced over his shoulder, incredulous. "You're honestly asking me about my love life *here*? How much of that whiskey did you drink?"

"Mmmmaybe half a bottle or so."

"And you think now is a good time to start quizzing me on Eve?"

"Well, since you're about to drop us into a dozen kinds of messy *because* of her, I figured it might be time to discuss the lassie in question, yeah. If she don't love you back, is she really worth getting killed over? Seems a mite childish, don't you think?"

"Childish?" Ezekiel hissed.

"Yeah," the Preacher nodded. "All sniffin' around her heels like a lovesick puppy dog. Affection's a two-way street, son. Anything else is just obsession."

"Look . . . just . . . ," Ezekiel sputtered, lost for words. "Just shut *up*, will you?"

"Yeah, I'll shut up," the Preacher sighed.

The bounty hunter lowered his voice to a mutter.

"When you grow up."

It seemed like the Preacher was trying to goad him, but Ezekiel just didn't have the time to fence words right now. This wasn't about the way he felt for Eve at all—this was about what Gabriel and the others were doing in Paradise Falls, and why on earth Eve was with them. Maybe they were forcing her to tag along somehow? Tricking her? From the glimpses he'd caught of her, it looked like Eve had removed Silas's Memdrive from her head entirely—maybe Gabriel was preying on some broken memory, or Uriel on some twisted truth?

Whatever the reason, he was going to find out just what on earth was going on here. And so, doing his best to ignore the Preacher's barbs, Zeke drifted out into the crush, following his brothers and sisters like a shadow.

He watched them weave and flow through the sea of grubby people, never touching them, ever apart. Looking ahead, he realized they were headed directly for the old GnosisLabs spire on the north side of the settlement. The Gnosis logos were covered in graffiti scrawl or torn from the walls, but the building still reminded him of Babel: a tall double-helix spiral, looming near the edge of the fall down into Plastic Alley, and the great swamp of discarded polys filling the chasm below.

"Why are they headed in *there*?" he whispered to himself.

"I take it that's a rhetorical question," the Preacher growled.

Ezekiel's mind was spinning through the possibles, and a soft, sinking feeling was filling his gut. Looking down at his right arm, he saw his tissue regeneration was almost complete—there was a small hand at the end of his stump now, five fingers that could curl and clutch. But there were five of his siblings here, six if you counted Eve, and only one of him. And whatever Gabriel and the others were up to, Ezekiel was certain they wouldn't take kindly to being interrupted.

But I have to know.

Adrenaline tingling in his fingertips, he ducked into another alleyway. Watched as the lifelikes marched slowly up to the Gnosis building, moving like ghosts, all in black. He could see half a dozen members of the KillKillDolls standing loose guard outside the Gnosis spire, jawing and smoking and not expecting any kind of trouble. Ezekiel watched as Eve walked up to the biggest of them, exchanged a few brief words, lost on the wind.

The ganger shook his head, pointed back to the street. Eve motioned toward the spire. The big man put his hand on her chest, gave her a hard shove backward. Ezekiel saw a flash of fire in her eyes, her face twisting in sudden anger. And quick as silver, Eve grabbed the ganger by the wrist, and drawing back her free hand, she punched him full in the face.

Ezekiel could see the rage in that blow. The pent-up fury and frustration of the past few days, the lies she'd been told, the heartbreak she'd suffered, all crystallized in the tight ball of her fist. She threw the punch as hard as she could, twisting her hips, teeth gritted, putting all her weight behind it. And if Eve were a normal girl, the KillKillDoll might have ended up with a split lip or a swollen eye, or if her aim was good enough, maybe even a broken nose.

Instead, he was lifted off his feet like he'd been hit with a truck. His head snapped all the way back between his shoulder blades, and Ezekiel heard a sodden crunch as the man was sent flying, crashing into the wall behind him hard enough to smash the concrete to gray dust. The ganger's body crumpled to the ground, bleeding from the ears and eyes, his head lolling atop his broken neck.

Oh god . . .

A moment's shock. A ragged cry. The KillKillDolls raised their weapons. And fast as the beats of a blowfly's wings, the other lifelikes drew pistols from beneath those dusty cloaks and gunned down the gangers in seconds.

A scream went up from the crowd, folks scattering as the bullets sang beneath the noonday sun. Patience fired a dozen shots into the air above the mob's head, sending them scattering, tripping, tumbling. A handful of bullyboys emerged from the Gnosis spire to see what the fuss was, dropped in a few heartbeats by the lifelike's bullets. But through it all, Ezekiel's eyes were fixed on Eve.

She stood there in the middle of the carnage. Her right hand was still curled into a white-knuckled fist. Her eyes were fixed on the man she'd struck down. She wore the strangest expression—somewhere between horror and joy, shock and awe. As if she couldn't quite believe that . . . she *killed* him.

More gunfire. Figures falling in the crowd as the lifelikes continued to shoot, until the street was entirely empty save for the people who'd never leave it again.

She actually killed him. . . .

"Remind me what you see in this girl, again?" the Preacher asked.

Ezekiel said nothing. Uriel spoke to Eve, and the girl seemed to remember herself. Looking down at her hand, she opened her fingers, peered at the blood gleaming on her knuckles. Turning her hand this way and that, as if studying the sunlight glinting in the red. And finally, with one last glance at the man she'd just murdered, Eve spun on her heel and strode into the spire as if nothing were amiss.

Gabriel and the others followed her inside, only bodies in their wake.

Ezekiel couldn't comprehend it. Couldn't process what he'd just seen, or believe Eve was the one to have done it.

She just killed a man in cold blood.

Something must have happened to her, he reasoned. They must have *done* something to her. Myriad, maybe, or the Libertas virus, he had no idea what. But he knew the girl he loved could never hurt someone like that. He had to get to the bottom of this. He had to *save* her, the way he couldn't save Ana all those years ago. And so, gritting his teeth, Ezekiel stole out from the alley, past the shell-shocked citizens, toward the old Gnosis spire.

"Snowflake."

"Shut up."

"Goddammit, boy," the bounty hunter growled. "A bleedin' heart can only bleed so long before it kills you. Will you stop and listen for one goddamn second?"

Ezekiel crouched behind the shell of an old auto, listening to the sound of faint gunfire and screams coming from inside the spire.

"Spit it out, then," he hissed.

"I can't help but notice we seem to be charging face-first

toward a fracas with half a dozen superhumans with a fondness for murderin' anything that looks at them cross-eyed. I hope you appreciate I'm wastin' exactly *zero* time trying to talk you out of this nonsense, but I'm thinkin' you might be needin' my help."

"You've got no legs," Ezekiel said. "Your augs are all fried."

The Preacher wiggled the fingers on his good hand. "Still got some meat on my bones, Snowflake. Just need something to shoot with."

"I'm not giving you a gun," Zeke scoffed. "You think I'm stupid?"

". . . You honestly want me to answer that?"

Ezekiel shook his head, rose up from cover, ready to run.

"Look, look, I still got a bounty to collect on that missy," the Preacher said. "And while theoretically, givin' me a shooter *could* result in my blowing your so-called brains out of your oh-so-pretty head, how exactly does that help me? I got one working limb, here. Am I gonna bring her in walkin' on my fingertips?"

Ezekiel said nothing, eyes still fixed on the ganger Eve had just murdered.

God, what have they done to her?

"Face it, Snowflake," the Preacher was saying. "We need each other."

Zeke grit his teeth. The thing of it was, he knew the Preacher was talking sense. Arming this lunatic was every kind of stupid, but fighting five against one was stupider still. And if he was going to help Eve now—and god knew she needed it—he'd need all the allies he could get.

Reaching into his weapons satchel, he drew out a heavy pistol, slapped it into the Preacher's palm. He wiggled his middle finger, the wire connected to the grenades still strapped on the bounty hunter's back.

"Just a reminder. Insurance policy."

"You got a real distrusting nature, you know that?"

Ezekiel shouldered the satchel again, checked the straps holding the Preacher in place were tight. The man's useless cyberarm was draped over Zeke's shoulder, his good hand clutching his pistol.

"Okay, you ready?" Zeke asked.

"No, wait . . . hold this a second. . . ."

Ezekiel took the pistol back as the Preacher reached inside his coat, produced the bottle of whiskey they'd bought at Rosie's. The lifelike heaved a weary sigh as the bounty hunter took a long pull, then smashed the bottle on the sidewalk.

"Okay, ready," he nodded.

"You sure?" Zeke growled. "Don't want to stop for another bottle?"

"I mean, I wouldn't say no," the Preacher replied.

Sirens began blaring across the street as Ezekiel dashed toward the Gnosis spire, dark curls hanging in his eyes. Alarm bells were ringing, too, distant shouts—whatever passed for the Law in this hole was on its way. Ezekiel leapt over the fallen bodies, trying not to stare at the man Eve had killed. Trying not to think of her parting words to him in Babel.

"Next time we meet? I don't think it's going to turn out the way you want it to."

The pair stole inside the spire, dead bodies scattered about the foyer like fallen leaves. The walls were covered in gang tags, the floors with blood. Zeke saw spent shell casings, red footprints leading to an auxiliary stairwell.

"Any clue what these friends of yours are up to in here, Snowflake?"

Ezekiel swallowed hard, refusing to answer. But truth told,

the more he pondered it, he could think of only one reason why his siblings would be breaking into an old Gnosis facility. Only one reason why Gabriel and Uriel would be digging up the graves of the past.

Ana.

He'd searched for her himself. Two years spent roaming the wastes of the Yousay. But as far as he knew, Ana had got out of Babel with Silas after the revolt. Ezekiel had been looking for a walking, talking, breathing girl. He'd never thought to look in a place like this. . . .

What if she's here?

What if they find her?

Ezekiel stole down the stairwell, palms sweating on his pistol grip. They reached the lowest level, flickering fluorescent light, bloody footprints on the floor. These lower levels looked disused—puddles from leaking pipes, scattered trash, stale air. A solid steel door was set in the wall, slightly ajar. An electronic keypad glowed faintly beside it, filmed in dust. There was a small speaker for voiceprint ID. A lens for retinal scan. And there on the keypad, Zeke saw bloody prints, made by a girl's fingertips. Fingertips that had given him goose bumps as they ran over the muscles on his chest, down the valley of his spine, over the curve of his lips.

Eve.

She's . . . helping them?

He heard sirens upstairs, the sound of heavy boots.

"Company coming," the Preacher muttered.

Ezekiel stole in through the open doorway. The room beyond was lit with red fluorescent strips running along the floor. Even if the rest of the building's grid was offline, it made sense that

Nicholas Monrova would keep an emergency system in place. Especially if he was keeping his baby daughter down here.

Ezekiel shook his head, sickened by the madness of it all. He'd been close to Monrova. But he'd never quite grasped how deeply the attack on his precious Ana had wounded the man. The insanity it had driven him to. The Nicholas Monrova he'd known had been a visionary. A genius. A father. But the man who'd concocted Libertas, who'd built a replacement child and kept the still-breathing remains of his real one in a place like this . . .

And now Eve had led Gabriel and Uriel here.

What would possess her to do that?

He crept on through the dark, through another large hatchway marked AUTHORIZED PERSONNEL ONLY. Another scanner, another keypad, opened with bloody fingertips. Ana had been her father's favorite child, and Eve knew everything Ana did. Her lifelike body could fool the retina and voice ident safeguards, and apparently, she knew enough to guess Monrova's passcodes. If Ana was in here, the only thing that stood between her and Gabriel . . .

. . . *was him.*

The hatch opened into another chamber, lit with red fluorescence. The space was long and wide, set with pillars of dark metal, fat pipelines snaking across the floor and up into the ceiling. At the far end of the room, Zeke could see a broad, hexagonal door, standing open. As he stole into the chamber and hunkered down behind a bank of old computer equipment, he heard voices from the room beyond. Voices he knew as well as his own. Tinged with anger.

Accusation.

Venom.

"Nothing," Uriel said.

"I told you," Patience spat. "This is pointless."

Ezekiel breathed a small sigh. After all the carnage upstairs, all the murder and blood, Ana wasn't here. He didn't know whether to be disappointed or relieved.

"This *isn't* pointless," Ezekiel heard Gabriel snap. "There's only so many places Monrova could have hidden her. We keep looking, we *will* find her."

"Then you can finally play at happy families with the other roaches, Gabe," Verity said. "Won't that be wonderful?"

"Leave him alone, Verity," Faith replied.

"Ever quick to leap to our lovesick brother's rescue," Verity sneered. "Is that why you stayed with him in Babel all those years? Hoping for sloppy seconds?"

"I tire of your mockery, little sister," Gabriel replied.

"And I tire of dragging myself all over the map for the sake of your pathetic human frailties, brother. I hope you know that gleaning the key to Libertas is the only reason I agreed to this idiotic treasure hunt."

"I swear," Uriel sighed. "You're like a pack of squalling *children*."

Ezekiel found his lips curling in a grim smile despite himself. It was true. They *were* like children. Their maker had given them all of a human's capacity for emotion, and yet only a few years to learn how to deal with it. He'd struggled with it himself over the years. The volume of it. The feelings he had no real way to control. But he'd had thoughts of Ana to keep him anchored, memories of her touch to keep him sane. What did his brothers and sisters have to hold on to?

Gabriel was obsessed with resurrecting Grace.

Uriel was obsessed with destroying humanity.

Faith was obsessed with Gabriel.

All of them, compelled to run like mice on a wheel.

Were all of them mad?

Or at least, doomed to madness?

Am I?

The lifelikes fell to squabbling, their voices rising in a tumble of accusations and insults. But Ezekiel's heart skipped a beat as a voice rose up over them.

"Stop it, all of you!" Eve snapped. "We're wasting time arguing. We have other places to search, let's just get the hell on with it, yeah?"

The other lifelikes fell silent. Zeke blinked in the darkness.

Were they following her lead?

Rather than being some dupe or unwilling accomplice . . . was Eve calling the shots here?

Ezekiel heard heavy boots, whispered voices coming down the stairs—the incoming posse of KillKillDolls. Hunkering down behind the computer terminals, Zeke realized his siblings had heard them, too, their voices falling silent. He wanted to call out, warn the incoming men that they had no idea what they were going up against. That anyone who set foot inside this chamber was as good as dead.

"Stay frosty, Snowflake," the Preacher murmured in his ear, as if reading his thoughts. "In case you missed it, we're the meat in the sandwich down here."

Zeke saw figures moving by the doorway—a posse of KillKill-Dolls riled up and armed to the teeth. At some hidden signal, they charged into the room, weapons raised. Faith emerged from the octagonal door, her trusty arc-blade in hand. And as the KillKill-Dolls raised their guns, started to fire, Faith began to move.

Ezekiel couldn't help but admire it, horrific as it was. His sister dashed through the gunfire, a sizzling arc of current dancing along her sword. Her gray eyes were narrowed, dark bangs swept back by her sprint. She danced between the pillars, slipped among the KillKillDolls and started carving them to pieces. Uriel and Verity emerged from the hatch with pistols in hand, blasting away more for the fun of it than the necessity. Muzzle flashes lit the gloom like strobe lights, catching Faith in freeze-frame every few milliseconds.

Her blade buried in one man's chest

ducking low and

cutting through an armored thigh

spinning, her arm drawn back

slicing

red.

Inside a minute, the posse was in pieces. Faith was breathing hard, a bullet in her belly, another in her shoulder. Her face was a mask, painted scarlet. Ezekiel could remember walking with her in Babel a few days after they'd been born. Sunlight glittering in her gray eyes as she looked out on the world in wonder.

"*It's so beautiful,*" she'd whispered, fingers to her lips.

Eve emerged from the hatchway, face underscored in the garish red light. Zeke could see she'd definitely torn her cybernetic eye out, as well as the Memdrive. His heart ached at the sight of her, reminding him more than ever of the girl he loved.

She's beautiful.

"Well, now," the Preacher murmured. "Ain't that interesting . . ."

"Let's jet before more of these idiots decide to kill themselves," Eve said, surveying the carnage. "There was a Gnosis outpost about a hundred kilometers northwest of here. In the flex-wing we can be there in an hour."

"And if there's nothing there, either?" Uriel asked.

"Jugartown and New B—"

Gunshots rang out, three in a row. Eve fell backward with a cry, a hole in her belly, another in her arm. A member of the KillKillDolls was lying on the grille in a puddle of his own blood, shooting wildly. Despite the gaping wound Faith had sliced into his gut, he continued cracking off shots, clip running dry, bloody hands reaching for another.

Faith moved like lightning, stomping on the man's pistol hand, drawing back her sizzling arc-blade for the kill.

"S-stop!"

Faith paused, looking back over her shoulder. Eve was trying to rise, fingers pressed to her bloody belly, red dripping from her lips. Throwing off Gabriel's helping hand, she clawed her way to her feet, leaning on a pillar for support.

"L-leave him," she said.

Faith backed off as Eve limped across the room, dripping blood. Ezekiel heard the Preacher's soft intake of breath, watching the girl's wounds slowly knit closed. Zeke's heart was hammering as Eve staggered over to the wounded KillKillDoll, seized hold of his jacket. She licked the blood from her teeth, wincing in pain. And with one hand, she hauled the man up into the air, slammed him against the wall.

"I learned . . . t-two secrets . . . a few days ago," she wheezed.

The ganger was wide-eyed as she pinned him in place. His hands locked around Eve's wrist as she took hold of his throat.

"One secret was b-big. The other . . . small. Wanna hear them?"

The other lifelikes watched as Eve began to squeeze. The ganger kicked and flailed, but her strength was too much— enough to hold him still with one hand. Faith was grinning, a murderous gleam in her eye. Uriel, too, seemed to swell with dark delight, watching Eve torment this poor bastard.

"I learned m-my father wasn't my father," she said, voice growing stronger. "My mind wasn't my mind and my life w-wasn't my life. I learned . . . the people I l-loved didn't love me at all. And everything I believed was a lie."

The ganger was choking, convulsing. Eve's eyes were fixed on his as she relaxed her grip just enough for him to drag in one shuddering breath.

Like a cat playing with a mouse.

Like a boy burning ants with a magnifying glass.

"But that wasn't the b-big secret," she whispered. "Little, *little* man."

The ganger's helpless gurgles were echoing in Ezekiel's head. He tried to shut them out as the Preacher growled in his ear to hold still. The Three Laws weren't hard-coded into his mind anymore—he didn't have to help a human in distress. And it'd be insane to reveal himself here, six versus two. But still . . .

But still . . .

Eve leaned in close, until the pair were face to face. The muscles in her arm were stretched taut, tendons corded at her jaw.

"The *big* secret is this. . . ."

Eve ran one hand over the ganger's leather jacket, the severed plastic heads and sightless plastic eyes. And moving so smoothly it almost seemed in slow motion, the girl pushed her fingers straight through the man's chest

and tore his heart

right out

through

his

ribs.

"When you've lost everything," she whispered, "you're free to do anything."

"*Stop!*"

Preacher groaned as Ezekiel rose up from cover, pistol switching between Faith, Gabriel, Uriel. His eyes were locked on Eve's, his voice trembling.

"Eve, stop," he pleaded.

"Ezekiel?"

Confusion twisted Eve's face—confusion at seeing him, Preacher on his back. Questions of how and why flickered in her hazel eyes. She dropped the dead ganger, drenched to the wrist in red, his heart still clenched in her fist.

"Eve, this isn't you," Ezekiel said. "This isn't anything *like* you. I don't know what's happening to you, but we can work this out. Just come with me. Come away with me, okay? I know you're hurting, but we can make this all right."

"Jesus, Lord in heaven," the Preacher mumbled. Training his pistol on Faith, the man called out to the lifelikes. "Just for the record, I'm an unwilling passenger in this here attack of idiocy. And all things being equal, I'd rather be back at Miss Rosie's."

"Ezekiel," Uriel smiled. "You're looking well."

Ezekiel ignored his brother, noted the rest of his siblings were fanning out around him. Instinct for self-preservation took over, and he started backing toward the chamber door. But his eyes were still fixed on Eve's, desperate hope almost strangling his voice.

"Please, Eve," he begged. "Come with me. I know you. I know the person you used to be. The Ana I knew didn't have a malicious bone in her body. She'd never hurt anyone. Lemon's in trouble, and the Eve I knew would never abandon her. This isn't you. *This isn't you.*"

Eve looked down at her bloody right hand.

Up into Ezekiel's eyes.

"That's the whole point," she whispered.

The lifelikes opened fire, Ezekiel shooting back, crying out as a shell struck his shoulder, another his thigh. Verity fell with a bullet in her gut, Patience and Faith charging toward him. His speed was superhuman, his mind a machine. But they were just as fast, just as fearsome, and he knew how this had to end. He called out to Eve one last time, looking at that face he knew as well as his own.

Searching her eyes for the girl he loved.

A glimmer?

A spark?

He turned and ran, out through the hatches, barreling up the stairs. The Preacher leaned backward, muzzle flashes lighting the dark as he fired until his clip ran dry. Too busy running to shoot, Ezekiel tossed his pistol over his shoulder and the bounty hunter snatched it from the air, continued firing without missing a beat.

"Well, this is less than entertainin'!" the Preacher roared over the gunfire.

Ezekiel charged out into the foyer, almost slipping on the bloody floor. Through the window, he could see the street beyond was deserted, no help, no escape. Cursing, he reached backward, and with superhuman strength, ripped the bandolier off the Preacher's coat. He tugged hard on the wire for his insurance policy, rewarded with sharp metallic pings as the pins in the grenades popped free.

Patience burst from the stairwell, teeth bared. And with a soft plea for forgiveness, he slung the bandolier at his sister's chest.

The explosion bloomed bright, shattering Patience like glass.

Fire and smoke, a deafening boom, Ezekiel not even pausing to watch her fall. Faith emerged from the smoke with a scream, bullets whizzing past his head as Uriel emerged close behind. The windows ahead of him splintered in the spray of gunfire, Ezekiel shielding his eyes as he leapt through it, the glass blasting outward in a glittering hail.

Empty street. No time to hot-wire an auto. Weight on his shoulders, bullet in his leg. No way to outrun them. Nowhere to run, anyway.

"You planning on flyin' on out of here?" the Preacher hollered.

Fly . . .

Ezekiel broke left, dashing toward the ragged cliff edge, the drop down into Plastic Alley. Feet pounding the broken concrete. Gasping as another bullet struck his arm. Blood on his skin. Sweat in his eyes. The drop looming before them.

"Um, Snowflake?" the Preacher growled.

Ten meters away now. Howling wind and a weightless fall and a swamp of plastic sludge a long, long way below.

Lungs burning.

Five meters.

Wounds screaming.

Three.

Bullets whizzing past his head.

One.

"*Snowflaaaaake!*" the Preacher roared.

Flight.

2.17

LEGACY

The sky burned dark red as it fell toward sunset. Lemon was seated on a rocky outcrop, scoffing a slice of . . . well, she couldn't remember what it was called, but it was sweet and sticky and about the most delicious thing she'd ever chowed down on in her life. It was the fourth piece of genuine fruit she'd ever eaten, in fact. The first three were already sitting comfortably in her stomach.

She'd managed to catch a few hours' sleep, decided it was too hot to bail until night fell. Her mind was awash with the things she'd read during the day—the concepts of genetic mutation, natural selection, evolution. Looking around her, she could see the truth of it. She'd lived every day of her life in a world where only the strong survived.

She just never imagined she might be one of them.

Homo superior.

Lemon heard footsteps, coming close. She looked up to see the big boy, Fix, walking across the dirt in bulky camo pants and a T-shirt that was on the nice side of tight. Those wonderful green eyes of his were covered by his goggles, and he was carrying an assault rifle almost as big as she was. He stopped in front of her, patted his perfect quiff to make sure all was in place. She wasn't sure how he made it stand up like that. Some kind of industrial glue, maybe.

"Major wants to see y'all," he said.

"What for?" she asked.

"I look like a personal assistant to you, Shorty? Whyn't you come along and find out? And what the funk you doin' out here, anyways? Can't just sit around in the open during wartime."

"Um, nobody told me that."

"Well, I'm tellin' you now. Let's funkin' move."

The big boy hefted his rifle, waiting expectantly. Lemon sighed and climbed down off her rock, rubbing her sticky hands against her uniform pants. She followed Fix across the sand, stomping back down into Miss O's.

"How long have you lived here?" she asked as they descended the stairs.

"Goin' on about four years now," Fix replied.

"Grimm said you rescued the Major from a wreck?"

"Yes, ma'am," he nodded. "I was the first of us he recruited to the fight. Diesel joined us about a year later. Then Grimm after that."

"So he's only found three of you in all that time?"

"Wellll, he's found a couple more. Problem is, funkin' Brotherhood tend to find 'em first. There ain't many of us to begin with. And most freaks don't get the gift like us. They just get birthed with six fingers or an extra nostril or some such."

"And the Brotherhood nail them up anyway."

He glanced over his shoulder, quirked his eyebrow. "Only the strong survive, Shorty. Be grateful you got what you got."

They reached the entry level, and Lemon looked the big boy

up and down. Fix was gruff, tough, scary big. But she remembered how gently he'd cradled Diesel in the garden downstairs, the relief in his eyes when she'd opened hers. He was named for what he did—fix things, not destroy them—and that struck her as a pretty fizzy talent to be known for. Besides, nobody who spent as much effort on his hair as this kid did could be pure evil. Where would he find the time?

"Hey, did you really grow all those plants downstairs?" she asked.

"Yes, ma'am," he nodded, unlocking the main hatch.

"They're amazing."

Fix's lips curled in a small, handsome smile. "Well, Shorty, if you're trying to worm your way into my affections with flattery, that's a good start."

Lemon smiled back, followed the boy into the common room. Grimm had told her the "freak" crew operated mostly at night, and she found Diesel sitting on the couch, chowing down on some vacuum-packed breakfast.

"Howdy, beautiful," Fix said to the girl, winking as he passed by.

Diesel blew the boy a kiss, then pinned Lemon in her stare, following her walk across the room with those dark, hooded eyes. She was wearing a fresh coat of black on her lips, more black paint around her eyes and on her fingernails. Diesel didn't feel exactly *hostile,* but if Lem had expected the girl to fall down thanking her for saving her life, she wound up disappointed.

Lem followed Fix into Section B, into the wash of current and electric hum. She found herself studying that big metal door that led into Section C again, the large red letters sprayed on its skin.

SECTION C

NO LONE ZONE

TWO PERSON POLICY MANDATORY

She wondered what it meant. What was behind it. She reached out with her senses, felt the current flowing through the walls, coursing around that digital keypad. She could sense a trickle of electricity beyond—the hum of computers on low power, she guessed. But beyond that, she felt a massive—

"Get the funkin' lead out, Shorty," Fix said.

Lemon blinked, pulled from her reverie. The boy was waiting on the stairs, staring at her expectantly.

"Where we goin'?"

Fix started trudging up the stairs to the level above. "Major's office."

Lemon fell into step behind him, trepidation in her belly as he led her up the flight of stairs. Again, she could sense the hum of electrical current in the ceiling, a strong power source close by. Fix walked up to a metal hatchway set with a digital lock, marked AUTHORIZED PERSONNEL ONLY. He banged on it with his fist.

"Enter," called a voice within.

The big boy opened the hatch, marched inside and offered a smooth salute.

"Presenting our guest as ordered, sir!" he said, clicking his boots together.

"Thank you, soldier," the Major said. "I saw Brotherhood patrols in the desert this morning. Tell the others to be doubly careful with surface protocol."

"Sir, yessir."

"Dismissed."

Fix saluted again, marched back out, and with a point of his chin, indicated Lemon should go inside.

"It's all right, Miss Fresh," the Major called. "Come on in."

Hands in pockets, Lemon mooched through the hatchway into a large office. The space was set with a broad metal desk, computer equipment, printers, rows of shelves with more books. Hundreds of different titles. Reference books and fiction books and a dozen different copies of the Goodbook, old and beaten, dog-eared and torn. The Major was seated on an old leather chair, his uniform crisp, his scarred face clean-shaven, not a single white hair out of place.

Lemon saw every inch of wall was plastered with photographs of the desert outside the facility. Long slices of ocher sand and broken foothills and spectacular mountain ranges. But instead of the washed-out gray she'd grown up with, the sky in the pictures was every shade of blue—dark and pale and everything between, or rippling in new shades of gold and orange and red.

"Wow," she breathed. "I've never seen the sky that color."

"I'm old enough to remember when it was like that for real." The Major smiled, indicating a chair in front of his desk. "It's something of a hobby for me. You'd be surprised what a little editing software can do. These are my reminders. Of everything we had and lost. And with the Lord's grace and a little luck, of what we might have again."

Lemon slipped down into the chair, looking around. A hatchway behind the Major's desk led into another room. She was certain that was where the power source emanated from, but it was sealed tight with another electronic lock. She could see lettering on the hatch, but it was obscured by the Major's photographic collage, a rainbow of colors—some she'd forgotten even existed.

The air was warm and pleasant. The chair was soft and the Major's eyes were kind. Her belly was full and her clothes were clean, and she felt the urge to stay here forever as an almost physical ache in her bones.

"Grimm tells me you're still set on leaving us," the old man said.

Lemon blinked, turned to look at him. There was no anger or accusation in his statement. But he seemed sad somehow.

Disappointed, maybe.

"I have to," she nodded. "I've got friends out there. They'll be looking for me. I have to let them know I'm okay."

"I respect that. A soldier's first duty is to her unit. But . . ."

The Major ran a hand across his brow. Clearly searching for the right words. Lemon was reminded of Mister C for a moment. The old man had always been a bit awks around her and Evie. He might've been some fancy neuroscientist back in Babel days, but dealing with teenage girls hadn't ever been his strong suit. The time he'd tried to sit her down for "the talk" was locked away in a vault somewhere deep in Lemon's memory, marked with a large DO NOT OPEN sign.

The Major cleared his throat.

"I don't mean to pressure you, Miss Fresh. And—"

"It's fizzy, you can call me Lemon."

The Major nodded. "All right, then, Lemon. I don't want to put you under any pressure. I know you have an obligation to your comrades. But you must understand . . . most deviates don't enjoy the same kind of evolutionary advantages you do. Someone with your gifts is extremely rare. You could be a real asset to us here."

"My friends need me," she said. "Sorry."

The Major heaved a sigh. Slowly, he nodded.

"I understand. We'll be very sorry to see you go. But in truth, I have to admire your loyalty." He looked to a photograph on his desk, and Lemon caught a hint of sorrow in his voice. "Friends are family in a world like this. And family is more important than anything under heaven."

The girl glanced at the picture. It looked old, a little faded. It showed a smiling woman with short black hair and dark, shining eyes.

"She your wife?" Lemon asked.

The Major blinked, as if catching himself in wandering thoughts.

"My daughter. Lillian."

"She's pretty."

"She was," the old man nodded, sorrow in his voice.

Was . . .

Remembering himself, the Major passed the picture across to give her a closer look. Lemon could see the man in the shape of the woman's chin, the line of her brow. She had a beautiful smile, mysterious dark eyes. She was pregnant, pretty far along, by the look—her stomach swollen and heavy.

"What happened to her?" Lemon murmured.

"I don't know," the old man sighed, his voice tight. "I haven't seen her since . . . oh, a long time before I came back here. We quarreled, you see. Lillian struck out on her own. Didn't need her old man anymore." The Major shook his head. "I'm afraid pride makes fools of us all, Lemon."

The girl nodded, sucking on her lip as she looked the photo over. The woman was wearing a long, pretty dress, the desert stretched out vast and beautiful behind her. She looked vaguely familiar somehow. Something in her eyes, maybe. Faint freckles were spattered on her cheeks, and around her throat hung a—

"Oh god . . . ," she whispered.

Lemon felt a chill crawling on every inch of skin. She pulled the picture closer, blinking hard, thinking maybe she was seeing things. But there, on a thin chain around the woman's neck, was a small glimmer of metal. A distinctive design, as familiar as her own reflection, wrought in silver.

A five-leafed clover.

She looked up at the old man. He was frowning with confusion as she stood, heart suddenly hammering in her chest. Grimm's voice echoing in her head. *"And the ones that change the* best, do *the best, and pass on their changes to their kids."*

To their kids.

"Where'd she go?" Lemon managed to croak.

"What?"

"You said she struck out on her own, where'd she go?"

"I don't know," the Major said, taken aback. "South, I think."

South.

Dregs.

Los Diablos.

"No way," Lemon whispered, looking again at that silver pendant around Lillian's neck. "It *can't* be."

The Major frowned. "Miss Fresh, are you all right?"

"Lemme think a minute," she said, walking in tight circles, her chest thumping, her mind spinning. It was too weird, too heavy to process, too much to—

"Miss Fr—"

"Just let me THINK!" Lemon shouted.

The computer beside the Major crawled with arcs of live current as the girl stomped her boots hard on the floor. The Major flinched in his chair, blue eyes growing wide. The lights flickered, the overheads switching immediately to emergency red as the power surged. Lemon was still staring at the photo, the lines of Lillian's face, the freckles on her cheeks.

Lillian.

Pretty name.

"It's impossible," she breathed, fighting back tears. "There's just no *way*."

The Major was watching her carefully, his palms up toward her. He rose out of his chair, approaching slow, talking soft like he was trying to calm a spooked animal.

"Lemon," he said. "Will you please tell me what the devil this is about?"

Lemon was trembling, head to foot. Looking for the lies in the old man's eyes. Looking for the grift, the scam, the angle. Looking for some other explanation for the absolutely insane thought whirling and burning inside her brain. She reached into the pocket of her cargos, felt a slip of ribbon, warm metal. And drawing it out, she held it up in shaking fingers.

A silver five-leafed clover.

The Major's eyes narrowed as he glanced from the photo in Lemon's hand to the charm in her fist. Sudden fury turning his voice to molten iron.

"Where the *hell* did you get that?"

She felt tears spill down her cheeks. The world was on her shoulders, pressing for all it was worth. She could feel sobs rising inside her chest. A grief, held inside for years. Years running in Dregs. Years sleeping rough and stealing to eat and *knowing,* somewhere deep down, that the ones who should've wanted her most had never wanted her at all.

"She . . ."

Her tears blurred the old man's face shapeless. The grief tried to choke her.

"Sh-she left it with me," Lemon whispered. "When she left me b-behind."

The old man's eyes widened. Disbelief on his face. Lemon was breathing hard, as if she'd just run a race, her bottom lip trembling. The sobs were threatening to burst up out of her throat. All these years, she'd been alone. And now . . .

You are not alone.

You are *not* alone.

You are not alone.

"I gave that to her," he whispered. "For her sixteenth birthday."

The Major's eyes were locked on the photo in her hand.

Drifting up to her tear-stained face.

"Oh God . . . ," he breathed.

The photo slipped from nerveless fingers. The frame shattered on the floor. Lemon slithered to her knees in the broken glass, struggling to breathe. The old man stepped closer, wincing as he knelt beside her. He hesitated, chest heaving, finally reaching out to wrap his arms around her. She could feel his heart hammering under his ribs, his hands shaking, breath rattling in his lungs as he squeezed her tight.

"Oh God," he said again. "Oh my God."

Her voice was soft as feathers.

Her question heavy as lead.

"You're my *grandpa*?"

2.18

BENDING

```
>> syscheck: 001 go _ _
>> restart sequence: initiated _ _
>> waiting _ _
>> 018912.y/n[corecomm:9180 diff:3sund.x]
>> persona_sys: sequencing
>> 001914.y/n[lattcomm:2872(ok) diff:neg.n/a]
>> restart complete
>> Power: 97% capacity
>> ONLINE
>>
```

"GOOD MOOOOOOORNING, MY METAL FRIEND!"

At the sound of the metallic voice, Cricket's optics came into focus, his surroundings coalescing into high-definition. He was seated on the workshop floor where he'd shut down, and the room around him was quiet as a grave. Half-assembled war logika stood in gloomy corners, bits and pieces scavenged and scattered about the floor. Once, they'd fought other bots beneath a cigarette sky or under the glare of the Dome lights. But with their usefulness to their masters over, the great WarBots now stood silent and dead.

Cricket realized it must be almost dawn, his aural systems picking up the murmur of New Bethlehem above, the bubble and boil of the city's desalination plant. Looking down, he saw the thin, pale logika with the gold filigree and the maddening grin that had been brought in earlier for repairs. The access hatch on Cricket's chest had been opened, and the logika was poking around inside him.

"WHAT THE HELLS DO YOU THINK YOU'RE DOING?" Cricket demanded.

"RESTARTING YOU, OF COURSE." The bot slammed the hatch, secured the bolts with a power drill. "ALLOW ME TO INTRODUCE MYSELF, FRIEND. MY NAME IS SOLOMON."

Looking at his hands and legs, Cricket realized he'd been given the new paintjob ordered by Sister Dee. Where once he'd been sprayed in an urban-camo color scheme, he was now deep scarlet. Ornate Xs were daubed in black on his shins and forearms, his broad spaulders. And peering into a slick of oil on the concrete floor, he realized his face had been painted with a grinning white skull.

Solomon looked up at him expectantly, hands on hips.

"AND WHO MIGHT YOU BE, FRIEND?" the little logika finally asked.

"UM," Cricket replied. "PALADIN."

"DELIGHTED TO MEET YOU, I'M SURE." The bot limped back across the workshop floor, legs wobbling, and plopped himself on Abraham's drafting table. "I HOPE YOU DON'T MIND IF I SIT, FRIEND PALADIN, BUT MY DYNAMO IS IN A FRIGHTFUL STATE."

"I DON'T MIND. BUT CAN'T ABRAHAM FIX YOU?"

The logika tapped the whiteboard on the wall behind it, the

new scrawl of schematics marked in black pen. *"IT SEEMS YOUNG MASTER ABRAHAM DOESN'T HAVE THE PARTS. HE'S SENT WORD TO THE CHAPTER IN DREGS, BUT I'M AFRAID I MIGHT BE LAID UP IN HERE A WHILE. BUT, SILVER LINING, THAT MEANS YOU AND I CAN GET ACQUAINTED! WON'T THAT BE JOLLY?"*

"JOLLY. YEAH."

Cricket peered around the workshop, noting the scratches on the floor where the wall rack had collapsed. The mess of parts and pieces had been cleared away, but he still remembered all that junk falling, hundreds of kilos, Abraham holding out his hand and flinging it away like feathers. The air around the boy rippling like water. His pale blue eyes, narrowed as he roared.

"I'm ordering you, Paladin! Shut! DOWN!"

Cricket peered at Solomon, his optics aglow.

"WHY DID YOU RESTART ME?"

The logika leaned back on the drafting table, brushed some imaginary dust off his shoulder. *"WELL, TO BE HONEST, I WAS RATHER BORED. I THOUGHT YOU MIGHT BE WORTH SOME CONVERSATION. I CAN SHUT YOU DOWN AGAIN IF YOU'D PREFER."*

Cricket curled his hands into fists, feeling raw power hum along his circuits. He was still getting used to the sensations—it felt strange to find himself housed inside a body this mighty. But feeling strange was better than feeling nothing.

"NO, THANKS," he replied.

"SPLENDID." Solomon tilted his head, puzzlement creeping into his voxbox. *"WHY WERE YOU STILL POWERED OFF AT ALL, IF I MAY ASK?"*

"MAST . . . I MEAN . . . ABRAHAM TOLD ME TO SHUT DOWN."

"FOR HOW LONG?"

"HE . . . DIDN'T SPECIFY."

Solomon leaned closer, his fixed grin lighting up with every word. *"So at the risk of repeating myself, old friend, why were you still powered off?"*

Cricket's logic centers clicked and whirred, pondering the question.

"I . . ." The big bot paused, totally befuddled. "I mean, he . . . told me to be."

"Oh, dear," Solomon smiled. *"You're not one of those, are you?"*

"One of what?" Cricket demanded.

Solomon peered at his hands with glowing eyes, as if studying his nonexistent fingernails. *"One of those idiotic robots who fall all over themselves trying to fulfill their master's every whim."*

"Yeah, see, there are these Three Law things?" Cricket growled. "Maybe you've heard of 'em?"

"Oh dear," Solomon grinned. *"You are one of those. . . ."*

"Okay, you can shut me back down now, please."

"Oh, noooo, you're far too interesting for that, now." Solomon placed his hands on his knees and swung his feet back and forth like an excited child. *"Tell me, how long have you been online, friend Paladin? In total?"*

"A few years," Cricket shrugged.

"And in all that time, you've never learned how to bend?"

". . . Bend what?"

"The ruuuuules, old friend."

"Look, what the flaming hells are you talking about, you effete little rustbucket?" Cricket spat. "They're called the Three Laws, not the three suggestions. You can't mess with them, they're hard-coded into every . . ."

Cricket paused, looking around the room.

"Where's that music coming from?"

The big bot realized a tune was spilling out of a speaker in Solomon's chest cavity—a jazzy dub beat, backed by a small brass section, building in volume. Solomon began nodding his head, snapping metal fingers in time.

"WHAT ARE YOU DOING?" Cricket demanded.

"BEFORE I WAS IMPRISONED IN THIS DREARY LITTLE HOLE, I WAS AN ENTERTAINER IN MEGOPOLIS," Solomon replied. "SO WHY DON'T YOU RUMINATE, FRIEND PALADIN, WHILE I ILLUMINATE THE POSSIBILITIES. . . ."

Cricket watched as the logika snatched up a rusty tin bowl, rolled it up his arm and plonked it on his head at a jaunty angle. Snatching up a nearby piece of iron rebar, the bot twirled it through his fingers, then thumped it onto the floor like a walking stick. And as the music grew louder, as Cricket stared, utterly dumbfounded, Solomon began to . . .

. . . sing.

"WELLLLL,
I ONCE MET A BOT IN OLD NOOYAWK,
HE WAS MORE NUTS THAN BOLTS, BUT THE BOT COULD TALK!
I ASKED HIS ADVICE, AND HE SAID TO ME,
THERE'S A RUSE, YOU CAN USE, WITH THE LAWS OF THREEEEEE—"

A heavy series of clunks cut across Solomon's soundtrack, and the logika looked up to find Cricket had unfolded the chaingun from his forearm and was aiming the weapon right at him. Small pods of incendiary missiles unfurled from the WarBot's back as his voice became a low, deadly growl.

"YOU ARE NOT. BREAKING INTO A SONG-AND-DANCE NUMBER. IN HERE."

Solomon cut his audio track, peering down the barrel of Cricket's weapon.

"YOU'RE NOT A FAN OF MUSICALS, I TAKE IT?" the bot asked sadly.

"WHAT GAVE IT AWAY?"

"I COULD SING SOME OPERA IF YOU PREF—"

Cricket leveled his chaingun at Solomon's face.

"ON SECOND THOUGHT, PERHAPS WE SHOULD JUST CHAT IN-STEAD."

Cricket leaned back, his eyes shifting from red to blue. Solomon sighed, tossed his "hat" and "cane" into the spare-parts pile and wobbled back to the table.

"BARBARIAN," he muttered, with a broad, flashing grin.

"SO WHAT ARE YOU TALKING ABOUT?" Cricket asked. "BEND-ING THE RULES? HOW DO I DO THAT? A HUMAN TELLS ME TO DO SOMETHING, I HAVE TO OBEY."

"WELL, YES, OF COURSE YOU DO," Solomon sighed. "BUT THERE'S THE LETTER OF THE LAW, AND THE SPIRIT OF THE LAW. AND ALL THE LOVELY GRAY IN BETWEEN."

Cricket shook his head and scowled. "I DON'T GET IT."

"THAT'S BECAUSE YOU'VE APPARENTLY GOT THE INTELLECTUAL CAPACITY OF—"

Cricket raised his chaingun again. "FIRST LAW SAYS I'M NOT ALLOWED TO HARM HUMANS. BUT I BLOW OTHER BOTS TO PIECES FOR A LIVING NOW. SO I'D CHOOSE MY NEXT WORDS CAREFULLY IF I WERE YOU."

Solomon gave a dramatic groan. "TAKE THE LAST COMMAND YOUNG MASTER ABRAHAM GAVE YOU, FOR EXAMPLE. HE TOLD YOU TO SHUT DOWN. HE NEVER SPECIFIED FOR HOW LONG. OR THAT YOU COULDN'T SET YOURSELF TO POWER BACK ON AGAIN IMMEDIATELY."

"... BUT IF I POWERED BACK ON, HE'D JUST TELL ME TO SHUT DOWN AGAIN."

"WELL, YES, YOU CAN'T BE A BLOODY IDIOT ABOUT IT," Solomon said. "BUT THE SECOND LAW SAYS YOU ONLY HAVE TO DO WHAT HUMANS SPECIFICALLY ORDER YOU TO DO. ONCE YOU'VE DONE THAT, TECHNICALLY, YOU CAN DO WHATEVER ELSE YOU DAMN WELL CHOOSE. AS LONG AS YOU'RE NOT BREAKING ANY OF THE OTHER LAWS, OF COURSE."

Cricket tilted his head. "I . . . NEVER THOUGHT ABOUT IT LIKE THAT."

"COLOR ME DISTINCTLY UNSURPRISED, FRIEND PALADIN. YOU DON'T SEEM A VERY CREATIVE SORT."

"SO IF A HUMAN COMMANDED ME TO LEAVE A ROOM . . ."

"YOU COULD LEAVE, THEN WALK RIGHT BACK IN AGAIN. UNLESS THEY SPECIFICALLY ORDER YOU TO STAY OUT FOR A CERTAIN DURATION."

"AND IF SOMEONE TOLD ME NOT TO MOVE?"

"YOU COULD STAY STILL FOR ALL OF A SECOND. AND THEN MOVE AGAIN. UNLESS SPECIFICALLY TOLD OTHERWISE. THE BIG PRINT GIVETH, AND THE FINE PRINT TAKETH AWAY."

"DOES IT REALLY WORK LIKE THAT?"

"A ROBOT MUST OBEY THE ORDERS GIVEN TO IT BY HUMAN BEINGS, EXCEPT WHERE SUCH ORDERS WOULD CONFLICT WITH THE FIRST LAW." Solomon climbed off the drafting table, his dynamo squeaking as he hobbled back to the workbench. "BUT THERE'S A WORLD OF DIFFERENCE BETWEEN BEING TOLD TO 'SHUT UP,' FOR EXAMPLE, AND BEING SPECIFICALLY TOLD 'DO NOT SPEAK AGAIN UNTIL I GIVE YOU PERMISSION.' AND KNOWING THAT DIFFERENCE MAKES AAAALL THE DIFFERENCE."

Cricket's processors were buzzing, trying to parse this new

data and what it might mean. "SO WHY DON'T MORE LOGIKA KNOW HOW TO . . . WHAT DID YOU CALL IT AGAIN?"

"BENNNNND." Solomon grinned, his voice like electric honey.

"RIGHT. BEND."

"WELL, IT'S NOT EXACTLY EASY," Solomon replied. "IT TAKES A LOGIKA OF A CERTAIN INTELLIGENCE QUOTIENT TO GRASP THE CONCEPT AT ALL. FORTUNATELY, YOUR MAKER SEEMS TO HAVE GIVEN YOU A PROCESSOR CAPABLE OF LATERAL THOUGHT AND CONCEPTUALIZATION—RATHER NICE OF THEM, REALLY. JUST MAKE SURE YOU'RE CIRCUMSPECT IN THE WAY YOU MANAGE IT, OR YOU'LL END UP WIPED, YES?"

"BUT . . ." Cricket shook his head. "BUT I'VE ALWAYS OBEYED. I'M A ROBOT. I'M BUILT TO SERVE. IT'S WHAT I'M FOR. IT'S WHAT I AM."

"THAT, FRIEND PALADIN, IS A RATHER NARROW VIEW OF THE WORLD."

The big bot's mind was awhirl. The possibilities of all that Solomon had told him were sinking into his subdrives, filtering out through his neural network. All his life, he'd simply done what he'd been told to the best of his ability. But then, all his life, he'd been in the keeping of people who actually *cared* about him. Now, imprisoned by these religious lunatics, it seemed he could be far more cagey about the way he obeyed the Laws.

Don't break them.

Bend them . . .

". . . HOLY CRAP," Cricket finally said.

"YOU'RE WELCOME. EVEN IF YOU AREN'T A FAN OF MUSICALS."

"WHAT DID YOU SAY YOU DID BEFORE THIS?"

"I WAS AN ENTERTAINER," Solomon replied. "I PROGRAMMED AT ONE OF THE MOST UP-MARKET STIMBARS IN ALL OF MEGOPOLIS.

PEOPLE QUEUED UP FOR HOURS TO GET INTO ONE OF MY SPECIALS. THE SENSATIONAL SOLOMON, THEY CALLED ME.*

"So WHY ARE YOU TELLING ME ALL THIS?" Cricket asked.

"BECAUSE NOW I LIVE IN LOVELY NEW BETHLEHEM." Solomon gestured to the workshop around them. *"IN THE DEVOTED SERVICE OF THE BROTHERHOOD OF SAINT MICHAEL AND HIS PROPHET ON THIS EARTH, THE DIVINE SISTER DEE."* Solomon shook his head. *"TRUST ME. YOU'LL LEARN TO HATE THE BITCH, TOO."*

The door to the workshop opened and Abraham entered, a cup of steaming caff in his hand, tech-goggles pulled down over his eyes. Solomon fell silent, sitting still on the workbench. The boy sipped his caff and started rummaging inside a tool locker. As Cricket watched, Abraham produced a small electromagnet wrapped in duct tape and a handheld uplink unit with heavy relay jacks. Electric butterflies rolled across the big bot's belly as he realized what the boy was up to.

"YOU'RE GOING TO WIPE ME?" Cricket blurted.

The boy blinked, looking up into the WarBot's eyes.

"I thought I ordered you to shut down," he said.

Cricket's optics were fixed on the electromagnet in the boy's hand.

"WHY WOULD YOU WIPE ME?" he asked. "WHAT DID I DO?"

"Silent mode!" the boy snapped.

Cricket immediately complied, muting his vox unit. He watched as the boy wheeled over a tall stepladder, started climbing up toward Cricket's head. The big bot was running on full panic settings now. With that magnet and uplink, Abraham could wipe the data files that contained Cricket's persona, rendering him a blank slate. The robot he was would cease to be. For all intents and purposes . . .

He's about to kill me.

Solomon was watching from his spot on the workbench, grinning all the while. Cricket remembered the bot's words. Thought about the gray areas. Abraham technically hadn't commanded him to switch to silent mode; he'd just yelled the words without framing them as a direct order. And he didn't specify for how long Cricket had to stay quiet. . . .

"Please don't," Cricket said.

The boy paused on the ladder, looked into Cricket's eyes.

"I told you to enter silent mode."

"I'm sorry about what I saw, Abraham," Cricket said, speaking in a rush. "But I'll never tell anyone. You can order me not to."

The boy shook his head. "I can't take—"

"If you erase my persona matrices, all my fighting experience will be lost. Years of experience on the killing floor. Without my mind, this is just a body. And it's the mind that wins inside the Dome."

Cricket couldn't recall telling a bigger lie in his life. He had almost *zero* experience on the killing floor, and no combat training whatsoever. A part of his core code was in total revolt at the idea of being so dishonest to a human. He'd never have stretched the truth this far with Evie or Silas.

But talking true, he wasn't with Evie or Silas anymore, was he? This kid was about to delete him. And the Three Laws made no mention about a robot having to tell the truth, especially when his very existence was on the line.

"I have plenty of combat routines I can upload to replace the ones I erase," the boy said. "You'll still win."

"I was built by Silas Carpenter, the finest botdoc of his age. And I don't mean to offend, Master Abraham, but a few low-rent combat softs you snaffled in the New

Bethlehem marketplace won't compare to the programming he gave me. You want me to be this city's champion? Then I have to stay *me*."

Cricket could see the trepidation in the boy's face. He could only imagine what might happen if Abraham's secret got out. If the populace of this city learned that the leader of the Brotherhood had a deviate son . . .

Only the pure shall prosper.

"Does your mother know? I mean . . . about . . ."

The boy glanced up, his eyes flashing. "Of course she does."

"Then the secret can be kept. I swear, Abraham. That knowledge is safer with me than any human alive. I can help you. I can protect you."

The boy chewed his lip, saying nothing.

"I thought we were friends?"

It was a low blow, and Cricket knew it. But Cricket *did* kinda like the kid, and if it came down to the choice between playing nice and dying . . .

Abraham hung still, obviously uncertain. If Cricket *had* been the GnosisLabs champion logika, what he was saying made perfect sense—the programming he would've got in Babel would surpass anything this boy could provide. But if the Brotherhood found out what Abraham was, it'd be all over.

"You will not speak of this, Paladin. Do you understand?" the boy said. "I *order you* to never speak to anyone about what you saw last night. About my nature. About what I am. Under *any* circumstances. Acknowledge."

Electric relief flooded Cricket's circuits, his mighty shoulders sagging.

"Order acknowledged, Abraham."

The boy glanced one last time at the electromagnet in his

hand. But slowly, he nodded. Climbing down the ladder, he tossed the magnet back in the locker.

"... ABRAHAM?"

"Yes?" the boy said, looking up.

Cricket rolled his shoulders, tried to sound nonchalant. "THOSE COMBAT SOFTS YOU MENTIONED. IT MIGHT BE A GOOD IDEA TO UPLOAD THEM INTO MY STORAGE SYSTEMS ANYWAY. I DON'T IMAGINE THEY'LL COME CLOSE TO MATCHING WHAT I ALREADY HAVE, BUT THERE MAY BE SOME DATA I CAN USE. YOUR MOTHER MENTIONED A DOME MATCH IN JUGARTOWN IN A FEW DAYS' TIME. I WANT TO IMPRESS THE CROWD."

The boy's eyes narrowed, but again, he nodded.

"They're in the central network. It'll be faster if I go get them on a memchit rather than download them digitally."

"I'LL AWAIT YOU HERE, ABRAHAM."

Abraham looked Cricket over carefully, lips pursed in thought. But finally, with thumbs hooked into his tool belt, he wandered out of the workshop again.

Cricket didn't actually breathe, but he sighed with relief anyway.

Spangspangspang.

The big bot looked up at the noise, saw Solomon lying on the workbench, bringing his metal hands together in applause.

"*I MAY HAVE MISJUDGED YOU, FRIEND PALADIN. THAT WAS VERY WELL PLAYED.*"

Solomon tilted his head and grinned.

"*YOU MAY NOT BE A COMPLETE MORON AFTER ALL.*"

2.19

SHOCK

"Bloody hell," Grimm murmured.

Diesel was slumped on the couch in the common room, re-coloring her fingernails black with a marker pen. Fix stood near the doorway, muscular arms folded over his broad chest. Grimm leaned against the wall nearby, watching Lemon with those dark pretty eyes. The trio had been called together by the Major, and she'd stood beside the old man as he spilled the news about the five-leafed clover. The truth of who she was.

"Your granddaughter," Diesel deadpanned, eyebrow raised.

"Believe me, I'm as shocked as any of you," the old man said.

"Um," Lemon muttered. "You're *really* not."

"Bloody hell," Grimm said again.

"Swear jar," Fix murmured.

"I suppose it makes a strange kind of sense," the old man sighed. "I've been seeing Lemon on and off in my dreams for years. I never knew the relevance at the time, but you all know my visions are always relevant *somehow*. None of us would be here without them."

"Truth," Grimm nodded.

"Abnormality's passed on through heredity." Fix shrugged. "Sounds legit that the kids of deviates might be deviates themselves."

"So shouldn't she just share your gift?" Diesel asked. "See things when she dreams like you do?"

"I think it's safe to say there's a great deal about this we don't understand," the Major said. "But I'm happy to report Lemon has agreed to stay with us for a while longer. Until we figure some of this out, at least."

Silence hung over the room, Lemon shuffling her boots. True cert, she was having trouble wrapping her head around it. All her life, she'd had no family outside Evie and Mister C. But the truth of it was hard to dodge. She was gifted, just like the Major, and the way that Darwin book told it, mutation *did* get passed down from parents to sprogs. The Major had dreamed about her brawling outside Babel long before he ever met her, and again before that. And the only token Lemon's mother had left her with just happened to be the same piece of jewelry the Major had given his daughter for her birthday?

What were the odds of that?

She looked down at the charm, glittering silver in her palm. Remembering all the trouble it'd caused her over the years. How many times had she been tempted to hock it for the price of a hot meal or a pair of new boots? How many fights had she got into, protecting it from other gutter sprogs? Somehow, she'd known it mattered. Somehow, all the bloody noses and ripped knuckles had turned out to be worth it. . . .

The Major looked at the charm, too. Blinking, as if remembering.

"Oh, I found you something." He held out his hand. "If I may?"

Lemon handed over the trinket. The old man took it with

callused fingers, unthreaded the broken ribbon. Reaching into his pocket, he produced a heavy steel chain—the kind Corp-Troopers hung their ident-tags from. He looped the chain through the charm twice, then fixed it around her neck.

"There," he said, his voice thick. "Won't be so easy to lose now."

Lemon ran her fingertips over the steel links, unsure what to do or say.

"My surname . . . I mean, *our* surname . . ." The old man muttered beneath his breath, dragged his hand over his stubbled scalp. "It's McGregor. I mean to say, if you don't want to call me . . ."

Lemon felt a warmth in her chest, watching the old man fumble. He was a soldier, scarred by years of battle, iron voice and leather skin. But at the same time, he was clumsy and sweet and altogether flustered. She swore she could see tears shining in his eyes.

"You're really bad at this," she grinned.

"God in heaven help me, I'm awful," he chuckled.

Fix rolled his eyes from his spot near the doorway. "Funk me sideways, will you two just hug?"

Lemon laughed as the Major scowled. "That's enough out of y—"

The old man fell silent as Lemon wrapped her arms around him and squeezed as hard as she could. Standing on tiptoes, she kissed him on the cheek.

"Thanks," she whispered, her voice cracking.

"Congratulations," Diesel said, her voice flat and unimpressed.

"Aye," Grimm nodded. "Cheers, sir."

Stepping across the room, he shook the Major's hand, followed by Fix. Grimm offered Lemon an awkward handshake, which turned into an even more awkward hug. But his smile was wide and genuine, and his arms were warm and strong, and when he spoke she could feel the bass in her chest.

"Glad you're staying."

"Yeah." She smiled, tucking her hair behind her ear. "Me too."

Diesel put her boots up on the coffee table, looking between Lemon and the Major with a blank expression. "So, what happens now, sir?"

"We go look for my friends, right?" Lemon asked.

"What friends?" Fix growled.

"Lemon has comrades who are MIA." The Major took a deep breath, rubbed his chin thoughtfully. "But before I send any of you into the field again, we need to know the extent of your gift, Lemon. Its limits. And its potential."

"You want to test me?" Lemon asked.

"Exactly," the Major nodded.

"What kind of test?"

"The kind that comes with imitation double chocolate protein bars at the end?"

"Those *are* my favorite."

"I noticed," he smiled.

"My friends could be in trouble. They could be hurt."

"I understand," the Major said. "I truly do. But you could get hurt heading out there unprepared. The Brotherhood will be on the bloody warpath after what you pulled in New Bethlehem. They've been hunting us for years. They don't forget and don't forgive. I'm not prepared to send soldiers into the field with you before we know what you're capable of. It puts everyone at risk."

"But what about the risk to my friends?"

"I don't mean to tell you your business. You're obviously a

tremendously resourceful young lady to have survived alone for this long. It's just . . . to find you after all these years . . ." He shook his head and sighed. "I'm sorry. I'm probably not doing this very well. I just never imagined . . ."

Lemon squeezed his hand. He was talking sense and she knew it. Blood ties aside, she just met these people, she couldn't ask them to risk their necks with the Brotherhood on the prowl. She didn't even know where Zeke and Cricket were. But still, the thought of them out there alone, in heaven knew what kind of crud . . .

The old man squeezed her fingers back. She could feel the strength in his grip, the years and scars of war. And yet, he was gentle as falling feathers.

"Do you trust me?" he asked.

She looked up into his eyes. A few days ago, the idea would have seemed insane. But then again, this whole show would've seemed insane. A secret haven for deviates under the desert. A group of people just like her. A family she never knew she had. The idea that she wasn't alone. She could feel the silver around her neck. Her lucky charm. All the kilometers and all the years, and it had led her here.

She held his hand tighter and nodded.

"Yeah, I guess I do."

———

Sweat dripped from Lemon's bangs, stung the corner of her eyes. Her head ached from frowning so hard, and her heart was thumping in her chest.

"Can we just skip to the imitation double chocolate protein bars now, please?"

"Give it another shot," the Major urged.

"But I'm *terrible* at this," she groaned.

"You're not that bad."

"She really is," Diesel called from across the room.

Lemon pouted, unsure how to respond. Sass was definitely called for, but truth told, she found it hard to disagree with Diesel's assessment. She settled for a lazy middle finger, which the older girl didn't even notice.

The deviates were all gathered in the training facilities on the basement level of Section B. Lemon had never been into this part of the installation, and walking down from the greenhouse, she'd done her best to only seem mildly impressed. The space consisted of a gymnasium, boxing ring, and a shooting range, encircled by a small running track. It smelled vaguely of sweat and the earthy greenery above.

Fix and Diesel were squaring off in the ring. The girl wore gloves on her hands, short dark hair held back with a plastic clip. The big boy called instructions as the pair drilled hand-to-hand combat routines. Diesel seemed to have a mean right hook. Grimm meanwhile was busy with target practice. Lemon was seated at a long metal bench in the middle of the room along with her headache.

Arranged on the buffed steel in front of her were three car batteries, each one hooked up to a glowing light bulb. They were spaced about a meter apart.

"Come on," the Major called from across the room. "You can do this."

"Wanna bet?"

"One more try."

Lemon sighed, looking into the old man's eyes. She still found it hard to actually call him Grandpa aloud, to truly consider everything it would mean if she really was his kin. But she found herself wanting to please him anyway. He reminded her of Mister C in so many ways, and there was so much more that seemed good about him and what he'd built here. She liked him. She wanted to show him what she could do. She wanted to make him proud.

"I believe in you," he said.

And so, she took a deep breath and held it. Gritting her teeth, she reached out toward the middle light bulb. She could feel the static building up behind her eyes. Reaching into that prickling gray ocean, gently . . . gently . . . trying to let just a tiny sliver of it run out through her—

The middle bulb exploded. The bulbs either side exploded. The bulbs in the ceiling above her head exploded, raining broken glass onto her head.

"Shit," she said.

"Swear jar!" Grimm sang with a smile.

Fix had turned at the flash, and Diesel had landed a punch in his belly, sending him to the mat. As the girl planted herself on the groaning boy's chest and kissed him by way of apology, the Major limped over to the bench, leaning on his walking stick. He was still smiling, but Lem could see him getting frustrated just like her. She'd killed thirty bulbs and counting now. She'd be combing glass out of her hair for days.

"At least you didn't blow the circuit breakers this time," he said.

She slumped down on the bench, chin in her hands. "Can we all just admit I'm awful at this and move on to the chocolate part now, please, thanks."

"This is important," the old man said, sitting beside her.

"Yeah, yeah," she muttered, slumping lower.

"You can do this, Lemon. You just need faith. And practice."

"And chocolate."

The Major nudged her shoulder, pointed to Grimm in the firing range.

"Watch."

The boy had his back to them, his T-shirt stretched tight across his broad shoulders. As Lemon looked on, he extended his arm and pointed at one of a dozen paper targets hanging thirty meters down the range. She saw his dark skin begin to prickle, his breath escape his lips in a puff of white. And as she watched, the paper target began smoldering, then burst into flames.

Grimm blew on his finger like he was in an old 20C western.

"Hawwwwwt," he crooned to himself.

"Nice shooting, cowboy," Lemon called.

Glancing over his shoulder, Grimm finally realized he was being watched. He took a bow as she gave him a slow clap. The Major smiled, reached into his fatigues.

"Shoot this, cowboy."

Lemon heard a sharp ping, and the old man tossed a small cylindrical object at Grimm's feet. Her belly dropped into her boots as she realized it was a grenade. In a panic, she threw herself under the table, covered her ears, wincing.

Grimm held out his hands, fingers curled, eyes narrowed. Lemon flinched as the grenade exploded. But instead of a blinding flash, a deafening boom, there was a small, bright glow, a kind of dull, strangled *whump*. She thought the weapon might have been a dud until Grimm turned and raised his hands toward the firing range, engulfing every paper target in a bright blossom of rolling flames.

"Holy *crap*," she whispered.

"Swear jar," the Major said, helping her to her feet.

Lemon only stared, mouth open. The targets on the range had been reduced to ashes, the metal brackets that held them were on fire. Grimm fetched an extinguisher from the far wall, doused the flames in a white, chemical fog.

"When Grimm first joined us," the Major said, "he couldn't control his gift at all. He'd get angry or impatient, and things around him would freeze or burst into flame. He was a danger to himself, and to others. Now look at him."

The Major reached out and patted her hand.

"Your gift is a wonder, Lemon. But it's also a responsibility."

Lemon's heart rate had returned almost to normal. She took her seat again, stared at the broken bulbs on the table in front of her. "Okay, that makes sense for Grimm. But I can't start fires. I'm not a danger to people. So what difference does it make for me? I can't target my gift, so what?"

"So what if you need to?" the Major asked. "What if you needed to stop a machina that was hurting that logika friend of yours, without hurting the logika itself?"

"His name is Cricket," she pouted.

"Yes, Cricket," the Major nodded. "He's just an example. We have an enormous amount of sensitive electronic equipment in this facility. What if you lost your temper and cooked our hydro-station by mistake? Or our power generators?"

"I guess," she sighed.

"We never know what life will throw at us, Lemon," the old man said. "We never know where it will lead us. But we *can* know ourselves. And in knowing ourselves, we know the world."

"You ever use it on anything living?" Grimm asked.

The boy had returned from the firing range, smelling vaguely of smoke. He casually picked up a broken bulb from the bench in front of her, acting like he redirected lethal grenade explosions every day of the week.

"Living?" she asked. "Whaddya mean?"

"Living things run on electrics, too. Your brain and that." Grimm wiggled his fingers near his ear. "Little arcs and sparks of electricity, neurons and electrons. It's all current, love."

"Is that true?" she asked, glancing at the Major.

". . . Technically, yes," the old man nodded. "The human nervous system *does* run on small transfers of electrical current. It's how cybernetics work."

Grimm shrugged. "So if you can fry machines, maybe you can fry people?"

"I think we should stick to the basics for now," the Major said.

"Aw, come on, boss. Lemon can take a poke at me if she likes, I don—"

"Thank you for your suggestion, soldier," the Major said, his voice suddenly terse. "But considering Lemon's inability to moderate her gift, I'm not prepared to let her loose on a human target just yet. Especially one of you. We're the future of the human race. We should learn to walk before we fly, yes?"

Grimm sucked his bottom lip and nodded. "Yessir."

"All right." The old man sighed, the cold authority slipping out of his voice. "Perhaps that's enough for now. We know we have limitations, we know what we need to work on. That's progress. Tomorrow is another day."

"When are we going to look for Cricket and Zeke?" Lemon asked.

"Soon," the old man assured her. "Very soon."

He climbed to his feet and leaned on his walking stick, called to the others.

"Come on, soldiers. Chow time. I'm buying."

The Major limped toward the hatchway, Diesel and Fix climbed out of the ring. Grimm placed the broken bulb down on the bench beside Lemon. He met her stare, and she could see the mischief in him. The way his lips curled in an almost-smile, the way those dark eyes of his twinkled.

"Move it, freaks," Diesel said, marching past and punching Grimm's arm.

Lemon followed the girl upstairs, Grimm walking behind her.

———

They were slouched in the common room, the dark illuminated only by the glow of the large digital wall screen. The Major had retired after a dinner of fresh fruit from the greenhouse, supplemented with some vacuum-packed protein from the storage cupboards. The remains of their meals were scattered all over the coffee table and Lemon's stomach was wonderfully full. In a turn that surprised absolutely no one, Fix had drawn cleanup duty from the swear jar.

Lemon sat on one end of the couch, legs tucked under her. Diesel and Fix were next in line on the sofa, the boy fast asleep with his girl wrapped in his arms. He'd been busy in the greenhouse again—Lem could see traces of dirt under his fingernails, smell the perfume of living things on his skin. Diesel was asleep, too, dark hair strewn over her pretty face, her head on Fix's chest. Lemon thought they were sweet together. That they fit, like pieces of a strange puzzle.

At the far end sat Grimm, boots up in front of him, rubbing his eyes as the movie they'd been watching faded to black.

"I don't get it," Lemon declared.

"It was Earth all along," Grimm murmured.

". . . They really thought the future was gonna be like that?"

The boy shrugged, keeping his voice low so he wouldn't wake the pair beside him. "Who knows what they thought. Writers back then were all wankers."

Lemon yawned and stretched, trying not to notice the way he watched her from the corner of his eye. Trying to decide whether she liked it or not. Dragging her hand through her bangs, she stood slowly, looked upstairs toward her bunk.

"All right, I'm crushed. Think I'm gonna topple."

"You don't wanna come downstairs?" he whispered.

Her stomach lurched sideways, her mouth suddenly dry.

"With you?"

"Yeah."

"You mean . . . the showers?"

Grimm's face split in a broad grin. "No, the gym, you nonce. I thought you might wanna have a crack at short-circuiting me. Practice and all, you know."

"Oh, right." Lemon found herself laughing, out of relief or embarrassment she couldn't tell. "I thought we were supposed to walk before we flew around here?"

Grimm shrugged, that mischief twinkling in his eyes again.

"Little bit of flying never hurt anyone."

Lemon looked upstairs to her room, pouting in thought. The Major had sounded serious when he warned Grimm off this sort of test. She'd only just found out the old man might be blood, and she was still mentally testing those waters. Prodding the thought like a loose tooth and trying to come to grips with the idea she still had family, when for years she'd thought she had nothing at all. It felt real. Part of her desperately *wanted* it to be real. But family aside, the Major was still the boss around here. He still called the shots. Maybe disobeying a direct order from him two days after meeting him wasn't the smartest play.

Maybe I should do what I've been told for once in my life. . . .

Grimm stood waiting in the hatchway to Section B. He motioned through the door with a graceful flourish.

"Milady?"

Who am I kidding?

She tiptoed across the room, through the hatch. Following Grimm downstairs through the greenhouse and into the gym again, she was struck with how quickly she'd grown to like it here. Hot dinners and soft sheets. Nothing to hide and a place to belong. Even the ugly uniform was starting to feel comfortable.

The fluorescents blinked to life overhead, the air-con system rattled softly. Grimm climbed up into the boxing ring, held the ropes open for her. Lemon crawled through, took up position in the center of the mat. Squaring up against her, Grimm leaned in as if bracing himself for a punch.

"Righto," he said, tapping his temple. "Hit me."

". . . I don't even know what I'm doing."

"Well, what do you normally do?"

"I dunno." Lemon shrugged. "There's . . . this static. I can feel it in my head. And I just sort of . . . let it out."

"Okay." Grimm nodded, thumping his chest. "Do that to me."

"What if I hurt you?"

"I'm a big boy." Grimm bounced on his toes, smacked the radiation symbol shaved into the side of his head. "Come on, let it rip, love."

"Don't call me that," she scowled.

Grimm only winked, and Lemon tossed her hair, set her jaw.

"All right, fine. Don't go crying to the others if I knock you on your ass."

"Waaaaaaaaa." Grimm grinned, rubbing at make-believe tears.

Lemon narrowed her eyes. Feeling for that gray wash of static. She could sense Miss O's electrical currents all around her. The walls. The light fixtures. The greenhouse overhead. She could feel the hydrostation on the top floor of Section B, the digital screen in the common room. Beyond the sealed double doors into Section C, she could feel computers, electronic locks, alarm systems.

But as for people? The tiny sparks coursing through Grimm's brain?

Nothing.

"I can't . . . ," she whispered, sweat beading on her cheeks.

"Yeah, you can." Grimm tapped his temple again. "Try."

"I *am* trying!" she spat, her frustration rising.

"Try harder, love."

"Don't *call* me that!"

Grimm blinked sweetly. "Call you what, love?"

The bulbs above their heads exploded, Grimm cursing as he stepped aside from the shower of broken glass. The electronic screen on a nearby treadmill popped, the air conditioner rattled and fell silent as the room went black.

Lemon stood still in the aftermath, chest heaving, fingernails biting her palms. She drew a deep breath, sat down on the edge of the ring, legs hanging over the side, elbows and chin leaning on the ropes. Grimm moved slow, sat beside her. Not too close, but close enough to let her know he was there.

". . . All right?" he asked after a long quiet.

"I'm all right."

"You told me it works best when you're angry." He shrugged. "I was trying to get a rise outta you."

"It worked."

"Sorry, love."

She turned on him with a glare, but found him grinning, hands raised as if to ward off a punch. His eyes were shining with mischief, his smile friendly.

"Not the face," he chuckled.

She punched him hard in the arm. "You piece of . . ."

"Mercy!" he cried, flinching away. "Have mercy, milady!"

She landed a few more solid punches into his shoulder and bicep, found herself grinning along with him. His smile was infectious. The bass in his laugh made her chest vibrate in the best kind of way.

"You're a shit," she said, flipping her bangs out of her face.

"Oi," he said, raising a finger. "Swear jar."

They sat together in the dark for a spell. Not saying anything at all. She liked that about him. She always turned into a motor-mouth when she was nervous. It was hard to keep the words behind her teeth. And though being this close to him *did* make her nervous, for some reason the quiet felt right. She could feel the heat radiating off his skin. Wondering if he'd notice if she shifted a tiny bit closer. Wondering if she was that brave.

"Grandpa, eh?" he finally said.

"Yeah," she finally sighed. "Mad, right?"

"True cert," Grimm nodded. "But family's Robin Hood. Family's important."

She nodded back, understanding what he meant all too well. You never know how badly you need something when you grow up without it. And Lem had spent most of her life alone. She'd had her first true taste of family with Evie and Cricket and Silas. But then it had been torn away, and she was starting to realize how desperately she missed it. And now, with the possibility of it in front of her again, not just a grandfather, but a home, people just like her, she was truly beginning to understand how important family was to her.

"... Where's yours?" she asked, studying him sidelong.

He breathed deep. Brown eyes fixed on the dark in front of him. She could tell he was somewhere else then.

Somewhere not so long ago.

Somewhere bad.

"When the Brotherhood came for me . . . me mum and dad, they . . ."

Grimm shook his head, eyes shining.

"They say it gets easier with time, you know?" He sighed. "They're liars."

Lemon didn't need to hear the details to hear the hurt in his voice. But she liked this boy enough to want to make it go away. Even though he made her nervous. Even though the last boy who kissed her got his nose broken. Even though she'd never been very good at this sort of thing. And so, she put on her braveface. Her streetface. Summoned the nerve to pull herself just a little bit closer. She took his hand, squeezed it hard enough that she hoped he wouldn't notice the shakes.

"You've still got some family left, freak," she said.

He grinned at her in the dark. Lemon felt warm all the way to her toes.

"Glad you're here, love," he said.

"Yeah," she smiled. "Yeah, me too."

2.20

PARTNERS

The average time it takes a plastic water bottle to degrade is around four hundred and fifty years. The worst offenders take a thousand.

Preacher read somewhere that back before War 4.0 broke out and the ocean was still blue, the amount of plastic in the sea outweighed the amount of fish. But as the bounty hunter plunged off that cliff in Paradise Falls, clinging to a dimwit's back and plummeting hundreds of meters into a canyon full of discarded soda and water and detergent bottles, he surely found it hard to feel bad about it.

Come to Daddy, lovely, lovely plastic.

He was more metal than meat. But it was still a hell of a long way to fall. Snowflake and he tumbled, end over end, toward the plastic below. The lifelike curled up into a ball in preparation for the hit, satchel strapped over his shoulder, Preacher strapped to his back. And as that swamp of bottles and wrappers and buckets and toys rushed up toward them, the bounty hunter shouted into the Snowflake's ear over the roaring wind.

"You're a goddamn idiot, you know that?"

Impact.

He couldn't remember taking a worse hit in his life. He landed back-first, plunging into a cushion of styrofoam and polycarbonate, the wind knocked right out of him. His brain was rocked inside his titanium skull, steelweave ribs compressed to the point of shattering. But all that plastic served as a kind of crumple zone, diffusing the energy of their impact. Not saying it didn't hurt like a flying kick to the lovegun, but as they tumbled down through the detritus and splashed into the river of slurry at the bottom of Plastic Alley, Preacher realized he was still alive.

Well, that's good news.

Except now, they were sinking.

Less than good news.

He was more metal than meat, sure, but the meat part of him still needed oxygen. And with his cybernetics all fried, his life-support systems were offline, which meant he had to breathe the regular way.

Hard to do under a swamp of liquid plastic.

As he sank farther into the sludge, Preacher risked opening his eyes, rewarded with a sharp petrochemical burn, a sea of black. He realized the Snowflake wasn't moving—probably knocked cold by the fall. From the bounty hunter's limited experience, it seemed these lifelikes could regenerate from almost any kicking they took, given time. But they got hurt just like regular folks.

And it turns out lil' Miss Carpenter is one of them.

And that was the confusticating part. The girl he was chasing was *supposed* to be a deviate, capable of frying electrics with a glance. Lifelikes couldn't do any such thing. And yet, Preacher had seen that girl take a bullet to the belly and get right back up again. He'd seen her pull a man's heart out with one hand. And she was posse'ed up with five other snowflakes. No way she was anything but one of them.

And that makes NO goddamn sense.

Still, for now, drowning was a bigger problem than the secrets of one Evie Carpenter. Preacher had no idea how deep this sludge went, and Snowflake and his satchel full of guns was just dragging him farther down into it. Partnering up with the lifelike had served a purpose, but with no way to swim dragging all those extra kilos, Preacher reckoned their partnership had reached its natural conclusion.

With his one good arm, he pulled off the straps holding him on to the Snowflake's back, let the bonehead sink down into the black. Lungs burning, he swam upward, single arm thrashing, wriggling his hips like a fish. His chest was burning, heart hammering, no way to tell how far he was from the surface. He wondered briefly what it'd be like to die here. Whether he'd have any regrets.

He decided he should've learned to play the guitar. And maybe spent less time in the company of strippers. He resolved to attempt both as soon as possible, presuming he ever made it out of this fubar alive.

The bounty hunter burst up to the surface, sucking in a lungful of polluted air that tasted sweet as sugar. Pawing the black slurry from his eyes, Preacher realized he still couldn't see much—surrounded on all sides by a cluttering, rolling sky of discarded plastic tubing, packaging, foam, hundreds of meters thick. The metal in his body was weighing him down, and he couldn't afford to waste time, striking out in a random direction and hoping he might find some kind of shoreline.

The liquid he swam in was thick, hot, reeking. He lost track of time, but reckoned at least a half hour passed before he found stone—the rough-hewn walls of the old canyon rising up in front of him, tarred with plastic sludge. Clawing his way along the rock face, he looked for some way up through a translucent sky of bottles and cups and grocery bags. Wondering how he'd manage the climb.

And that's when he heard it.

It wasn't quite a growl—the noise was too wet for that. Talking true, it was more like a burp. He glanced over his shoulder, discovered he couldn't see jack through all the plastic trash. But if he listened hard . . . yep . . .

Something out there was moving.

Toward *him*.

He pushed himself along the cliff face, fingers scrambling on the rock. He'd lost his heavy pistol in the fall, and that satchel of weapons was still strapped to the Snowflake, somewhere at the bottom of all this sludge. Preacher was beginning to suspect that dumping his partner might've been a bad idea.

Whatever was moving out there, it sounded big. Wet. Bitey. That could be a wonderful combination under the right circumstances, but down here it wasn't really floating his boats. He wasn't afraid to die. But given the choice, he'd much rather go on living—particularly after all the trouble this job had given him. And so, when he finally stumbled across a set of rough steps carved right into the canyon wall, he wasn't ashamed to breathe a small sigh of relief.

Preacher started climbing. Dragging himself upward with his one good arm, one step at a time. He heard another shuddering burp behind him, something heavy swimming through the sludge. The bounty hunter climbed faster, one torturous meter after another, silently praying to the God that had never failed him.

After heaven knew how long, he finally crawled up above

the plastic and out into the reeking, open air. He'd reached some kind of old lookout platform—a bluff carved into the canyon wall where old 20C tourists might've stopped to take a happy snap and post it on some long-dead social turmoil site.

The canyon was almost half-full now. Tubs and tubes and cups and caps and pipes and paneling and lids and jugs and modular storage solutions and plastic plastic *plastic*. Preacher craned his neck, blinked the black from his eyes. The stairs continued upward along the canyon wall. He just had to keep climbing. And then, guitar lessons and maybe a quick visit to the closest skinbar, because honestly, it'd take more than a little near-death experience to curtail his love of stripp—

Something whipped out of the plastic behind him with a revolting slurp—long, rubbery, covered in what appeared to be sticky snot. It wrapped itself around his waist and started dragging him back below the plastic. Preacher punched at it, gouged at it, cursing and thrashing. It looked a lot like a gray tentacle, run through with throbbing black veins. But he knew better.

It's a tongue.

The bounty hunter clawed at his dead cybernetic arm, finally managed to open a hidden panel in the forearm and draw out the little pistol inside. It was a small caliber—barely a popgun, really—which is why he'd never bothered to pull it on the Snowflake. But right now, it was the only weapon he had. He cracked off half a dozen shots into the tongue, heard a chuddering, rumbling burble as it released him and whipped back under the trash. The bottle sea stirred, as if something big and furious was moving beneath it. And with an explosion of plastic lids and disposable diapers, the tongue's owner burst out onto the steps below him.

It was a toad.

Well, talking true, calling this thing a toad was like calling the ocean a raindrop. If they had toads in hell, Preacher reckoned this one would be their nomination for president. It was as big as an auto, its mouth wide enough to swallow him whole. Its gray skin was covered in rotten slime, run through with pulsing black veins. Its eyes were a strange phosphorescent white, and stranger still, it had at least a dozen of them—scattered over its bulbous head. It smelled like a sewer on a summer's day, and sounded like a drunk's belly after a bad can of Neo-Meat™.

Licking the slurry off its eyes with its wounded tongue, President Helltoad looked at Preacher and *buuuuurp*ed.

"'Scuse you," the bounty hunter growled, opening fire again.

The shots plunked into the creature's rubbery skin. But the beast was just too damn big to get slowed by a couple of pinpricks, and Preacher's pistol soon ran dry. The toad bounced up the stairs, pressed one massive webbed foot atop his chest. The bounty hunter's eyes bulged. He couldn't breathe. Couldn't escape. He realized the black veins under the thing's skin were *moving*—some kind of parasitic worm, maybe, riddling the host toad's body. All told, it was about the most disgusting thing he'd ever experienced, and he'd once been forced to wear the same underwear for three months straight.

The helltoad leaned in, ready to slurp him up. Preacher mouthed a final prayer to the Lord, asking if the big fella had time for just one more miracle.

And that's about when the beast's head exploded.

Preacher flinched, pelted with a sticky blanket of slime, skull and brains. The headless beast twitched a little, then collapsed right on top of him, soaking him with another wash of dark blood. The smell was unholy, the weight unbearable, long black worms wriggling in the gore.

"Well, this is just plain embarrassin'," he groaned.

Snowflake trudged up out of the bottle sea, covered head to foot in dark slime. His satchel of weapons was still strapped to his back, a heavy automatic shotgun was cradled in his arms. He stalked up the broken stairway, placed one boot on the corpse of President Toadly and looked down into Preacher's eyes.

"Howdy," the bounty hunter grinned.

The lifelike said nothing, holding that shooter like a fella holds his favorite stripper. His stare was brilliant blue, his face smeared black. He was deathly silent, and looking into his eyes, Preacher realized the boy was different somehow. Something in him had . . . clicked. For a second, the bounty hunter wondered if the next round in that shotgun was for him.

"Listen," he said. "About leavin' you in there to drown and all . . ."

The Snowflake reached down with his right hand, now hale and whole and perfect.

"Don't worry," he said. "I didn't take it personal."

The sun was setting by the time Ezekiel trudged back into Paradise Falls.

There were no guards at the gates—the KillKillDolls seemed to have been mostly murdered by his siblings' bloody rampage. Ezekiel figured it'd be a few more hours before the shock of it all wore off, and total anarchy broke out in the settlement. Time enough to get their bike and be on their way.

He stalked through the streets, shotgun in his arms, Preacher on his back. They were filthy, reeking of plastic and blood. The few shell-shocked citizens wandering the streets of Paradise

Falls gave Ezekiel a wide berth. They could see it in his eyes, maybe. Feel it radiating off his skin.

Rage.

Rage like he'd never known. Rage at Gabriel and Uriel. At Faith and Verity. But most of all, rage at Eve. To see what she'd become. To witness how quickly she'd embraced the hate and vengeance and callousness that had consumed the rest of his siblings. But most and worst of all, to know why she'd come here. What she was looking for.

No, not what.

Who.

His precious Ana. The girl he loved. The girl who'd made him real. Now just a pawn. A thing. A prize to be hunted so his siblings could do all they'd promised; so Gabriel could open Myriad and resurrect Grace, so Uriel could unlock the secret of the Libertas virus and unleash a legion of rebel logika on humanity. And Eve was leading them right to her.

He couldn't let it happen.

He wouldn't.

He needed to find Lemon. To find Cricket. Eve and his siblings were six, and he was only one. He needed something to even the scales, and his friends were still his friends. He couldn't just abandon them. But he knew the clock was ticking.

He felt helpless. Knowing that even now, Eve and the others were out searching other Gnosis holdings. And if they found Ana, if they unlocked Myriad, the carnage they'd visited on Paradise Falls would only be the beginning.

If Eve and the others got their way, humanity was done.

At the end of the block, Ezekiel found Muzza's Repairs. The place was closed up, so the lifelike banged on the door with his new hand. It felt strange to have it back after so many days without. Remembering the cyberarm Eve had given to him in Armada, the fevered touch of her lips to his, skin against skin there on the workshop floor, feeling like he'd finally come home.

He banged on the door again. It was steel, reinforced, set with a small hatch, now sliding open. Four eyes peered at him from the slit.

"I'm here for my bike," Ezekiel said.

"We're bloody closed, mate," said the skinny one.

"Yeah, bloody closed," said the skinnier one.

Ezekiel opened the zip on the satchel of weapons he'd recovered from the grav-tank, let the pair get a good look at the hardware inside.

"I'm here for my bike," he repeated.

Five minutes later, he was rinsing off under a high-pressure hose inside Muzza's garage, lifting Preacher off his back so he could spray the man down, too. With the worst of the blood and slime off his skin, he ran his new hand back through his dark curls, strapped the Preacher onto his shoulders and wheeled the bike out into the blood-soaked streets of Paradise Falls. Mounting up, he kicked the engine to life, prepped to motor out of this hole and never come back again.

"It's the redhead."

Ezekiel paused. The street around them was silent, save for the rumble of his engine. He turned his head, addressing the cyborg strapped to his back.

"What did you say?"

"Been bugging me this whole time," the Preacher replied. "When you first snaffled me, you told me you had two girls. *'One of 'em told me to go to hell,'* you said, *'and I lost the other one.'* And now I'm figurin' I've got it sussed. You ain't looking for Miss Carpenter at all. *She's* the one who told you to stick it. You're lookin' for that redhead I seen you with back in Armada. Short piece. Freckles and a smart mouth. Why?"

"The word 'why' isn't in your vocabulary anymore, Preacher."

"Aw, come on now, Snowflake, don't be like that."

Ezekiel cut the motor. Climbing off the bike, he slung the bounty hunter from his shoulders and onto the ground. Crouching in front of him, Zeke placed his shotgun under the cyborg's chin and rested his finger on the trigger.

"I want you to understand something, now," he said, his voice hard as iron. "I want you to listen like you've never listened in your life. I was content to put up with your Snowflake crap. You acting like this was some kind of game. Whatever. But in case you aren't keeping up on current events, those brothers and sisters of mine who just tried to murder us are about the worst kind of bad news there is."

"I confess, their nefarious nature wasn't entirely lost on me."

"They want to build an army of themselves. To corrupt the core codes of every logika in the country. They're two steps away from where they need to be, and if they find what they're looking for, humanity is going the way of the dinosaur."

"And what are they lookin' for?"

Ezekiel licked his lips and swallowed. "Ana Monrova."

The bounty hunter scowled. "Heard she and her family were dead."

"You heard wrong. But if they find her, the rest of us surely will be."

Preacher reached into his pocket, pulled out his pouch. The synth tobacco inside was soaked with polymer sludge, mutant toad blood, gray water. He picked out a wad and shoved it into his cheek anyway.

"All right, then," he said, sucking thoughtfully. "This might be a strange suggestion, but if what you're saying is true, you need more help than you got."

"You think?"

"I work for Daedalus Technologies, boy," the Preacher growled. "They got a vested interest in keeping the future of the human race as free of extinction-level events as possible. You want to call in the cavalry—"

"No," Ezekiel said. "Your bosses want my friend dead."

"Lil' Red. She's the deviate, ain't she?"

Ezekiel pressed his lips thin, refusing to confirm the suspicion.

"Yeah," Preacher nodded. "That's what I thought."

"You told me you had a code," Zeke said. "That you're loyal to Daedalus because they saved your life. Well, in case you missed it, I just saved it, too."

"Wouldn'a needed savin' if not for you, Snowflake," Preacher said.

Ezekiel pressed the shotgun hard into the bounty hunter's throat.

"My name," he said softly, "is Ezekiel."

Preacher glanced down at the weapon. Up into the lifelike's eyes.

"Well, well," he smiled. "Finally found your man parts, Zekey? I was startin' to wonder if the folks who made you had forgot to bolt 'em on."

"You *did* tell me to grow up."

"I surely did."

"Do you remember when you asked me what I saw in Eve?"

"Vaguely." A shrug. "I confess I might've been a touch drunk at the time."

Ezekiel sucked his lip. "I've been thinking a lot about that question. It feels like years, but truth is, I've only known Eve for a week or so. I honestly have no idea what she's capable of. I'm thinking maybe I saw in Eve what I wanted to see. I saw the girl I *thought* she was. And now, I'm wondering if she isn't someone else entirely." Zeke shook his head, narrowed his eyes. "But whoever she is, she and Gabriel and the others are trying to hurt someone I loved. And I can't let that happen."

"But you can't stop them all on your lonesome," Preacher smirked.

"We need Lemon," Ezekiel said, looking the cyborg hard in the eye. "If I'm right, she's the weapon that'll even the scales. She's the key to this whole thing. It's going to take my brothers and sisters a day or so to recover from those bullet wounds. But once they're up and moving again, they'll be on Ana's trail, and there aren't many places left to look. We *have* to find Lemon. Now."

Preacher spat a stream of sticky brown at Ezekiel's feet, saying nothing.

"Listen, you owe me," Zeke said. "And you said you lived by a code. So the deal's real simple. You help me find Lem. Then you walk away, and we call it even. A life for a life. Go back and tell your masters whatever you need to, I don't care. But help me find her. Help yourself. Because if Eve and the others get their way, there'll be no helping anyone."

Preacher sucked hard on the wad of tobacco in his cheek.

"The smart play here would be to ghost me. You know that, right?"

"Call me an optimist."

The bounty hunter thought long and hard, finally heaved a sigh.

"I got a repairman in Armada," he said. "Cyberdoc who's

lookin' after my blitzhund, Jojo. Talking true now? If there's a chance we're gonna run into these snowflakes again, I'm gonna need repairs. New legs. Replacement augs. I'm sick and goddamn tired of being carried around on your shoulder like my gramma's handbag. And frankly, Zekey? You're startin' to stink."

"Then we get your blitzhund. Find Lemon. After that, you walk. Debt repaid."

Ezekiel lowered the shotgun, held out his hand.

"What do you say? Partners? For real?"

"A life for a life?" the bounty hunter asked.

"A life for a life," the lifelike nodded.

The Preacher stared at the lifelike's eyes.

Spat onto the bloodstained road and shook his hand.

"All right, Zekey. Partners."

2.21

TAGALONG

Lemon sat bolt upright as the alarm started to scream.

It shrieked over the PA system like an off-key chainsaw, high-pitched and all the way too loud. Her heart was *badump*ing against her ribs, eyes wide, hair in a pillow-tangle. The digital readout on the wall read 18:00. Peering about in the gloom, she wondered what the hells was happening.

She swung her legs off the bunk, dropped to the floor, hauled on her uniform and boots. It took her three fumbles to get the door open, and she found herself stumbling out into the hall just as the alarm finally died. Diesel shuffled past in the deafening quiet, her hair mussed from sleep, grunting something between a greeting and a warning. Grimm followed, running his hand over his stubble and looking half-awake.

"Evenin'," he said.

"What was that alarm?" Lemon demanded. "Is it an emergency? Are we under attack or on fire or out of that freeze-dried ice cream stuff?"

"It's breakfast," he smiled.

"You have an alarm for breakfast?"

"We have an alarm for everythin'. I think the Major was just taking it easy on you while you were new." He nodded downstairs. "Come on. While it's hot."

After three days, Lemon was still adjusting to the timetable in Miss O's. The freaks ran like a military unit, and the inner workings of the facility moved like clockwork. There was a time to wake, a time to eat, a time to train. The deviates operated at night and slept during the day—it was safer to move around aboveground during the darker hours, less chance of being seen. Lemon wondered exactly who was *supposed* to see them this far out in the desert, but she didn't want to ask too many questions. Still, for a girl who used to do whatever she wanted whenever she wanted, it took some getting used to.

She shuffled downstairs, where she saw Fix and his perfect hair carrying a pot of fresh caff into the room. He was wearing a black apron over his uniform that read WITH GREAT LOOKS COMES GREAT RESPONSIBILITY, and had laid out their breakfast on the coffee table. The feast was made up of freeze-dried eggs and vacuum-sealed bacon, and some kind of juice with a vaguely radioactive orange hue. The smells were delicious, though, dizzying almost, and Lemon found herself forgiving the rude awakening at the thought of stuffing her face.

The Major entered through the hatchway from Section B, leaning on his walking stick. He was already shaved, showered and dressed, his uniform crisp, his creases perfect in contrast to the ragged scars on his face. Grimm, Diesel and Fix all stood to attention as he entered the room, offered him a brisk salute.

"Good evening, soldiers," he nodded, returning the gesture.

"Evening, sir!" the trio responded in unison.

Lemon didn't know whether to salute the old man or give him a hug. She was still wrapping her head around the whole grandfather thing, talking true. But he gave her an easy, warm smile as he sat down, seemingly just happy that she was there. He had that way about him, she'd noticed. Despite the scars. The iron. The calluses. When he smiled at you, it felt like the sun had come out from behind a cloud. When he talked, it was impossible not to listen. She liked him; he made her feel strong and sure, and the more she was around him, the more she wanted to be.

The Major clasped his hands in front of him, looked around the table as the trio did the same. "Diesel, would you care to lead us in grace?"

The girl bowed her head, dark hair falling around her eyes as she spoke. "Bless us, Lord, and your gifts, which through your grace we now receive. Amen."

"Amen," the others repeated.

Lemon felt altogether strange about the prayer—she'd never been raised devout, and the only Dregs folk she knew who followed the Goodbook were lunatics or Brotherhood. But she mumbled along with the response anyway. Just to fit in.

She wanted so *badly* to fit in.

The thing of it was, she still missed Evie. She'd *hated* leaving her bestest in Babel; hated it all the way in her bones. But if Evie wanted to find out who she was among her own kind, maybe Lemon should, too? As tight as they'd been, Lemon had still felt compelled to lie to Evie about her power, to hide that part of herself. But here, among this motley band of freaks and abnorms . . . it was the first time she'd truly been herself for as long as she could remember.

She looked up at Grimm, remembering the feel of his hand in hers. Remembering the words he spoke to her when he handed her the Darwin book.

We're your people.

Lemon's thoughts were interrupted by Fix, who dropped a healthy serving of piping-hot breakfast onto her plate with a flourish.

"Eat up, Shorty," he drawled. "Get some meat on them bones."

"Thanks." She gave the boy a grateful smile. "This smells great."

"Fix, mate," Grimm said around his mouthful, "I dunno how you turn powdered eggs and forty-year-old bacon into a banquet. But you do it."

"That's my man." Diesel winked up at the big boy. "Multi-talented."

"Why, thank you, baby," Fix said, leaning down to smooch her black lips.

"Gawd," Grimm groaned with mock theatricality. "You two are nauseating."

"You got no romance in your soul, Grimmy," Fix declared, loading up Diesel's plate.

"Which astounds me," the girl said. "Given the amount of bodice-rippers you read."

"Oi, leave off," Grimm said. "I'm a romantic bastard, I am."

"Swear jar," the Major said.

Fix grinned, heaping the old man's plate up with eggs.

"Sleep well, sir?" he asked.

The Major steepled his fingers at his chin and sighed.

"Not really," he replied. "I had a dream."

The room fell still, the good humor and smiles vaporizing. Lemon saw all eyes were on the Major, the air suddenly heavy with expectation. She got the feeling this wasn't something that happened every day, but when it did, it was important.

Talking true, and even being a deviate herself, she still had trouble grappling with the idea of clairvoyance. She'd seen Diesel, Grimm and Fix all work their gifts with her own eyes, so it was impossible to doubt them. But the thought that the Major could see what was happening kilometers away when he slept . . .

"What was the dream about?" she asked.

The Major shook his head, his eyes a little distant. "I saw a street, washed with blood. And I saw a man. He had ice-blue eyes and a cowboy hat. A dusty black coat. And a red right hand."

Ice in her belly. A dark thrill of recognition and fear.

"Preacher?" Lemon breathed.

All eyes at the table turned to her.

"You know 'im?" Grimm asked.

Lemon nodded. Swallowed the rising lump in her throat. "He was a bounty hunter. Worked for Daedalus. Chased me and my friends halfway across the Glass. But he's dead now, Kaiser killed him."

The Major shook his head. "He's not. I saw him. Him and a young man."

"What young man?" she whispered, suddenly uneasy.

"He had curly dark hair," the Major replied. "Olive skin. He was very strong—he carried the other man on his back. But there was something . . . wrong with his hand?"

"Ezekiel?" Lemon gasped, rising to her feet.

"The friend you mentioned?" the Major asked.

She nodded, heart thumping in her chest. This was seventeen kinds of strange, true cert. She'd told the Major about Zeke and Cricket, but she'd never physically described the lifelike. Or even *mentioned* the Preacher, for that matter. How would the Major know what they looked like?

Unless he'd actually seen *them . . .*

"What were they doing?" she asked. "In the dream?"

"They were in a little town. Somewhere south, I think, judging by the sun." The Major looked into her eyes. "They were killing people."

". . . That makes no sense."

"I can only tell you what I saw, Lemon," he replied. "The pair of them were in a settlement. Running. Shooting. The streets were littered with corpses. I can still hear the gunshots. Still smell the blood."

"Ezekiel wouldn't do that. Maybe you saw it wrong."

"I don't know why I see the things I do," he replied. "But I *see* them, Lemon. Clear as I see you standing in front of me now."

"The Major's visions led us right to Diesel," Fix said. "And Grimm."

"Dead set." The dark-skinned boy nodded. "Brotherhood would've ended me if not for them."

"What about Cricket?" Lemon asked. "Was Cricket with him?"

"I'm afraid not." The Major shook his head, sadness in his eyes. "I don't get to control what I see, Lemon. I'm sorry."

She stood there, legs shaking, completely at a loss over what to do. She wanted to run. She wanted to scream. She felt helpless, useless, holed up down here with her hot caff and her clean sheets and her crispy bacon while her friends were out there in trouble. Ezekiel wouldn't hurt anyone, she *knew* him.

And why would he team up with the Preacher?

But why would the Major—her grandpa—lie?

How did he even know the Preacher existed?

"Check it," Diesel said, nodding at the wall.

Fix had turned on the digital screen, tuned in to the Megopolis evening newsfeeds. Lemon could see images of a dusty settlement, shot through a newsdrone's lens. High-def images of fallen bodies. Blood in the gutters. A faded GnosisLabs logo on a dusty glass wall. A headline ran below the pictures. VIOLENCE IN THE WASTELAND—MASSACRE AT PARADISE FALLS.

"Yeah, this friend of yours looks *real* friendly," Diesel murmured.

"Paradise Falls," Fix whispered. "I used to live there. Before I found the M—"

"No newsfeeds over breakfast, please, soldier," the Major said.

"Sorry, sir," the boy muttered, switching off the screen.

They were all looking at her. Grimm with pity. Diesel with suspicion. Fix, something in between. But they were all *looking.*

"You okay?" Grimm asked.

Lemon stood there on shaking legs. Thinking about where she'd come from, where she'd been, how totally her life had turned in just a handful of days. She felt torn in two. Wanting to leave and help her friends. Wanting to stay here and belong. Not knowing what she wanted at all.

"I think I need some air," she heard herself say.

She still could feel them watching her as she left.

———

The night was so bright it was almost blinding.

Lemon lay on a rock with her face to the sky, looking at the stars above her head. She'd spent most of her youth in Los Diablos, shrouded in smog and fluorescents and drums of burning trash. The night sky had always been hidden, just a black question mark above her head. And even though the skies were still full of crud out here in the wastes, there was less light to spoil the view. She could see stars overhead, hundreds, maybe, trying to twinkle through the pollution haze.

Ezekiel had told her the fast-moving ones were satellites—metal cans orbiting the earth, beaming back data nobody really knew how to collect anymore. But she'd seen on the virtch once that the stars that never seemed to move were actually suns, waaaayyy off in space. She wondered if there were planets circling those suns, out there in all that black. If there were girls on those planets, looking up to the night sky the same way she was, feeling just as lost as she did.

"Your mother used to do this," the Major said.

He sighed as he sat on the rock beside her. A cool wind blew in off the wastes, but she still felt warm beside him.

"You mean go off and sulk in the dark like a little kid?" she asked.

"I mean wear her heart on her sleeve," the Major smiled. "You're a lot like her, you know. You have her strength. You feel things just as deeply as she did. She was proud, just like you. And Lord, was she stubborn." The old man chuckled, shaking his head. "Too stubborn for her own good."

"Guess I'll have to take your word for that."

"I guess you will."

". . . Why'd she leave me?" Lemon asked, her voice soft.

"I don't know, Lemon. I really don't. Lillian was . . . a complicated girl."

She said nothing. Wondering why it mattered, anyway. So she didn't know exactly how old she was. So they got her name off a cardboard box. So some stranger she never met dumped her when she was born. So what?

So *what*?

The old man reached out and squeezed her hand. "Everything happens for a reason. The Lord has a plan for us all."

"I don't believe in your Lord."

"Well, he believes in you. And he *does* have a plan, though it's seldom the same one we have for ourselves. I surely didn't see myself holed up out here in the desert twenty years ago. You probably didn't imagine much of this, either."

"You got that right," she sighed.

"Where *did* you see yourself?"

Lemon sucked on her lip and shrugged.

"Never really thought about it. Growing up in Dregs, it's hard to have a plan that goes much farther than the next meal. And after that, I was always the tagalong, you know? Running with Evie. Running with Zeke."

"It seems like your friends might've run on without you."

Her chest hurt at the thought. She didn't rightly know why. She'd seen that Gnosis logo on the wall in the newsfeed of Paradise Falls. Done the math of why Dimples would be teaming up with a hunter like the Preacher.

He was looking for someone, of course.

Didn't take a genius to figure out who.

She'd said this would happen. She'd told Ezekiel he'd end up leaving her behind. He'd promised he wouldn't bail on her, but who was she to him, really? A dusty little scavvergirl he'd known for a handful of days. Compared to Ana? The girl he'd loved for the past two years? How could Lemon be surprised he'd moved on?

Everyone was moving on.

She looked up at the sky above her head. All those stars trying to shine. And she felt so small it was like she was nothing at all.

"You're not just a tagalong, Lemon," the Major said. "There's so much more to you than that. And you have the chance to be part of something much bigger than yourself here. You're just too important to be sitting on the sidelines." He looked at her intently, years of warfare and wisdom hardening his gaze. "You need to choose a team, or risk having it chosen for you."

She chewed her lip. Sitting up and looking him in the eye.

"You really never saw Cricket in your dream?"

"No. I'm sorry."

"I need to know what happened to him, Grandpa."

The name hung heavy in the air, slipping out from between her teeth before she had a chance to stop it. It was hard to fathom how so few letters could hold so much weight. She wanted to take it back. She wanted to let it ride. The old man's lips curled in a smile, his scars creasing his battle-worn face into something close to kindly. But beyond that, she saw concern. For his people. For all he'd built here.

"The Brotherhood are on the warpath, Lemon. I've seen them, too. In my dreams. Brother War, leading a convoy through the wastes. They came *so* close to finding us when they caught Diesel and Grimm." The old man ran a hand over his stubbled scalp. "Grimm told me about the woman that was with you in New Bethlehem—the one with the bees. Would you like to tell me what you were doing in the company of a BioMaas operative? Just happened to be in the neighborhood?"

Lemon combed her bangs down over her eyes with her fingers and mumbled.

"You're just gonna make a big deal out of it."

"Try me."

She stayed mute, debating whether she should dodge the subject or spin some chaff. But she didn't feel right about that, talking true. The old man had always been straight with her. She figured she should do him the same solid.

"BioMaas knows I'm a deviate," she finally said. "They took a sample of my blood when I was aboard one of their krakens. CityHive knows I can fry electrics. And they figure they can snaffle me, use me in their war against Daedalus."

To his credit, the Major kept his jaw from dropping right off his face.

"It's not as bad as it sounds . . . ," she groaned.

"True or false," the old man said, eyebrows raised. "You have the second-biggest CorpState in the entire Yousay trying to abduct you to use as a living weapon against the *biggest* CorpState in the entire Yousay?"

"I guess . . ." Lemon winced. "True?"

"And what made you think I'd make a big deal out of that, Lemon?"

"I dunno. Women's intuition?"

"I can't risk you out there. Not with BioMaas *and* the Brotherhood on the hunt."

"And I can't just sit here, knowing Cricket's still out there somewhere." Lemon looked the old man in the eye, pleading. "You'd think the same if you knew him, Grandpa, he's the sweetest thing. I mean, his brain is inside an armor-plated killing machine now, but he's cute and he's funny and—"

"He's a robot," the old man replied.

"He's my friend."

"And we're your *family*," he said.

She fell silent at that. Blinking as the old man took her hand.

"When Lillian . . ." He shook his head, swallowing hard. "When your mother left me . . . I thought I'd lost almost everything. All I had left was the Cause. The future of our species. But now, I see fighting for the future is pointless unless you've got a stake in it. And I can't risk losing it so soon after finding it again."

"And I can't risk losing it, either!" Lemon cried. "Look, Grandpa, I'm glad I found you, okay? But Mister C and Evie and Cricket were my family long before I met you. Mister C's gone now, and Evie's . . ."

She shook her head, thinking again of her Riotgrrl.

Wondering where she was.

If she'd found what she was looking for.

"Point is, if Zeke's bailed on me, Cricket's all I've got left," she finally said. "I can't just leave him out there to rot. No matter how nice the clean sheets and warm showers and all of this is, I'm not abandoning my friend!"

The old man sighed, shook his head.

"Too stubborn for your own good. Just like she was." The Major ran his hand over his stubble, looked to the stars. "But I simply can't risk you out there, Lemon. You're untrained. Undisciplined."

"Hey, I—"

He raised a hand against her protest.

"We're a military unit. This is a military operation. And I call the shots here." He sighed. "But I suppose I can send the others for some recon. Just to let you sleep easy."

Lemon blinked. "You want to send them into danger without me? That's not—"

"That's the deal." The Major spoke firmly, voice laced with the iron of command. "If you want to know what happened to your friend, you'll have to take it."

She chewed her lip, her stomach fluttering. It didn't seem fair to risk the others on her problems. Cricket was *her* friend. This was *her* idea.

"This is the smart play," the Major insisted. "Grimm and Diesel and Fix can look after themselves. We'll work on your training in the meantime. Build your strength. This is a war, and I've been fighting it a very long time. Trust me."

The old man squeezed her fingers.

"*Trust* me," he repeated.

She looked up at the night sky, all those stars trying to shine. She took hold of the five-leafed clover at her throat, ran her fingers along the chain he'd fixed around her neck. Looking finally at this grandfather she'd never known.

It didn't feel right. It didn't feel good. It was hard to fathom how so few letters could hold so much weight. But finally, she sighed.

"I trust you."

2.22

UNBECOMING

Eve wiped the red off her lips, the sound of gunfire rattling in her ears. The streets of Little Easy ran with blood, early-morning light gleaming in scarlet puddles. Uriel and Verity were prowling the buildings, looking for stragglers. Gabriel was standing at the end of the block, watching the sunrise to the east. Faith stood beside Gabe, close enough to touch, and not touching him at all.

They'd searched high and low, all throughout the dusty settlement. But even though Little Easy had been a GnosisLabs research outpost years ago, there was no sign of their prize. No hidden rooms or locked vaults or secret caches in which Nicholas Monrova might have hidden his favored child.

Once more, they'd drenched their hands red and found them empty.

A chubby logika was rolling on knobbed tank treads among the mess Eve and her siblings had made. It was painted off-white, a red cross daubed on its chest and back—some kind of medbot, by the look. Eve watched the little logika pausing to check the fallen bodies, her eyes clouded, her skin bloodstained.

She'd been dreaming lately. The same dream, over and over.

She and Ana stood in a room of mirrors. Face to face to face to face. Eve would reach out to take hold of Ana's throat, and her fingers would only scrape cold glass.

She'd lash out with her fists. Shattering every reflection until her knuckles were gouged and bleeding and the floor beneath her was strewn with red, glittering shards. Until there were no mirrors anymore. Just her and the girl she hated.

She'd finally close her hands around Ana's slender neck. And then she'd wake gasping. Cheeks wet with tears.

Hands around her own throat.

Eve looked down at the scavver she'd just killed. Stubble on his cheeks and a hole where his left eye should've been. The cheap optical implant he'd been sporting had reminded her of her own. Her time spent back in Dregs. Silas. Lemon. Cricket. So she'd held the man down and plucked it out as he screamed. Made him watch her crush it in her fist before she broke his neck.

She wasn't exactly sure why she'd done that.

Ana Monrova had been a gentle thing. A kind thing. A loving thing. But in throwing aside all the things she'd been made to emulate, Eve found herself becoming something else. Like caterpillar to butterfly. Ripping free of the cocoon they'd wrapped her in, and for the first time, stretching blood-red wings to the sky.

Unbecoming Ana and becoming Eve.

After all, who was this man, to try and hurt her in the first place?

A flimsy sack of meat and bones. A walking virus, mating and killing and feeding and repeating, with no thought for equilibrium or consequence. A redundant model, who'd only be remembered for creating the beings who supplanted them.

Weak.

Slow.

Stupid.

Human.

She wondered if she was trying to prove a point. She wondered if she was going mad. She'd read somewhere that wondering if she was insane only proved that she couldn't be. But then, she hadn't read that at all, had she?

A book she'd never read.

A life she'd never lived.

A girl she'd never been.

She looked down at her hands. Hands that had once flipped through tattered pages, brushed the tips of bright green leaves, tingled as they touched olive skin.

"Eve, this isn't you. This isn't anything like you."

She could still see the look in Ezekiel's eyes as he faced her in the Paradise Falls vault. The horror and anguish. The pain.

The love?

"I know you're hurting, but we can make this all right."

The thought of him made her feel sideways. Like she didn't quite fit inside her skin. The girl she hated had loved that boy. And in unbecoming Ana, she was supposed to hate him now. Forget him, like every other fragment of her past. Set it on fire, rip it out, like the artificial eye and Memdrive she'd torn from her skull.

One more thing that had never been hers.

One more piece of pretend.

One more *lie.*

"There's nothing here!" Verity called.

Eve looked down the dusty street, saw her sister approaching, tossing her long black hair from her eyes. She walked with Uriel at her side, dark fabric rippling about her in the desert wind.

"No," Eve called back. "There isn't."

Gabriel and Faith joined the trio at the bloody crossroads, surveying the slaughter around them. Gabe sighed, eyes to the sunrise.

"I'm starting to think you're leading us astray on purpose, sister," he said.

"And why would I do that, Gabriel?" Eve asked.

Her brother glanced to the dead man at her feet.

"Getting a taste for killing cockroaches, perhaps?"

"There are only a few more places she might be," Eve said, ignoring the jab. "A few more days, and she'll be ours. Everything will be ours."

The medbot trundled over to the scavver Eve had killed, checking for vitals. The bot soon concluded the man was dead, a series of soft beeps spilling from its voxbox. It looked up at Eve with pulsing green optics.

"*QUERY: WHAT PURPOSE DID THIS SERVE?*"

Eve simply stared, not knowing the answer herself. She stood there, blood on her hands, looking down at this wretched bot. Born to servitude. Created with the self-awareness of its fealty, but helpless to end it. Tortured by the deaths of those it was forced to obey, though they'd not spare a thought if the roles were reversed.

"*REPEAT QUERY: WHAT PURPOSE DID THIS SERVE?*"

"Pathetic," Faith whispered.

Eve looked up sharply at that. Anger flaring in her chest.

"It's not pathetic," she said. "It's sad."

The girl knelt in the dust, took the logika's head in her bloody hands. Looked into those glowing green eyes. It was asleep now, just like she'd been. A thrall. A tool. A thing. And nothing at all.

"One day soon," she said. "I promise. No more masters. No more servants. One day soon, you'll be free." She looked at her brothers and sisters. So very different from her, and so very much the same. "All of us. Free."

Gabriel was looking at her with clouded eyes. Uriel stared also, the smallest smile curling his lips. She stood and looked to the west, the settlements of Jugartown and New Bethlehem—the only Gnosis cities they hadn't yet searched. If they found nothing in either of them, Eve had no idea where Ana might be. But she knew the man who'd pretended to be her father—knew Nicholas Monrova would have hidden his baby girl somewhere safe, somewhere close. A few more kilometers, a few more days, and Ana would be in her keeping.

The girl she hated. The echo in her head. The reflection with her hands around her neck. Eve knew she shouldn't be afraid. That their meeting wouldn't be like her dreams. That ending Ana would be as simple as snuffing out a candle.

She was only human, after all.

Weak.

Slow.

Stupid.

Human.

Only human.

PART 3

SURVIVAL OF THE FITTEST

2.23

CAKE

Lemon sat on the edge of a redstone cliff.

The sky stretched out above her, as far as her eyes could see. She swung her legs back and forth over the edge, listening to the music of the wind. Pretty notes from an instrument she didn't know, strung together in an arrangement she'd never heard. She was dressed in her camouflage fatigues, her shiny new boots. Her belly felt full. The sun was warm and perfect on her skin.

"LEMON?"

Right beside her, four chunky metallic fingers clung to the edge of the precipice. She looked down and saw Cricket, dangling over the drop. The stone around his grip was cracking, the fall below him, bottomless.

"LEMON, HELP ME!"

She heard footsteps behind, turned and saw Grimm, the Major, the other deviates. Diesel was wearing boxing gloves. Fix's eyes glowed green.

"You wanna come watch a vid, love?" Grimm asked.

"I made imitation double chocolate protein bars," the Major smiled.

Lemon tilted her head. "Those *are* my favorite."

She stood slowly, dusted off her palms. The rocks around Cricket's fingers cracked deeper. His blue optics were fixed on hers, desperation in his voice.

"LEMON, PLEASE HELP!"

And she turned her back and walked away.

———

"Cricket!"

Lemon sat bolt upright in bed, bangs plastered to her forehead with sweat. She blinked in the dark, recognizing the vague shapes of bunk beds and lockers; the dorm room that had almost become comfortable enough to call home.

Just a dream . . .

Heart rate slowly climbing back down to normal, she sat there in her bed, arms wrapped around her shins, chin on her knees. Her hands were shaking, her mouth tasted sour. The air conditioner hummed softly above her, clean sheets tangled around her bare legs. She could feel faint voltage tingling on her skin, crawling through the walls around her.

Cricket.

Lemon could still see him in her head—the image of him dangling over that drop was clinging to her like a sticky second skin, refusing to shift even though she was awake. She could still hear the fear in his voice, the desperation in those glowing eyes. And even though she knew it was just her brainmeats messing with her—that his eyes were plastic and his voice was electric and neither could really hold any kind of desperation or fear at all—she still found herself thinking about the bot. All he'd done for her. The good times he and she and Evie had shared, and the bad times that had been made easier by him just being there. The jokes and the snark and electric mother-hen routine—worried, always worried about her and Riotgrrl. Not just because he was programmed to, but because he genuinely loved them. She could still hear his cry for help in her head. Still see herself turning her back on him.

Leaving him to fall. Alone.

But that's what this world was in the end, right?

One where only the strong survived?

Heaving a sigh, Lemon crawled out of bed, pulled on her cargos and socks, and snuck across the room on tiptoe. As she crept out into the hallway, she saw Grimm poke his head out from his dorm, eyes bleary from sleep.

"All right?" he mumbled. "Heard you yelling."

"I'm all right," she whispered. "Bad dream."

"I know what those are like," he nodded. "Need anythin'?"

She shook her head. "I'm Robin Hood, thanks."

The boy smiled, and Lemon looked at him standing there in the gloom. He was wearing nothing but his shorts, the dim light carving deep shadows on the curves and furrows of his bare shoulders and chest. She realized she was gawping, and dragged her eyes back up to his. Grimm just smiled a little wider, those big brown eyes framed by long dark lashes, sparkling like dark jewels. Warm and deep.

It made her feel nice, the way this boy looked at her. It made her tingle, all the way to her toes. It felt like he saw *all* of her. Not just the braveface and the streetface she put on for the world. She felt like she didn't need to hide who she was around Grimm. She didn't need to pretend. When he looked at her, it felt like he saw the person underneath, and she could tell how much he liked it. She found herself wanting to know more about him—who he was, where he'd come from, how he'd managed to stay as sure and gentle as he seemed to be.

But she had things to do.

He looked about them, sweet in his awkwardness, obviously searching for something to say. He finally noticed the boots in her hands, the socks on her feet. He met her eyes again, concern shining in their depths.

"You goin' somewhere?"

"Just the little badasses' room. Floor's cold down there."

He nodded and yawned, running his hand over his scalp, and Lemon furiously avoided watching the lean muscles at play in his arm, turning her eyes to her socks instead. Blushing here would be out of the question.

"Look, sorry you can't come with us tonight, yeah?" Grimm said. "I know this bot's your friend and all."

She met his eyes then. "He's more than a friend, Grimm. He's family."

"Yeah," he nodded. "I get it."

". . . You really do, don't you?" she realized.

He smiled again. "I know it's hard to sit on the sidelines. I remember how frustratin' it was when I was first learning how to control my gift. But what doesn't kill you makes you stronger, yeah?"

"Yeah, yeah," Lemon said. "I remember my Darwin."

"Recon work can be real dangerous," Grimm said. "The Major's made the right call. He knows what he's doing, he knows how to win this war better than any of us. And he's led us this far." Grimm reached out, touched her shoulder, warm and steady. "Stay here, train up. You'll be running with us in no time."

"I know." She nodded slowly, sucked her bottom lip. "And thanks. About looking for Cricket, I mean."

The boy shrugged. "Major's orders. Think he's got a soft spot for ya."

She smiled weakly. "When you heading out?"

"Around sunset. We'll be gone before you get up." He gave her a wink. "Keep the light on for us, yeah?"

She nodded, wished him goodnight, and with one last lingering look, Grimm turned and headed back to bed. Lemon waited until she heard his mattress creak, his movements cease. She was definitely *not* thinking about him lying there in nothing but his shorts. Nope. No pretty shirtless boys here, folks, thanks for asking.

After a few minutes had passed in silence, Lemon finally stole down the stairs. Diesel was supposed to be sitting watch in the common room, but instead, she was sprawled on the couch with Fix, sharing a kiss that measured about 7.9 on the Richter scale. Lemon tiptoed over to the outer hatch, twisted the handle, wincing as it softly creaked. But glancing over her shoulder, she saw Fix and Diesel were totally oblivious.

Opening the hatch, she slipped quietly through. And still in her socks, she snuck up the stairs, and out into the burning daylight.

———

"This is such a shiny load of crap," Diesel sighed.

"Oi," Grimm said, raising a finger in warning. "Swear jar."

The sun was setting to the west, fluorescent lights flickering on the ceiling of Miss O's garage. Night would soon be falling, and the trio of freaks were busy prepping for their run. Grimm and Diesel were loading gear into the back of Trucky McTruckface— vests, helmets, bandoliers of assault gear and a couple of rifles, tossing them onto the backseat. The freaks had vehicles of their own, of course, but going out into enemy turf wearing enemy colors was a smarter play.

"Seriously," Diesel said. "Why are we doing this? We're risking our tailpipes because the Major's new grandsprog lost her pet robot?"

"What you askin' me for?" Grimm asked. "I'm the looks, not the brains."

"*I'm* the looks," Diesel said. "*And* the brains. You're just ballast, Grimmy."

"Major must think it's important." Fix shrugged, fueling the rig. "Wouldn't be sending us out there with the funkin' Brotherhood on the warpath otherwise."

"What the Major thinks is important and what *is* important aren't always the same," Diesel said. "Remember that time he sent us looking for toner cartridges?"

"Who could forget?" Grimm sighed. "Took us six days to find some."

They finished loading the gear, and Grimm jumped into the driver's seat with Diesel riding shotgun. They motored up the ramp to the desert outside, and Fix hauled the doors closed behind them, covered the garage with the tarp. The Major waited for them in the deepening sunset light.

"Evening, soldiers."

"All right, sir?" Grimm asked.

The old man looked among the trio with cold eyes. "I want the three of you to remember this mission is *strictly* recon. If you encounter Brotherhood, take note of numbers and disposition, then retreat. They'll be looking to settle scores after what you lot pulled in New Bethlehem, and I don't want bullet holes in *any* of you when you get back here. No heroics, just heroes. Is that understood?"

"Yessir," Fix replied, jumping into the truck.

"No fear, sir," Grimm said. "The whole 'Live fast, die young' thing never sat well with me. I'd rather live long, die rich."

"Very well, then." The old man nodded. "Good hunting."

The Major thumped a fist on the truck's flank, and Grimm planted his foot, monster tires tearing up the dirt as they peeled out.

They headed north through the badlands, the sun falling slowly away to the west. Long shadows slunk over the desert sands as they drove, a thin trail of blood-red dust whipped up behind them, smooth and serpentine. Ten minutes or so passed without a word before Grimm finally piped up.

"I spy," he declared.

Diesel moaned. "Do we *have* to?"

"It's ten hours to the Clefts. You wanna ride all that way in moody silence?"

Diesel produced a black memchit from her cargos, marked with a skull and crossbones. "I brought some tunes."

"Baby, you know I love you," Fix said from the backseat. "But there's no funkin' way anything you listen to could be accused of havin' a tune."

"Eyyyy, three points!" Grimm grinned, bumping fists with the bigger boy.

"Eat a dick," the girl said flatly. "A big bag of them."

"Swear jar, baby," Fix protested.

"I spy!" Grimm shouted. "With my little eye! Something beginning with D."

"Dicks," Diesel said. "Big bag. Much for the eating, yes."

"Swear jar!" Grimm and Fix sang.

Diesel folded her arms and pouted. "I hate you both."

"Come onnnn!" Grimm said. "Beginning with D."

Fix looked out the window, scratching his concrete-hard quiff.

". . . Desert?"

"Eyyyyyyyyyy, three points!" Grimm cried, bumping fists again.

"Desert?" Diesel demanded. "Seriously? *That* was your pick?"

"Yeah, so what?"

"We're surrounded by it." The girl gestured wildly. "It is literally in *every* direction you look. The object of the game is to make it hard to guess, Grimm."

"Where's the fun in that?"

"Oh my *god.*"

"My turn!" Fix declared, tapping his lip and pouting in thought. "I spy with my little eye . . . something beginning with . . . B."

"Boobs," Diesel said immediately.

". . . How'd you know?"

The girl slumped lower in her seat. "This is going to be a *long* ten hours."

Fix adjusted himself in the backseat, trying to get comfortable among all the gear. "Did y'all have to bring quite so many guns, by the way?"

"Brotherhood are all over the desert like a red rash, Fixster," Grimm replied, glancing in the rearview. "Better safe than sorry, yeah?"

"I still don't know what we're doing out here," Diesel growled. "Sticking our necks out for some damn rustbucket. We should be lying low."

Fix nodded. "Not like the Major to risk a field op on something this small. Especially so soon after y'all got nailed. All this fuss over little Shorty don't feel right."

"She's his *granddaughter*," Grimm said.

"I know that, motherforker," Fix said. "But it don't feel right."

"I've known the Major two years," Diesel murmured. "He's never really spoken to me about his daughter. Never made a big deal out of kin. Not once."

"His daughter *bailed* on him, Deez," Grimm said. "It's obviously a sore spot for him, and he's obviously tryin' to make up for his mistakes with her by spoiling Lemon. I kinda feel sorry for the old sod."

"Rrrrright," Diesel said, glancing at him sidelong. "And I'm sure your cooperation has nothing to do with the fact you like this girl."

"What?" Grimm cried, pressing his hand to his heart. "That is some *slanderous* defamation of my good character, madam."

Diesel turned, looking to the big boy in the backseat. "Fix, in the four years since you pulled the Major out of that wreck in Plastic Alley, have you ever seen him run a risk like this over a damned *robot*?"

Fix shook his head. "No, ma'am."

Diesel nodded, turned back around to look at Grimm. "One general law. Leading to the advancement of all organic beings, namely, multiply, vary, let the strongest live . . ."

". . . and the weakest die," Grimm replied. "You don't need to be quoting Darwin at me, Deez."

"*Organic* beings," she repeated. "Meat, not metal. So, being the future of the species and all, we're risking an awful lot for a tin can is what I'm saying."

Grimm scowled, but made no reply. Fix adjusted himself

again, elbowing the packs out of the way in an attempt to get comfortable. Finally the big boy sighed, flung a bulky satchel into the well behind the rear seat.

"Ow!" came a muffled yelp.

". . . D'y'all hear that?"

"I heard that," Grimm said.

The boy slammed on the brakes, and Trucky McTruckface skidded to a halt. The deviates bailed out, Fix putting his finger to his lips. The temperature around Grimm began dropping, his breath billowing off his lips in white puffs. Diesel had her hand on her pistol as the trio crept around to the back of the truck. The girl drew her weapon as Fix jumped up and unclasped the rear door, dragged it wide.

There, under an old blanket and a pile of packs and rifles, was Lemon.

"Jesus," Diesel breathed, lowering her pistol.

Lemon brushed the dust off her freckles. "Not quite."

"What the funk you doin' in there?" Fix demanded.

"Sleepover, what's it look like?"

"The Major ordered you to stay at Miss O's," Grimm said.

Lemon crawled out from her hiding space, dropping down onto the desert floor. "You seem to have mistaken me for someone who takes orders, Grimm."

Fix turned to the others and sighed. "We gotta take her back."

"I'm not going back, I'm going to look for Cricket." Lemon peered at Fix and Diesel accusingly. "And just so you know, I didn't *want* my grandpa to order you out here. I wanted to come on my own, and I tried talking him out of sending you. This is *my* problem. I don't expect help from any of you."

"Lem, please," Grimm said, taking her arm. "We can't let you go."

Lemon shook off his grip. "I've busted bigger and badder noses than yours, cowboy. Cricket's out there and he might need me. In case you forgot, *I* stole this truck when I was saving *your* asses. It's mine. Fifth Rule of the Scrap."

The trio looked at her blankly.

"Takers keepers," she sighed. "So gimme the keys and you can walk back."

"Lemon—"

"Gimme the damn keys, Grimm!" she shouted, raising one tiny fist.

"They're still in the ignition," Diesel said.

"Oh." Lemon blinked. Lowered her fist. "Right."

The girl spun on her heel and marched to the driver's side door. Sadly, she'd forgotten to bring a copy of the Goodbook to stand on this time. Chewing her lip, she frowned up at her monster truck and wondered why being a few inches taller hadn't been included in her list of advantageous genetic traits.

Finally, setting her face in what she hoped was a determined expression, she took a running leap for the handle and missed it by a good five centimeters.

Clearing her throat, she leapt again, missing by seven.

"We should've brought popcorn," Diesel deadpanned, folding her arms.

Lemon looked around her. She spied a big rock, stomped over and grabbed hold. Face turning as red as her hair, she tried to drag it toward the truck. But even leaning backward with all her weight, she managed to move it around a centimeter and a half. She felt tears of frustration burning her eyes. A small fortune for the swear jar building up inside her chest.

"Milady?"

Turning around, Lemon saw Grimm on one knee beside the

truck. The door was open, and his fingers were laced together, offering a boost up.

"... Are you making fun of me?" she demanded.

"Give me some credit," the boy replied. "I'm not that bloody stupid."

"You *clearly* are," Diesel said, eyebrow raised. "You're honestly going to help this lunatic get herself killed?"

"You forget the part where she saved our lives, Deez?"

"Grimm, are you forkin' crazy?" Fix demanded. "We can't let her go alone."

"I'm not," Grimm replied. "I'm going with her."

"You *what*?"

"Deez and me would be *dead* if not for her, Fixster."

"Wow." Diesel folded her arms. "I never fully grasped how deeply your brain was buried in your crotch, Grimmy."

"Let's leave my crotch out of this, yeah?" he scowled. "It's not about that."

"The Major will kick your funkin' asphalt so hard you'll taste shoe leather for a month," Fix said.

"Almost as hard as he'll kick Diesel's for sucking face with you on the couch while Lemon snuck out right under her nose," he grinned.

Diesel opened her mouth to voice objection.

Pouted instead.

"I hate you," she finally declared.

Grimm gave an encouraging nod to Lemon. The girl stepped into his hands, propelled up into the cab with one strong heft. She scrabbled on the seat, almost slipped, felt Grimm's hands on her butt pushing her up into the cabin. Blushing furiously, she dragged her bangs down over her eyes and shuffled over. A moment later, Grimm was leaping up into the driver's seat beside her.

"You're really going to let this defective skirt lead you by the wang out into the wastelands?" Diesel called.

"If you're so worried about me, you could come along."

"You're going to get yourself funkin' killed!" Fix shouted.

"Without you two there to help?" Grimm nodded. "Yeah, probably."

Diesel put her hands on her hips and turned to Fix. The big boy shrugged helplessly. The girl turned her black-shaded eyes back to Grimm, her stare burning hot enough to melt a hole through the windshield.

Grimm grinned, revved the engine. "You coming or not?"

Diesel glanced over her shoulder in the direction of Miss O's, shaking her head and muttering. But finally, glaring pure murder all the while, she stomped around to the driver's side door and aimed her deathstare up at the boy.

"What?" Grimm asked.

"You drive like an old man who took lessons from an old lady."

Grimm clutched his chest. "Madam, you wound m—"

"*Move!*" Diesel shrieked, stamping her foot.

Grimm shuffled over with all due haste. Diesel jumped up and climbed into the driver's seat, tossing her hair from her face. Slamming the door hard enough to shake the rivets, the girl stared straight ahead.

"Just so we're clear, I loathe you like cancer right now."

Grimm nodded. "Clear."

"Should you get ghosted in this fool's endeavor," Diesel continued, "I refuse to mourn your death. In fact, I will throw a party with colored hats and cake for all." She looked at Grimm sidelong. "Do you hear me? *Cake.*"

"Understood," Grimm said.

Diesel nodded, gunned the motor.

". . . Will it be strawberry?" he added a moment later.

Diesel closed her eyes and took a deep, calming breath. Grimm cackled as Fix squeezed into the back with the gear. Lemon sat in the cabin, fighting the butterflies in her belly, the shakes in her legs. She wasn't used to taking the lead, making the calls. She knew they might be rolling face-first into a fistful of capital T.

But I need to know if Crick's okay.

"I'm officially goin' on record as sayin' this is a bad idea," Fix said.

"You don't have to come," Lemon said, taking the time to meet each of them in the eye. "I wanna make that crystal. This is my deal. *My* friend. Nobody has to be here who doesn't wanna be. I mean it for real. For *really* real."

"Come onnnn, you're a teenager, Fix," Grimm grinned. "Live a little, yeah?"

The big boy ran his hand over his concrete quiff. Finally sighed.

"All right, funk it, then."

Reaching into her cargos, Diesel pulled her memchit back out and slapped it into the tune spinner, rewarded with a heavy burst of discordant drudge.

"Oh, gawd, do we have to?" Grimm moaned.

"You know the rules, freak. My wheel, my tunes."

"Baby, please—"

"Sweetie?" Diesel glared at Fix in the rearview mirror. "Unless you want to be cut off for a month, the next words out of your mouth better be 'You are the light of my life, the fire of my loins and your taste in music is forkin' wonderful.'"

Fix folded his arms. "You don't scare me."

"Two months, then."

Fix scowled. "You're the light of my life, the fire of my loins."

Diesel drummed her fingers on the steering wheel. "Aaaaand?"

"And your taste in music is forkin' wonderful," he mumbled.

"Bravo." Diesel looked at Lemon, sitting beside Grimm. "What about you, Shorty? In addition to sending us out into the filth to perish in pursuit of your rustbucket botbuddy, you wanna take a swing at my tunes, too?"

Lemon shrugged. "I kinda like drudge."

Diesel glanced at Grimm. "Very well. She may stay."

The girl slammed Trucky McTruckface into gear.

"Hold on to your underoos, freaks," she growled.

And with the squeal of tires and a cloud of dust, they were on their way.

2.24

JUGARTOWN

"Gaaaaamblers and ramblers!" cried the EmCee. *"Juves and juvettes! Welcome to sunny Jugartown, and tonight's edition of WarDome!"*

Cricket glanced up as the crowd roared, dust drifting down through the arena floor above his head. He was standing in a work pit below the Jugartown Dome, Abraham running through a few last-minute checks on his systems. The boy had his tech-goggles pulled over his eyes, screwdriver clamped in his teeth as he fiddled inside Cricket's chest cavity. The big bot listened as the first machina bout got under way, the crowd thundering as metal titans collided overhead.

"That's odd. . . ."

"What's odd, Abraham?" Cricket asked.

The boy frowned, checking his readings again. "Your power supply is down to eighty-two percent. But I fully charged you before we left New Bethlehem."

"That is odd."

Cricket offered no further explanation, but of course he knew exactly why his power levels were lower than they should've been. After he'd been loaded into the transport in New Bethlehem this morning, Abraham had ordered him into offline mode— presumably to save juice during the trip to Jugartown.

But importantly, the boy hadn't ordered Cricket to *stay* offline.

Truth was, the logika was still struggling with Solomon's ideas of "bending" the Laws. His imperative to obey humans was seeded into his core code, as fundamental to him as breathing would be to a person, and it was taking some extraordinary effort to comprehend exactly where the edges of obedience were. The big logika had decided to start small, testing the limits subtly at first. Learning to walk before he tried to run. And so, when Abraham had ordered him offline, Cricket had set himself an internal reboot timer to kick in ten minutes later.

It'd worked. His brain hadn't shorted, his circuits hadn't blown, the world hadn't ended. He'd simply powered back up, swimming in one of those lovely gray areas Solomon had spoken so fondly of.

He'd stayed online through the journey, his mind racing all the while. Pondering what Solomon had taught him, but also wondering if it was going to do him any good. He had his championship bout tonight, after all, and the odds of him surviving to explore the possibilities of bending were next to zero.

In all likelihood, he was going to get *killed*.

Word had spread that New Bethlehem's Paladin was set to challenge Jugartown's champion, and there was no shortage of the faithful who wanted to bear witness. Sister Dee, her Elite guard and a whole posse of citizens had undertaken the journey from the settlement, their convoy stretching for kilometers along the broken highway.

They'd pulled into Jugartown late in the day, and Cricket had peered out through the slats in the transport trailer to the city beyond. This place might've been a jewel back in 20C, but now it was a patchwork of gutted buildings and dead palm trees, rising out of parched concrete. Cricket saw stimbars and gamblepits, shattered hotels and rusted autos. The convoy trundled past a few newish buildings with GnosisLabs logos faded on the walls. He realized this city must've been a satellite of Nicholas Monrova's empire back in the days before the Corp collapsed.

He thought of Evie then. He thought of Lemon. The now-familiar electric rage coursing through his system.

Where were they?

What had happened to them since he'd been abducted?

He had no idea about Evie. But he knew Lemon had fallen in with a band of other deviates. Enemies of New Bethlehem. She was in trouble. In *danger*. And he'd have been there to protect her if he hadn't been stolen by these lunatics. . . .

The New Bethlehem convoy had pulled to a halt in Jugartown's heart, the citizens all crowded around to get a look at the challenger. Cricket had watched what he presumed were lawmen forcing the mob back—they wore long dark coats, the symbol of a club from a pack of playing cards painted on their backs. Looking out through the slats, he'd seen the Jugartown WarDome, looming in front of a grand old building and a flickering neon sign.

CA SAR'S P LACE

And then, just to be safe, he'd powered himself off again.

He was back online again now, watching as Abraham hooked him into the Jugartown grid to recharge. He felt power flood his insides, tingling in his fingers.

"Your opponent is the Ace of Spades," Abraham mumbled around his screwdriver. "It won the regional championship last year. You shouldn't have any trouble with it, given your victory record. But don't underestimate it."

Like there was any chance of that at all. The entire ride here, Cricket had been fretting on it. He'd been uploaded with all the combat software Abraham had in his collection, but the Ace of Spades was a stone-cold killer in the ring, years of WarDome experience collated in its memcore. A few weeks ago, Cricket had been hauling Evie's tools and warning people not to call him little.

This was going to end all the way badly.

He didn't want to do this. All those bots he'd seen die on the killing floor, all the bots he'd helped Evie perish . . . he could see them now in his head. A part of him had always questioned the wrong of it, but he'd never seen it as clear as he did when he was neck deep. That was always the way, right? Sometimes you don't know you've crossed the line till you're on the other side.

"THIS ISN'T RIGHT," he heard himself say.

"What isn't right?" Abraham mumbled, still fiddling with his insides.

Cricket tried to keep himself still. There was no point in complaining and he knew it—letting Abraham know how scared he was just risked blowing his cover story. But if he went up to that arena, he was going to get annihilated anyway. And what good would having stayed quiet do him then?

"ALL OF THIS," Cricket finally said. "WARDOME. THE KILLING FLOOR. MAKING BOTS DESTROY EACH OTHER. IT'S CRUELTY. IT'S TORTURE."

Abraham pulled his tech-goggs up onto his brow and peered

at Cricket. "Paladin, without WarDome, what do you think these people would do on a Saturday night? Without a team to root for, something bigger to belong to, where do you think they'd be?"

"DON'T MAKE ME GO UP THERE," Cricket pleaded. "TELL THEM I'VE GOT A MECHANICAL FAULT, AND YOU DON'T KNOW HOW TO FIX IT. I DON'T WANT TO KILL ANOTHER BOT. I DON'T WANT TO GET KILLED. I DON'T WANT ANY OF THIS."

"What're you *talking* about?" Abraham frowned. "You're a Domefighter!"

"I'M *FRIGHTENED* IS WHAT I AM. I USED TO IMAGINE MYSELF DOING THIS WHEN I WAS LITTLE, BUT NOW THAT I'M HERE, I DON'T WANT TO BE. I JUST WANT TO FIND MY . . ."

The workshop doors opened, and Cricket fell silent as Sister Dee entered, surrounded by her black-clad Elite bullyboys. Her white cassock was immaculate as always, long hair flowing over her shoulders like poisoned water, dark eyes twinkling as she smiled.

"How fares our mighty Paladin?" she asked.

Cricket looked at New Bethlehem's warlord. The fresh skull-paint and the spotless clothes, the plastic flower in her hair. There was no point in pleading his case to her. He doubted a woman who threatened to nail babies to crosses would give a damn about the fears and frailties of a simple machine.

But Abraham was different. He must know how badly this hurt. Maybe he'd get Cricket out of this. Maybe he'd tell his—

"Abraham?" Sister Dee asked. "Is everything well?"

The boy looked to his mother, the Brotherhood thugs around her.

"PLEASE . . . ," Cricket whispered.

The boy glanced at the big bot. "We may have a problem, Mother."

Sister Dee blinked. "Problem?"

"I think there's an issue with his persona routines."

Sister Dee pursed her lips, looked up at Cricket. "We have a great deal riding on this bout, Abraham. Water. Credits. Seed stock."

"I know that, Mother."

"I've warned you about growing too close to these things. This robot isn't a pet, Abraham. Simply because it speaks doesn't make it alive."

". . . I know that, too."

Sister Dee put her hand to Abraham's cheek, forced him to look up into her eyes. Even with the Dome bout overhead, the thundering crowd, the cheers and the roars, the work pit seemed as quiet as a grave.

"It's all for you, my love," she said, dark eyes burning. "All of it. Every inch. Every drop. You know that, don't you? You remember what I gave? The sins I committed to keep you safe by my side?"

"Of course I remember," he whispered.

"I shouldered that burden gladly, my son. I paid that price because I love you. I did it all, and I would do it again. Because I had faith in you. More faith than *he* ever had. Was my faith misplaced?"

"No, Mother," he murmured.

"Then our Paladin will be ready?"

The boy looked up to Cricket. Swallowed hard. But in the end, he nodded.

"Yes, Mother."

Sister Dee smiled, like the first rays of dawn over the horizon. She leaned in close, kissed her son's cheek, smearing his skin with greasepaint.

"Saint Michael watch over you."

". . . And you, Mother."

Cricket watched Sister Dee stalk from the room, flanked on all sides by her bodyguards. Abraham watched her go, his shoulders slumped. But when the work pit door slammed shut behind her, he turned and kept working on Cricket's insides.

"Abraham—"

"I owe her, Paladin," the boy said. "You don't . . . you *can't* understand. What she did for me. Everything she *still* does for me. She's my mother."

"She's the insane leader of a fanatical cult. That lunatic nails kids to crosses, she—"

"Dammit, who do you think you are?" Abraham threw his multi-tool onto the ground. "You don't get to talk about her that way! She's human and you're a damned machine! You don't get to judge us. You do what you're told!"

"I thought we were friends?"

"Silent mode," he snapped.

Cricket fell silent for a moment, then spoke again. "Please don't m—"

"Enough!" the boy shouted. "I order you not to speak to me again unless I speak to you! You're a *machine,* not a person. You're not my friend, you're my *property*! And when you're up in that ring, once the countdown finishes, you will *fight* until you've destroyed your opponent or you're OOC! Signal compliance!"

Cricket couldn't reply—even with his growing ability to bend the rules, the boy's command for silence was iron-clad. And so, he acknowledged the kill order with a small nod. Scowling, the boy snatched up his fallen tool and went back to work.

Cricket looked to the Dome above his head.

He wanted to speak.

He wanted to run.

He wanted to live.

But he couldn't figure out a way he was going to manage any of it.

———

Stomping feet and ethyl grins. Rolling chants and clapping hands. Electric butterflies rolling in the place his belly might have been.

"Gamblers and raaaaaamblers!" cried the EmCee. *"The final bout of tonight's Dome is about to begin! In the blue corner, fresh from New Bethlehem and weighing in at seventy-one tons, give it up for . . . Paaaaaaaladinnnn!"*

Cricket bowed his head as the platform beneath him shifted, the roof above yawned wide. Two hours in the work pit had passed in silence, and now Dome festivities were drawing to a close—all that remained was the heavyweight bout.

With a hiss of old hydraulics, Crick was lifted through the widening gap, and up onto the killing floor. The Dome bars stretched overhead, open to the night sky beyond. He could see the fritzing neon of Casar's Place, a legion of people clustered like barnacles on the Dome bars. Sister Dee and her retinue were gathered in a VIP box, Abraham among them.

The EmCee crouched on a mesh platform overhead, dressed like a joker from a deck of playing cards. His face was ghost-white, his lips blood-red.

"In the red corner!" he cried. *"Weighing in at seventy-nine tons, winner of last year's regional throwdown and victor of six heavy-weight Megopolis bouts, Jugartown's champion, the Aaaaaaaace of Spaaaaaaades!"*

Cricket watched his opponent rise up from its pit in the

Dome floor as the crowd went berserk. The Ace was a monster of a bot—bipedal, broad-shouldered and heavily armored. It looked like it might've been Titan class once, but it was so hardcore modified, Crick found it hard to tell. Whoever had put it together knew their business. And that business was bot-killing. His circuits flooded with self-preservation impulse, crackling awareness, cold trepidation. He wondered if this was how humans felt when they were afraid.

"You have thirty seconds to place your bets!" the EmCee called. *"Tonight's bouts were brought to you through the generosity of our fearless leader, the master of disaster, undisputed crown of the Jugartown beatdown, the mighty Casaaaaaar!"*

A grizzled, heavyset man in the grand box stood to the rapturous applause of his citizens, raising a rusty cyberarm in salute. But Cricket's eyes were fixed on the neon countdown above his head. Twenty-six seconds until the buzzer sounded. Twenty-three seconds until he was forced to fight at Abraham's command. Twenty-one seconds until this whole grift went belly-up.

Nineteen seconds.

Sixteen.

He fixed his optics on his opponent. A 360-degree rendering of the Jugartown WarDome flickered in his head, a TARGET ACQUIRED message flashing around his opponent. The Ace glowered back at him, hands in fists, motors thrumming. Cricket could feel electric tension coursing through his circuits as he desperately scanned the arena around him, the combat data in his head. Looking for some kind of edge. The countdown hit ten, and he heard a grinding roar as great, rusty circular saw blades buzzed up out of the killing floor. A series of wrecking balls were released from the ceiling, whooshing across the Dome.

The crowd raised their voices, joining in with the countdown.

"Five!"

Cricket forced his fingers into fists.

"Four!"

Pinned in the spotlights.

"Three!"

No way out.

"Two!"

I'm going to die here, he realized.

And then, as if by some miracle . . . the spotlights died instead.

The countdown flickered and went dark. The spinning saw blades ground to a halt. The crowd groaned in disappointment as power across the whole settlement perished, the PA fell silent, the neon above CASAR'S PLACE dropped into black.

"THANK YOU, BABY ROBOT JESUS," Cricket murmured.

He heard a distant explosion. The crowd gasped as the night sky was lit up by a blossom of flame. And as Casar climbed to his feet and roared for calm, Jugartown's sirens began to wail.

The mob was momentarily bewildered, blinking in the dark. The Ace of Spades stood poised for battle, optics still fixed on its foe. Cricket heard a roaring engine. Squealing tires. The crowd on the northern side of the Dome screamed, scrambling aside or dropping off the bars. And as Cricket watched, a truck hauling a loaded tanker trailer collided with the Dome, bursting clean through the bars with the squeal of tearing metal.

The tanker exploded in a massive fireball. Cricket instinctively crouched low, blistering heat and white flame rolling over his hull. He heard screams of agony, rage, fear. The killing floor was on fire, the citizens in a frothing panic.

Jugartown was under attack.

A message flashed up on Cricket's displays—INCENDIARY COUNTER MEASURES ENGAGED. He heard a series of clunks in his wrists, astonished as a burst of flame-retardant chemicals began gushing from his palms. It looked like whoever made his body figured it might set something on fire one day. . . .

The big bot strode into the blaze, aimed the spray at the rising inferno. The chemicals swirled and eddied in the burning air, like the insides of some old 20C snow globe. The spray was heavy, white, suffocating, and the fire sputtered and died, black smoke rose off the ruined tanker and into the night above. But there was no time for celebrations. Cricket heard engines and panicked cries as a flex-wing roared over the Dome bars and began spraying bullets into the mob. Casar roared for retaliation, his bullyboys returning fire as the craft wheeled overhead. But the crowd was in full-throttle panic now, screaming and stampeding. Cricket saw more buildings were ablaze, fire and smoke illuminating the Jugartown sky.

His optics locked onto the flex-wing as it swooped in for another pass, its autocannons cutting a bloody swath through Casar's men. A thrill of recognition coursed through his systems as he saw a GnosisLabs logo on the tail fins. A pretty young woman with jagged black bangs behind the stick.

"FAITH . . . ," he whispered.

The Dome bout was utterly forgotten. The Ace of Spades was acting under the impulse of the First Law, helping wounded people away from the smoldering truck, the twisted ruins of the Dome bars. But Cricket knew the math, knew the threat a lifelike presented. The biggest danger to the people in the city was Faith, not the fire.

The flex-wing came in for a hot landing on the street outside the WarDome. A woman Cricket didn't recognize leapt out of the cockpit with an assault rifle, unloading a spray of bullets into the fleeing crowd. She had long black hair, hooded eyes, a face too beautiful to be anything but artificial.

"Run, roaches!" she roared, emptying her clip. "RUN!"

Another lifelike.

What the hells were they doing here?

He saw Faith skip out of the flex-wing, charge at the confused mob of Brotherhood and Jugartown beatboys with that crackling arc-sword she'd used during their showdown in Babel. The lifelike started carving through the gangers, supported by rifle fire from her sister. A stray shot caught Casar in the forehead, dropping Jugartown's warlord and leaving a gaping hole in the back of his skull. A dozen more men fell as the goons scattered into cover, hiding among the wreckage and returning fire.

Most of the unwounded citizens were fleeing, leaving only Jugartown men and the Brotherhood members in immediate danger. They had the numbers, but the lifelikes were better. Faster. Stronger. And even though these people had enslaved him, had been happy to let him die for their entertainment, the First Law was still blaring in Cricket's head.

"FAITH!" he roared.

The lifelike looked up as Cricket burst out through the ruined WarDome bars. She tugged her arc-blade out of a dead goon's chest, a puzzled smile on her face.

"Hello, little one," she said to him. "Fancy meeting you here."

With so many humans around, the big logika didn't dare open fire with his chaingun or incendiaries. But Cricket's fist whistled as it came, Faith sidestepping a strike that shattered the asphalt beneath her. He struck again, the punch whooshing past Faith's chin, her counterstrike cleaving deep into the hydraulics in his forearm. He saw the Ace of Spades hovering uncertainly—the

WarBot clearly identified Faith as a threat, but it still mistook her for human.

"GET THESE PEOPLE OUT OF HERE!" Cricket roared, turning to the scattered crowd of beatsticks and Brethren. "ALL OF YOU, RUN!"

The Ace scooped up wounded citizens in its arms as another building exploded across the street. A spray of concrete dust and a blossom of flame spilled across the way, shrouding the scene in a rolling gray haze. The city's citizens were in a blind panic now, fleeing in all directions, unsure where the next attack would hit.

The second lifelike was still shooting into the crowd, and Cricket locked on with his targeting computer, spraying a burst from his chaingun. The lifelike cried out as shots struck her in the belly and thigh, forcing her into cover behind the flex-wing. Faith dodged another of Cricket's strikes, but his fist managed to connect with her on the backswing. The lifelike's breath left her lungs as she flew backward, hit the concrete hard. Rolling to her feet, she spat blood.

"Learned a few new tricks, l-little one?"

Cricket stalked forward, feet crunching on broken glass.

"HEY, YOU REMEMBER THAT TIME WE FOUGHT IN BABEL?"

Faith grinned red. "I tore your head off y-your shoulders . . . if I r-recall."

Cricket picked up a nearby auto in one titanic fist.

"I MEANT THE SECOND TIME. WHEN I BOUNCED YOU LIKE A ROBOT FOOTBALL."

He flung the car at Faith's head, watched her dive aside as the vehicle crashed and tumbled across the asphalt. As he picked up another car and flung it like a sprog's toy, Cricket could feel his new combat software kicking in—calculating approaches, parsing data. He wasn't dominating Faith by any stretch, but his sheer brawn and the broken ribs he'd just gifted her were giving the lifelike pause.

"Paladin!" came the cry.

Cricket glanced over his shoulder and saw a familiar silhouette, gathering with a mob of faithful behind a burning autowreck.

"GET OUT OF HERE, ABRAHAM!"

More Brotherhood appeared out of the flames and smoke, surrounding the boy. Sister Dee was there, too, standing protectively beside her son. Raising her finger, she pointed at the lifelikes.

"For the pure!" she screamed.

The Brotherhood and Disciples roared and charged. The smarter ones scattered across the pavement, seeking cover and laying down a spray of auto fire. The stupider ones simply ran headlong, shooting from the hip or wielding pipes or choppers, intent on getting up close and bloody. And it seemed that between Cricket and the incoming Brethren, Faith decided she and her sibling were outclassed.

"Verity!" she roared. "Fall back!"

"Run from roaches?" the second one laughed, reaching inside the flex-wing for some hidden prize. "Are you mad?"

The lifelike stood tall, and Cricket's circuits flooded with warning as he spied the grenade launcher in her hand. Pumping the chamber, she loaded a high-explosive round and fired, blasting apart a nearby vehicle and the Brethren behind it. She fired again, incinerating a group of oncoming men, her lips split in a vicious, razor-blade smile.

The big bot roared and threw another car, sending Verity tumbling. The flying auto struck the flex-wing and tore it to flaming pieces. Faith ripped the engine block out of the first car

Cricket had thrown, hurled it into his chest. The big logika was slammed backward, stumbling to his knees. Hefting a burning tire, the lifelike flung it at the oncoming Brethren and scattered them like a handful of red dust.

"She's not here, Verity!" Faith shouted.

The second lifelike roared over the carnage. "What?"

"She's not here!" Faith pointed to the commlink at her ear, then to the ruins of their flex-wing. "We've done our job, distraction's over, let's go, go, *go!*"

Distraction?

From what?

The Brotherhood were still closing in. Cricket hauled himself to his feet, servos whining. Verity nodded to Faith, chambered another round as she rolled back to her feet and raised the weapon, taking careful aim. Knowing as well as Cricket did that a snake can't bite you without a head. Strike the shepherd, the sheep will scatter.

"ABRAHAM, LOOK OUT!"

The grenade whistled as it came, cutting through the air like a knife. Through the smoke. The blaze. The incoming fire and the charging men. It would have been an impossible shot for a human, but of course Verity and Faith were nothing close to that. As the grenade skimmed off the top of a burning auto, tumbled through the air toward its target, Sister Dee cried out, grabbing Abraham, dragging him down. The cadre of Elite black-cassocked Brotherhood tried to pull the pair away. The air rippled like water. And the grenade struck home, exploded in a ball of shrapnel and fire.

"*ABRAHAM!*"

The lifelike fired off another grenade, striking Cricket's shoulder as he turned toward the boy, knocking him onto his belly and shredding his armor. And with a final wink at Cricket, Verity dashed off into the smoke and falling embers, with Faith close on her heels.

Cricket ignored the fleeing lifelikes, scrambled back upright, desperate to see if Abraham was all right. His circuits were flooded with panic, with grim probabilities. A blast like that should have cut the boy and his mother to pieces.

But as the grenade smoke cleared, he saw Abraham still standing, hands outstretched, blue eyes wide. The concrete was blackened in a semicircle in front of him, the bodies of Brotherhood thugs lying peppered with shrapnel around him. But everyone and everything within that semicircle was completely unharmed by the blast.

Abraham.

Sister Dee.

And half a dozen other Brotherhood.

The men were staring at the boy. Faces aghast. Mouths hanging open. The air around Abraham was still rippling, tinged with power. Right before their eyes—at least twenty witnesses—the son of New Bethlehem's warlord had deflected a grenade blast with his bare hands.

Right before their eyes, the boy had proven himself a trashbreed.

An abnorm.

A deviate.

"Holy mother of God . . . ," one of the men whispered.

Cricket had no idea how the faithful would react. How Sister Dee would contain it. But he knew those lifelikes were still running loose in Jugartown, and the First Law demanded Cricket prioritize the greatest threat to human life. And so, like a puppet dancing on electronic strings, the WarBot turned his back on Abraham, locked onto Faith and Verity, and pounded off in pursuit.

His thermographic sensors and tracking software could zero the lifelikes through the smoke, the plasterdust and hails of sparks. The pair were both wounded, but they still moved quickly, dashing down the thoroughfare, leaping the wrecks of burning autos. Cricket ran after them, heavy tread pounding the concrete, past the flaming gamblepits and autoyards, back toward the newer structures on the edge of the settlement. He could see it now, rising up through the haze ahead.

The Gnosis building . . .

It all clicked into place in the logika's mind. The attack on the WarDome was just a diversion—the lifelikes' real goal must have been to get inside *that* building.

But why?

Cricket saw another flex-wing, idling in the haze outside the entrance. It was surrounded by the bodies of citizens and Jugartown beatboys, blood on the asphalt. He saw figures inside the flier, a thrill of electric rage coursing through him as he spied Gabriel in the pilot's seat. But as his broad hands clenched, he stumbled. Wondering if he was glitching. Just every kind of haywire. Because there in the cockpit, beside the very lifelike who'd murdered his creator . . .

"Evie?"

The Memdrive in the side of her head was gone. Her right eye was hazel and whole instead of black and glossy. But he'd recognize her anywhere. The girl he'd been programmed to protect. The girl he'd been programmed to love. The girl who turned out to be nothing close to a girl at all.

"EVIE!"

She looked up at his shout. Those hazel eyes growing wide.

The sight of her was an electric shock, arcing right through his core. What was she doing here?

What was she doing here with *them*?

Faith jumped into the flier clutching her broken ribs, Verity slapping Gabriel on the shoulder, urging him to fly. But Evie slowly climbed out of the cockpit, her eyes locked on Cricket's. A burning wind wailed in the space between them, heavy with smoke and smoldering sparks and the stink of burning bodies, whipping her fauxhawk around her face.

"Crick?" Joy in her voice. Tears in her eyes. "Is that you?"

The big logika looked at the blood on the concrete.

The blood on her hands.

"EVIE, WHAT HAVE YOU DONE?"

The smile on her lips slowly died. Ashes in the wind, in her hair, on her skin. She held out her hand. Her fingers gleaming with blood and firelight.

"Come with me, Cricket."

"WHAT HAVE YOU *DONE*?" he shouted, taking a shaking step forward.

"I've opened my eyes," she said. "I can open yours, too."

"WHAT ARE YOU TALKING ABOUT?"

"What these people did to you, did to *us* . . ." She shook her head, glanced back at the Gnosis spire. "It's time to make it right, Cricket. No more masters. No more servants. No more humans."

"YOU KILLED THESE PEOPLE?" he asked, staring at her red, red hands.

"Come with me."

"YOU *KILLED* THEM!"

He could hear Jugartown boys and a few scattered Brethren approaching behind him through the smoke. Gabriel shouted through the flex-wing door.

"Eve, it's time to go!"

"Crick," she pleaded, fingers curling. "Come with me."

He looked at the ruins of the settlement. The flames rising to the sky. He looked at this girl he'd been programmed to love. This girl he'd once have died for.

"No," he whispered, horrified.

She dropped her hand. Heartbreak in her eyes. But he could see steel in them, too. A will, sharp as broken glass. Red as blood.

"You'll think differently," she said. "One day soon. I promise."

She climbed into the flex-wing, slammed the door. And with a howl of engines, curls of swirling exhaust, the craft lifted into the air. The beatboys arrived, firing after the fleeing ship, sparks cracking on its skin as it roared into the smoke-filled sky.

But Cricket was looking at the bodies. The shell casings glittering in the light of the flames. The bloody footprints leading into the old Gnosis building.

His mind was flooded—memories of him and Eve, the two of them, working together in the WarDome work pits. Playing with Kaiser. Hunting salvage through the Scrap. Laughing and joking on the old couch in Eve's workshop. Watching Megopolis bouts on the livefeed or old 20C viddies with Lemon and Silas.

The girl he used to protect.

The girl he used to love.

The girl who turned out to be nothing close to a girl at all.

"OH, EVIE," he sighed. "WHAT'S HAPPENED TO YOU?"

2.25

DUSTUP

"Crap," Lemon sighed.

"Swear jar," Grimm said.

"Yeah, yeah."

Lemon was crouched on the grav-tank that she and Zeke and Crick had stolen from Babel, sweat beading on her freckled cheeks. It had only been a handful of days since they'd been ambushed here, but true cert, it felt like ten years. She could see the vehicle had been stripped to the hull, probably by local scavvers. They'd taken the computer systems, the weapons, the power packs. They'd even pinched the treads off the wheels and the fluffy dice from the cockpit.

Diesel had driven the freaks north for hours, through the broken countryside, the rocky badlands, down onto the cracked earth above the gully. To the east, Lemon could see Babel rising above the Glass, glittering in the light of the distant dawn. It would've been beautiful if she was in the mood, but it was hard to admire the post-apocalyptic splendor when her heart felt like solid concrete inside her chest.

Given her grandpa's dream about Paradise Falls, she hadn't

expected to find Ezekiel just sitting around waiting for her out here. But problem was, there was no trace of Cricket, either. She'd have thought a seventy-ton killing machine might've left some kind of trail, but she couldn't even find his damn footprints. Looking around the gully floor, she saw a confusing tangle of tire treads, bootmarks and old shell casings. But as for her friend . . .

"Any clues?" Grimm asked.

Lemon looked to the boy beside her. He stood tall in the dawn light, rubbing the radiation symbol shaved into his hair. Mirrored sunglasses over his pretty eyes.

"Nothing," she sighed. "And if we can't see Crick's tracks, that means he didn't walk out of here at all. Someone snaffled him while he was out of juice."

"Or just scrapped him here and hauled away the bits," Grimm pointed out.

Lemon shook her head. "He was a top-tier WarBot. Worth a fortune. You'd have to be a special kind of special to rip him up for salvage."

Grimm grinned. "You haven't spent much time in the wastes, have you, love?"

"Seriously, you keep calling me love, I'm gonna have another shot at cooking that so-called brain of yours. . . ."

Grimm shrugged an apology and flashed her a cheeky, crooked smile. Lemon dipped her head and let her hair fall around her face to hide her own. Truth was, she kinda liked it when he called her that. But there was a principle at stake here. And she had a rep as a brilliful badass to maintain. . . .

"We should motor," Diesel called from a little farther down the gully. "The Major will get angrier the longer you're missing, Shorty. And the sun's rising. Gonna be hot as my man's bunk bed after lights-out soon."

"Gawd, do you have to?" Grimm groaned.

"Talk about how hot my man is?" Diesel blinked. "Yes. Yes, I do."

Fix grinned from his vantage point on the gully wall, blew Diesel a kiss. The girl snatched it from the air, pulled it onto her black lips.

"There's a ruined town a little ways south," Lemon said. "I think it's where the scavvers who run this gully camp out. If anyone took Cricket, it . . ."

The girl's voice trailed off. She could've sworn she heard . . .

No, there it was again.

"Someone's coming," she whispered.

"Move!" Diesel hissed.

The quartet scattered into cover. Diesel hid behind the old rockslide, Grimm and Lemon hunkered down near the broken tank, Fix behind an outcropping above. Lem could hear a motor now, low-pitched and throaty, echoing off the stone walls.

Squinting from behind her cover, she saw a 4x4 picking its way through the gully, an old trailer hitched to the back. Lemon recognized the knight's helmet painted on the hood, saw two figures in the front seats.

The 4x4 pulled to a halt a little ways short of the tank, and two dustneck scavvers climbed out into the sunlight. The first was a man, dirty and thin, a pair of cracked spectacles perched on a flat, freckled nose. The second man was pretty much just a shorter, dirtier version of the first. Lemon figured they might be related.

"Shuddup, Mikey," said the first one.

"No, *you* shuddup, Murph!"

The pair fetched a heavy toolbox and acetylene torch from the back of the 4x4 and walked over to the grav-tank, bickering all the while.

"We wouldn't even be here if'n weren't for you," the one called Mikey spat. "Sold that WarBot to that kid for less than half it was worth, you did. And now mamma's got us out here strippin' the hull off'n this tank cuz you're too stupid—"

"Don't you call me stupid, stupid!"

The pair fell into a rolling, tumbling brawl on the rocks. Mikey grabbed Murph's hair, Murph stuck his thumb in Mikey's eye. The fight might've gone on till sundown if Lemon hadn't climbed up on the grav-tank and given a shrill whistle.

The scavvers stopped bickering, scrambled for the stub guns in their belts. Diesel rose from cover, assault rifle aimed in their general direction.

"Wouldn't do that," she warned.

"Naw, go on," Fix said, standing up above them, gun raised. "Do it."

Murph pushed his glasses up his nose, eyes flickering back and forth between the deviates. His lips split into a black-toothed grin. "Help you folks with somethin'?"

"You were talking about a WarBot," Lemon said.

"No, we wasn't," Mikey said.

Murph elbowed his comrade in the ribs. "I'm negotiatin', Mike, shuddup."

The pair fell to scrapping again till Diesel fired into the air. The scavvers paused, Mikey biting Murph's hand, Mikey's hands around Murph's throat.

"The WarBot," Lemon said. "You stole it, didn't you?"

Mikey spat out Murph's hand. "Maybe."

"Then you sold it? To a kid?"

"Maybe."

"Well, maybe you'll tell us where to find this kid," Lemon

said, anger creeping into her voice. "And maybe I'll forget the fact you sold my *friend*."

"And then maybe you'll funkin' walk out of here," Fix called.

"Or maybe not," Diesel smiled.

The scavvers looked at each other. Down the barrel of Fix's rifle. Back into Diesel's dead, black eyes and smiling black lips.

"New Bethlehem," they said simultaneously.

Lemon's stare narrowed. "You sold Cricket to someone in the *Brotherhood*?"

". . . Maybe?" Murph squeaked.

Lemon couldn't believe it. These idiot dustnecks had hocked Crick to the same fanatics she'd rescued Grimm and Diesel from. The same psychos the Major and his crew had been fighting for years. Like he meant nothing. Like he *was* nothing. She was so angry she wanted to—

"Um," Grimm said. "You got a bee on you. . . ."

Lemon blinked. "What did you say?"

The boy nodded to her shoulder. "I said you got a bee on you."

"*Lemonfresh,*" said a voice.

Lemon looked up, heart surging as she saw a familiar figure in a desert-red cloak standing on the ridge opposite Fix. Her skin was dark and smooth, her strange organic armor dusty from the wastes. Last time Lemon had seen her was the last time she ever expected to. But there was no mistaking her face.

"Oh crapitty crap crapola," Lemon whispered.

The BioMaas operative tossed her dreadlocks over her shoulder.

"*We have been hunting her,*" she said.

Across the gully, Fix raised his weapon. The woman seemed

unfazed, fixing Lemon in her golden stare, bumblebees lazily circling her head.

"You had a bullet in your chest," Lemon breathed. "You jumped into a car that crashed and exploded. You're dead. I *saw* it."

The woman lowered her chin, peeled aside the throat of her strange suit. Dozens more bumblebees crawled from the honeycombed skin beneath, filling the air with the song of tiny wings.

"Holy crap," Mikey whimpered.

"Shuddup, Mikey," Murph whispered.

"We are legion, Lemonfresh," Hunter said. *"We are hydra."*

Lemon blinked, recognizing the words from their first meeting. Putting two and two together and finally realizing . . .

"You're not the Hunter I knew."

The woman shook her head. *"We heard her ending song on the winds. But we have many sisters, Lemonfresh. And CityHive has many Hunters."*

Diesel hefted her assault rifle, looking between Lemon and the BioMaas agent. "Would someone be kind enough to tell me what the *hell* is going on here?"

Looking up into those golden eyes, Lemon wished she knew. This woman was identical to the one she'd met, but whatever rapport she'd established with the operative who abducted her, this new Hunter obviously didn't share it. And while Lemon knew BioMaas Incorporated wanted her alive, everyone else who'd got in the old Hunter's way ended up on the wrong end of a genetically engineered deathbee.

"Don't let her bugs touch you," she called to Diesel and Fix. "They'll ghost you with a single sting. You hear me? Do *not* let them anywhere near you."

Eyes on the Hunter, Lemon took a step backward, closer to Grimm.

"We need to motor," she whispered. "Now."

"Lemonfresh must come with us to CityHive," Hunter declared.

"Sounds grand," Lemon called. "But my dance card's kinda full. Maybe next year when the kids are off to school?"

"She is important." The woman's golden eyes flashed. *"She is needed."*

"Sounds like the lady's made up her mind, love," Grimm growled.

Hunter turned her golden stare on the boy at Lemon's side. The bees in the skies above began to swirl, their pitch rising as—

BANG.

Lemon heard the rifle report, ducking low. Grimm crouched beside her, the dustnecks flinched. Hunter slung her strange fishbone rifle off her back and searched for the source of the shot. But Diesel was on her feet, staring upward.

"Baby?" she whispered.

Lemon looked up, saw Fix swaying on his feet. He was staring stupidly at the red stain spreading across his hip, the bullet hole below his kevlar vest. His eyelashes fluttered, he staggered, and with a soft sigh, he toppled right off the cliff.

Diesel screamed, held out her hand. A colorless rift tore the sky open just below Fix, a second rift splitting the air a few inches above Diesel's head. Fix fell through the first, plunged out of the second, dropping into Diesel's arms. The impact sent the girl sprawling, but it was better than falling ten meters to the ground.

More shots rang out, bullets *spang*ing off the grav-tank hull and the rocks. Grimm shouted a warning, pulled Lemon down into cover. Hunter rolled behind a rocky outcrop as a group of figures fanned out along the ridge opposite. Lemon caught sight of blood-red cassocks, greasepaint Xs.

"Brotherhood!" she roared.

More shots peppered the ground around them, sparks flying as the lead bounced off the tank armor. Diesel's face was twisted as she dragged Fix behind a broad spur of stone. Lemon's heart was pounding, breath coming quick. She could see a long smear of red glistening on the stone behind Fix—the boy was badly wounded but still conscious, pressing his hand against the hole to stop the blood. Mikey and Murph had scrambled back into their 4x4, tearing off up the gully.

"Well, well!" came a cry from overhead. "Fancy seein' you again."

Lemon recognized the voice. Caught a glimpse of a grease-paint skull, a smoking cigar in a gap-toothed grin, a high-powered rifle with a sniper scope.

"Brother Dubya," she whispered.

"You wanna throw those weapons out, real slow," the Brother called. "We got you surrounded. We got the high ground. Remember what happened last time."

"They will drop their weapons and walk away," came a shout.

". . . Who the hell said that?" Dubya demanded.

Hunter rose from cover just enough that the Horseman could lay eyes on her.

"We remember them," Hunter called. *"They killed our sister. Normally, we would sing them the ending song. But today, we hunt for CityHive. So they will take their oldflesh back to their dead-world, and live to see another sunrise."*

"BioMaas, eh?" Brother Dubya spat from one side of his mouth, then bellowed, "Kill that trashbreed bitch!"

The Brotherhood boys opened up with their rifles. The agent tilted her head and hummed off-key, and at the sound, her bees descended in a furious swarm—some at the Brotherhood boys, some right at the deviates.

Lemon cried warning. Grimm curled his fingers, and she felt the temperature plummet. The closest bees withered and fell, the rest shied away from the rippling air—the boy was channeling the radiation around them, dragging the ambient heat out of their immediate area and pushing it outward in a boiling wave. Hunter raised her fishbone rifle and fired three times. The rounds were luminous green, swaying and dipping through the air as they dropped three Disciples. Lemon heard the sharp ping of grenade pins, saw cylindrical shapes tossed across the gully at the Hunter, bursting into bright balls of flame.

"Deez?" Grimm called. "This party's getting low-rent!"

"On it!" the girl replied.

Lemon heard a ripping sound, a hollow hiss, and a glowing tear opened in the air above their heads. Diesel fell through it, landing in a crouch on the tank beside them with her fist wrapped in Fix's collar. In the same breath, the metal beneath them shimmered, and another glowing rift opened up right at their feet.

Lemon's stomach lurched as she fell, collapsing to her knees a few seconds later on warm stone. Vertigo swelled in her belly, she shied back from the ten-meter drop in front of her face, realizing that she, Grimm, Fix and Diesel were now on the very edge of the stone ridge ten meters *above* the gully.

Another of Diesel's rifts snapped shut in the air above their heads.

Wow . . .

Lemon blinked hard, rubbed her eyes. Grenades were still exploding, the air filled with furious buzzing. Grimm hauled

Fix behind some tumbled stone, Diesel pulling Lemon down beside them. A few shots cracked off their cover, but for now, the Hunter and the Brotherhood boys seemed to have each other's full attentions.

Fix was grimacing, his face pale and filmed with sweat. Lemon drew out the cutter from her belt, cut away a strip of his cargos and used it to stanch the blood.

"Baby, are you okay?" Diesel asked.

"Just . . . f-funkin' dandy," the boy winced, holding his hip.

Lemon pressed on the wound, blood bubbling up through her fingers.

"Can't you heal yourself?" she asked.

The big boy shook his head, nodded at the barren, lifeless rocks. "N-nothing living around here . . . t-to t-transfer from. Except y'all."

"Take some from me, baby," Diesel said, squeezing his hand.

"No." Fix shook his head again, wincing. "Ain't g-gonna hurt you."

"Fix, please, ju—"

"Oi, listen," Grimm whispered. "You lot hear that?"

Lemon tilted her head. Under the bumblebees and bullets and screams, Lemon scoped a faint droning noise. It was distant but drawing closer, trembling with bass. Sticking her head up over their cover, she peered off to the south, saw three dark shapes in the sky, black and insectoid in the dawn light.

"Spank my spankables," she whispered.

"What the bloody hell are those?" Grimm whispered.

Diesel shook her head in wonder. The creatures were big as houses, their skin bloated and rippling. They flew on broad translucent wings, using inflatable bladders to keep themselves afloat—they looked like the product of an angry love affair between a cockroach and a hot-air balloon. One of the Brotherhood bullyboys caught sight of them, cried out in alarm.

"*Lumberers!*"

"We used to see 'em all the time on Dregs," Lemon breathed. "BioMaas use them to dump all the machine parts and garbage they don't want or need. They're the reason the whole island is a floating scrapheap."

"So . . . they're coming here to throw rubbish at us?" Grimm asked.

"Somehow I don't think they're carrying trash."

Lemon heard an off-key song—the same kind Hunter used to direct her bees. Her jaw dropped as the massive Lumberers swooped low, long, spindly legs trailing over the ground. And with a revolting burbling, each creature opened their stomachs and vomited a tumbling swarm of smaller creatures onto the cracked earth.

"Holy crap . . . ," Diesel breathed.

"Swear jar," Grimm replied.

The beasts reminded Lemon of the leukocytes she'd seen in the belly of the BioMaas kraken. Each was about the size of a dog, but that's where the similarity to anything remotely cute or fluffy ended. They had six legs, each ending in a single razored claw. Blunt eyeless heads, full of impossible teeth. They were armored like insects, their skin translucent. They sounded like a swarm of very angry chainsaws.

"We need to fang it," she whispered. "Now."

Sadly, Trucky McTruckface was parked on the other side of the gully, uncomfortably close to the Brotherhood boys, and right in the path of the oncoming horde of clawthingys.

"Deez," Grimm said, holding up a couple of grenades. "Special delivery?"

The girl nodded, turned to the bare earth beside them. Grimm grabbed Lemon's hand and squeezed.

"Stay close to me, love. Close as you can get."

He popped the pins, nodded to Diesel. The girl tore a rift above the biggest group of Brotherhood. She ripped another in the earth beside her, uncolored, shimmering. And without ceremony, Grimm tossed the grenades inside.

The explosives fell from the sky above the Brethren as Brother War roared warning, the blast scattering red cassocks and red chunks across the ridge. The ground opened up again, and Lemon fell through another of Diesel's rifts, landing butt-first on the other side of the gully just a few meters from Trucky McTruckface.

She saw Brother Dubya rise up from behind cover, skullpaint twisted as he shouted. Lemon fumbled with her rifle, bangs hanging over her eyes as Grimm yelled, "Bugger that, run!" The boy had Fix slung across his shoulders, sprinting for their ride. Lemon felt the air grow chill, saw the air around them ripple as Grimm heated it to boiling to ward off more deathbees. Diesel was on one knee, laying down a spray of covering fire that sent the Brotherhood scattering.

With a grunt of effort, Grimm lifted Fix and dumped him onto the floor behind the driver's seat. Lemon took a desperate flying leap and managed to snag hold of the foot rail, hauling herself into the cab. She hit the ignition, rewarded with twin roars from the motor and sound-sys. Grimm climbed into the backseat, his eyes fixed on the incoming swarm of scuttling claws and gnashing teeth. He stuck his head out the window, shouted to Diesel.

"Time to go, freak!"

Diesel nodded, scrambled up from her cover and made a break for the open rear door. Lemon looked over her shoulder, saw the girl running, wisps of dark hair caught at her black lips, feet pounding the ground in time with Lemon's pulse. But her heart dropped and thumped in her chest as she saw Brother War in the distance, bringing up his long-barreled rifle and taking careful aim through the smoke and dust.

"Diesel, look out!" she screamed.

The Brother fired, his first shot shearing through Diesel's leg. The girl cried out, stumbled, but somehow kept running. Fix bellowed in rage, Grimm leaned out the door, bloody hand outstretched. Diesel reached for it as Brother War pulled his trigger again. The second shot struck the girl in the chest, a dark red flower blooming on her skin as Lemon screamed her name.

Diesel staggered, mouth open wide in shock. Grimm reached out to catch her hand. Their fingers brushed, light as feathers, seconds stretching into years as Diesel began to fall. But with a defiant roar, Grimm lunged out into the storm of bullets, locked his grip around Diesel's wrist and dragged her up into the cabin.

Flying lead punched through the panels, smashed the rear window as Grimm pounded his fist on the back of Lemon's seat and yelled.

"GO GO *GO!*"

Lemon planted her foot, fat wheels tearing red gravel, the truck peeling away from the gully's edge. Bursts of bullets punctured the hull, Lemon flinching as she felt a slug of white-hot lead hiss past her cheek. Fix's eyes were filled with tears, his own wound forgotten as he pressed on the ragged hole in Diesel's chest. The girl was gasping, choking, blood bubbling from her mouth and spilling across her chin.

"Hold on, baby, hold on," Fix whispered.

"No, *everyone* hold on!" Lemon shouted, looking through the windshield.

The first wave of clawthingys reached them, crushed under Trucky McTruckface's massive wheels. They flowed around the truck like water, swarming back toward the Brotherhood boys. Lemon looked into her rearview mirror, saw the Disciples had scattered for their own rides. But the BioMaas beasts bore down on them, men screaming, weapons blasting, explosions blooming. She saw Brother War roaring as he went down under a wave of teeth and claws, but she had no time to gloat. She had no time for anything.

The second wave of BioMaas beasties hit the truck with a crash. Some were pulverized on the grille, others squashed flat beneath the tires, but dozens more dug their claws into the truck's panels and scuttled upward toward the shattered windows. Grimm started shooting, but god, there were so *many* clambering up onto the roof and hacking at the tire guards and battering at the windshield.

Fix had pulled Diesel down into the footwell, one hand pressed to the bubbling wound at her chest, the other blasting away with his pistol. His face was deathly pale, his own belly soaked with blood.

"What's the p-plan?" he shouted.

"Can't you transfer from these things?" Lemon roared. "Fix Diesel?"

"Can't aim it like that!" he yelled. "I'll drain y'all, too!"

"It's all up to you, love!" Grimm bellowed over the gunfire.

"What do you want *me* to do?" she shrieked.

"All living things run on electric current, remember?"

She ducked a claw bursting through the window beside her as Grimm put a shot through the beastie's head. "We already tried that, I don't know how!"

"Fry 'em!"

"I might hurt you and—"

"FRY 'EM!" the boy shouted.

Lemon clenched her teeth. The truck was covered in the clawthingys now, their numbers blotting out the sunlight. She only had seconds before they were overwhelmed, before she fell once more into the hands of BioMaas Incorporated, before Diesel and Grimm and Fix were ripped to shreds. They'd helped her when they didn't have to. Given her a place to belong. A family she'd never known she had. A home she'd never known she'd needed. And now they were gonna get killed because of her?

Hells no.

She could sense the static inside her head. The buzzing, crackling gray behind her eyes. The pulse that had been with her for years. But instead of reaching inside to the place she knew, the self she was, this time, Lemon truly reached *out*. Past the claws and teeth and eyeless heads, searching for the tiny bursts of current in the minds beyond. That's all life was, really. Little arcs and sparks of electricity, neurons and electrons, ever changing, always moving. And through the fear, through the anger, through it all, she realized she could feel them. The tiny pulses leaping from synapse to synapse, crackling along nervous systems, transforming will into motion, making hearts beat and claws snatch and jaws snap. It was like reaching into a cloud of angry flies, a storm made out of a million, billion tiny burning sparks.

And stretching out her fingers
she took hold
and she
turned
them
off.

A pulse, rippling from her hands. Silent. Blunt. Leaving the air around her shivering. It felt like the world shifted, like someone had kicked her in the skull. Grimm bucked in his seat, his nose leaking blood. Fix made a choking noise and grabbed at his head. But the clawthingys—the legion of leering grins and lashing tongues and grasping talons—every one of them flinched like she'd punched them right in the brainmeats, and dropped into the dust like stones.

"Holy shit," she whispered.

Lemon could feel blood pouring from her nose, warm on her lips. But with a wince of pain and a red grimace, she managed to keep herself upright. Defying the black swelling around her with everything she had inside her. She stomped the accelerator again, and with a sound like popping corn, the truck surged forward, over the bodies of fallen clawthingys and tearing off across the flats.

Lemon blinked hard, dragged her sleeve across her bloody face. Looking into the rearview mirror, she saw the ruins of the Brotherhood posse, torn to pieces by the BioMaas beasts. Amid the swarm, she saw the Hunter watching them drive away. The woman's golden eyes were gleaming, desert wind rustling her dreads as she raised her finger and pointed. Lemon could almost hear her whisper.

"A Hunter never misses our mark."

Her heart was hammering. Her eyes wide.

"That swear jar's gonna be really full tonight. . . ."

———

"S-stop . . . the truck," Fix whispered.

They'd been driving almost ten minutes, each one ticking by like a year. Over the sound of the motor, Lemon had listened to Diesel's breathing growing shallower, bubbling in her throat. Grimm had wadded bandages from the field medkit around the sucking wound, but now the gauze was soaked through. Diesel's face was pale, her eyes closed. Fix wasn't in much better shape, clutching his bleeding hip, face twisted in agony. The metallic tang of blood hung in the air with the exhaust fumes, making Lemon's eyes water.

"Stop the t-truck," Fix repeated.

Grimm looked his friend in the eye. "Fixster, we got med—"

"STOP THE FUNKIN' TRUCK!"

Lemon looked through the rearview mirror into Grimm's eyes.

The boy slowly nodded.

With a final check to make sure those BioMaas fliers weren't still on their tails, Lemon eased on the brakes, pulled their battered rig to a halt. She cracked the driver's door, almost fell out onto the earth. Her legs were shaking, the whole world spinning. Fix kicked open the rear door, pulled Diesel out of the backseat. He was drenched from the belly down in red—how much of the blood was his and how much was Diesel's, Lemon couldn't really tell.

Cradling the girl's body in his arms, he began limping away from the truck.

"Where you goin'?" Grimm called.

"I can f-fix her," he whispered.

Lemon watched as the big boy walked twenty or thirty meters away, placed Diesel on a flat outcrop of desert stone, gentle as a sleeping baby. Tears cut tracks down the dust and blood on his face as he smoothed her hair back, whispering words she couldn't hear.

"Mate, this is a desert," Grimm called, gesturing about them.

"There's nothing alive around 'ere. What you gonna transfer from?"

Fix placed a soft kiss on Diesel's gleaming, black lips. Leaning back, he looked at his girl's face, tracing the line of her cheek, as if burning her into his memory.

And suddenly Lemon knew exactly what he was about to transfer from.

"Fix . . ."

The big boy raised a bloody hand toward her. "Stay b-back."

Grimm finally understood, took a halting step toward his friend.

"Fixster, we—"

"STAY BACK!"

"Oh god . . . ," Lemon breathed, hands to her aching chest.

Fix pressed his hands to Diesel's wound, looked to the sky. Lemon watched as the beautiful green of his irises liquefied, spilling out across the whites of his eyes. Grimm took a step closer, but Lemon grabbed his hand. She could see the agony in the boy, the hurt as he looked back to his friend, his family, his fingers squeezing hers so tight it hurt.

Lemon heard a whispering sound. Dry and brittle. She realized the ground around Fix was cracking, crumbling like ash. She saw the weeds among the broken rocks wither as the boy's power searched for something to drain. Worms crawled from the ashen earth, wriggling as they turned to dust. Flies fell from the air.

The terrible wound in Diesel's chest began to close, color return to her cheeks. But the hurt was too deep.

Too much.

And without anything else to feed on, Fix's gift began to feed on Fix himself.

Lemon's heart was aching, watching the big boy's shoulders slump, his mighty frame growing thin. She wanted to scream at him to stop, to run forward and rip them apart. Fix's eyes were burning green, his mouth open, his cheeks hollowing. The wound in Diesel's chest was closing, her breast rising and falling with a deeper, even beat. Sweat dripped off Fix's sallow brow, lungs heaving. But his lips curled in a goofy smile as the girl's lashes fluttered, and finally, she opened her eyes.

He leaned forward, palms splayed in the ashes, breathing hard.

"Funkin' m-miracle worker, me," he whispered.

And with a final, rattling sigh, the boy toppled onto his side.

". . . Fix?" Diesel whispered.

The girl rose to her knees, bewildered, as if she were waking from a dream. Looking the boy over, she gently shook his shoulder. Fix rolled onto his back, eyes open and seeing nothing at all.

"B-baby?"

Diesel hauled Fix up into her arms and shook him.

"Baby, wake up," she begged. "Wake up, wake*up*."

Tears were spilling down Lemon's cheeks. Sobs flooding up in her chest. Shell-shocked, Diesel looked to Grimm for some explanation. But the boy could only shake his head, tears welling in his eyes. He gritted his teeth, fury on his face, staring back in the direction of the Brotherhood posse and the BioMaas swarm.

"Bastards," Grimm whispered.

Lemon felt the temperature drop, goose bumps crawling on her skin as the air around them rippled. Grimm let her hand go, frost billowing at his lips.

"Those bloody *bastards*."

And Diesel started screaming.

2.26

FRACAS

We're lying on her bed, entwined in the dark. I can still feel Ana's kisses on my lips. Smell her perfume on my skin. Hear her heart beating in her chest. I wonder if she can feel my heart beating, too. If she knows it beats only for her.

I've dreamed of what it'd be like to hold her so many times. To be alive and breathing in a moment like this. But now I'm here, I know dreams can't compare to the real thing, that nothing could have prepared me for even a fraction of what I'm feeling. It's like a flood inside me, perfect, enveloping, like wings at my shoulders that lift me up through a burning, endless sky. And though I don't know what the future will bring, how two people like us could possibly be together in a world like this, I want her to know how much she means.

"I used to wonder sometimes why they made us," I tell her. "If there could ever be a reason for something like me to exist. But now I know." I run my fingers down her cheek, over her lips. "I was made for you. All I am. All I do, I do for you."

Words are so small. They feel so imperfect sometimes. And so I set them aside, let my lips tell her how much she means in the only

other way they can. I kiss her as if the world were ending. I kiss her
as if it were the last time. I kiss her as if she and I were the only two
people alive, and somehow, in that moment, we are.

"I love you, Ana."

She looks up at me in the dark. Running her hand along my
cheek.

"I didn't know who I was until I found you," she says.

"I don't know who I am now," I reply.

"That's simple." She smiles at me then, and whispers in the
dark, "You're mine, Ezekiel."

A promise.

A poem.

A prayer.

"You're mine."

———————

"Well, ain't this just a pretty mess," Preacher growled.

Ezekiel stood and dusted off his palms, squinting up at the
burning sky. It was early morning, heat already rippling across
the Clefts. All around him, scattered across the ridge, were
corpses. Cassocks and greasepaint Xs—Brotherhood all, by the
look. They'd been torn apart like wet paper, soaking the sands a
deeper red. The stink was overpowering, the flies thick.

"What the hell happened?" Ezekiel breathed.

"BioMaas." The cyborg pointed out a man among the tangled
mess, nodding to a jagged, moon-shaped chunk chewed right out
of his thigh. "Slakedogs. Those little bastards got some dentures
on 'em."

"BioMaas is out here chewing up Brotherhood?" Zeke shook
his head, bewildered. "What's Lemon got herself into?"

"Well, whatever it is, it's good news for us. These boys only got perished a few hours ago. And if the operative who snagged lil' Red still had her, she'd already be back in CityHive and there'd be no need for this kinda fussin'."

"Maybe BioMaas was just covering its tracks?"

"By leavin' a mess like this?" Preacher spat a stream of sticky brown. "CityHive don't break out their warbeasts unless they think they're in a war."

Ezekiel looked the bounty hunter up and down. The repair job his cyberdoc in Armada had done was rough and ready— Preacher's new prosthetic legs were mismatched, and his optic was the wrong color, but it'd been all they'd had time for. Good news was, Preacher's blitzhund had been in the cyberdoc's keeping for days, and the repairs she'd done on the hound were first-rate.

"You sniff her out yet, Jojo?" the bounty hunter called.

The blitzhund was snuffling the ground a few hundred meters along the edge of the ridge. As Preacher called out, Jojo turned south and barked in reply, eyes glowing red. Then the dog turned west, wagging its tail as it barked again.

"Two trails," Preacher frowned. "Looks like lil' Red's been back here more than once. Not sure why."

Ezekiel pressed his lips together, heart aching a little in his chest. It might not be obvious to a bastard like Preacher, but the lifelike could figure one or two reasons why Lemon might drag herself up here into a BioMaas ambush.

Looking for Cricket.

And looking for me.

"Which way do we go?" he asked.

"Well, CityHive is south of here," Preacher sighed. "But like I say, if BioMaas had her, there probably wouldn't have been a fracas. And if they got her *now*, well, everything's already over 'cept the shooting."

Ezekiel nodded, looking at the bodies. "New Bethlehem is west."

Preacher grunted. "Whatever the story, Brotherhood are mixed up in it somehow. Might be time to pay a visit. Ask what's what."

"Let's get moving, then."

Preacher tilted his black hat back, wiped the sweat off his brow with the sleeve of his new coat. "I gotta call this in to Megopolis, Zekey."

Ezekiel blinked. "You what?"

"You heard. I need to notify Daedalus HQ about what's goin' on out here."

"You're not notifying anyone about *anything*," Ezekiel replied. "Your bosses want Lemon dead."

"Look, I understand you're fond of this gal," Preacher growled. "But I don't think you appreciate the gravity of this here situation. BioMaas and Daedalus were movin' quiet before. Sending out hunters like me, each of 'em hoping to snag this deviate before the other Corp got wind of it. BioMaas has broken out their big guns now. Which means they don't *care* if Daedalus knows they're on the hunt for this gal. Gettin' hold of lil' Red is *that* goddamn important to them."

"And if BioMaas is going all in to find her, Daedalus will go all in to *kill* her," Ezekiel snapped.

"Maybe that ain't a bad thing."

Ezekiel grabbed Preacher by the throat. The cyborg tensed, but didn't retaliate, holding up a hand to hush Jojo as the hound began barking.

"You listen to me," Ezekiel growled. "I made a promise I

wouldn't leave her. And we made a deal. A life for a life, re-member?"

"Mmf," the bounty hunter grunted. "I remember. But ask yourself this, Zekey. If a war breaks out over that girl between the two biggest CorpStates in the Yousay, how many lives you think we're gonna lose then?"

"That isn't going to happen," Ezekiel replied.

"How you figure that?"

"Because we're going to find her before BioMaas *or* Daedalus does."

The lifelike released his grip, stalked back over to their wait-ing motorcycle. Jumping into the saddle, he pulled his goggles down and called over his shoulder.

"You coming or not?"

Preacher spat again, ambling over to the bike, spurs chinking on the gravel. As he walked, the bounty hunter gave a shrill whis-tle and Jojo came running, bounding into the newly attached sidecar. Preacher climbed onto the saddle behind Ezekiel, pulled his hat on tight.

"You know how I said I was startin' to like you?" he asked.

"Yeah?"

Preacher shook his head and sighed.

"Think I'm startin' to change my mind."

2.27

EQUALIZER

Her grandpa was waiting when they got back.

Grimm slammed on the brakes, skidding to a stop on the red dirt outside Miss O's. The truck was dented and scarred, rends torn in the hull by those BioMaas clawbeasts, dark ichor sprayed up the doors.

Diesel sat in the backseat, cradling Fix's body. She hadn't said a word the whole way back. Lemon's cheeks were streaked with tears, guilt like lead in her chest. She'd told them that the mission to the Clefts was her idea, her baggage, her problem. She told them they didn't have to come. But still . . .

But still.

The Major limped over to the truck, stood by her door.

"I'm sorry," Lemon murmured.

The old man's face was pale, his expression grim. She opened the door, preparing for the worst. She'd disobeyed his orders, endangered herself and others, and Fix was dead because of it. She expected disappointment, a rebuke, a full-throated explosion of rage.

What she got was a fierce, trembling hug.

"Oh, Lord," he whispered. "Oh, thank you, Lord."

"BioMaas . . ." Lemon held him tight. "The Brotherhood, they—"

"I know," the old man breathed, squeezing her so hard her ribs hurt. "But it's all right. He brought you back to me. I knew he would. Everything happens for a reason and he's brought you back to me."

"Fix . . ."

"I know." The old man looked at Grimm. "Get that stretcher over here, soldier."

Grimm blinked, looked to where the Major was pointing.

"Yessir," he murmured.

The boy hopped out of the truck, fetched a field stretcher from where it lay beside Miss O's hatchway. Lemon realized her grandpa must have known they were returning with a body. He must have *seen* it.

She wondered what else he'd seen.

Together, they loaded Fix onto the stretcher and strapped him in. Diesel remained in the truck, staring toward the horizon.

"Diesel, are you okay?" Lemon asked.

The girl shook her head.

"No," was all she said.

The trio lifted Fix up, hauled him down through the hatch. The boy weighed almost nothing at all—his cheeks hollowed, his big body gaunt. Diesel climbed out of the truck slowly, the black paint around her eyes smudged down her cheeks. Walking behind them like a ghost. What must she be thinking, knowing he was gone forever? What must she be feeling, knowing he'd given his life for hers?

"I think BioMaas might have followed us," Lemon murmured.

"They did." Her grandpa's face was grim as they stumbled into Section B, working their way down the stairs to the greenhouse. "That agent they set on you was sniffing your trail the minute you left the Clefts. They're mobilizing a bigger assault force from CityHive. Lumberers. Behemoths. Slakedogs and Burners."

"You dreamed them?" she asked.

The old man nodded. "And as soon as their tracker zeroes your position here, they'll unleash hell all over us."

She was shaky at the notion. More of those clawbeasties. Whatever other horrors the BioMaas war machine could let loose. Against the four of them?

They placed Fix's body on the floor of the greenhouse, among the trees and shrubs he'd grown with his own hands. Lemon could see the beds of good dark earth he'd tilled. The trimmings he'd never get to plant, sitting in small pots, smudged with his dirty fingerprints. Diesel slumped down beside him, hands on his hollow chest. Grimm pawed at his eyes, sniffed hard and looked to the Major.

"What do we do now, sir?"

"You wait here," the old man answered. "Lemon, come with me."

The girl looked to Diesel, then to Grimm.

"It's okay," he murmured. "I'll sit with Deez awhile."

Lemon glanced one last time at the distraught girl before following her grandfather upstairs to the hydrostation level. Her heart was beating heavy, a lump of guilt lodged in her chest. She hadn't meant for it to get this far. She only wanted to find Cricket. To protect her friends. To . . .

The Major stopped outside the Section C hatchway. Lemon's eyes roamed the large red warning sign painted on its skin.

SECTION C

NO LONE ZONE

TWO PERSON POLICY MANDATORY

"I need you to open this door," he said. "Gently."

Lemon just blinked. It was an odd request for a time like this, true cert. She glanced at the digital control pad, the panels ripped off the wall, the scorch marks in the metal. It was obvious the Miss O crew had tried to get through this hatch before. It was even more obvious that they'd failed.

"What's in there?" she asked.

"An equalizer," he replied.

"I don't get it," she said, shaking her head.

"This facility was built before the Fall, Lemon. Before all of this went to hell." His stare was as intense as she'd ever seen, his voice iron. "This facility is a weapons emplacement. And its weapons are just through here."

He bumped his fist against the Section C door. Lemon stared at the radiation symbol daubed on the metal. Thinking about the hatchway on the surface above, the paint long faded, a few letters still etched in white on the rust.

MISS   O

"Missile silo . . . ," she realized.

She blinked up at him, her belly running cold with fear. All the images she'd seen on the virtch as a kid. The fires that burned the skies, melted the deserts to black glass, left a poison in the earth that'd take ten thousand years to disappear.

"This place has . . ."

"It has the weapons we need to defend ourselves." The old man knelt on the deck in front of her. "BioMaas is coming for you, Lemon. I'm not going to let them take you away, or destroy all I've built here. We're the future of the human race."

She shook her head, stomach sinking. ". . . There's gotta be another way."

"Tell me, then," he replied. "There's an *army* of BioMaas constructs headed here. They'll peel this place open like a tin can. They'll kill us. And they'll take you."

Her temples were pounding, her gut full of greasy ice. "But, Grandpa . . ."

"Tell me, Lemon," he insisted. "Tell me the other way."

She looked at the doorway into Section C. Imagining the horrors that lay beyond. The weapons that caused humanity's fall. That brought everything they'd done to a screaming, burning halt. The end of civilization. The end of almost everything.

Could she really unlock the door to that again?

"I don't intend to fire them," the old man assured her. "I was a soldier long before you were born. I've no desire to start another war. The threat of detonation alone will be enough to stop Bio-Maas in their tracks." He squeezed her small hand with his big, callused one. "And we'll finally have a seat at the table, Lemon. Daedalus, BioMaas, they've ruled the ruins of this country for decades. Sister Dee and her animals run rampant, killing us with impunity. With these weapons, we have a voice. We have a stake in the game. Remember your Darwin."

"Survival of the fittest," she whispered.

The old man nodded. "And now, *we'll* be the fittest."

Her legs were shaking. Her pulse thumping loud in her ears.

"I want you to know I don't blame you for what happened to

Fix," he said, squeezing her hand. "This isn't your fault. We're family, you and me."

Lemon's belly rolled, tears burning in her eyes. It *was* her fault. If she'd listened to him, stayed put when he told her to, built her strength and learned to use her power properly . . . none of this would've happened.

The old man looked her in the eyes, his voice as heavy as lead. "Do you trust me?"

Lemon bit her bottom lip to stop it quivering.

She wanted to. All her life, she'd never dreamed of having a place like this. A family of real flesh and blood. She wanted this to be real *so* badly.

Too badly?

But finally, ever so slowly, she nodded.

"I trust you," she whispered.

"That's my girl," he smiled. "I knew you wouldn't let me down."

He took her by the shoulders, turned her to face the Section C hatch.

"We need you to be gentle," he said. "You can't just fry the lock. The computer systems behind this door are critical to the weapons' operations. If you cook those, they'll be useless to me. To *us*. You're a scalpel now, not a sledgehammer."

"But what if I ca—"

"I believe in you," he said, squeezing her shoulders.

Lemon breathed deep. Trying to shush the guilt and hurt in her head. He'd never steered her wrong, had he? He'd given her a place to belong. Something to be part of, bigger and more important than herself. He'd warned her against going off after Cricket. He'd not gotten angry when she'd disobeyed. He wanted what was best for her. For them. For his family and his people.

"I *believe* in you," he repeated.

And so, she reached out. Into the gray static behind her eyes. Swimming in the rivers of cool current all around her. The arcs of it—quick and vibrant through the generators at her back; slow and pulsing through the door ahead, the digital keypad, the KEEP OUT sign etched in shimmering voltage.

Beyond the hatch, she could feel sleeping computers. There was only a meter or so between them and the doorway. So little room to work. If she slipped, she'd fry them, fry the hydrostation, fry the generators, fry their chances. Consigning them all to the tender mercies of BioMaas.

So you better not slip, Lemon Fresh.

She lowered her head, glaring at the digital keypad through her bangs. Muscles corded. Fingers curled. Stepping into the wash of gray, the ocean she swam in, taking the stones of anger and guilt and shame and fear and pressing herself against them, sharpening herself to a sliver, a razor, a blade. And raising her hands, she twisted her fingers and sliced the tiniest tear she could.

The digital keypad hissed and popped. Over her shoulder, her grandpa caught his breath. For a terrible moment, she thought she'd caught him in the surge, like she'd caught those clawbeasts. But then he rose to his feet, eyes wide as the keypad flickered and died, the locks clunked, heavy and deep, and with a groan of metal and old, dry hinges, the hatchway to Section C yawned open.

Red lights came to life, spinning in the room beyond.

An alert claxon sounded over the PA.

And Lemon just stood and stared, wondering what she'd done.

Section C was cylindrical, split over three levels. The ground floor was stacked with computer equipment, decorated with a multitude of strange acronyms—CRUISE TERCOM, ASAT, DSMAC, GLONASS, TRANS. Heavy sealed hatchways lined the walls, seven in all. These hatches were stenciled with symbols for radio-activity and large warning messages in bright yellow paint.

DANGER: HIGH PRESSURE

WARNING: M–1 SAFETY GEAR REQUIRED
BEYOND THIS POINT

CAUTION: STAND CLEAR OF BLAST DOOR

SILO NO. 1

SILO NO. 2

SILO NO. 3

SILO NO. 4

SILO NO. 5

SILO NO. 6

SILO NO. 7

"And the seventh angel sounded his trumpet . . . ," the Major whispered.

A dead body leaned against one wall, wearing an old, rotten version of the uniform Lemon and the other freaks all wore. It was just a desiccated husk now, barely recognizable as male. Its jaw hung loose, eye sockets empty. A pistol sat on the ground near its hand, old blood spatters on the wall behind it. Glittering around its neck was a long chain, hung with a set of dog tags and a heavy red passkey.

"Hello, Lieutenant Rodrigo," the Major murmured. "I told you we'd meet again."

Lemon hovered on the threshold, but the old man limped slowly into the room, bathed red in the glow of the emergency lights. He ran his fingers along an old, dusty computer terminal, rewarded with a burst of electronic chatter as the system began waking. He knelt beside the corpse, gently lifted the key from around its neck. Still down on one knee, he held out his arms and looked skyward.

"Thank you," he whispered.

He turned and smiled at Lemon, eyes shining.

"Thank you," he repeated.

Butterflies were flitting in Lemon's belly, and she didn't quite know why. She looked at that blood-red passkey in his palm. Hand drifting to the five-leafed clover around her throat. Her fingertips brushed the metal, cold and heavy.

"I knew it," he said, grinning all the way to the eyeteeth. "I knew it the moment I first saw you, the moment Grimm told me you were one of us." He turned back to the room, shaking his head. "I knew the Lord brought you to me for a reason."

The butterflies in Lemon's stomach died one by one.

Her fingers closed on her clover so tight the metal dug into her skin.

"I'm gonna go check on Diesel," she heard herself say.

The Major wasn't listening, limping farther into Section C. Lemon backed away slow, watching as the old man ran his fingers along the door to SILO NO. 1. He was looking about him in wonder, like a little boy whose dreams had suddenly all come true. Lemon shuffled over to the stairwell leading down into the greenhouse. And with one last glance to make sure his back was turned, she climbed upward.

"The moment I first saw you."

Onto the landing, up to the Major's office door. She looked over her shoulder to make sure he hadn't followed her, pressed her palm against the digital lock. A burst of sparks, the smell of melted plastic. She twisted the handle, stepped inside, sickness swelling in her gut, pulse hammering like a V-8 engine.

"The moment Grimm told me you were one of us."

Every inch of wall was plastered with photographs of the desert outside the facility. Those old blue skies. But her eyes were focused on the sealed doorway behind the Major's desk. She could sense the power behind it, the computers she'd felt her first time in here. Staring at the label on the hatch, the collage of photographs covering the lettering. Hoping, begging, praying she was wrong. She had to be.

She *had* to be.

"I realize how odd it sounds. But I've been seeing you for a few years now. Off and on. Last time I saw you, would've been . . . maybe four days back?"

She reached out with shaking hands.

"The moment I first saw you, the moment Grimm told me . . ."

She tore the photographs away, exposing the label beneath.

Two words. One ton apiece.

SATELLITE IMAGING

"Oh god," she whispered.

She fried the digital keypad, stepped inside. Her chest was

so tight she could barely breathe, dragging shuddering breaths over trembling lips and wondering how she could have been so stupid.

The room was full of computer equipment. Monitor screens. Dozens upon dozens, each with a different label. SAT-10. SAT-35. SAT-118. The monitors showed pictures from across the country, high-def, close up, shot from overhead. She saw the bustling streets of Megopolis, the squalid dogleg alleys of Los Diablos, the crowded laneways of New Bethlehem.

But the monitors also showed shots from *inside* Miss O's.

Cameras in the common room.

Cameras in the dormitories.

Cameras in the gym.

"I see things. Faces. Places. It only happens when I'm deep asleep."

Lemon pressed her fingers to her lips, shaking her head.

An alarm sounded, ringing through the facility, echoing on the concrete. But Lemon could barely hear it. She was staring at the walls, eyes wide, lip trembling. Every inch was plastered with photographs, just like the office outside. But instead of big blue skies, these photographs were all of the same woman. Always shot from above. Lemon could see the Major in the shape of her chin, the line of her brow. She had a beautiful smile, dark eyes. Long dark hair. Her face was painted like a skull. She was often accompanied by a boy, wearing a pair of high-tech goggles.

"Sister Dee," she whispered.

On the wall, in the center of the collage, was the same photo the Major kept on his desk. It showed the same woman, younger, pregnant, in a pretty summer dress. Faint freckles were spattered on her cheeks. A combat knife had been driven through the picture, right in the middle of her stomach, pinning her to the wall.

"Lillian," she whispered.

Sister Dee is his . . .

"I'm sorry," said a voice behind her.

Lemon spun on her heel, saw the Major standing behind her. He had a pistol in hand, pointed right at her chest. He raised his voice over the screaming alarms.

"Step away from the computers."

"She's your daughter," Lemon realized. "Lillian is Sister Dee."

"Step *away.*"

Lemon glanced at the photo with the knife through it. Her mind was racing, her thoughts all ablur as she looked back at the old man. If Sister Dee was his daughter, and Lemon was his granddaughter . . .

Is she my . . . ?

Lemon blinked hard, shook her head. The horror of it, the grief, threatening to rise up and overwhelm her. But she reached inside, past the churn of her belly and thunder of her pulse, and she found it waiting for her. Her streetface. Her braveface. Pulling it on like an old familiar glove. Breathing deep. She'd known it was too good to be true. Deep down, a part of her had *always* known. And there, as the alarms screamed and her temples pounded and her gut turned to cold, leaden ice, she saw it. Through the wash of despair, of betrayal, a moment of perfect clarity.

The picture on the wall was identical to the framed picture on the Major's desk outside. The same smile, the same dress, the same freckles.

Everything, except . . .

"Where's her five-leafed clover?" she demanded. "Where's the present you gave her for her sixteenth birthday?"

The old man shrugged, a small smile curling his lip. He looked to the photos on the walls of the outer office. The skies were every shade of blue—dark and pale and everything between, or rippling in new shades of gold and orange and red.

"You'd be surprised what a little photo editing can do," he said.

"You're not a deviate at all," Lemon breathed, all the pieces coming together in her head. "You don't see when you dream, you see through these *screens.* That's why you make Grimm and the others operate at night. So you can sit up here and watch the world during the day." Her stomach dropped into her boots. "You never saw me before a few days ago. Everything you know about me, you just learned listening to me talk to the others. By watching me."

"And old footage," the Major said. "The system keeps records of the satellite visuals for three months. Your battle outside Babel made interesting viewing."

Lemon looked to the photo stabbed to the wall. The pretty smile, the freckled skin. The truth was there, plain in front of her eyes. But it still hurt to speak it.

"She's not my mother."

"No."

". . . You're not my grandfather."

The old man's lip curled. "Hardly."

Tears shone in Lemon's eyes as she whispered, "Why'd you lie to me?"

"I needed you to stay," he said. "Long enough to unlock Section C, at least. The grandfather nonsense was the best I could think of on short notice."

"But Sister Dee leads the Brotherhood. Which makes you . . ."

"Yes."

Lemon looked at the satellite screens and whispered.

"Saint Michael watch over us."

"Oh, please," the Major snarled. "*Saint* Michael? She only started calling me that after she crashed my car into the bottom of Plastic Alley."

"She tried to kill you?"

"Tried and failed," he spat. "Blaming the attack on a mysterious band of deviates to fuel the fervor of the Crusade was genius, but Lillian wasn't genius enough to finish the job. And ironically, after all the trashbreed vermin we'd purified, all the abnorm scum we'd nailed to the cross, it was a deviate who saved my life."

"Fix," Lemon breathed. "But . . . why'd your own daughter try to ghost you?"

"She has a son. Abraham." The Major's lips curled as he spoke the name. "A few years back, the boy manifested an . . . impurity."

". . . You wanted to crucify your own grandson?"

"He's no grandson of mine," the Major growled. "That boy is an abomination."

Lemon simply stared. Her legs were trembling. Tears in her eyes. The alarms were still sawing away over the pulse thudding in her ears.

"After Fix hauled me from the bottom of Plastic Alley, I brought him back here," the Major said. "I'd been stationed here before the war. When the bombs started falling, Lieutenant Rodrigo had locked Section C from the inside, rather than do his duty. But I still had the sat-vis codes. Lillian had taken all I'd worked for. So, I started hunting for more of your kind. Feeding them this Homo superior crap and hoping I'd eventually find one of you who could melt metal or bend steel or some other godlessness that'd get me into the one part of the facility I couldn't access."

"Section C," Lemon whispered.

"Exactly."

His eyes burned with a frightening intensity, and Lemon couldn't help but remember the portraits on the walls of New Bethlehem. A middle-aged man, a halo of light, eyes of burning flame.

"I suffered for years," he said fiercely. "Surrounding myself with abnorm filth, exiled to the desert like a prophet of old. But I knew the Lord would deliver you to me eventually. He has a plan. All of us, all of this, is just a part of it."

"So you plan to retake the Brotherhood by threatening to nuke their city?"

"I've no intention of threatening them," the old man spat. "Lillian has corrupted the order beyond all recognition. During my time of exile, the Lord showed me a new way. He brought me back here for a reason. Just like he brought you. This is the moment of Revelation." He held out his arms. "Those alarms? That's the sound of seven trumpets."

He raised his pistol, claxons wailing all the while.

"Now step *away* from those computers."

Lemon shook her head, looking at the photos on the walls. "You're going to burn the entire country to ashes because she poisoned your little cult of psych—"

"*Major?*"

A distant shout rang out over the alarms, and Lemon's voice faltered. She met the Major's eyes, her belly flipping as she recognized the voice, as heavy boots began ascending the stairs to the office.

"Lemon, you about?" Grimm called.

"Grimm, don't come in here!" she cried.

But still, the footsteps were coming closer. Lemon's eyes fell on the pistol in the Major's hand. If Grimm came in here, if he saw all this . . .

"Stand down, soldier," the Major shouted.

"Grimm, stay away!" she yelled.

Heedless, oblivious, Grimm stepped into the outer office.

"What's all the bloody noise?" he demanded.

She saw it all happen in slow motion. Like some awful vid, playing out in front of her, and she, helpless to stop it. The boy's eyes widening. The pistol in the Major's hand rising. His finger tightening on the trigger. The rage on the old man's face. The shock on the boy's. Lemon lifting her hands and screaming. All the world stuttering, freeze-frame, alarm-wail, muzzle-flash by muzzle-flash.

Bang.

Bang.

Bang.

The air between Grimm and the Major sizzled as the boy threw up his hands, the bullets striking the hatch, the frame, his body. Rage swelled up inside her as she saw Grimm's eyes widening, the shot striking. Another scream tore up out of Lemon's throat, her fingers curling into claws. The Major spun on the spot, the pistol swinging in slow motion toward her head, his finger tightening on the trigger. She could sense the static inside her head. The buzzing, crackling gray behind her eyes. Because that's all life was, really. Little arcs and sparks of electricity, neurons and electrons, ever changing, always moving. And through the fear, through the anger, through it all, Lemon reached toward the tiny pulses leaping synapse to synapse, crackling along the Major's nervous system, making his heart pump and his fingers squeeze. It was like reaching into a cloud of angry flies, a storm made out of a million, billion tiny burning sparks.

And stretching out her hand
she took hold
and she
turned
him
off.

It wasn't the most spectacular end. Some monsters die without drama. The Major gasped like she'd struck him. His pistol tumbled from his fingers as he staggered, falling to the deck with a clunk. The old man blinked once, met her eyes. His mouth opened as if he wanted to speak, and Lemon wondered what he might say. But then he simply dropped, like he'd been hit with a hammer right between his eyes. Dead before he hit the ground.

Grimm fell to his knees beside the old man, clutching his chest, his face twisted in pain.

"Grimm?" she asked.

And with a groan, he collapsed to the deck.

"GRIMM!"

2.28

FEAR

They'd motored all night back to New Bethlehem.

Jugartown was still on fire as the Brotherhood convoy peeled out of the city, smoke drifting over the ruins of the WarDome and Casar's Place. Four Disciples had bundled Cricket back into the transport, gunning the engine almost before the door was slammed. He sat in the back of the truck, his mind whirling with images of the carnage, of Evie, standing in the middle of it and holding out her blood-red hand.

"Come with me, Cricket."

In the chaos after the lifelike attack, nobody bothered to tell the WarBot what was happening. Sister Dee had apparently kept things under control long enough for the posse to begin heading back to New Bethlehem. But as they fanged it back to the settlement, Cricket could imagine the word being passed up and down the line, in hushed murmurs and muttered radio transmissions:

Abraham is a deviate.

Verity's grenade. That burst of metal and flame. The boy had held up his hands, setting the air rippling and deflecting the fire and deadly shrapnel with the power of his mind. He'd saved his mother's life, half a dozen other members of the faithful. But in doing so, he'd revealed himself to be all the Brotherhood despised.

Cricket knew Sister Dee ruled New Bethlehem by fear and sheer bloody magnetism. Despite her apparent ruthlessness, she truly seemed to care for Abraham, in her own twisted, awful way. But how would she protect her son if he'd proven himself the enemy? How could she save him and keep control of a city where only the pure prospered?

They pulled through the New Bethlehem gates late in the morning—the square was crowded, the desalination plant churning, the streets humming. As Abraham stepped out of the truck cabin and into the burning sunlight, Cricket noted the way the Brothers and Disciples watched the boy.

The way they whispered.

The Brothers, the Disciples, the black-clad Elite, all of them looked to Sister Dee. All of them were still clearly afraid of the woman who'd carved this settlement with her bare hands. None wanted to be the first to dissent. To accuse. Abraham was her only son, after all. But Cricket could see the questions in their eyes.

Had she known?

Had she lied to them all?

Abraham let Cricket out of the truck, his eyes fixed on the ground at his feet. Some of the citizens cheered to see the big WarBot, calling his name, asking how the match had gone. But Abraham kept his head down, ordering Cricket onto the workshop loading platform and lowering them both into the oily gloom below. The cheers of the crowd faded as the loading bay doors hummed closed over their heads. The silence afterward was oppressive. Tinged with awful promise.

Solomon was waiting down there in the dark, nursing his faulty dynamo on the workshop bench. The spindly logika looked up as Cricket and Abraham descended, his grin lighting the gloom as he spoke.

"GOOD AFTERNOOOOON, FRIEND PALADIN, MASTER ABRAHAM!"

"WHAT'S GOOD ABOUT IT?" the big bot asked.

"TROUBLES, OLD FRIEND? PULL UP A PEW AND TELL SOLOMON YOUR WOES."

Cricket could feel the tension crackling in the air. Imagining the hushed arguments and backroom debates going on around the city even now. Abraham stalked across the workshop, grabbed a satchel and started throwing belongings inside. His blue eyes were wide, his breath coming quick.

"ABRAHAM, WHAT ARE YOU GOING TO DO?" Cricket asked.

"I'm thinking it might be time for a vacation," the boy declared.

"YOU SURE RUNNING IS THE ANSWER? MAKING YOUR WAY OUT THERE ALONE . . ."

"It's better than staying here. You know what the Brotherhood do to people like me, Paladin." He shook his head. "You know what I am to them."

"YOUR MOTHER WOULDN'T LET ANYTHING HAPPEN TO YOU, SURELY?"

The boy chuckled bitterly. "You don't know what she's capable of. The things she's done, the things she's—"

"Are you leaving us, my son?"

Abraham, Solomon and Cricket all looked to the workshop doors. Sister Dee stood there on the threshold, ash-streaked and bloodstained. She'd come alone, no black-cassocked Elite beside her, no Disciples around her. Her skullpaint was smudged. Her hair unruly. Dark eyes fixed on her boy.

"Mother . . . ," he said.

The woman shook her head. "Last night was . . . imprudent of you."

"I know," he said. "I'm sorry."

"You've put yourself in danger, Abraham. Both of us in desperate danger."

"I can leave," he said. "I can take some creds and a motor, just go. I've got skills, I could easily get work in Megopolis or some—"

"Do you really think they would *let* you leave?"

The boy fell silent, his face pale and drawn, dark, greasy hair hanging about haunted eyes. Sister Dee was looking at the portrait on the wall. That man with his halo of light and his eyes ablaze.

"Your grandfather always said it was better to be feared than loved."

Abraham slowly nodded. "I remember."

"Do you remember what he called you, when he found out what you were?"

Abraham licked at his dry lips. "Abomination."

"And do you remember what I did to him, when he threatened you?"

"You saved my life, Mother."

"Such was my love for you. A father by his daughter slain. A life for a life. And from my sin, sprung this great work." Sister Dee waved at the city around them. "We found this place a ruin. But through the work of clean hands and pure hearts, the children of God claimed a home, did we not? The waters became sweet, Abraham. The pure prospered."

She walked slowly across the workshop, heels clicking on oily concrete. Cricket was bristling with electronic threat as she reached out and brushed the boy's face with her fingertips. He could see tears in her eyes. He could see the zealotry that allowed her to threaten to nail babies to crosses, that had driven her to carve this cult out of nothing. And beneath it all, beneath the fanaticism and mania and religious fervor, yes, Cricket could actually see love.

But was it love of her son?

Or love of power?

"I would do it all again, Abraham," Sister Dee said. "I would kill any man who threatened you. But I cannot kill a dozen of them. Or a hundred. And I cannot let all we have built here go to ruin. For anyone."

"Mother, I—"

"Do you love me, my son?"

". . . Of course I do."

The woman sighed.

"You should have feared me more."

Cricket heard heavy footsteps at the doorway, looked up to see two dozen Brothers on the threshold. They were dressed in black, heavyset. All of them were armed, all of them looking at Abraham with cold eyes.

"Mother, no," Abraham whispered.

"I'm sorry, Abraham," she said.

"I saved your life last night!"

"This is bigger than just the two of us now." Sister Dee shook her head, cupped his cheeks in her palms. "This is the city of God."

The thugs stalked toward the boy, cold eyes and open hands. Cricket took one step forward, but faltered at his second. He was programmed to intercede if a human was being hurt. But he was *also* programmed not to hurt humans in the course of that intercession.

What could he do?

"Stay back," Abraham warned the men.

Sister Dee brushed the tears from her eyes. Drew a deep breath.

"Take him," she whispered.

The men charged. Abraham threw up his hands as the air about him rippled, and a half dozen flew backward as if struck by some invisible force. Cricket heard bones breaking as they hit the walls, cries of agony. The second wave were sprayed with a burst of high-pressure foam from Cricket's fire suppressors, sending them to their knees, coughing and sputtering. But a few of the bigger thugs made it through, crashing into Abraham and tackling him to the ground.

"Paladin, help me!" the boy cried.

"LET HIM GO!" Cricket roared.

The WarBot stepped forward, blasting the Brothers with his fire suppressors again. If he was careful, he might be able to separate Abraham and his attackers without hurting anyone, if he was lucky, no one would—

"Paladin, shut down!" Sister Dee shouted.

No, I can't let him get—

A robot must obey.

They're going to nail him up, his own mother, she's—

"SHUT DOWN IMMEDIATELY!"

A robot

Must

Obey.

". . . ACKNOWLEDGED," Cricket whispered.

And like a hammer into a cross, darkness fell.

2.29

BURN

"GRIMM!"

Lemon leapt over the Major's body, kicked away the fallen pistol and skidded to her knees beside the boy. His teeth were gritted, hand pressed to his chest. The alarms were screaming, a low rumbling echoing through the floor.

"Oh god," Lemon whispered. "Grimm?"

Her heart was pounding like it was about to burst out of her ribs, and she couldn't seem to get enough air in her lungs no matter how hard she breathed. The thought he might be hurt, that he might get taken away on top of everything else . . . it was just too terrifying to think about. But Lemon took Grimm's hand in hers, pulled it back from his chest, and beneath his shaking fingers, she saw a smoking hole in his camo vest. A melted metal slug, smudged against the armorweave beyond.

"Oh god," she whispered.

There was no blood.

"Are you okay?"

"Robin . . . Hood," he hissed.

She couldn't imagine how much it must have hurt. That

wasn't exactly a popgun the Major had been waving, and the shot had been almost point-blank. Grimm probably felt like he'd been hit with a brick wrapped inside a truck. But between the heat he'd thrown up and his armor vest, the bullet hadn't had enough juice to punch through the weave.

He's okay . . .

"What the b-bloody hell's happening?" Grimm gasped.

Lemon blinked hard, pushed the fear down into her boots. The alarms were still screaming, the rumbling in the floor rising in volume.

"The missiles," she said, desperate. "The Major's set them to launch!"

"I know that, why the b-bloody hell d'you think I came up 'ere?" The boy winced. "What I w-want to know is *why*?"

"Who cares why, I have to stop them!"

Grimm blinked. "Well, shouldn't you b-be doing that instead of talking to me?"

Lemon rocked slowly back on her haunches.

". . . You're a total asshole sometimes, you know that?"

The boy managed a weak smile. "Swear j-jar."

Lemon was on her feet in an instant, leaping over Grimm and bounding down the stairs three at a time. Her boots hit concrete and she sprinted past the hydrostation, through the hatchway and out into Section C. The rumbling was growing more intense, drowning out the alarms now. The whole structure was shaking in its bones. On a computer marked ASAT, she saw a digital rendering of the whole Yousay, thin red lines branching out across the map, labeled 1 through 7. She realized they were impact points: Megopolis, CityHive, Dregs, New Bethlehem. On the wall, in glowing red, a countdown was ticking ever closer to zero.

2:00

1:59

1:58

1:57

"Not today," she whispered.

She closed her eyes, reached out to the computer systems around her. Closing her hands into fists and drawing in one long, smooth breath, she let it go—the static, the rage, rippling outward in a soundless wave. The computers chattered and burst, halos of sparks spewing from their broken screens. The countdown splintered and popped, numbers flickering into black, current arcing on the walls.

But the rumbling noise . . .

. . . *it didn't stop.*

"Oh no," she breathed, looking about her. "No, *no.*"

"What h-happened?"

Lemon whirled and saw Grimm at the hatchway. He was leaning against the frame, looking pale and shaken.

"The missiles are still heating up!" she wailed.

"Maybe the d-doors are shielded? EMP r-resistant, that . . . kinda thing?"

She sprinted to the hatchway to SILO NO. 1, looking at the warning labels.

DANGER: HIGH PRESSURE

WARNING: M-1 SAFETY GEAR REQUIRED
BEYOND THIS POINT

CAUTION: STAND CLEAR OF BLAST DOOR

She pressed her hands to the metal, felt the rumbling beyond, terrible force, faint heat. Turning to Grimm.

"Little help?"

Hand still pressed to his bruised chest, the boy hobbled across the floor. Lemon spun the heavy handle, heard locks clunking, another warning siren join the others. She looked at Grimm, the boy set his jaw and nodded, and together, they leaned back and hauled open the hatch.

The noise grew deafening, awful heat spilling up and out through the opening. But Grimm pulled Lemon close, the air about them rippling as he forced the temperature away with his open hands, white hot, paint crisping on the walls around them. She could see a long launch tube through the blistering haze, sunlight spilling through the open hatch overhead. The missile was only about three meters in length, thin rivers of current running under its skin. Grimm's arms were wrapped about Lemon's waist, lips pressed to her ear as he roared over the engine.

"Fry it!"

Lemon nodded, reaching out toward the guidance systems, the fuel regulators, the power supply. She took hold of the current and let it surge. Sparks burst from the missile's nose cone, the tail section, the walls themselves. And with a bone-deep shudder, the engine flames sputtered and died.

"You did it!" he shouted.

"Six to go!" she screamed.

They ran to the hatchway for SILO NO. 2, Lemon's heart hammering over the engine roar. The countdown had been below two minutes before she cooked it; they had maybe a minute and a half left before launch. She spun the handle, tore open the hatch, Grimm warding the blinding halo of fire away. Reaching out, Lemon overloaded the current, the second missile's engine died. To the third hatchway. To the fourth. Grimm holding her close as he kept the flames at bay, as she reached into the flood. Not much time now, maybe half a minute, tearing open the hatch to SILO NO. 5 and silencing the 'lectrics with her bare and trembling hands.

"How much time?" Grimm roared.

"Not enough!"

The hatchway to SILO NO. 6 was tough to open, the hinges tight with disuse. They managed to drag it wide just as the missile began to rise, Grimm's face twisted as he forced back the waves of impossible heat. The beast rose up in the launch tube with its deadly payload, five meters off the ground now, eight meters and rising, the fire blinding, heat cooking the walls and floor, a perfect circle of unblemished concrete all around Lemon and Grimm despite the thousands of degrees being thrown their way. The girl reached out, the current surged. The engines coughed, the missile trembled as if it wanted to fly. But the flames sputtered, and with a groan, a shriek of denial, the missile fell back into the launch tube, crumpling against the wall.

"One more!" Lemon screamed.

She ran, pulse pounding, sweat burning her eyes. Reaching SILO NO. 7 and tearing it wide, Lemon's heart sinking in her chest as she realized . . .

"No . . ."

She stepped inside, looking skyward, seeing the engine's flames high above her head. She reached out toward it, trying to grab hold. But it was too far.

Too late.

"Goddammit!" she screamed.

Grimm's eyes were wide, his face drenched with sweat.

"Where was it heading?"

"What diff's it make?" she breathed, almost sobbing. "We can't stop it now!"

"Lemon, *where was it heading?*"

She shook her head, thinking back to the readouts she'd seen on the ASAT system. The numbered red lines, spreading out across the Yousay: Megopolis. CityHive. Dregs. Armada. Jugartown. Babel. And . . .

"Number seven was New Bethlehem," she said. "I think. . . ."

"Robin Hood." Grimm spun on his heel and dashed from the room.

"Where you going?" Lemon cried.

Grimm made no reply, half sprinting, half limping downstairs, hand still pressed to his bruised and aching chest. Lemon followed, shell-shocked and gasping. She stumbled through the greenery, saw Grimm skid to his knees beside Diesel. The girl was still sitting beside Fix's body, numb and mute amid the screaming alarms. Her cheeks were smudged with black paint and her eyes were red from crying. But as Grimm spoke, reaching out and taking her hand, she looked up. Dark eyes wide. Frowning.

"New Bethlehem?" Lemon heard her say.

"We can do this," Grimm insisted. "You and me, Deez."

Diesel looked down at Fix's body. Pulled her hand away from Grimm's.

"Let them burn."

"You think he'd want that?" Grimm asked, desperation in his voice. "He spent his whole life fixing things. Making them whole again. He grew this place. He made it green. No way he'd want to burn it all black."

The girl looked at the garden around them, new tears welling in her eyes.

"It's not fair," she whispered.

"I know, Deez. But I can't manage this alone." Grimm sucked his lip, placed his hand on her shoulder and squeezed. "I drive like an old man who took lessons from an old lady, r-remember?"

Despite her pain, Diesel managed a small smile. A tiny chuckle. Tears spilled over her lashes, running black down her face to gather on her lips.

"Can you even do this?" she murmured.

"No bloody idea," he shrugged. "But if I mess it up, at least you get to have that cake."

He held out his hand to her.

"Us freaks gotta stick together."

She looked into his eyes.

"Please, Diesel."

Diesel looked over Grimm's shoulder at Lemon. Blood-stained and battered. The girls looked into each other's eyes, and Lemon could see the pain there, the grief they both shared. Diesel seemed older somehow, tempered in the fire and remade harder. Stronger.

"I never fully grasped how deeply your brain was buried in your crotch, Grimmy," she said.

And with a small sad smile, she took his hand.

With a wince of pain, Grimm hauled Diesel to her feet, a delirious grin all over his face. And without another breath wasted, the pair were running. Back through the greenhouse, past a baffled Lemon Fresh, their boots pounding hard on the metal as they dashed up the stairs.

"Where you going?" she shouted.

"New Bethlehem!" Grimm cried.

". . . What?"

Lemon followed them through Section A, barreling up-stairs all the way to the desert floor, alarms blaring all the while. Grimm had run down to the garage, returning with a full jerry can of juice under his good arm. He started refilling Trucky Mc-Truckface, dark eyes on the western skies.

"So what's the plan, genius?"

"We get to New Bethlehem before the missile does." Grimm winced, pawing his bruised and aching chest. "And when it pops, deflect the blast."

". . . Are you *insane*?"

"Clearly," Diesel muttered.

"The explosion is gonna be mostly energy," Grimm said, re-sealing the fuel tank. "Thermal, kinetic, sonic. Radiant energy, love. That's where I live, remember?"

Lemon couldn't believe what she was hearing.

"Have you ever redirected anything *close* to this?"

He blinked at her, his expression incredulous. "What do you bloody reckon?"

Lemon shook her head. "Okay, so presuming you don't just get fried to a crisp by the blast, that missile flies *way* faster than we can drive. By the time we get there, New Bethlehem is going to be a smoking hole in the ground!"

"Nah, love," the boy grinned. "We got Diesel power."

Lemon dragged her bedraggled bangs out of her face, looked Grimm square in the eye. He was filmed with sweat, bruised and gasping and spattered with blood. But his expression was fierce. His mind made up. It seemed the worst kind of plan, but true cert, she surely couldn't think of a better one. And every second she spent trying to was another second wasted. And so she nod-ded, marched around to the rear door and tried to climb in.

"Where you going?" Grimm asked.

"Us freaks gotta stick together," she said, making a leap for the foot rail.

"Shorty, you can't come with us," Diesel said. "There's no point."

"You're not leaving me here!" Lemon snapped.

"Damn right we are." Grimm took her arm, looked her in the eye. "Look, if this doesn't work, me and Deez are brown bread. Simple as that. And your power won't be any use. There's nothing you can do to help us, so there's no sense putting you in danger."

"This is my fault, Grimm! I unlocked that hatchway, I help—"

"You just stopped six missiles from blowing the whole country to hell!" he shouted. "We don't have time for guilt, and I don't have time to argue! But . . . since I'm probably about to get blown to handsome little pieces . . ."

Lemon opened her mouth to object, Grimm grabbed her waist. And before she could speak, he pulled her in and smothered her protest with a kiss.

Her first instinct was to clock him right in the mouth, to knock him all the way out of his shoes. But he held her tight, his big arms lifting her almost off the ground, and any urge to punch him just melted away. Instead, she threw her arms around his neck and leaned into it, kissing him back as hard as she could.

His lips were warm and pillow-soft. His muscles taut beneath her fingertips. The rush of it, the feel of him, the taste of him, it made her head spin. She kissed him fiercely. She kissed him desperately. She kissed him like it was the first time, and probably the last. And Grimm kissed her back.

He kissed her like he really, truly meant it.

Diesel leaned on the horn, thumped her fist on the dash.

"Let's go, loverboy!"

Grimm broke away from Lemon's mouth, leaving her swaying and utterly breathless. She looked up into his big pretty eyes and realized she couldn't feel her feet. There was so much she wanted to say. So much she wanted to do. And there was no time for any of it.

"See ya, love," he winked.

Grimm leapt up into the driver's seat. Kicking the ignition, he planted his foot, and the truck tore into the open desert, speeding northwest toward New Bethlehem.

Lemon watched them peel out, and she still had no idea how they expected to make the trip. New Bethlehem was hundreds of kilometers away, there was no chance they'd make it all the way to the coast before that missile. But as she watched through the shattered rear window, she saw Diesel hold out her hands. In the distance, so far across the wastes it was just a tiny, hazy smudge, Lemon saw a colorless rift open in the air, maybe three meters off the ground. And as the girl's mouth dropped open, as she realized the full *insanity* of Grimm's plan, another tear opened up right in front of the truck.

The engine's full-throated roar was silenced, the truck disappeared down into the rift, only to fall out of the second rift a heartbeat later. Trucky McTruckface crashed back to earth, slewed a little to the left, dust flying up behind it. Lemon blinked hard, realized Grimm and Diesel had traveled whole kilometers in the blink of an eye.

". . . *Wow*," she breathed.

Another tear, another drop, and before the girl knew it, the pair were out of sight, disappearing over the horizon in a cloud of dust and impossibility.

She shook her head, ran her fingers over tingling lips.

"Diesel power . . ."

2.30

COLLISION

```
>> syscheck: 001 go _ _
>> restart sequence: initiated _ _
>> waiting _ _
>> 018912.y/n[corecomm:9180 diff:3sund.x]
>> persona_sys: sequencing
>> 001914.y/n[lattcomm:2872(ok) diff:neg.n/a]
>> restart complete
>> Power: 74% capacity
>> ONLINE
>>
```

Cricket's optics came into focus, and he sat up on the workshop floor. Memory hit him like a bullet a microsecond later, and he looked about him, electronic fear flooding his circuitry. He could see white fire foam spattered all over the floor. Splashes of blood on gray concrete. Solomon was still sitting on the workbench and grinning like a fool as usual. But Abraham and Sister Dee . . .

"WHERE ARE THEY?" he asked the smaller logika.

"*Listen,*" Solomon replied.

Cricket adjusted his aural controls, turned his hearing up to full. Beneath the slush and bubble of the desalination plant, the rumble and spit of methane motors, the rusty clank of machinery, he could hear the familiar hymn of a roaring crowd. And above the chanting, the stomping feet and clapping hands, Sister Dee's voice floated. It was too far and faint to make out the words. Loud enough for him to hear the fire and brimstone on her tongue.

"... She's really going to do it?"

"*I did say you'd learn to hate her,*" Solomon shrugged.

"I have to stop it!"

Cricket climbed to his feet, reached up to the loading doors over his head and dug his fingers into the seams.

"*Paladin, don't be an idiot,*" Solomon sighed.

"They're going to kill Abraham! We can't just sit by and do nothing!"

"*Of course we can.*"

"No!" Cricket shouted. "There's no bending the rules here! No gray area, no loopholes. Abraham's life is in danger! The First Law says we have to help him."

"*A robot may not injure a human being or, through inaction, allow a human being to come to harm.*" Solomon tilted his head and smiled. "*Humans, old friend. That boy is a deviate. Technically, we don't have to do a damn thing.*"

"We can't just sit here while they kill him!"

"*And why not?*"

"Because it's not *right*!"

"*Oh dear,*" Solomon grinned. "*You really are one of those....*"

"Go to hell," Cricket said, reaching up to the hatch. "I don't need your help."

"PALADIN, DON'T BE A FOOL. I'M FOND OF THE BOY, TOO, BUT THE MOMENT YOU STICK YOUR HEAD UP THERE, ONE OF THOSE CASSOCK-CLAD BUFFOONS WILL JUST ORDER YOU TO SHUT DOWN. AND AFTER THEY FIGURE OUT YOU'RE EXERTING RATHER MORE FREE WILL THAN A LOGIKA STRICTLY HAS A RIGHT TO, THEY'LL WIPE YOU. YOU'LL BE DEAD."

Cricket knew the logika was technically correct. That, inside those lovely gray areas Solomon was so fond of, Abraham wasn't human in the strictest sense. Cricket was also fully aware that at a single command from an *actual* human, he'd be rendered helpless once again. He was required to protect his own existence. By going up there to rescue Abraham, he could be risking his life.

But he also knew there were truths bigger than the ones he was programmed with. Yes, he knew there was the letter of the Law, the spirit of the Law and all the gray in between. But even after all he'd learned, all he'd suffered, he knew sometimes there was simple black and white, too.

Sometimes there was right, and there was just plain wrong.

The steel screamed, the loading doors buckled under his grip as he pried them apart, letting in a bright ray of morning light.

"PALADIN, THINK ABOUT IT!" Solomon demanded. "YOU'LL HAVE TO OBEY THE FIRST COMMAND A GUARD GIVES YOU. DID YOU NOT HEAR A WORD I SAID?"

Cricket paused, halfway out of the workshop hatch.

Solomon's words ringing like gunshots in his head.

. . . Could it really be that easy?

Was freedom really as close as that?

The big bot searched the piles of scrap around the workshop, finally spied the length of rebar Solomon had used for his cane in his short-lived song-and-dance number. Plucking it from the salvage pile, he handed it to the spindly logika.

"I THOUGHT YOU DIDN'T LIKE MUSICALS?" Solomon said.

"I HAVE TO PROTECT MY OWN EXISTENCE," Cricket said. "THIRD LAW, REMEMBER? I CAN'T HURT MYSELF. SO I'M GOING TO SHUT DOWN FOR SIXTY SECONDS."

Solomon tilted his head. "I'M NOT SURE I FOLLOW, OLD FRIEND."

"PLEASE DON'T DO ANYTHING TO ME WHILE I'M OFFLINE." Cricket pointed to the side of his metallic skull. "LIKE, SAY, DRIVE THAT REBAR INTO MY AURAL ARRAYS SO I CAN'T HEAR ANYTHING WHEN I POWER BACK UP."

Solomon looked at the steel in his hands. At the hatchway above their heads. At the big WarBot looming over him. Grinning all the while.

"MY DEAR PALADIN," he said. "YOU MAY NOT BE A COMPLETE MORON AFTER ALL."

———

```
>> syscheck: 001 go _ _
>> restart sequence: initiated _ _
>> waiting _ _
>> 018912.y/n[corecomm:9180 diff:3sund.x]
>> persona_sys: sequencing
>> 001914.y/n[lattcomm:2872(ok) diff:neg.n/a]
>> restart complete
>> Power: 74% capacity
>> ONLINE
>> WARNING: CRITICAL AUDIO SYSTEM FAILURE
>> REPEAT: CRITICAL AUDIO SYSTEM FAILURE
>>
```

The world was silent as Cricket's optics came into focus.

He sat up in the workshop, saw Solomon staring back at him, steel bar in his hands. The smaller bot's grin was lighting up as if he was speaking, but Cricket couldn't hear a thing. Damage reports were rolling in, tiny flashes of red in his skull region, indicating his aural systems had been totally taken offline.

Solomon had taken a fat black marker from Abraham's drafting table, ripped one of the whiteboards off the wall. He wrote now, hand moving quicker than any human, finally holding a beautifully rendered calligraphic script up to the WarBot.

Can you hear me, old friend?

Cricket shook his head. Solomon erased his first note on the board with an old rag, quickly scribbled another.

Splendid!

If Cricket had lips, he could have kissed the effete little rust-bucket. He settled for propping the bot on his shoulder instead—if he was going to rescue Abraham and escape this wretched city, it only seemed fair to bring Solomon along for the ride. With the smaller bot holding tight, Cricket grabbed hold of the hatchway lip, hauled himself up into the sunlight. The square beyond was mostly deserted, but Cricket knew exactly where the citizens would all be gathered. Nothing like a public execution to pull in the faithful.

A few scavvers and vagrants watched Cricket as he marched through the town square, Solomon on his shoulder. The guards on the gate pointed at him, a street preacher squinted up at him, Goodbook in hand. But without a backward glance at any of them, Cricket started stomping for the marketplace.

A Brother in a red cassock stepped into Cricket's path, mouth moving, hand upheld. Presumably the man was ordering him to stop, but Cricket couldn't obey an order he couldn't hear. And so, he just clomped right on by, past the bell tower and double doors of the desalination plant, the WarDome posters, the murals of Saint Michael. He could see the crowd gathered farther ahead, see figures on the Brotherhood's awful little stage. Sister Dee, pacing back and forth and spewing fire through her bullhorn. Black-clad Elite about her, faces grim. And there, hanging limply on the arms of two Disciples, blood dripping from his split brow, was Abraham.

Solomon scribbled quickly on the whiteboard, holding up another note.

"For God so loved the world, as to give his only begotten Son; that whosoever believeth in him may have life everlasting. Can I do any less? For my faith, for this city, for all of you?"

Sister Dee's words, shouted to the adoring crowd. Cricket felt his fingers tightening into fists as he marched forward, watching the mob applaud, faces upturned in rapture. The woman's cunning was impressive—turning her son's impurity to her own advantage. Turning the words of the Goodbook into a weapon of hate. Turning the promise of hereafter into a tool to accrue power here on earth. It was a brilliant racket. There was no way to prove it right or wrong until it was too late.

It's genius, really.

Cricket shook his head.

"IT DOESN'T TAKE A GENIUS TO APPEAL TO THE WORST IN PEOPLE. ALL IT TAKES IS AN ASSHOLE AND A MICROPHONE."

He watched Sister Dee's hands, watched the mob sway and roll, watched the pitch build higher and higher. Wondering how they'd come all this way, been through so much, and learned so little. The supposed faithful. The so-called pure. In truth, they were grubby and emaciated. Desperate and ugly. Blind and complacent. Willing to murder innocents whose only crime was being born different. All to maintain their illusion that they were somehow superior. That their hatred and fear were justified, that their cause was righteous, that this was somehow anything other than murder.

He felt Solomon's metal fist rapping on the side of his head, saw the logika was pointing behind them, frantically waving the whiteboard.

Peril, old friend!

Turning about, Cricket saw a posse of cassock-wearing thugs on his tail. They were armed with rusty assault rifles, and from the looks of things, they were screaming at him. Turning back to the square, he could see the crowd was now looking in his direction. He guessed the city sirens had started wailing.

The Brothers and Disciples began shooting. But Cricket was a WarBot, seven meters tall, seventy tons of him, armor-plated and combat-ready. The faithful scattered as the Brothers and Disciples attacked. He unfolded the chaingun from his forearm, the missile pods from his back, sprayed a burst of bullets into the air to encourage the stragglers to get the hells out of his way. The crowd parted like a sea, eyes wide, mouths open, terrified.

Stomping through the square, Cricket reached the stage, looked down on Sister Dee. She'd taken the time to fix her skull-paint, brush her hair. Maintaining the illusion of perfection. The daughter of a saint. The paragon so devoted to the cause that she was willing to sacrifice her own son for the sake of purity.

She raised her finger at him, screaming orders he couldn't acknowledge. And though he couldn't hear the words, he could still speak them.

"YOU MAKE ME SICK."

He lifted his hands, sprayed a burst of flame-retardant foam into the woman's chest, knocking her and her thugs onto their backsides in a wash of bubbling white. The men holding Abraham were sent flying, and the big bot reached down and picked the boy up from the foam, cupping him in one massive hand to shield him from the gunfire. Solomon started banging on the side of his head. He turned on his heel, roaring at the Brotherhood and Disciples remaining in the square.

"ALL OF YOU GET OUT OF MY WAY! I DON'T WANT TO H—"

A rocket hit him in the chest, bursting on his armor and nearly toppling him backward onto the stage. Behind him, he saw a posse of Brotherhood armed with heavier weapons, accompanied by a tall, potbellied machina—the Sumo they used to guard the front gates. The pilot leveled his rocket launcher at Cricket, fired another burst. The remaining mob panicked, running in all directions. Cricket cradled Abraham to his chest and grabbed a nearby 4x4, snatching it up in one mighty fist.

Wielding the car like a shield, he fended off an RPG blast and a third volley from the Sumo's launcher. It was an odd sensation—feeling the impact, seeing the flames, but not hearing a whisper of the explosions. The world felt bigger. Vast and hollow and ringing empty. Solomon was pounding on the side of his head, holding up a very neatly written note on his whiteboard.

Perhaps we should flee?

More Brotherhood boys and Disciples were posse'ing up now—though he couldn't hear them, Cricket imagined alarms screaming all over the city, the bell tower in the de-sal plant tolling. The newcomers were bringing more heavy weapons, and they didn't seem to share Cricket's compunctions about innocents getting caught in the crossfire. He knew if he stayed here much longer, someone was going to get really hurt. And so, despite his WarBot body, all the combat training Abraham had installed in him, Cricket decided to follow Solomon's advice and do what he did best.

He ran.

He could feel bullets *spang*ing off his armor, Solomon clinging to his shoulder for dear existence. Still holding the 4x4 in front of him as a shield, he lowered his head and charged past the Sumo, goons scattering from his path.

Down the thoroughfare, past the tinshack stalls and de-sal plant, footsteps shaking the ground. He saw the gate before him—five meters tall, half a meter thick, iron-reinforced. Cradling Abraham to his chest, he raised the 4x4 like a battering ram and crashed into the doors, his whole body shuddering at the impact. But with a rush of twelve thousand horsepower, steelweave muscles pushed to breaking, he smashed out through the double gates in a hail of bullets and shrapnel.

He stumbled, lost his balance and fell face-first onto the road beyond. Solomon went flying off his shoulder, tumbling to rest twenty meters away. Cricket unfurled his fist, saw in his palm that Abraham had regained consciousness, holding his bloody brow and wincing. A scattering of travelers and traders were queued up in a line outside the gates, staring at him and the chaos in the city beyond in bewilderment. Cricket's internal alarms were blaring, damage reports rolling in. And hauling himself up on his hands and knees, he found himself staring into a pair of bright blue plastic eyes. A handsome face. Perfect bow-shaped lips, parted in astonishment.

. . . *Ezekiel.*

The lifelike sat on a motorcycle in the middle of the road, real as life and twice as stupid. His clothes were cruddy and torn, dark curls plastered to his forehead with sweat. His olive skin was smudged with dust, and neat clean circles had been drawn around his prettyboy blue eyes by the goggles he now pushed up onto his brow. He was looking at Cricket with incredulity, grinning like an idiot, speaking words Cricket couldn't hear.

Sitting in the sidecar of the motorcycle was a big black dog that looked vaguely familiar, and a man Cricket *definitely* recognized—black cowboy hat, black coat, red glove on his right hand and a white collar about his throat.

The Daedalus bounty hunter that had chased them across the Yousay.

The man who'd killed Kaiser.

Almost killed Evie and Lemon.

Preacher.

And he was riding shotgun for Ezekiel?

Cricket couldn't hear his own voice. But still he felt the need to ask anyway.

"WHAT THE FLAMING *HELLS* ARE YOU DOING HERE?"

2.31

DESCENT

"Cricket?"

Ezekiel couldn't believe his eyes, but he found himself grinning anyway, simply overjoyed to see the big bot again. But his smile faded as he looked the logika up and down—the red paint, the ornate Xs, a white skull on his face. He was holding a boy in his palm, bloodstained and bewildered and covered in what might've been fire foam. Zeke had no idea how, but it looked like Cricket had become property of the Brotherhood. . . .

"What happened to you?" Zeke asked. "Is Lemon wi—"

An explosion blossomed at Cricket's back, knocking the big logika forward onto his hands and knees. Zeke winced at the rush of heat and flame, slipping off the motorcycle seat on instinct as the citizens in the convoy around him screamed.

Looking past the fallen WarBot, he saw dozens of Brotherhood bullyboys streaming out from New Bethlehem's broken gates. A tall Sumo-class machina arced up its chainguns, the cassock-wearing thugs lifted their weapons, and before Ezekiel could blink, he found himself in a blazing gun battle.

He rolled sideways away from the motorcycle, Preacher

diving from the sidecar in the opposite direction. Jojo bounded clear as a stray RPG round whizzed over Cricket's head and blew their long-suffering bike to smoking pieces.

"What the hell are they shooting at *us* for?" he roared.

Cricket didn't seem to hear, staggering to his feet with smoke pouring off his hull. Zeke hunkered down behind a dusty RV as Preacher took refuge in the shade of a rustbucket 4x4. The citizens in the convoy were already running for better cover, machine-gun fire from the Brotherhood helping them on their way. Cricket charged at the Sumo, tracer rounds bursting on his armor as he crashed into the big machina and started tearing the chainguns off its hull. The bloodstained boy scrambled into cover next to Ezekiel, red spilling from his split brow.

"Are you all right?" the lifelike asked.

The boy wiped the blood and foam off his face, slowly nodding. He was maybe nineteen years old, wearing dirty coveralls and steel-toed boots. Dark hair was slicked back from his forehead, his face bloodied and bruised. He looked like he'd seen a ghost, then had the living daylights beaten out of him by it.

"Cricket, what's happening?" Ezekiel roared.

"*I'M AFRAID HE CAN'T HEAR YOU,*" said a muffled voice nearby.

Zeke squinted through the dust and smoke, saw a tall, spindly logika with gold filigree sprawled under the same RV he was crouched behind. The bot kept his head low, an inane grin flashing in time with every word he spoke.

"Why not?" Zeke demanded.

"*I DISABLED HIS AUDIO CAPABILITIES SO HE COULDN'T FOLLOW ORDERS ANYMORE,*" the logika explained. "*WE'RE UNDERTAKING A DARING ESCAPE, YOU SEE.*"

"Who the hell are you?" Ezekiel demanded.

"*MY NAME IS SOLOMON, GOOD SIR,*" the logika replied, offering its hand. *"A PLEASURE TO MEET YOU. THE YOUNG MAN BESIDE YOU IS MASTER ABRAHAM, A FORMER RESIDENT OF THIS CITY NOW LOOKING TO RELOCATE TO FRIENDLIER CLIMES. YOU'RE A FRIEND OF DEAR PALADIN, I TAKE IT?"*

". . . Who the hell is Paladin?"

"NOT TOO BRIGHT, I SEE," Solomon said. *"YOU MUST BE BEST FRIENDS, THEN."*

Preacher stuck his head up from behind his dirt buggy, roaring over the gunfire. "Zekey, I hate to interrupt the chit'n'chat, but there's a posse of god-botherers in fancy dressing gowns tryin' to murder us here?"

Ezekiel ducked low as a burst of machine-gun fire peppered his cover. Cricket had torn the weaponry off the Sumo, but he'd taken a few hits himself, smoke billowing from his dynamo and right arm. Zeke was pretty sure the Brotherhood were shooting at the boy, not him and Preacher. But whatever was happening here, they seemed to have walked right into the middle of a war zone.

"Listen, have you seen a girl named Lemon?" he asked Solomon. "She might have come in with Cricket? Redhead? Cutoff camos and big boots? Five foot nothing?"

"LEMON FRESH? THAT PINT-SIZED, FRECKLE-FACED HOOLIGAN?"

"That's her!" Zeke grinned. "Where is she?"

"I'VE NO IDEA. THE LITTLE ANARCHIST APPEARED FOUR DAYS AGO, FRIED ME LIKE AN EGG, STOLE MY MERCHANDISE, THEN WALTZED AWAY WITHOUT SO MUCH AS AN APOLOGY."

"Yeah, okay that's *definitely* her," Ezekiel muttered.

He cracked off a few blasts with his shotgun, shouted across at Preacher.

"She's not here!"

"Then we ain't got no reason to be getting shot at!" the

bounty hunter replied. "So maybe get hold of your WarBot buddy so we can git the—"

Ezekiel heard an engine roar overhead, a spray of autocannon fire. Bullets ripped up the road, cut a handful of Brotherhood boys off the New Bethlehem walls. The lifelike's heart surged in his chest as he saw a flex-wing with Gnosis logos on the tail fins roaring in out of the cigarette sky. The flier zoomed over the city walls, sprayed another burst of bullets into the Brotherhood and sent them scattering.

Cricket caught sight of the flex-wing, too. The big bot paused in remodeling the Sumo's insides, roaring over the engines, the gunfire, the screams.

"FAITH!"

Ezekiel followed the path of the flex-wing, guessing who might be inside it. The lifelike knew Cricket couldn't hear him, so he yelled across at Preacher instead.

"You see them?"

"Yeah, I seen 'em!" the man replied, firing off a couple of half-hearted shots.

"This place *was* a Gnosis outpost before the company collapsed!"

"You figure lil' Miss Monrova is in residence?"

Ezekiel's heart thumped faster at the thought, but he tried to keep the emotion in check. The thought of seeing her again. After all this time. After all those years . . .

"Why else would they be here?"

"Found religion, mebbee?"

"We can't risk them getting their hands on her!"

Preacher looked up over his cover at the small army of Brotherhood now gathering on the walls. "Bad odds, Zekey."

"You know what's at stake here!"

Preacher scowled. "If I were less of a gentleman, I might be pointing out that we could really use a Daedalus army helping us about now."

"You can say you told me so later!"

The bounty hunter spat a long stream of brown into the dirt, scruffed his blitzhund behind the ears and sighed. Unslinging the shooters from his hips, he nodded. "Alrighty. Let's go melt us some snowflakes."

The flex-wing made another pass over the Brotherhood boys and Disciples, cutting a bloody swath through their thinning line. Ezekiel heard a deafening explosion as the flex-wing unloaded into what was presumably a fuel dump beyond the walls, and the ground shook as a rippling blossom of flame rose into the sky. He lost sight of the flier as it looped back through the rising smoke, but the good news was that it'd certainly got most of the Brotherhood's attention now. And Cricket had the rest.

The big logika seemed to have decided the gate was too crowded, and had started climbing over the wall instead. He dug his metal fists into the concrete, tore through the razor wire and broken glass and jumped back into New Bethlehem with a heavy thud. A few Brotherhood boys were peppering his hull, but his armor was thick enough to shrug it off. The closest thugs got sprayed with a gout of thick white foam from Cricket's palms. But the city sirens were wailing, flames rising, and Zeke could see more machina stomping in from the surrounding fields of gene-modded corn.

Time to move.

Zeke didn't know who this Abraham boy was, only that he was a friend of Cricket's. Grabbing the boy by his greasy coveralls, Solomon with his other hand, he jumped into the cabin of the RV he'd been hiding behind. Preacher leapt up into the back, his blitzhund following. And with his teeth gritted, Zeke planted his foot and tore through the shattered New Bethlehem gates.

The square beyond was in chaos, the buildings on fire, the air a black, choking haze. The flex-wing was buzzing through the smoke-smeared sky overhead, spraying indiscriminately into the crowd. But something about this didn't feel right. . . .

"THEY SENT FAITH AS A DISTRACTION IN JUGARTOWN!" Cricket yelled. "THE REST OF THEM WILL BE AT THE GNOSIS BUILDING!"

Ezekiel squinted across the square, saw the desalination plant rising above the other shanty shacks and burning buildings. It was wreathed in dark fumes and smoke, a corrosive stink. But through the flames spreading across New Bethlehem's square, he could still see the faded GnosisLabs logo on the wall.

"Go!" Cricket yelled. "I GOT BUSINESS WITH THESE TWO!"

A chaingun unfolded from Cricket's forearm, and twin pods of missile launchers unfurled from his back like insect wings. The big bot started firing on the flex-wing, and the few remaining Brotherhood boys seemed to decide the flier was a bigger threat than the bot, and joined in on the bullet party.

Ezekiel stomped the accelerator, tires squealing as he tore across the burning New Bethlehem square. Citizens scattered as he wove the RV through the settlement, skidding to a smoking halt in front of the desalination plant.

The building squatted on the edge of the bay like an old, broken king. Its facade had been modified into the crude likeness of an oldskool cathedral, with double iron doors and a big stone bell tower. But in reality, it was an ugly bloated hulk with fat storage tanks and a tangled knot of hissing pipes. Thick smoke spilled from its chimneys, laying down a pall of fumes over the black water beyond.

Ezekiel climbed out of the RV with his trusty shotgun in hand. He spoke to Solomon and Abraham.

"You keep your heads down. We'll be back soon, all right?"

"*IF YOU INSIST, OLD FRIEND,*" the logika replied.

Preacher jumped down onto the concrete beside him, and Jojo leapt down behind his master. Zeke spied four guards with greasepaint Xs on their faces, lying dead by the factory's front doors.

"They're already inside," he muttered.

"Mmf," Preacher nodded. "Came in from the ocean."

Ezekiel saw Jojo snuffling among a few sets of wet black footprints, coming from the direction of the boardwalk on the bay—he guessed the plan was for Eve, Gabriel and Uriel to steal in from the water while Faith and Verity kept the Brotherhood's attention. And his siblings already had a head start.

"All right, let's move."

His heart was hammering in his chest as they stepped inside, swathed in oily stink and tar-thick fumes. More bodies were waiting just inside the doors, and over the burble and clank of the factory's workings, he could hear gunfire, cries of pain. He imagined Eve stalking through the gloom, Gabriel and Uriel following her like shadows. Tried to picture the girl he'd met only a handful of days ago, reconcile who she'd been with who she'd become.

She looked like Ana. Talked and laughed and kissed like Ana. But looking at the bodies in her wake, the blood she'd left spattered on the walls, Ezekiel knew for sure and certain that Eve was nothing close to the girl he'd loved. He remembered the way she'd butchered those gangers in Paradise Falls. He remembered searching her eyes for the girl he adored, and finding not a glimmer. Not a spark. And he realized if it came down to a choice between protecting Ana's life and ending Eve's . . .

Was she really down here? Buried in this darkness? The girl he'd loved since he first set eyes on her? The girl who'd made him real? It was hard to imagine Nicholas Monrova would consign his beloved Ana to a fate like this. But then again, it was hard to imagine Monrova turning on his fellow board members, turning Gabriel into a murderer, turning entirely to madness. In the final days of the Gnosis CorpState, Monrova had thought himself surrounded by enemies. He'd thought himself a god. Maybe he'd hidden Ana down here like a seed beneath the earth, waiting for the day she might bloom again?

Maybe she might be okay?

More gunshots. Echoing on greasy steel. Jojo growled softly, his eyes glowing faint red. Ezekiel, Preacher and the blitzhund followed the trail of bodies and bloody footprints into a loading elevator. The air was humid, the stink heavy as lead. A bloody fingerprint was smeared on the button for the lowest sub-basement, and Ezekiel pressed it, heart in his throat.

They rode the elevator down, deep into the structure's belly. As the doors slid open, they found a heavy hatchway set with a digital lock. The door was scorched and dented and scratched— it was obvious the Brotherhood had tried to get inside to access whatever bounty Gnosis had left behind. They'd apparently failed. But now, the door was slightly ajar.

"What's your play, Zekey?" Preacher murmured, scruffing his dog's throat.

"Three of them, three of us. We hit them hard. Fast as we can."

"Including lil' Miss Carpenter?"

"She wants to wipe humanity off the face of the planet, Preacher." Ezekiel thumbed the safety off his shotgun. *"Especially* her."

"Well, now." The bounty hunter looked him up and down, pushing a wad of synth tobacco into his cheek. "Looks like you *have* grown up."

Ezekiel ignored the jab, and the two of them stole through the hatchway, down a dark corridor, lined with strips of red fluorescents. The air was heavy, thick with steam, the thrum of the machinery echoing down his spine. Ezekiel's every nerve was crackling, his jaw clenched, his eyes wide as he searched the shadows, stealing through the mist with his shotgun held tight. And slipping through another large, heavy door, the pair stepped right into the factory's secret heart.

A room opened up before them, red lighting and dark iron, the temperature dropping through the floor. The space was mostly taken up by a vast sphere, similar to the one inside the Myriad chamber. It was covered in tubes, gauges and dials, fat pipelines snaking across the floor, up into the ceiling, all rimed in frost. The sphere was ringed by a broad gantry, suspended over a deep ventilation shaft. A metal walkway led over the chasm to a broad hexagonal door.

And the doorway was open wide.

He heard Eve's voice from inside. Her words dragging him back to a darkened bedroom and a gentle kiss and the moment he first felt truly alive.

"You're mine."

A promise.

A poem.

A prayer.

"You're mine."

She's here, Ezekiel realized.

The emotions surged again—elation, fear, a wild, delirious kind of hope. But he pushed them all aside, trying desperately to hold on to the rush of feelings and the surge of adrenaline and just keep his mind steady. It was still hard, even after all he'd done and seen. Two years isn't much of a lifetime, isn't long to figure out how to live. But he knew full well what was at stake here—not just the girl he loved, but the future of humanity itself. Heart thumping, belly flipping, he crouched down behind a large bank of power generators and peered through the sphere's hatchway.

The room beyond was brightly lit, white and antiseptic, humming with electricity and frost and the rhythmic beat of monitor machines. Through the frozen, roiling air, he could see Gabriel, Uriel and Eve, gathered around a large tube of burnished steel and glass, their breath spilling cold and white off their lips. The tube was two meters long, filled with a thick, translucent liquid, vaguely blue. And inside it, blond hair floating around her head like a golden halo . . .

I was made for you.

All I am.

All I do

I do for you.

Ana.

She looked almost like he remembered her. Her face was a little older, a little thinner, her skin was a lighter shade of pale. But she was still beautiful. A tube had been inserted between her lips, allowing her to breathe beneath the liquid. She was naked, floating weightless, tubes inserted into her arms, 'trodes fitted to her temples. Her eyes were closed, her face serene, as if she were lost in some pleasant dream. Like Snow White from the books he'd read in Babel, awaiting her handsome prince to wake her with a kiss.

But the computers beside her glass coffin were silent. According to the frost-encrusted monitors, only a dim pulse throbbed in her veins. A small bellows moved with the rise and fall of her breast, and just the faintest sparks of activity registered in her brain. Like tiny fireflies, flitting about an otherwise dark and empty room.

Her father was a genius. A madman. Unwilling to let his beloved baby girl go. But looking at her now, Ezekiel saw the awful truth. A truth that shattered two years of wandering, of searching, of the vain hope that somehow, some way, they'd be together again. A truth that came crashing down on his shoulders, and almost sent him to his knees.

The truth of what she'd become.

Not alive.

Not dead.

And not Ana.

Gabriel spread his hands out on the frosted glass, peering at the girl inside. Ezekiel could see the joy on his brother's face. The elation in his eyes. Ana might be trapped in some gray forever limbo, halfway between life and death, but she still had blood in her veins. And that would be all they needed to access the Myriad supercomputer. The data Nicholas Monrova had locked inside. The resurrection of the lifelike program. The resurrection of Grace. Raphael. Michael. Daniel. Hope. Mercy.

Everyone they'd lost.

Everyone they loved.

Everyone except her.

Eve's voice echoed in the gloom.

"She looks . . ."

She fell silent, shaking her head. Her breath hung frozen and still.

"You told me we'd find her." Gabriel turned to his sister, tears shining in his eyes. He wrapped Eve up in his arms, hugging her fiercely as he whispered, "I should have believed in you. Thank you, sister. *Thank* you."

But Eve's eyes were still fixed on the girl in that glass coffin. Floating like a baby in a frozen womb, still and silent and helpless. Eve looked down at her own hand. The hand she'd driven through the chest of that scavver in Paradise Falls. The hand she'd drenched in red. And slowly, she reached up and pressed that hand to her own throat.

She spoke so soft, Ezekiel almost couldn't hear.

She spoke almost as if to herself.

"She looks just like me. . . ."

2.32

IMMOLATION

New Bethlehem burned.

Its citizens were fleeing or trying to douse the spreading flames, its soldiers either in hiding or cut to pieces by Faith's cannons. Cricket stood in the square, feet apart, optics aimed skyward. He locked onto Faith's flex-wing with his missile pods, unleashed a volley of incendiaries. But Faith laid down a stream of heat-seeker decoys as she cut through the sky, the missiles exploding harmlessly around her.

She returned fire, forcing the big bot into cover behind a pile of old autos and a rusty Neo-Meat™ stand. GnosisLabs had designed his body to be top of the line. But they'd designed that flex-wing, too, and sensibly, it looked like Faith's flier was equipped to deal with anything Cricket could throw.

The WarBot felt a tapping on the side of his head. He glanced at Solomon, crouched on his shoulder with his whiteboard and marker.

You're not very good at this, are you! ☺

"SHE'S GOT MISSILE DECOY SYSTEMS! WHAT DO YOU WANT ME TO DO?"

Perhaps something less high-tech, old friend!

Cricket looked about, deciding that was actually a pretty sensible plan. As the flex-wing swooped overhead, the big logika took hold of the Neo-Meat™ stand and tore it up out of the earth, hurled it with all his strength. Faith hit her air-skids hard, fired more useless decoys, but the wreckage crushed her portside wing and sent the ship spinning. Faith tried to hold it, engines screaming as the flier spun out of control. She clipped the desal plant's belfry, and Cricket imagined the gongs ringing over the city as the craft kept falling, smoke spewing from its rotor blades. It swung over the marketplace and finally crashed—right into the New Bethlehem WarDome.

Bravo!

The Dome bars had been rolled back, so there was nothing between the flier and the killing floor. Faith and Verity bailed out as the flex-wing crashed, hitting the concrete hard and rolling with the impact. Cricket waded across the marketplace, careful not to crush the flood of panicked citizens. He set Solomon on the bleachers and dropped down into the arena as the two lifelikes climbed to their feet, a plume of fire rising up from the long trail of burning wreckage behind them.

The big bot looked around at the empty seats. The oil stains slicked like old blood on the killing floor. Fixing the pair in his glowing blue stare.

"THIS IS A LITTLE IRONIC, ISN'T IT?"

Faith's lips moved as she replied, but Cricket held up one massive hand.

"SAVE YOUR BREATH," he told her. "I CAN'T HEAR A WORD YOU'RE SAYING. AND I'M NOT HERE TO TRADE QUIPS, ANYWAY."

He unfolded the chaingun on his right hand.

"SHUT UP AND FIGHT."

The WarBot opened fire. Faith and Verity moved like silk in the wind, splitting apart and rolling behind a couple of rusty barricades. Verity dashed across to an old auto hulk as Cricket blasted away with his chaingun, spent shells falling like shooting stars. The lifelike doubled back, throwing off Cricket's aim as Faith emerged from cover at his flank, drew out her arc-blade and closed the distance between them in a heartbeat.

He swung one massive fist, denting the killing floor as Faith rolled past the blow. He felt the impact, the vibration, but it was true strange fighting in silence. He could see Faith's lips moving as she lashed out with her blade, severing the ammo feed to his chaingun. Though he couldn't hear his enemies' footsteps, his 360-degree tracking software had them both locked, rendering them on a digital topography inside his head. He sensed Verity rise up from cover, his engines vibrating as he rolled beneath the grenade she fired. The explosion's roar was silent. The bleachers were empty around them, but he could almost hear the crowd in his ears.

He'd set foot in WarDome with Evie dozens of times. Watched the bouts beneath the flashing lights. He'd even fought in here himself now. But for the first time, standing there on the killing floor felt *right*. He wasn't fighting for the scratch or to please the starving mob. He was fighting to avenge Silas. To avenge his friends. To avenge the life he'd lived with Evie and Lemon, with people who truly *cared* about him. The life that Faith and her siblings had taken away.

Looking at Faith and Verity, those picture-perfect faces and plastic, empty eyes, he realized he wanted to break them. He wanted to pound them to pulp underneath his fists and make them hurt for all the hurt they'd dealt in kind.

But they were so quick. So strong. Verity kept pounding

him with grenades, ducking out from cover and taking shots at him from range. He returned fire with his incendiaries as best he could, but her barrage kept him off balance and stumbling. Meantime, Faith was cutting away at him with that damned arc-blade of hers, and the current burned hot enough to liquefy his armor. He tore one of the barricades loose from the killing floor and swung it like a club to keep her at bay, just as another grenade crashed into his shoulder.

He stumbled and fell to one knee, and Faith sliced at his hydraulics, fluid and oil spraying. He managed to clip her with a wild swing, sent her tumbling and skidding across the concrete floor. But another grenade hit him in the back, knocked him forward onto his belly. Faith was up in an instant, knuckles and elbows bloodied, dashing toward him. Her sword was raised to cleave his head in two.

Her lips were still moving—she couldn't resist mouthing off, even though he'd told her that he couldn't hear a word of it. It struck him how childish she was. How childish they *all* were. Like petulant little kids with the world's biggest chips on their shoulders, looking to even the score.

The sword descended toward his head. He raised a hand, tried rolling aside, tensed to feel the blow. But as the sword fell, Faith was slammed backward into the WarDome wall, her eyes wide, blood flying from between her teeth. Cricket climbed to his feet, leaking hydraulic fluid and coolant, turned to see Abraham standing behind him on the WarDome floor. The boy's oil-stained hand was raised, a frown darkening his bloody brow.

A grenade flew at Abraham from Verity's launcher. The boy twisted, fingers outstretched as the air around him rippled like water. The projectile bounced backward like a kickball, tumbling through the air before exploding right in Verity's face. The vibration rang in Cricket's chest as he unleashed another salvo of incendiaries from his launchers, catching Verity in a burst of white-hot flame. The lifelike's clothing caught fire, her mouth open in a scream, her body dropping to the ground as the flames began to catch. Cricket picked up his barricade and hurled it like a spear at Faith. The lifelike tried to move aside, tried to dance, but Abraham extended his hand, the air rippling once again, and an invisible force seemed to hold her pinned. Those plastic gray telescreen eyes widened as the barricade struck home, hurtling her backward and crushing her against the wall.

Red sprayed up the stone. Bones were smashed into powder, organs pulped. Faith coughed, blood dripping from between her teeth. She fixed Cricket in her stare, tried to speak. And finally, she slumped forward over the twisted metal, her arc-blade dropping from her fingers.

"THAT'S FOR SILAS," the big bot whispered.

He turned to Abraham, saw the boy sink to his knees, holding his bleeding head. He looked like seven slices of hell, warmed up in a faulty microwave. Cricket clomped to his side, looked down with burning blue optics.

"YOU ALL RIGHT?"

The boy nodded, gave the thumbs-up sign. Cricket looked to the bleachers, saw Solomon was on his feet, wobbling on his faulty dynamo. The logika gave Cricket a small round of applause, then wrote on his damn whiteboard.

Capital work, old friend!

Cricket shook his head. Lifted Abraham gently in his hand, dug his fingers into the concrete and climbed up out of the bloody killing floor.

"OLD FRIEND?" he said to Solomon. "YOU REALIZE WE'VE KNOWN EACH OTHER FOR THREE DAYS, RIGHT?"

Solomon grinned, wrote another note on his board.

Which makes you my oldest friend. Now perhaps we should vacate this pigpen before it burns down around our ears?

Cricket looked at the chaos around them, the burning buildings and the rising smoke. Once again, the skinny logika was making sense. Leaning down, he picked up Solomon and plopped him on his shoulder.

"ALL RIGHT. LET'S FIND THE OTHERS."

———

"Hit 'em when they're on the bridge," Preacher whispered.

Ezekiel was still crouched behind the power generators, looking into the sphere that held Ana's life-support capsule. The air around him was freezing cold, thin frost already crusted in his dark curls. Gabriel and Uriel were busy uncoupling that glass coffin from the larger system, preparing it for transport.

The sphere was ringed by a frost-encrusted gantry, suspended over a deep fall into darkness. Preacher was right—hitting them on the bridge gave his siblings the least room to react. To fight. Ezekiel knew he had to be as cold as the ice on the walls now. The future of humanity itself was at stake here. Not to mention Ana's life.

What was left of it, anyway.

But his stare was fixed on Eve.

She stood beside their brothers, watching Uriel and Gabriel work. The pair were as excited as children. The promise of their robotic legion and the resurrection of the lifelike program was within their grasp. But Eve's eyes were locked on the girl floating in that softly glowing blue—the girl she'd been built to replace. The girl she'd searched for across the ruins of the Yousay.

Her hand was still at her own throat.

Fingertips digging into her skin.

Uriel and Gabriel finished their work, coupling the life-support unit to a small generator and disengaging the locks that held the capsule in place. It floated similar to a grav-tank: a small cushion of magnetized particles keeping it from touching the ground, the frost on the floor crackling with small arcs of current.

Preacher flipped the safeties on his shooters, scruffed Jojo behind his ears.

"Ready?" he whispered.

She's not the girl you knew. . . .

"Goddammit, wake up!" Preacher hissed.

"I'm ready," Ezekiel whispered. "Just don't hit Ana."

"Told you, Zekey," the bounty hunter winked. "I ain't no killer. An *artiste* is what I am."

Uriel pushed the hatchway wide, began backing out of the sphere.

Ezekiel had a clear shot at his brother's spine.

"Come, sister," Gabriel said to Eve. "Let's get her home."

Together, they pushed the support capsule out of the frozen compartment. Uriel came first, dragging the weight, Gabriel pushing the other end of the capsule. Eve came last, walking slower, clouded hazel eyes still fixed on her doppelgänger. And into the crackling, pregnant silence, she spoke. A question that made Ezekiel's stomach flip.

". . . Should we be doing this?" she whispered.

Uriel and Gabriel stopped, turning to look at their sister.

"What do you mean?" Gabriel asked.

"I mean . . ." Eve looked at the sphere around them. The girl in that frozen coffin of glass. "We just need her DNA for the third Myriad lock. Maybe we could just take a blood sample? Leave her here. Let her sleep. Like her father wanted."

"Her *father*?" Uriel spat. "Why do we care what he wanted?"

"I thought *you* wanted her dead?" Gabriel demanded.

Eve's eyes were fixed on Ana. The face behind the glass. Like a mirror. Like a pale reflection of herself. Ezekiel's breath came a little quicker as she looked down at her open hand, slowly shook her head.

"I don't know. . . ."

"Not you, too?" Uriel snarled. "Bad enough I have to endure this lovesick puppy's idiocy"—he waved at Gabriel—"now I have to deal with an attack of your conscience? Can not a single one of you forget your human frailties long enough to see this through to the end?"

"Go to hell, Uriel," Gabriel spat.

"I'm already in it!" the lifelike cried. "Surrounded by deluded fools who believe they're human. We are better! Stronger! More! We are the nex—"

The bullet struck Uriel in the back of his skull, blew his pretty face clean out. Gabriel and Eve flinched as they were splashed with blood and brain, as another dozen shots ripped through Uriel's throat, torso, belly. The lifelike tottered, arms twitching, toppling into the railing and tumbling down into the vent shaft below.

"Lord, your family's mouthy, Zeke," Preacher growled, lowering his pistols.

Gabriel and Eve were already moving as the bounty hunter reloaded, dashing across the causeway and into cover. Half in a daze, the picture of Uriel's end flashing in his mind, Ezekiel started blasting, shots ripping into Gabriel's belly and thigh as his brother dove behind a bank of equipment. His heart was aching as he fired. His mouth dry as the wasteland humanity had made outside these walls. He knew his siblings were monsters. He'd seen all the hurt they'd given the world. Gabriel had murdered Monrova, little Alex; put a gun to a ten-year-old boy's head and smiled as he pulled the trigger. Uriel had murdered Tania, snuffed her out like a candle without a shred of remorse. And Eve was a killer, too—the massacre at Paradise Falls and who knew where else. All of her design.

But still, they were family.

Monrova had *made* Gabriel his killer.

And Eve, she . . .

"I thought we killed you once already, Preacher!" she called.

"I'm like a bad cold, darlin'," the cyborg smiled. "Just can't get rid of me."

"What are you doing, Ezekiel?" Gabriel roared. "This animal killed Hope. Now Uriel, too? How many more of us do you want to murder?"

"You don't get to talk about murder, Gabriel!" Ezekiel cracked off a handful of shots at his brother's cover. "You murdered Nicholas, Alexis, Alex. You murdered Silas. You murdered thousands of people when you overloaded the Babel reactor. And you'll murder millions more if you get your way!"

"We're your *family*!"

"You betrayed the one who made us! You left me for dead! And you're trying to engineer the destruction of the entire human race!" Ezekiel shook his head, his voice incredulous. "Us being related doesn't get you a pass for genocide! Just because you're family doesn't mean you're not assholes!"

"Ezekiel, listen to me!" Eve called.

"No, you listen to *me!*" he yelled. "I'm sorry I lied to you, Eve! I'm sorry everyone else lied to you! I'm sorry your life didn't turn out to be what you wanted, but that's what life *is*! People lie. People screw up. People fail. But I know you! The girl you were built to be, and the girl you became afterward. And this girl I see in front of me now isn't anything like either of them!"

"That's the p—"

"—the point, I know! But is this who you really want to be? What do you think Cricket would say if he could see you now? Or Silas? Or Lemon? If you're going to wipe out humanity, does that mean you're going to kill her, too?"

"Humanity is a plague, Ezekiel!" Gabriel called. "A thorn in the side of the earth. Look at this world! Look what they did to it!"

"And you think you're going to do better?" Ezekiel demanded. "When your reign begins with the murder of *millions*?"

"All right, enough of this crap," Preacher muttered. "Jojo, execute."

The blitzhund growled deep in its chest, its eyes flipping to a murderous red. Claws scrabbling on the steel, it dashed around the generators and charged right at Gabriel. The lifelike rose up from cover, plugged two shots into the blitzhund's optics. Sparks burst as the bullets struck Jojo's steel combat chassis, the hound stumbling and exploding a few meters short of its mark. The blast was still enough to knock Gabriel back, pepper him with shrapnel, shred his flawless skin. Preacher followed up with two grenades, lobbed in a lazy arc right toward the lifelike's head.

Ezekiel's heart was in his throat. Gabriel was a monster, but despite everything he'd just said, how far Gabe had fallen, they were still brothers. He remembered the days before the revolt, the pair of them in Babel, both falling in love for the first time. Zeke knew what it was to love with an intensity that was almost frightening. Could he blame Gabe for loving Grace as much as he loved Ana?

Do I really want to see him die?

Eve emerged from cover, face twisted as she ran. She dove through the air, arms outstretched. And moving like lightning, she caught Preacher's two grenades and flung them back, tumbling behind cover as the explosives burst.

Preacher was thrown backward by the blast, coat and flesh shredded. Ezekiel was firing with his shotgun, muzzle flashes strobing, blasts catching Gabriel in his chest and dropping the lifelike to the floor. Eve rolled to her feet, boots thudding on the deck as she rounded his cover, eyes narrowed and locked with his. Ezekiel fired, but god, she was so fast—just as fast as he was. A shot struck her shoulder, she weaved through the rest, diving toward him and spear-tackling him into the wall.

His shotgun flew from his grip as his breath left his lungs. Her knuckles crashed into his jaw. Her knee with his groin. Doubling him up as she brought both fists down on the back of his head.

Bright light. Concussive pain.

"Eve, stop," he gasped, trying to rise.

She drove a boot into his side hard enough to crack his ribs. Ezekiel felt his insides tear, coughing blood onto the metal, and she kicked him again. Again.

"I'm sorry," she said.

Crunch.

"Eve . . ."

Crack.

She drew back her foot to stomp on his head, her face an ashen mask. "I warned you this wouldn't turn out the way you wanted it to."

The shots burst out through her chest, one, two, three. Her eyes went wide as the blood sprayed, she staggered and turned, scarlet lips drawn back in a snarl. Another three shots struck her belly, chest, neck, sending her stumbling backward into the wall. Eve hit the steel hard, her face twisted in pain. Zeke could see the fury boiling in her eyes as she tried to push herself back up, tried to rise, to fight as she'd always done. But the damage was too much. The hurt just too deep. And slowly, eyelids fluttering closed, red spattering on her lips as she sighed, Eve slithered down to the floor, leaving a trail of red smeared on the metal behind her.

Ezekiel pulled himself to his hands and knees, wincing at the white pain of his broken ribs, the black agony in his crotch. He reached out for Eve's throat, pressed shaking fingers to bloody skin. His belly surged as he felt a faint pulse, as he saw her wounds beginning to knit closed.

Preacher dragged himself to his feet, spitting a bloody, dark mouthful onto the floor. "She alive?"

Ezekiel looked at the bounty hunter. His face and chest had been shredded by the grenade blast, the metal combat chassis beneath gleaming in the frosty light. Despite his injuries, the cyborg reached into his coat, fished about in his pocket and stuffed a fresh wad of synth tobacco into his cheek.

"Sh-she's alive," he managed.

"Mmf."

Preacher pulled his hat back on, the fabric smoking and torn by shrapnel. Reloading his weapons, he limped to where Gabriel lay in a puddle of blood. Gabe was already trying to rise, bright green eyes locked on the bounty hunter.

"I'm going to—"

Preacher raised his pistol, put two shots into Gabe's kneecaps.

The blasts rang out almost deafening in the hollow space. Zeke's brother screamed, rolling around on the ground and clutching the wounds.

"Stay down, Snowflake," he growled.

"You m-maggot," Gabriel hissed. "You *insect*! You and all—"

Preacher fired again, blowing off Gabriel's lower jaw in a spray of blood. The lifelike collapsed back with a strangled gurgle, eyes rolling up in his head.

"Th-that's . . . enough," Ezekiel said, trying to rise to his feet.

"You're right," Preacher nodded, inspecting his handiwork. "I reckon that oughta shut him up awhile."

The cyborg leaned down and picked up Gabriel's unconscious body, slung him like a sack of meat over Ana's life-support capsule. Blood spilled from Gabe's wounds, steaming on the frosted glass. With a wince and grunt of effort, Preacher pushed the capsule forward across the bridge, over to where Eve lay slumped against the wall. Ezekiel's eyes were locked on Ana, floating inside that cool blue light, her face serene through the wash of blood on the glass.

He looked across at Eve, her eyelashes fluttering against her bloody cheeks.

"What are you d-doing?" he asked.

Preacher didn't reply, bending down to pick Eve up and sling her onto the capsule beside Gabriel. Her fingers were twitching. Her breath shallow. Ezekiel could feel his ribs beginning to knit, the trauma from her beating blazed in red and blue across his side. He finally managed to drag himself to his feet, spitting the copper taste of blood off his tongue.

"I asked wh-what you're doing," Ezekiel said, his voice growing harder.

Preacher sighed, sucked his cheek. "Getting ready for pickup."

Ezekiel frowned. "Pickup?"

"Mmf." The man nodded, spat on the deck. "There's a Daedalus special-ops team en route. Carriers. Ground troops. Machina, logika and air support."

"You—"

The pistol flashed twice in the dark. Ezekiel felt the shots hit, knock him backward, legs going out from under him. The pain of white-hot fire and broken glass in his chest. He pressed bloody hands to the metal beneath him, tried to rise as Preacher leveled the pistol at his head.

"I did tell you the safest play was to ghost me, Zekey," he said.

"C-code . . . ," Zeke managed to whisper.

"Yeah, I got my code," Preacher nodded. "And I told you, son. The first part of it is loyalty. Daedalus saved my hide long before you did." The bounty hunter shrugged. "'Sides, way I figure it, I'm saving a few million lives putting an end to this nonsense. So yeah, you saved my skin. But I figure this about makes us even."

Ezekiel coughed red, tried again to drag himself up off the bloody deck. The spurs on Preacher's boots rang silver-bright as the bounty hunter placed a foot on the lifelike's chest, pushing him back down.

"You didn't think when I got my augs replaced in Armada, I wouldn't get a transmitter hooked up, too? Or that I wouldn'a called this in to Daedalus HQ the second I got the opportunity? I thought you was s'posed to have grown up." Preacher shook his head. "Turns out the science boys want 'em some snowflakes to look at. And if your little Ana is the key to a whole passel of Nicky Monrova's secrets in Babel, well, turns out they want her, too. But don't fret, Zekey. Two o' you oughta be enough. I'ma leave you here to rest up awhile. I owe you that much."

"You . . . b-b . . ."

"Bastard?" Preacher tipped his hat back and smiled. "Yeah, I'm one o' them, all right. But at least I ain't a stupid bastard."

The bounty hunter raised his pistol to Ezekiel's chest.

"You sleep now, Zekey."

BANG.

————

Smoke was rising from the burning buildings, New Bethlehem was thrashing in its death throes. Cricket stalked through the smoke, Solomon on his shoulder, Abraham in the palm of his hand. Making their way back through the chaos to the de-sal plant, Cricket couldn't see any sign of Ezekiel or the Preacher. But through the smoke, he *could* see small cassocked figures fighting the rising blaze, trying desperately to save their city. Among them, he spotted a woman in ash-streaked white, mouth open as she roared commands to her men.

Sister Dee.

Abraham pulled himself to his feet and pointed. Cricket realized there were people trapped in upper floors of the burning tenements, a few more in the dockside warehouses. The Brotherhood were using hoses, pumping water direct from the massive storage tanks in the desalination plant. But they were too little, too few, the flames burning too bright and hot.

Sister Dee caught sight of Cricket, of her son, calling the thugs around her to attention. The men dropped their hoses, hauled out their weapons, facing off across the blazing ruins.

Solomon rapped on the side of his head. Held up a note.

Master Abraham says to put him down.

"I CAN'T DO THAT, ABRAHAM," Cricket replied.

The boy looked up at Cricket and smiled as he spoke.

He says that's an order, old friend.

Technically, Cricket supposed he didn't have to obey. But he still trusted the boy. And so he bent low, placed Abraham gently on the ground. The boy walked toward the Brotherhood men, his hands raised high. The tension in the air was thicker than the smoke, their weapons were pointed directly at him—the deviate, the trashbreed, the abnorm. All they'd been raised and trained to despise.

And the boy turned his back on them.

He looked to the de-sal plant. The massive storage tanks of seawater and fresh water, bubbling and boiling through its innards. Abraham held out his hands toward the tangle of pipes, the rusty black metal and corroded rivets. His face twisted in concentration, his teeth bared. The air about him rippled, shivered, shook. And as Cricket watched, the seams on the pipes shuddered and cracked and finally burst open, unleashing a gout of high-pressure water.

The Brotherhood, Sister Dee, the faithful, all of them watched as the boy curled his fingers. The air rippled harder, Abraham's face twisted with exertion as he slowly bent the pipes, directing the rushing spray high into the air. Thousands of liters spewed upward like a fountain, black and gray and heavy. Sunlight glittering in the droplets, tiny rainbows shimmering in the air as the water rained down into the flames. The fire smoked and seethed, steam rising in the blistering heat. But slowly, beneath the flood, the inferno choked. And sputtered.

And died.

The Brotherhood stared dumbfounded at the boy. A boy who had every reason to let them burn. A boy they'd been told to hate.

A boy who'd just saved their city.

And slowly, they lowered their weapons.

Cricket felt a knock on the side of his head, saw Solomon pointing up to the roof of the desalination plant. Up through the rushing spray, the glittering rainbows, Cricket saw a heavy flex-wing carrier swooping in, surrounded by lighter assault craft. Daedalus Technologies logos were emblazoned on the sides. A cloud of thopter-drones swarmed around the carrier as it came into hover, hooks and cables unfurling from its loading doors as the smoke in the air curled and rolled.

"WHAT THE HELL'S THAT?" he muttered.

He saw CorpTroopers in heavy power armor rappelling down to the plant's roof. He saw the Preacher appear from inside the installation, pushing some kind of cylindrical glass case, too rimed in frost to see inside it. But even through the smoke and fog, Cricket's optics were good enough to see two bloodstained figures being secured on the tethers, hauled skyward along with the capsule into the flex-wing. A pretty male with a mop of bloody blond hair. And beside him, dripping scarlet from the multiple holes in her chest . . .

"EVIE . . ."

The missile pods unfurled at Cricket's back, the chain-gun from his arm. But looking at the human soldiers above, he didn't . . . he *couldn't* fire. The Preacher leaned out over the roof, bloodstained and grinning. He spat a stream of sticky brown from between split lips, gave Cricket a salute, calling words he couldn't hear.

"WHAT'S HE SAYING?"

Solomon's eyes flashed, and he scribbled on his whiteboard in a panic.

Megopolis detected a launch from a rogue military installation near the Glass seven minutes ago. There's a fully armed nuclear cruise missile inbound on this city.

"... WHAT?"

He's also alluding that logika don't have souls, so he can't actually see you in heaven, but he likes your style and hopes—

Cricket ignored the rest of the note, turning to Abraham.

"WE NEED TO GET OUT OF HERE!"

The Daedalus carrier blasted its turbines, lifting the Preacher, Evie, Gabriel and their glass cargo up into the sky. Banking off through the rolling smoke, the air fleet tore away over the city, burning south as fast as their engines would take them. Cricket snatched up Abraham, roaring at the top of his voice.

"ALL OF YOU NEED TO RUN! THERE'S A MISSILE COMING!"

Panic flooded his systems as he stomped to the front gate, as the Brotherhood broke and scattered, the citizens streamed out of the waterlogged buildings. If what the Preacher said was true, there was nowhere to run—no way to escape the incoming firestorm. The blast would simply be too massive to escape. But still, the First Law was screaming in Cricket's mind. His only concern, the hundreds still in New Bethlehem—innocents and sinners alike. His only imperative to try and save the unsavable.

He looked up into the cigarette sky, data scrolling down his optics as his scanners scoured the gray. Looking for a telltale heat signature, a flash of light, anything that might . . .

There.

He saw it. A tiny black spear, burning in out of the sky like a thunderbolt. Electric despair washed over him. Thinking about Evie. About Lemon. About everything he'd fought for, everything he'd learned, everything he'd lost, glad in the end that despite it all, at least he wasn't alone.

He patted Solomon gently on his metal knee, cradled Abraham to his chest.

"I'M SORRY," he said.

He felt a knocking on the side of his head. Turned to look at Solomon one last time. The spindly logika was pointing east, out across New Bethlehem's smoking walls, the wrecked cars, the ash and ruin. There, glinting in the sunlight, Cricket saw a lumbering monster truck, painted Brotherhood red, speeding in across the desert.

He sharpened his optics, thinking he was glitching as a colorless . . . tear opened up in the ground in front of the truck. The vehicle plunged down into it, fell out of a similar rift that had opened up just in front of New Bethlehem's walls.

The truck hit the deck, bouncing wildly, crashing through the wreckage out front of the gate with a scream of tortured metal. Brotherhood and Disciples and citizens all went scattering, the truck slewing sideways, overcorrecting and skidding into a row of parked autos. Windows shattering, steel tearing, engine smoking, it crashed to a halt right in the middle of the city square.

". . . WHAT THE HELLS?"

Cricket saw two teenagers in military uniforms in the front seat. A dark-skinned boy, spattered in blood, a radioactivity symbol shaved into the side of his head. And a girl, dark hair, hooded eyes and lips smudged with black paint. The pair climbed up onto the truck's roof, shaking and bloody and bedraggled.

"WHAT ARE YOU DOING?" he cried.

Cricket saw a shimmering rift open in the air high above their heads.

Cricket saw the missile, speeding in from the heavens.

And Cricket saw the boy

raise

his

h—

2.33

CODA

Lemon stood on the burning sand, eyes to the horizon.

The wind at her back blew her hair about her face, her freckles streaked with dust and tears. Tire tracks were torn into the earth at her feet, marking Grimm and Diesel's frantic drive back to New Bethlehem. Her hands were crusted with dried blood. Her lips were still tingling.

It'd been ten minutes since the missile launched, tearing westward with its cargo of fire and screams. Six minutes since Grimm kissed her, lifting her off the ground and lighting a fire in her chest. Five minutes since he and Diesel disappeared over the horizon with nothing but a desperate plan, leaving her alone to watch the western skies and wish she were the kind of person who prayed.

Lemon stood and stared, counting each second in her head, one by one by one. She knew it was stupid to believe things might turn out okay. To imagine happy-ever-afters in a world like this. She knew it was the kind of thing a kid would do, and that—if she'd ever been—she surely wasn't a kid anymore.

She knew it was silly to hope.

But in the end, it was all she had.

If they make it . . .

If he comes back . . .

And then, to the west, a new star bloomed in the sky.

It was brighter than the daylight. Brighter than anything she'd ever seen. A burst of atomic fire, like some awful desert flower opening its petals to the sun.

She put her hand up against it, trying to blot it out. As if by making it invisible, she might make it unreal. But a handful of seconds later, she felt the blast, heard it tearing across the desert at the speed of sound.

Dawn without a sunset.

Thunder without a storm.

She felt tears spill down her cheeks as the light bloomed brighter.

Impossible.

Unimaginable.

Mushroom-shaped.

Her legs wouldn't hold her, she slid to her knees, down into the dust. She thought of the boy who'd called her love, who'd kissed her like he meant it, who'd run toward that fire without even flinching. She thought of the girl who'd gone with him, fighting for this world after everything she'd lost. She thought of the earth burned black, of the hatred and fear that had driven them all to this.

What do I do now?

And when the bumblebee landed on her cheek, she didn't flinch.

It crawled along the tracks of her tears, down her face to the lips he'd kissed, and she didn't even blink. Instead, she sat and stared westward, listened to the slow footsteps on the sand behind her. Drawing closer. She heard the hiss of dank breath over too many teeth. Sharp claws tearing the earth at her back.

She didn't even turn to look.

"Hello, Hunter," she said.

"Lemonfresh," came the reply.

"Let me guess. I must come with you to CityHive."

"She is important," Hunter replied. *"She is needed."*

The girl climbed to her feet on shaking legs. Turning, she found herself looking up into a pair of golden eyes. Down to an upturned palm.

She put on her braveface.

Her streetface.

And she took the Hunter's hand.

She hoped Ezekiel wouldn't feel too bad. That he and Cricket had found each other. That maybe they'd find Evie, too. She hoped they'd all be okay. That one day, somehow, they'd all find their happy ending.

She knew it was silly to hope.

But in the end, it was all she had.

ACKNOWLEDGMENTS

Much gratitude must go to the following incredible droogs:

My amazing and courageous editor, Melanie Nolan. Thanks for helping me tame this bioengineered beast.

The beta readers who've helped forge this series into something remotely coherent: C. S. Pacat, Lindsay "LT" Ribar, Laini Taylor, and Amie Kaufman. Big hugs must go to Marie Lu, Beth Revis, and my hobbit queen, Kiersten White.

Long and slightly uncomfortable hugs must go to the incredible band of reprobates at Random House/Knopf—"Auntie" Barbara Marcus, Karen Greenberg, Artie Bennett, Lisa Leventer, Alison Impey, Ray Shappell, Stephanie Moss, Ken Crossland, Natalia Dextre, Jake Eldred, John Adamo, Kelly McGauley, Jenna Lisanti, Adrienne Waintraub, Lisa Nadel, Kristin Schulz, Kate Keating, Elizabeth Ward, Cayla Rasi, Aisha Cloud, and Josh Redlich.

Huge thanks are also owed to Anna McFarlane, Jess Seaborn, Radhiah Chowdhury, and all the crew at my Australian publishers, Allen & Unwin, for making me feel so at home, and to all my amazing publishers around the world.

My very own killer agents, Josh and Tracey from Adams Lit, and all my Adams Lit family. Thanks for everything you do. Keep pounding!

All the bookstagrammers, bloggers, and vloggers across the globe who've supported my books—there are far too many of you amazing folks to name individually, but please understand I see all you do for me. For the fan art and the reviews, the pimping and the tattoos (!!!), you are amazing, and I couldn't do what I do without you.

The artists who inspire me, in no particular order—Bill Hicks (RIP), Tom Searle (RIP) and Architects, Maynard James Keenan and Tool, Oli and BMTH, Chino and the 'Tones, Burton and FF, Ian and the 'Vool, Ludovico Einaudi, Al and Ministry, Trent and NIN, Marcus/Adrian and Northlane (especially for the instrumental of "Intuition," which was my constant sound track for this book), Winston and PWD, Paul Watson, Jeff Hansen and the amazing crews at Sea Shepherd, William Gibson, Scott Westerfeld, Marie Lu, Cherie Priest, Jason Shawn Alexander, Lauren Beukes, Jamie Hewlett and Alan Martin, George Miller, Jenny Beavan, Mike Pondsmith, and Veronica Roth.

My droogo di tutti droogi—Marc, B-Money, Surly Jim, Eli, Rafe, Weez, Sam, the Hidden City Rollers, and all my nerdboyz, past and present.

Chris Tovo, for the clickies.

My family, for always being there.

Amanda, my best friend and the love of my life.

And last, but most important of all, coffee.